TRUANCY CITY

TRUANCY CITY

ISAMU FUKUI

A Tom Doherty Associates Book

New York

TOR
TEEN

TRUANCY CITY

Copyright © 2012 by Isamu Fukui

A Tor Teen Book
Published by Tom Doherty Associates, LLC
175 Fifth Avenue
New York, NY 10010

www.tor-forge.com

Tor® is a registered trademark of Tom Doherty Associates, LLC.

ISBN 978-0-7653-2263-0 (hardcover)
ISBN 978-1-4299-8674-8 (e-book)

First Edition: November 2012

Printed in the United States of America

0 9 8 7 6 5 4 3 2 1

I dedicate this story to
Vito Bonsignore, Rembert Herbert,
Eric Grossman, Michael Waxman,
and every educator who earned my respect
against all the odds.

CONTENTS

CONTENTS 8

TRUANCY CITY

The tent was sweltering as the young woman opened the flap and ducked inside. It had been particularly humid in the area, and her gray combat uniform was woven out of nylon cotton, a fabric that didn't perfectly insulate against the summer heat. Her troops liked to joke about the clothing getting hot enough to roast meat, but the woman herself showed no sign of discomfort as she sat down at her desk and thumbed on one of a series of monitors around her.

As the monitor flickered to life, a gaunt and disheveled man appeared onscreen. Upon seeing the woman, the man scowled and squeezed a chrome lighter with one hand.

"*You.* I should have known."

"It's been awhile since we last spoke like this, Mr. Mayor," the woman said. "That was nearly four years ago, correct?"

"Not long enough. I would have preferred never to see you again."

The young woman smiled faintly at the monitor, her stormy gray eyes glinting.

"Don't tell me you haven't been expecting a visit from us, Mr. Mayor."

"Actually, I'm wondering what took you so long." The Mayor flicked his lighter open. "Nearly a year since the war went public? The rebels are already knocking at my front door. You're much slower than I'd heard . . . *Iris.*"

If the young woman was annoyed by the mocking use of her name, she hid it well. Unperturbed, she leaned back in her chair and ran her fingers through her dark, wavy hair, neatly trimmed to regulation length.

"If the decision were mine alone I would have come four years ago, at the first sign of trouble," Iris said. "Things are a bit different now. I had to make sure to bring an army with me."

"I heard you were made a General of some sort," the Mayor said. "Shouldn't you have that army in your back pocket?"

"If only." Iris sighed. "I more often feel like it's the other way around."

The Mayor clicked his lighter shut. "Why are you calling?" he demanded. "Why now?"

Matching the Mayor's shift in demeanor, Iris sat up straight. Her voice, once politely neutral, now turned cold and hard.

"I didn't wish for this conversation any more than you, Mayor," she said. "Protocol requires me to warn you that you have until sundown to surrender and yield whatever control of that City you have left." Iris smiled wryly. "If you refuse—and I expect that you will—then you will be forcibly detained and the military will achieve control by itself."

"Good luck with that. You'll need it," the Mayor said. "I take it that you're camped just across the river, then?"

"I'm afraid that's none of your business."

"Well then," the Mayor growled, leaning forward, "all I have to say to you and your wretch of a father is this—*come and get me!*"

Iris brushed her forehead with her knuckles in a mild show of annoyance. The Mayor sat stoically, clearly expecting an additional outburst of some kind. But when Iris spoke again, her voice was oddly hushed.

"Where are the boys? Are they still alive?"

At that, the Mayor's face flushed red with anger.

"I'd die myself rather than tell *you* anything about that."

The screen went dead. Iris slammed her fist against the desk.

"Yes," she muttered. "You will."

W ho was that?"

The Mayor sighed and turned to face his guest, a boy sitting on the other side of his mahogany desk.

"A representative of the true Government of this City," the Mayor replied, "and someone I had hoped you would never meet. It's a long story."

"I've got time."

"But the City doesn't," the Mayor said sharply. "It's too late to explain the entire history of the Government, and frankly I don't know it all myself. What I can tell you is that they cannot be crossed. They are powerful beyond your imagination; their rule encompasses hundreds, perhaps thousands of cities. Their military makes our Enforcers look like a joke."

"So our City is just one of the many under their control?"

"Yes and no," the Mayor said. "This City is special, one of a few that the Government isolated decades ago. A sort of societal petri dish."

"Why?"

"Because of a wave of civil unrest that nearly destroyed the Government." The Mayor flicked his lighter open. "They have since purged all records of that incident, and even I don't know the details. What I do know is that in the bloody aftermath, the Government decided to take extreme measures to make sure that nothing like it would ever happen again." The Mayor smiled now. "The only problem was, no one could agree on *which* extreme measures to take."

The boy inclined his head. "So they created the Cities as experiments."

"Not exactly," the Mayor said. "The Cities were already there. The

Government merely isolated them from outside influence and tested a different philosophy in each. Until four years ago, this City was considered the most promising of all."

"And what was the philosophy behind this City?"

"It was simple." The Mayor clicked his lighter shut. "The founders believed that *education* was the key to controlling a population."

Strapped across Iris' back was a black pole about three feet in length, which she removed as she emerged from her tent. She pressed a button on the handle and two metal ends instantly extended from either side of the pole, resembling a staff. Tapping one end against the ground, she glanced over at the shade where a colonel, a member of her staff, had been waiting.

The Mayor's guess had been correct—her tent was one of hundreds that formed a temporary encampment at the riverside. A mercifully cool breeze rolled across the water and over the camp as Iris approached the saluting colonel.

"All units are ready for immediate deployment, General," the colonel said. "Will we observe the grace period, or has the Mayor rejected it?"

"The Mayor rejected it, but I don't intend to let him set our schedule," Iris replied. She watched a beetle crawl across the ground. "We will attack at sundown to take full advantage of the darkness."

The colonel frowned, but nodded anyway. "Yes, ma'am."

Iris glanced at him. "Something on your mind, soldier?"

"I was wondering why we didn't just overwhelm them to begin with. We could have put an end to the fighting sooner."

Iris watched the beetle stumble over a rock. Some commanding officers did not tolerate having their orders questioned at all. Never the most orthodox leader, she personally made the distinction between disrespect and curiosity. It was an approach that cultivated loyalty.

"There was no reason to interfere while the Educators and the rebels were so conveniently expending resources fighting each other," Iris said. "Remember, we have only twenty thousand troops to subdue any resistance and secure all fifty-seven districts. Had we rushed recklessly into the crossfire there's no telling what losses we may have suffered."

"So why don't we wait a little longer for both sides to completely collapse?"

"There is nothing more to be gained by waiting now. The outcome of the war was decided last night. The Mayor's last fortifications have fallen, and the Truancy is advancing upon District 1 even as we speak."

Iris gestured towards the river. Across the glittering water, the ominous shapes of skyscrapers loomed like giant tombstones. Many of them showed obvious signs of damage, and rising smoke plumes indicated that fighting was ongoing in the City.

"What you are looking at now is a failed society," Iris continued. The beetle examined her shoelace. "That City was based upon a bedrock of education. Now that that foundation has been shattered, those people don't know what to do with their newfound freedom, and so they run wild like the unruly children they are."

"If you don't mind me saying, General, that wasteland doesn't look much like freedom to me."

"Anarchy, then," Iris said dismissively. "Whatever you want to call it, that City has just about finished tearing itself apart. Now that both sides are exhausted, we can move in and pick up the pieces at our leisure."

"So what are your orders?"

"Keep all forces on standby. No flyovers, nothing that risks giving away our presence," Iris said. "I want everything to be quiet right up until the moment we move in. Remember, most of the City is still unaware of our existence."

The man nodded. "And what about our assets within the City?"

For the first time, the General hesitated. The beetle began skittering away. "Is there still no sign of our primary objectives?"

"None."

"Then tell the assets to keep looking. They have until tonight to find something or I will be deeply disappointed."

"And what happens if they *are* found?"

With precise restraint, Iris swung her staff, pinning the beetle to the ground without crushing it. She pressed a second button on the handle, and the staff discharged an electrical shock that instantly fried the insect.

"If either one of them is spotted," she said, "inform me immediately."

T hat woman was my sister?"

The boy sounded much calmer than the Mayor had expected.

"Iris is half related to you by blood, if that's what you mean," he said wearily. "She betrayed you before you were born. It was because of her that you were sent here, to live with me."

"Why would she do that?"

"Who knows?" The Mayor shrugged. "I suspect it might be because she saw you as a threat to whatever ambitions she harbored at the time. As you saw, she's come a long way. She has the full military might of the Government behind her now, and she hasn't forgotten that you exist."

"So all this time . . ."

"I was protecting you, and the City, from the Government." The Mayor flicked his lighter open. "It's funny, you know. When this City turned into an experiment it was proposed that we do away with the idea of parents and children altogether. All children would have been raised by the Government. You see, they knew that the bond between parent and child is instinctual."

"Why was that proposal rejected?"

"I'd like to say that it was because they were worried about losing sight of humanity altogether, but it was really because they believed that the parents could be a useful tool," the Mayor said. "The Government's goal was to suppress the troublesome instincts of children early on, to curtail their independence, their spirit. They sought to use the parental bond towards that end, to make parents agents of the Government."

"But still they feared that bond."

"They did, for they knew that if uncontrolled it could mean the undoing of all their hopes." The Mayor smiled. "As indeed it was, you know."

The boy shifted in his seat. "I'm sorry."

"Don't apologize; neither you nor your brother had any way of knowing the truth." The Mayor waved a dismissive hand. "I, however, do not have the excuse of ignorance. If I had been the parent the City expected me to be, if I hadn't cared about you two so much, none of this might have happened. But I don't regret it. It means that I was human after all."

"Can anything be done to stop them?"

At that, the Mayor lifted his lighter and lit it. A tiny flame danced between the two figures.

Boy and man. Father and son. Student and Educator.

For a moment they looked at each other through the flame.

"I'm afraid that it's too late." The Mayor clicked his lighter shut and the flame vanished. "They are already here."

12 Hours Earlier . . .

The Last Day of the War
Between the Truancy and the Educators

PART I

STUDENT

1

The Successor

"They say that every classroom is a battlefield."

The teacher was facing away from the class and towards the blackboard as he spoke.

Some students took advantage of this inattention to scribble notes or make faces at one another. From his seat at the front of the class, however, one boy with red hair listened with rapt attention. His desk was clean, his uniform crisp, his hair cut precisely according to school guidelines. His hands were clasped behind him and his eyes strayed not once from the front of the room.

"You are all soldiers of a sort, you who sit before me," the teacher said. "I cannot see you, of course, but I do not have to. You are no different from those that have come before. You have promise and potential, but without education you would only know how to waste it."

A girl in the front row stirred uncomfortably. The teacher lashed out backwards, slamming his ruler on her desk. The redhead smiled smugly as the girl snapped back to rigid attention. Still the teacher did not turn to face the class.

"You see, unshaped and unruly creatures as you are, you are by nature wayward and wild. You do not even recognize me yet as your benefactor," the teacher continued. "The task of an Educator is thankless in this way, but it is also essential. It is not mere rhetoric when our Mayor says that students are the future, but it is *our* job to determine what sort of future it will be. Such matters are too important to leave in the hands of children."

There were murmurs of discontent this time. The redhead remained at perfect attention as the teacher slashed the air with his ruler to restore silence.

"I cannot hear your complaints," he warned them, "for I have no ears. Of course I expect many of you to resist. It is the way of students to flee from their own salvation, to struggle against their saviors. You are drowning in a sea of ignorance, and it is up to us to pull you up from its depths. We will do this by force if we must."

With that the teacher finally turned towards the class. For the first time Cross could see that the man had no face. There was only a blank oval of smooth flesh.

"*This* is the nature of education," the teacher said. "It is and has always been a war waged against you young monsters—a war to rescue you from yourselves."

The redhead blinked. The man had no mouth. How could he speak? Was he speaking? Were these even his words?

The man drew closer.

"Well, Cross? Which side of the war are you on?"

Cross stood slowly and regarded the faceless man. He could feel the eyes of his peers upon him. He opened his mouth and the answer flowed easily.

"Your goals are my goals. I have no purpose but what you give me. Only through education can I find that purpose."

The faceless teacher nodded with approval.

"A fine answer. Music to my *ears*. I can see that your mentor Edward has been a very positive influence on you."

Cross smiled at the praise. He could feel the resentment of the other students in the room, but he didn't care. Nothing he did ever seemed to make them happy. Teachers, at least, could be pleased.

"Thank you, sir."

From somewhere far away a bell began to ring. Without waiting to be dismissed, the other students got up and began to file out the door. Cross stayed where he was, until only he and one other boy remained in their seats.

The other boy looked at Cross with emerald eyes.

"Good boy. You're not going anywhere just yet." Edward grinned. "After all, there's so much yet to be done for my legacy."

Edward held up a mirror. Against his will, Cross looked into it.

He tried to scream, but he couldn't. . . .

He had no face.

The bell was still ringing when Cross awoke.

Through the noise and the darkness he struggled to gather his bearings. Vague images from his nightmare flashed before his eyes, and for a few confused moments he half expected to find Edward looming in the shadows over him. Then there was a crack of light from an opening doorway, and the stirrings from the other bunks brought the memories rushing back.

Edward was dead. He had been for a long time.

Cross rubbed his eyes. It had been nearly a year since the young rebels of the Truancy had first risen up en masse to seize control of the City. A year since Edward, an ambitious student and Cross' mentor, had sided with the Mayor and answered the Truancy's challenge with his own Student Militia.

A year since the Truancy's founder Zyid had called for peace on the night of his greatest offensive. Neither Edward nor Zyid had survived that night. The cease-fire that followed had deteriorated quickly, as Cross had known it would. Now, a year later, peace was still elusive.

No sooner had Zyid's death been announced than word of his replacement, a mysterious boy named Takan, had circulated. And Edward had barely been gone a day before the Mayor had insisted that his protégé should succeed him—thus Cross had ascended to a leadership and responsibility he had never desired.

Swearing under his breath, Cross slid out of bed and into his shoes. Someone turned the lights on and was rewarded with a chorus of groans. Cross ignored them and focused on recalling the current situation through a fog of sleep.

The room he was in now had a year ago been an old classroom of the District 2 School. It had been long since converted into a dormitory, and the school itself transformed into a base for the students who chose to fight to defend their City.

They were losing that fight.

"All students, report for duty immediately," the intercom blared. "This is an emergency. I repeat, all students, report for duty immediately."

Cross looked around and saw that the other students were still dragging themselves out of bed. Heaving himself to his feet, Cross dashed out of the room without a word to those supposedly under his command. The only backwards glance he spared was for the clock on the wall. It read 20:06. He'd had a long patrol that morning and had slept right through the entire day.

Cross ran for his locker. The hallways were dimly lit by dying fluorescent lights and buzzing with blue uniformed students in various states of preparedness. Reaching his destination, Cross entered his combination and quickly retrieved his equipment. Rifle. Knife. Sidearm. Body armor. Flashlight. Pieces of himself.

Feeling complete now, Cross rubbed sleep from his eyes as he headed for the front doors where he knew his personal unit would gather. Sure enough, two of them were already there. The first was a lean, wiry boy with straw-colored hair and a sniper rifle slung over one shoulder. The other was a girl with brown hair held back by a blue bandanna.

"Rise and shine, boss." The boy bowed with exaggerated deference. "You sure look bright and cheerful this fine—"

"Not in the mood, Sepp," Cross snapped. "Have you heard anything about what's going on?"

"Well, sir, it would appear that the Truants are attacking. I hear that they're very unhappy and would like us all to die."

Cross let out a noise of exasperation. The girl cracked a smile.

"All we know is that they've massed around the eastern overpass," she said. "It sounds like they're a lot of them out there, but last I heard they haven't even tried to tackle the barricade yet."

"Well, that's some good news," Cross muttered. "Thanks, Floe."

The girl gave an airy salute. Rather than the uniform pants used by most girls in the militia, Floe had opted instead for a matching skirt and a hip sack. At five foot five she was the shortest member of his unit.

The news she'd offered was important. The Truancy's long campaign had cut off Educator-controlled districts from one another and strangled them until only a fortified core remained. Those fortifications had held so far, but they were all that stood now between the Truancy and total victory.

All tiredness forgotten, Cross found himself itching to get into the fight. Black vans were beginning to pull up by the curb outside.

"There's our ride," Cross said as other units began to form up and exit through the front doors. "We're still missing Joe. Has anyone seen that—"

"I'm here, I'm here!" a deep voice shouted, its owner shoving his way through the crowd. "Yeah, I'm a little late, whatever, let's go, come on!"

Joe was a large, muscular boy with a shaven head. Without waiting for a reply, he charged out as though he had been first. Rolling their eyes, the others followed. Now fully assembled, Cross' group piled into one of the waiting vans. Cross clambered in last and shut the door behind him.

Together the four of them made a formidable team, one that Cross felt was a match for any group of Truants. He had selected each of them for a different reason. Joe had impressive strength and could be absolutely vicious in battle when he got going. Sepp was one of the best shots in the Militia and could pick off Truants from many blocks away with his rifle.

As for Floe . . . Cross glanced over at the brunette, who was busy adjusting the sight on her rifle. Cross had personal reasons for picking her, but she had also defected from the Truancy and thus knew more about the enemy than any other student.

"The Truancy never had all this standardized gear." Floe admired her knife as the van began moving. "But we did get to play with some neat toys."

"Like what?" Joe grunted.

"Like these." Floe pulled a glass bottle out of her hip sack. A cloth was stuffed into its neck, and Cross recognized it as an old Truancy favorite—gasoline and motor oil, mixed into an explosive cocktail.

"Aren't those illegal?" Sepp said.

"I have no idea what you're talking about." Floe stuffed the bottle back into the pack.

"It's not like they'd arrest her for that," Cross said. "The Educators should let us use them openly. They're easy to make, and they give the Truancy an edge."

"Might as well have us all just *be* Truants," Joe muttered.

Cross glared. "Shut up, Joe."

An awkward silence fell over the van. Cross had never liked Joe as a person. The large boy had made the mistake of taking Cross for a pushover during his first day with the Militia. When their first and only fight put Joe in the infirmary for two days he had become much more respectful, though Cross knew Joe was still sore over the incident.

"Hey, you kids back there all ready to go?" the driver called. "I'm about to hit the gas so you all better buckle up!"

The students reached for their seat belts as the driver took a particularly sharp turn. Stop signs and streetlights flew by so quickly that Cross was glad that there was a curfew to prevent pedestrians from getting flattened.

"What have you heard about the situation?" Cross asked the man.

"Probably not much more than you," the Enforcer said, hitting a speed bump. "The overpass seems to be holding, which is good, 'cause the most important thing for us is to hold the high ground there—but the ground is just swarming with Truants. We can't pull too many Enforcers away from the other districts in case this is just a diversion."

"So that's why we're being called in."

"Exactly, kiddo. Now hold on tight, we're almost there."

A few moments later, the van screeched to a halt. Cross was already sliding the door open before the wheels had stopped turning. He leapt out. The others quickly followed. Sepp looked a little green from the ride and took great gulps of air with his hands on his knees.

They were standing at the base of a ramp that provided access to the overpass above. Not too far off in the distance, Cross could see tiny flashes of gunfire and movement—that was where the front lines were. The Truancy would have a hard time drawing closer with the overpass so well defended.

His heart racing with excitement, Cross was about to order his team straight onto the overpass. A rocket slammed into the van they had just gotten out of. There was a flare of heat and light, and then the force of the blast sent Cross crashing to the ground.

His head spinning, Cross dove behind the van's wreckage as gunshots rang out. He saw muzzle flashes coming from ground level. The Truants were in the buildings that lined the overpass.

Cross soon found himself joined by Sepp and Floe—Joe had found other cover nearby. They blindly returned fire.

"Ugh, with our attention on District 8 they must've snuck in over the District 5 border," Floe said. "They're everywhere now!"

"Split up," Cross said. "Sepp, go find a roost. Floe, you stay down here and keep an eye on the buildings, don't try anything stupid. Joe, come with me, we'll go—"

"Wait, look up there!"

Floe's eyes were wide with fear. Cross turned. Just a few blocks down, on the roof of a relatively low building, a figure stood clearly illuminated by a red neon sign. Against the dark blue sky, Cross could make out wild hair, a matching brown trench coat, and the faint gleam of what had to be a white sword.

Cross breathed. "Is that—"

"Takan," Floe said grimly. "Their leader."

"Sepp, can you get a shot off from here?" Cross demanded.

Sepp reached for his rifle, but never got the chance to aim. Another rocket landed nearby, and Cross' unit ducked for cover as shrapnel shredded the air. By the time they raised their heads again, Takan was gone.

"Of course it wouldn't be that easy," Cross muttered, his ears ringing. "He's taunting us. But if he's here at all, that means this fight is the real deal."

Already more vans and Enforcer patrol cars were arriving. Students and Enforcers spilled out of them, filling the streets, forming defensive positions, and charging up onto the overpass. A subordinate, one of the Student Militia's coordinators, ran up to Cross.

"Orders, Captain?" the student asked.

Cross frowned. This was the part he hated the most. He didn't like everyone looking to him for answers—he was good at carrying out orders, not giving them. He never thrived on being in charge as Edward had.

"Send half of the students onto the overpass to reinforce our defenses there, and spread the other half out down here," Cross said. "Try to push the Truants back to those buildings."

The student nodded and ran off to relay the commands.

"Don't underestimate Takan," Floe warned, glancing up at the neon sign. "If he joins the battle himself, it's gonna be messy."

"This was never going to be clean," Cross replied, raising his rifle. "All right, Joe, you're with me. Everyone, get going. Let's hunt some Truants!"

Floe joined the other students advancing upon the unseen Truants in the buildings. Sepp darted off on his own. Cross felt a familiar thrill as he charged up the ramp and onto the overpass. Peering off the side, he let off a three-round burst at a Truant that had strayed too far from cover.

Cross fought for the sake of fighting. He didn't enjoy the killing itself.

It was the danger and excitement that came from being one mistake away from death. He didn't really remember why he was *supposed* to be doing it. He didn't care why. Cross lived for the moment.

As the Student Militia reinforcements arrived, the Truants backed off. Only sporadic fire came now from the shadowed buildings. The brief respite gave Cross and Joe a chance to peer over the edge of the overpass, into the darkness of the Truant-infested District 5. That area had already been abandoned before the war had started, but now it lay in utter ruin with only the burnt and crumbling skeletons of buildings left standing.

"Can't say I like what they've done with their occupied territory," Cross said. "Everything they touch seems to turn into a smoking wreck."

"I hear the guys have their own name for it."

"Do they?" Cross turned to look at Joe. "What is it?"

The large boy grinned and fired a shot off into the darkness. A tiny wisp of smoke rose from the barrel of his gun.

"They call it Truancy City."

2

UNLEASH THE BEAST

aron peered off the side of the rooftop with binoculars pressed tightly to his face. A veteran Truant, he had come to enjoy watching the ebb and flow of battle.

"How's it look down there, Aaron?" Takan sat crouched nearby.

"There's an awful lot of them," Aaron replied. "Looks like they've emptied their headquarters. Almost as many students as there are Enforcers. You okay with that?"

"We settled this a long time ago." Takan gazed at the red glow of the sign. "The students made their choice—they can go down with the Educators if that's what they want."

Aaron was about to reply when his cell phone began vibrating. He flipped it open.

"Yeah? When? How many? All right, thanks, I'll tell him." Aaron shut the phone and turned to Takan. "Word from our spies. The Militia is dividing their forces, half for the ground and half for the overpass."

"And?"

"And that's it."

"That's it? Well that's boring." Takan smirked. "Is it Edward's replacement leading them out there?"

"They didn't say, but it probably is Cross."

"Cross, huh? By all accounts he's fierce, but he's got none of his predecessor's finesse," Takan said. "How are the preparations for the Beast?"

Aaron put the binoculars down and scratched his neck.

"Your, uh, additions should hold," he replied. "She's all fueled up and ready to go. The crew is just waiting on your order."

"Good. It's almost time. Get ready for it, Aaron."

Aaron shifted. "Can I just ask one thing?"

"Make it quick."

"Why isn't Zyid's brother along for the ride? This attack is important, isn't it?"

"He's not really one of us, you know. I can't exactly order him around." Takan shrugged. "Besides, he's got other things to worry about."

"Like what?"

"Like how to get into City Hall and persuade the Mayor to surrender. Hopefully this attack will make his job easier and we won't have to go through with Plan B."

Understanding dawned on Aaron's face. Before he could say anything, a fresh cacophony of gunfire sounded. He raised his binoculars again.

"Looks like the Militia is fully deployed on the overpass."

"Like moths to the flame." Takan sighed. "If they want to test the strength of their defenses so badly, I'm happy to oblige. Unleash the Beast."

A t the farthest end of the overpass, secure atop a twelve-foot-tall structure of reinforced concrete and steel, Patrolman Iverson blew lazily on his coffee. It was against regulation to be drinking coffee while a battle was going on, but no one ever took that rule seriously. Iverson himself had seen a dozen Truancy strikes come and go, but not once had the enemy dared to approach the impenetrable barrier on the overpass.

Setting his mug down, Iverson turned to the sentry next to him. "Hey, you can handle staring at nothing by yourself for a minute, right?"

"Yeah, sure. What's the matter?"

"Too much coffee."

The other sentry snorted, and Iverson descended from the barricade. At the edge of the overpass, Iverson unzipped his fly and began relieving himself off the side. The city streets were dark and abandoned below. No one lived this close to the border anymore. The distant sounds of battle were easy to ignore.

"Hey, wait a minute, I think I see movement."

Iverson glanced up at the sentry on the wall, who was now reaching for his binoculars. The other Enforcers were still dozing, or in the guardhouse listening to music and waiting for the commotion to die down.

"Are you sure?" Iverson said, zipping up his pants.

"Yeah," the man said. "Yeah, Truants, in the distance. They've got something with them. I think—"

A distant shot rang out, and the man toppled off the barricade and onto the pavement, a bullet through his head. Iverson stared at the fallen body in disbelief.

Explosions abruptly rocked the unattended barricade. The Truants were using rockets, but Iverson knew that they'd need more than that to break through. Iverson readied his rifle and darted up the barricade as other Enforcers spilled out of the guardhouse. One of them, he hoped, would remember to radio for help.

Atop the barricade, Iverson's stomach dropped as he saw dozens of dark shapes approaching fast. Behind them he thought he could see something huge approaching as well, a massive shadow in the night. Before Iverson could get a better look at whatever it was, bullets whizzed by, forcing him to duck.

Iverson and the other Enforcers returned fire, even as the barricade shook beneath them from more rockets. Closer now, a few Truants fell to the Enforcers' bullets. Then one of them lobbed something, and Iverson panicked as the grenade landed perfectly in their midst.

The blast threw Iverson from the wall, his ears ringing. He had landed atop the crumpled body of one of his fellows. Unable to stand, Iverson raised his head and realized that he could hear roaring now, a great mechanical cry of engines and gears.

He tried to back away, just in time to see something huge slam into the damaged barricade and burst through it like sand. In his last moments Iverson froze, and only one thought registered in his mind.

The barricade is gone, it's gone! They have a highway right into the core districts! We're finished—

He caught a glimpse of rusted metal and barbed wire, and then the machine was upon him.

Got one!" Joe laughed. "Man he was chubby. Easy target. Whatever the Truancy was feeding that guy, I want some."

Cross ignored him, focused on trying to provide cover fire for the students advancing below. Unable to escape the withering fire from the overpass, the Truants were beginning to pull back to the safety of the buildings. They had barely put up a fight against the student counterattack, and for a moment Cross wondered if it would really be that easy.

Joe was now taking exaggerated gulps from a hip flask in between pulling his trigger. It was deliberately stupid, and probably meant as a challenge. Cross promised himself that he would take care of it later.

The radio blared. "Everyone, you have an eye in the sky coming in."

That was a surprise. The City had lost so many helicopters to Truancy rockets that the remaining few were rarely used. That they were willing to use one now meant that they must be desperate for information. The Truancy's night attack had taken them by surprise, and it was hard to tell what their plan could possibly be.

Cross could hear the distant buzz of the helicopter overhead, high out of range of the Truancy's rockets. Then Joe pointed at something and shouted.

"What the *hell* is that?"

Heads turned. Worried murmurs broke out. In the distance Cross could make out something charging down the overpass. It was clearly some kind of machine, and whatever it was, it was large enough to block off almost the entire width of the road. Flashes of gunfire and explosions briefly illuminated parts of it, but not enough to make it recognizable.

"Is that thing ours?" Joe demanded.

"I don't think so," Cross said, cold dread forming in his gut. "I think it may mean that the barricade has fallen."

"Well, gee, maybe we should, I don't know, *find out*?"

Ignoring Joe's sarcasm, Cross glanced over the edge again just in time to see Floe vanish into a building along with several other students. Satisfied that she'd be safe, Cross ran towards the advancing machine. A few brave students followed in his wake.

As the pavement flew beneath their feet, aerial reports from the helicopter began filtering in on the radio.

"—lot of them in from District 5, but the line's not too thick. They're pressing pretty hard towards the overpass! Yeah, it looks like a lot of them are already taking shelter *under* the overpass, so watch out for—"

"Ask him about that monster *on* the overpass, dammit!" Joe said. "Is the barricade gone or not?"

There was more static, then:

"—can't be happening, it looks like Truancy vehicles are *on* the overpass, following behind . . . what the hell *is* that?"

Joe rolled his eyes and smacked his forehead in frustration.

"Pilot, this is the Captain of the Student Militia," Cross spoke into his radio. "There's some sort of armored vehicle on the overpass, moving fast. I think the Truancy is advancing behind it."

"I see it. Moving in for a closer look."

The droning sound of the helicopter grew louder, and Cross knew that somewhere above them the pilot was descending. The black Truancy machine was getting closer now, sparks flying as it smashed debris out of the way.

Just then it slammed into an abandoned car, and the resulting fireball illuminated its entire shape.

Joe stopped still. "Hey, isn't that a—"

"A bulldozer?" the pilot cried on the radio, evidently having gotten close enough to get a good look. "It's some kind of freak bulldozer! Hold on a sec."

A moment later, the helicopter cast a searchlight down at the machine. As its full form came into view, Cross felt his heart skip a beat. It was indeed an enormous bulldozer, a behemoth that had to have been salvaged from an old construction site, now twisted to the Truancy's violent purposes. The Truants had painted the machine black, and sprayed their hated red symbol onto it. Barbed wire had been strung over the whole thing, and armored plating had been wielded on to protect the driver.

Armed Truants rode atop the machine's bulk, shielded in the front by additional metal plates. They roared their challenge at the helicopter hovering above, and before Cross could shout a warning, one of them raised a rocket launcher and fired. There was fire from above, a scream on the radio, and Cross could only stare in horror as the helicopter crashed down onto the overpass itself. Moments later, the bulldozer plowed right through the wreckage.

Lit by flames, the machine seemed almost alive in that moment. Joe let out a terrified yell and turned to run. Survival instinct kicking in, Cross followed suit, though he knew they hadn't a hope of outrunning the machine. Adrenaline pulsed through his veins as he realized just how much trouble they were in. A drop off the side of the overpass would be fatal, and, far from the nearest ramp, Cross could think of no way to challenge the mountain of metal itself.

Just then, his eyes fell upon an abandoned car on the road ahead. His heart surged with hope.

Floe had followed the other students into the darkened building when the first shots rang out. The student directly in front of her crumpled to the floor. Floe swore and dropped to her belly, feeling for a pulse but finding none. More rifles flashed in the dark. A small flame was lit, and Floe immediately knew what it was—she raised her rifle and fired at the source, detonating the firebomb before it could be thrown.

Liquid fire sprayed everywhere, cutting through the darkness, and the Truants that were not caught in it were forced to flee out the door where most of them were cut down. Exhaling, Floe stood again. One of the Truants was still on fire and moving. Knowing that nothing could be done for him, Floe shut her eyes and put him out of his misery. As she lowered her rifle, she realized that she was shaking.

They're not your comrades anymore, they're your enemies! Floe told herself. *You've seen and done worse, don't fall apart now!*

"Hey, Floe." Sepp's voice blared on the radio and snapped her out of her trance. "I think I see some Truants heading back towards the overpass. Looks suspicious. Can you check it out?"

"Yeah . . . yeah, I think the helicopter mentioned that too." Floe recovered quickly, then turned to the other students. "I'll return to the overpass myself. The rest of you keep going, avoid getting close to District 5 in case they've set traps. Try to search the building with the lit neon sign—we spotted the Takan there earlier."

The other students obediently pressed forward as Floe doubled back. As she emerged from the building, it became clear that Sepp had been right; a small force of Truants had gone around and was now occupying the students' old position under the overpass. The Enforcers that had stayed behind had now been pushed back, exchanging fire on the other side. Floe reported this to Sepp.

"Are they nuts?" Sepp wondered. "This leaves them totally vulnerable to a pincer attack."

"They don't do these things on a whim," Floe said, biting her lip. "They must be after something."

"Well, take a closer look and see if you can find out what they're up to," Sepp said. "I can't spot them under the overpass from here, but I can cover you."

"That's probably the best idea."

"Happy hunting."

Floe checked her weapon, and then began creeping to the left. The Truants under the overpass hadn't noticed anything yet, and with any luck she would be able to get close enough to do some serious damage. Noticing some dark figures in the way, Floe realized that the Truancy had posted lookouts.

A cry to her far right, followed by silence, told her that Sepp was keeping his word. The other Truants were now moving to investigate, and one of them passed close by where Floe was hidden. She raised her rifle.

"A bulldozer? It's some kind of freak bulldozer! Hold on a sec."

Cursing herself for her carelessness, Floe reached down to switch off her radio. Too late. When she looked up again, she found two male Truants leering down at her, rifles pointed at her face.

"Drop the gun," one of them said. "It'd be a real shame to have to kill a pretty student like you."

The foot soldiers of the Truancy were as hormone-driven as ever, Floe thought as she laid down her weapon. The intelligent thing to do would have been to shoot her on sight. As one of them stepped closer, she readied the knife she kept hidden up her sleeve.

Just then, two things happened at once. In the distance the helicopter crashed onto the overpass, and a bullet struck one of the Truants in the head. As the second Truant turned to see what was going on, Floe lunged, slashing the boy's hand with her knife. The boy yelped, and she seized his rifle, slamming the stock into his face.

The Truant dropped to the ground, and Floe kicked him to make sure he stayed down. She cuffed the boy's arms behind his back, gagged him with a rag, and removed his shoes. Then she looked around to see where the shot could have come from. In the darkness and chaos, all she could tell was that it wasn't anyone nearby.

Remembering her radio, Floé flipped it back on and switched to her unit's private frequency.

"Sepp, was that you?"

"Sure was."

"Thank you."

"Just call me your white knight."

Floe hitched the radio back to her belt. Her Truant prisoner was stirring now, looking up at her somewhat apologetically. She drew her knife again and pulled the gag from his mouth.

"What are you guys doing here?" she demanded. "Why are you so intent on getting under the overpass?"

The Truant seemed to consider this for a moment, and then smiled. "You know, you're a very attractive—AURGH!"

Floe had kicked him between the legs.

"Not in the mood for jokes," she said. "Tell me the plan."

The boy looked resentful now. "Why should I?"

"Because if you don't . . ." Floe raised her knife. "I'm going to do some nutcracking."

The boy paled. "You wouldn't."

Actually he was right, but Floe saw no reason to let him know that.

"You want a demonstration? Do you prefer left or right?"

She crouched down as though she meant business. The Truant flinched.

"All right, all right," he said. "What's it matter anyway? You can't stop us. We've already strapped the explosives to the columns."

As those words registered, Floe felt cold dread in her stomach. Everything fell into place all at once. She reached for her radio and switched to an open frequency.

"Everyone, this is an emergency, the Truancy has planted bombs on the overpass support structures; they can collapse the whole thing at any moment!"

You drive!" Cross shouted as he piled into the backseat of the abandoned car.

"Why me?" Joe demanded, getting behind the wheel.

"I don't know how!"

Cross immediately regretted admitting that. Joe snorted derisively, but the growing roar of the machine behind them forestalled any further conversation. Cross shot out the rear window while Joe struggled to get the car started. The bulldozer was in plain sight now, and gaining fast.

His mind racing, Cross understood now that the battle was as good as lost. No matter how it ended, there would be no holding the Truancy back.

Within hours the Truancy would be able to advance behind their machine all the way into District 1. Meanwhile, the explosives would collapse the overpass behind them, protecting their rear.

A student fired a rocket at the oncoming bulldozer. The shot exploded against the blade, but the machine just kept coming. The student was cut down by gunfire even as he turned to run, while another decided to take his chances and jumped off the edge of the overpass.

"Got it!" Joe roared in triumph as the car engine came to life.

The bulldozer was almost upon them, its massive bulk overshadowing their tiny vehicle. As Joe hit the gas, it became clear that the car was in no shape to do much more than maintain the distance from the bulldozer. The Truants began yelling obscenities and insults as their gunfire peppered the car.

As if moved by puppet strings, Cross rose and fired a shot. One Truant was knocked off the bulldozer as his fellows cursed and ducked.

Cross withdrew again, heart pounding from that small victory. He shut his eyes and let his breathing ease. The whole situation felt faraway and surreal, like a dream where he could see his death coming but could do nothing to stop it. Time seemed to slow. It was an eerie, wonderful, terrifying feeling.

"Everyone, this is an emergency, the Truancy has planted bombs on the overpass support structures; they can collapse the whole thing at any moment!"

Floe's voice on the radio was like a bucket of cold water, reminding Cross that he had work to do. Looking out the front windshield, Cross saw that they weren't far from the Student Militia's main lines. He realized what had to be done.

"Sepp!" Cross shouted into his radio. "Sepp, are you there?"

"Yes, sir. What do you need?"

"Can you target the explosives on the overpass support columns?"

"Some of them."

Cross shut his eyes tight and grinned.

"Can you shoot one as that *thing* crosses over it?"

There was a pause as Sepp seemed to understand. "Yeah, but—"

"Do it! Don't argue!"

It took Joe a moment to understand what Cross had just ordered. When he did, his head snapped around and the car swerved dangerously. "Hey, wait a minute! If he does that then we'll also be—"

There was a great rumbling sound and the ground shook beneath them. Cross' head slammed hard into the car roof, and everything went black.

• • •

From his hiding place behind some trashcans, Aaron watched as more students appeared around the corner with guns drawn. Before they could react, Takan threw a bottle through the air and then shot it with his pistol. The students were showered by burning liquid. Even as they caught fire, Takan was among them, his white blade drawn—

Aaron turned away, having no need or desire to see the rest. Had he not known Takan personally, Aaron was not ashamed to admit that he might have been scared.

"It's over, Aaron. You can come out."

Aaron emerged to find Takan taking a swig from a glass bottle. Mineral water, fancy stuff they'd looted from a shop nearby. He didn't seem to be ruffled in the slightest.

"I didn't expect so many of them to get this far," Takan said, pouring the rest of the bottle out onto the burning ground. "The rational thing for them to do would've been to try to turn back and try to retake the overpass columns."

Aaron shrugged. "Who knows what they were thinking? Maybe they were after you in particular."

"I figured that letting myself be seen would intimidate them." Takan frowned. "Maybe that backfired. You should return to Truancy City. The battle is going according to plan any—"

The roar of an unusually large explosion reached their ears, and Aaron felt an involuntary shiver travel down his spine. He knew exactly what that sound meant, and judging from Takan's face, his leader did as well. They ran out of the alley and saw it immediately: one of the massive support pillars had been destroyed, a chunk of the overpass fallen. The Beast was nowhere to be seen.

"I think we have a problem," Aaron said.

Takan had a dark look on his face. "Could it have been one of your people? An accident?"

"Impossible, I'm the only one with a detonator." Aaron shook his head. "And besides, the timing . . ."

"Is too convenient." Takan nodded. "Then I assume that the students or Enforcers did it themselves. Sacrificing their key defensive structure to delay our attack. Talk about cutting off the nose to spite the face."

"Well, it seems to have worked," Aaron said. "We've lost the Beast."

"That is unexpected," Takan admitted. "But with the overpass gone we can now advance on foot and reach District 1 within the week. And we always have our sleeper agents."

"So, regroup?"

"Yeah." Takan sheathed his sword. "As soon as our people get clear, detonate whatever explosives are already set. We might not be able to use the overpass ourselves, but we've blown a gaping hole right into the heart of their territory. The Mayor is in no position to refuse our offer now."

Aaron reached for his cell phone. "And if he does?"

"Then we move on to Plan B." Takan shrugged. "We'll have given them a fair chance, and we can't wait forever. If the Mayor fails to see reason, we'll just wipe them out. The Educators, the Enforcers, the Student Militia. Everyone who still wants war."

3

DARKEST CHILDHOOD

I n his countless hours spent unconscious, Cross had experienced many dreams. Some of them were recurring. It was easier for him when the scenes were from his past, for though he had no control over those, he at least knew how they would unfold.

The scenes played out the same way each time.

They were always nightmares.

T ime's up, class, let's see how you did."

Cross winced and dropped his pencil, his assignment lying half-finished before him. He didn't have to look around to know that everyone else had completed their work, and they didn't have to look at his to know he hadn't. He'd developed something of a reputation at his school, and though Cross knew it wasn't his fault, he never felt safe explaining why.

The other students around him were chatting now, probably about him. Cross did his best to ignore them. It was always like this, in every class, in every grade. He was always alone in the classroom. He glanced down at his hands, the cause of his current misery. Ugly purple bruises slashed across each palm, making it very painful to write.

Ms. Obeita, his fat fourth-grade teacher, waddled over to collect his paper. He quickly tried to hide his hands, but the ugly marks were hard to miss and Obeita was a sharp woman.

"How did you get those on your hands, Cross?" she demanded.

"I got them while playing during recess, ma'am," Cross lied.

"Again? You're such a careless and sloppy boy," she muttered, snatching his paper and glancing at it. "There will be no more recesses for you. You can stay inside and do extra work instead, and I'm afraid I'm going to have to notify your father."

Cross felt a cold lump form in the pit of his stomach. "Yes, ma'am."

As the teacher walked away, Cross began to feel dizzy and short of breath. The laughter of his classmates was drowned out by the throbbing in his head. Recesses were no great loss; he only ever got bullied in the courtyard anyway. Yet his head still spun, because he knew that his father was going to be called.

Cross looked down at his small hands. This was going to mean more bruises.

· · ·

o, you showed off your bruises to the teacher, eh, boy? Thought that she'd protect you from me, was that it?"

"No dad, it wasn't like—"

"DO NOT CALL ME THAT!"

Cross had braced himself for the blow, but the sheer force of it still knocked him to the floor. "S-sorry, Mr. Rothenberg, sir."

"You pulled me off duty for this, boy!" Rothenberg raged, pacing around the living room. "I happen to be working on a very important case! Do you think I *want* to be here right now? Do you think I *want* to waste time on disobedient trash?"

"No, s-sir," Cross mumbled, fighting back tears.

"Then why do you make me do it?" Rothenberg demanded. "If you'd just learn to behave yourself then I wouldn't have to do this! Are you trying to waste my time? Apologize!"

Cross couldn't help it. The tears came pouring of their own accord, defying his every attempt to suppress them.

"I'm sorry," he sobbed. "I'm sorry I'm sorry I'm sor—"

"Stop crying!" Rothenberg roared. Cross tried, but the flood would not be held back. "I said, *stop crying*!"

Cross gasped as Rothenberg landed a kick to his stomach. The blow was so powerful that it shocked his tears away.

"Look at me when I'm talking to you!"

It was just a nightmare, *just a nightmare*. Cross repeated that mantra in his head as he turned his head to look up at his enraged father, who now held a leather belt in his hands.

"I'm gonna give you a choice, boy," Rothenberg said. "Ten lashes with your hands closed, or five with them open. Choose!"

Cross almost started crying again, but stopped himself just in time.

"Ask for one, or you'll get both!" Rothenberg snarled.

Cross shut his eyes and held out his fists, trembling.

"Ten closed, p-please."

he sidewalk was cold and unforgiving as Cross hit the ground again. His breaths came ragged, misting in the winter air.

"Hah, looks like he's all worn out now. How many times did you hit him, Chuck?"

"Just ten. Heck, I'm surprised he took that much."

"Thought you were real clever, didn't ya, Cross? Thought you'd ditched us, huh?"

"Hold his arms tighter, Jim, I can't aim right like this."

Cross gritted his teeth as he took another punch to the gut, hating how this had become a weekly routine. With his father absent most of the time, it fell to Cross to cook and clean after himself. This meant going out for groceries and stretching what little allowance he had. Most kids just laughed when word got around that Cross did housework. Two upper graders, however, had since made a habit of ambushing him on his way back from the store.

"Why'd you have to struggle, Cross? Now you're gonna pay for getting mud on Jim's pants."

"Yeah, you have any idea how long it's going to take my mom to wash this off?"

About forty minutes by hand, if she uses the right detergent, Cross thought.

Cross had tried hard to avoid them this time. He'd taken a long detour around the edge of District 18, only to discover that they'd been following him all along. His patience had snapped, and Cross had tried to fight back. Foolish.

Staring up at the frozen gray skies, Cross took their blows as his groceries scattered across the street. His eyes remained dry. It never occurred to Cross that anyone might help, that this time might be different from all the others.

Then an unfamiliar voice called out.

"Are we going to have a problem, or are you all going to get the hell out of my way?"

The two bullies glanced up, and even Cross rolled over to look at the newcomer. It was a boy, wearing a gray student's uniform and short blond hair. Emerald eyes glinted in the pale sunlight, and his thin eyebrows were slanted in contempt.

"Mind your own business, blondie," Jim said. "Get outta here before you end up like this kid."

Cross privately thought that the boy should take the advice. He was clearly younger than the bullies, and physically didn't seem like much of a match.

"That sounds like a raw deal." The blond boy actually yawned. "Here's a better one. You get out of my sight now, or I will remove you from it."

"Isn't this kid from one of the lower grades, Jim?" Charles asked, squinting. "He's got quite a mouth on him."

"Guess his parents never taught him when to keep it shut."

The boy shifted impatiently, and suddenly Cross felt a chill that had nothing to do with the winter weather.

"My parents, being the extraordinary fools that they were, are dead," the blond said. "Get out of my way unless you want to join them."

"Hah!" Jim's features lit up. "I remember now, he's one of those orphan kids!"

Cross found that vaguely interesting. All orphanages were run by the City, and contained kids whose parents couldn't or wouldn't take care of them. A gathering of misfits and outcasts.

"Yeah." Charles chortled. "I bet he— hey, whaddya think you're doing, blond boy?"

If his ribs weren't hurting, Cross would have gasped. Within an instant, both of the older boys lay sprawled on the sidewalk. Jim cursed and writhed as Charles rose to his feet and stared at his foe.

"You stupid little blond!" he snarled.

Charles lunged, intending to tackle the smaller boy to the ground. Like lightning, the orphan leapt clear, and Cross winced as Charles crashed into the ground face-first.

"My name's not 'blond,' fool." The boy kicked the fallen bully in the ribs, twisted delight on his face. "It's Edward. Remember it."

Cross remembered it.

It happened while he was scrubbing the floor of the apartment's bathroom, the revelation as sudden as it was random. Cross had always felt that the name Edward was familiar, but as someone far too awkward to fit into any social circle at school it had taken him some time to place it.

As he squeezed out his rag, Cross finally recalled that Edward was one of the popular kids at the District 18 School, a star at . . . something. Maybe a lot of things. Belonging to different social strata, they had never met before the incident with the groceries—though Cross had sometimes heard the name spoken in the hallways in tones of awe. There was no doubt in his mind that they were the same boy.

Taking down older kids that easily . . . I wish I could do that.

As Cross began work on the toilet, a sudden knock at the door snapped him out of his reverie. Cross tensed. It wasn't like his father to knock, but who else would possibly pay a visit here?

Cautiously, Cross removed his rubber gloves and hurried to the door. The knock came again, louder, and Cross quickly decided to open it before whoever was on the other side got angry.

The door swung open, and a uniformed Enforcer stepped inside.

"Are you Cross?" he asked.

"Yes, sir."

"I'm Enforcer Abrams," the man said. "Custody of you has been turned over to the local orphanage. I'm to escort you there. Pack your things."

The impact of the words was so sudden that Cross felt a little disoriented.

Dozens of questions swirled in Cross' head, threatening to make him burst from the pressure.

"Wha . . . I mean, yes, sir, but what . . . what . . ."

Cross couldn't find the words to express himself. He didn't even know what to express.

"Your father has been injured in his duty as an Enforcer," Abrams said unhelpfully. "Hurry up and pack your things. I'll explain on the way to the orphanage."

A Legend Returns

Y ou shouldn't be here, you know."

Sepp frowned as he and Floe picked their way through the dormant battlefield. The sun was just beginning to creep over the horizon, and the dawn was a swirled mess of blue and red.

"Why?" Sepp asked. "I'm not that ugly, am I?"

"You know what I'm talking about," Floe snapped. "You could have retreated with the rest of the Militia instead of following me behind enemy lines like this."

"You're not the only one who wants to find Cross and Joe," Sepp said. "This is my unit too you know."

Floe said nothing to that, but kicked an empty can in her way with particular ferocity. Sepp sighed and looked around sadly.

As far as the eye could see, the City had been completely devastated by the battle. Fires had reduced entire blocks to ruins, and some of them were still burning. The buildings they left behind were little more than charred husks—burnt monuments against a sky of ash. Rubble, trash, and the wreckage of cars littered the streets, relics of one battle or another.

Some of those ruins had once been neighborhoods that Sepp had known in his childhood. Now they were beyond recognition. Clucking his tongue, Sepp bit back a curse against the Truants. Floe had once been a Truant.

"Thanks for the backup out there," Floe said suddenly, her voice neutral now. "That shot was really clutch."

Sepp smiled. "No problem. I owe you some thanks too."

Floe turned to look at Sepp skeptically. "For what?"

"For improving the view. Sniper duty is so drab and unpleasant without you in the scope."

Floe shook her head. "You are incorrigible."

"I'm not familiar with that word. Does it mean 'very handsome?'"

"No."

"Ouch." Sepp clutched a hand over his heart. "You could have at least lied to spare my feelings."

The large gap in the overpass was in sight now, like a great chunk had been bitten out of the structure by a giant. Sepp scrambled up a piece of what had been a support column and gave Floe a hand up. After clearing more debris they arrived at the center of the blast.

Lying amidst the twisted concrete and steel was the wrecked hulk of the bulldozer. Like a slain animal it lay on its side, smaller pieces of it strewn around, smoke rising from its corpse. Mercifully there was no sign that the Truancy had come to salvage the machine yet—and judging from the extent of the damage, it was unlikely that they would gain much by doing so.

"Look for a car," Sepp said. "It should be somewhere nearby."

Sure enough, they found the battered automobile in the shadow of the bulldozer. It was upside down and half buried by rubble, but still in one piece. Floe bit her lip as she ran for the car and practically ripped the door open. Sepp thought she looked almost distraught as she pulled Cross from the wreckage.

For a moment Sepp was sure that their leader was done for. He showed no sign of movement and was bleeding from the head.

Floe pressed her ear to his chest and relief spread across her face.

"He's alive!"

Sepp grinned. "That's great news."

There was a groan from the driver's seat. Floe peered through the car window. "So is Joe."

Sepp blinked. "That's . . . news."

Floe nearly snorted with amusement but caught herself in time. Lifting Cross, she began to make her way up and out of the crater.

"Come on," she said. "We need to get out of here in case the Truancy gets curious about what happened to their dream machine."

"But we're behind enemy lines," Sepp pointed out. "Where can we possibly go that'd be safer than here?"

"We'll figure something out. Drag Joe out of there, will you?"

Sepp frowned and looked down at the car. He could catch a glimpse of Joe's massive outline through the window.

He groaned. "Heroics should come with a weight limit."

The news of the loss of the overpass threw District 1 into complete disarray. The Enforcers scrambled to prepare new defensive lines and carry out evacuations without any clear plan. Civilians fled en masse towards City Hall. Everyone expected to see Truants in the streets within hours. It was as though the end had already come.

As the chaos unfolded, no one noticed a lone figure clothed in black slip into a dark alley. The dawn had taken away the cover of night, but no one was looking for one shadow while throngs of thousands filled the streets.

Crouching behind a garbage can, Umasi waited and listened.

How long has it been since I last set foot in District 1? Two years? Three? Things sure have changed.

A group of Enforcers were trying to enforce a curfew to drive the crowd back from the steps of City Hall, but the civilians were being uncooperative for once. The disturbance would work to his advantage.

Straightening up, Umasi began moving, careful to avoid making any sound. Although his eyesight was already poor, he wore sunglasses that left him nearly blind. He had trained himself to rely heavily on hearing. Making his way around to the back of City Hall, he finally located what he was looking for—an old trapdoor service entrance that led into the basement. It hadn't been used for years.

The lock was rusted and easily gave way to a steel crowbar. With a smile of satisfaction, Umasi adjusted the black windbreaker buttoned around his neck like a cape. A pair of identical ceramic swords dangled at his sides.

The trap doors creaked open. After four years of self-imposed exile, it was finally time that he returned home.

The first conscious thing Cross became aware of was a slap to the face. The second thing was another slap to the face.

As the third one came Cross seized the oncoming arm by the wrist. Instinct told him to leverage his grip to break the limb, but he managed to suppress the urge. He cracked one eye open and groaned.

"What the hell are you doing, Floe?"

"Just testing your alertness," Floe said innocently. "And your patience too, I suppose. Surly as ever. You're going to be fine."

Cross tightened his grip. "What's going on?"

"You were having a bad dream."

Cross grunted. "It was better than this."

"I'll bet," Floe agreed. "May I have my arm back?"

Cross released her arm and sat up. They were on a station platform somewhere. A subway. The lights had long since gone out in this part of the City but a small bonfire had been built close to the edge of the platform so that the smoke would rise out of the ventilation holes above.

Floe was kneeling beside him with a look of concern on her face. Sepp was lying on his side, watching them idly through the fire, feeding it occasional planks of wood. Joe was awake as well, brooding by himself on a bench by the wall.

There was a painful pounding in Cross' head and he found it hard to concentrate. He gingerly touched the top of his head. His hand came away with dried blood.

"What happened?" Cross asked.

The others cast dark glances at one another.

"The Truancy is advancing fast towards District 1 now," Sepp said. "Without the overpass it'll take them a few days, but I don't see a whole lot that can be done to stop them. Meanwhile, we're stuck here in enemy territory."

"Enemy territory?" Cross repeated.

"That's right, boss," Sepp said. "Nothing between us and home but a few thousand Truants and the front lines of the war."

There were a few moments of brooding quiet. The only sound was the crackling of the fire. Sepp tossed another plank onto the heap.

"Are they looking for us?" Cross asked. "The Truancy, that is."

"I don't think we were seen. I doubt they even know we're here." Floe began digging through their packs. "Listen, I know you all might not have much of an appetite, but we should eat now while we have the chance."

No one was hungry, but the suggestion made sense. They pried open some canned rations and heated them over the fire. Within minutes they were scooping food up with their hands. Joe ate double his share but seemed to complain the most.

"I hate this damn slop," he said as he shoveled it in his mouth. "This stuff makes cafeteria food taste good."

Sepp merely poked at his food. "At least we put up a good fight. I'd say that for every student that went down we took two Truants with us."

"Maybe." Floe sipped at her canteen thoughtfully. "But it was never our combat ability they really feared. It was more the *idea* of us. Our very existence proves that they don't speak for all students. I can tell you firsthand that Edward gave them a real ideological crisis when he first came to power."

"I'm not Edward," Cross muttered.

"And a damn shame that is too." Joe was still licking his container. "What is this crap? They call this meat?"

"Hey, it'll give you a new appreciation for home cooking." Sepp punched Joe lightly on the shoulder. "Heck, my little sister could do better than that junk."

"She's only six, isn't she?" Floe said.

"Yeah." Sepp smiled. "But she's probably more mature than me. She lives near the western border with my mother. My father's an Enforcer, and I'm in the Militia, but of the whole family she probably minds gunfire the least. For her it's like fireworks every night."

"Aren't you worried about her?" Floe asked. "With the Truancy advancing and everything—"

"Of course I'm worried," Sepp said. "I've always been worried. Part of me wishes I could be with them right now, but staying with this unit is the best way I can protect them and everyone else. It's why I joined up in the first place. I couldn't stand doing nothing while the Truancy destroyed everything."

Cross remained silent. The talk of family made him feel uncomfortable. With nothing to add, he chewed the last of his food mechanically.

"That's all very noble of you Sepp." Joe threw his empty container aside. "But while we're talking about why we joined up, I've been dying to hear *your* reason, Floe. Haven't heard you mention it yet."

Floe looked away. "I'd rather not talk about that."

"Figures."

"I got my reasons, Joe, and the Educators thought they were good enough."

"Well if they're so good, why don't you share them with us?" Joe said. "Risking my neck is bad enough without wondering if there's a Truant in our unit."

Floe glared. "You never complained when I was out there watching your back!"

"Stupid me, huh?" Joe laughed. "The Truancy seemed to do a pretty good job predicting our movements back there. How do we *know* you're on our side? You won't even tell us why you support us!"

Sepp began to look a little alarmed. "Hey guys, why don't we all just—"

"So tell us why *you* joined, Joe!" Floe retorted. "Let me guess, you were failing school hard, right? Instant graduation. You're here because you're too dumb to be anywhere else!"

Joe jumped to his feet. On the other side of the fire Floe got up as well, unintimidated by the difference in height. Cross was in a bad mood and his head was still hurting, but he had no choice but to intervene.

"Both of you shut up!" he snapped. "You're acting like children!"

Joe rounded on Cross.

"You wanna fight too, *boss*?"

Blood began pounding in Cross' head again, and his instinct roared for him to say yes, to beat Joe so completely that he would never dare to challenge Cross again.

"You wouldn't stand a chance and you know it," Cross said coldly. "We are not enemies, Joe, and you'd better think twice before changing that. Floe isn't your enemy either—she's proven herself plenty of times. She fights for the same reason the whole Militia does."

"Oh? And what's that?" Joe demanded. "I don't know about you, but I kill Truants 'cause they try to kill me!"

"We kill each other *because* we're at war, that's not *why* we're at war." Cross spoke as though addressing a child. "Edward explained this when he first formed the Militia. We're fighting to prove that we can think and choose for ourselves. We're fighting to prove that not every student is a Truant!"

There was silence for a few moments. Seizing the opening, Sepp began clapping. The sound rang hollow in Cross' ears.

"That's right, we're all friends here," Sepp said. "Now why don't we just cool off for a couple of hours and then figure out what we're going to do? I can stand watch—"

"I'll do it," Cross said. "You all take your naps."

Joe still seemed to be sulking as he lay down on a bench, but the situation had been diffused. Suddenly exhausted, Cross stood up and slipped through the station turnstiles. Taking up watch inside the ticket booth, he began to think about the rhetoric he had used and how easily it had come.

It was all meaningless, of course. Proving individuality through conformity was a contradiction. Edward had even said as much in private when he manufactured the rhetoric a year ago. And so Cross didn't believe in any of it himself—how could he, when he knew it was all a lie? A lie that, somehow, had become his life.

Cross looked at the glass of the booth, searching for his reflection. For some reason he expected to find that it had no face. If not the Student Militia, what did he really believe in? Cross' headache worsened as he slipped back into memories of his time with Edward.

Pathetic!"

Cross winced as he hit the floor. A pair of emerald eyes glinted as Edward scowled at him from above.

It was a position Cross had gotten used to. Though his days at school went mostly unchanged, his new life at the orphanage was dominated by Edward. At their first meeting the ruthless boy had confessed his mad ambition for power. Ever since then he had been trying to persuade Cross to join him.

The two of them had been fighting tonight. This was a game Edward insisted they play, one that Cross would always lose.

"You know your techniques, Cross, but you don't use them for real," Edward said, crouching down. "Your father had you so beaten that you can't even defend yourself. You're a wimp."

Cross sat up. "Sorry."

"My patience has limits, Cross," Edward said. "I know you have it in you to fight back. I saw you struggle with those thugs when we first met."

"That was only because I lost my temper."

"Exactly!" Edward's gaze intensified. "You're not particularly talented, Cross. You can't even think for yourself. Do you know why I bother wasting time on you like this?"

"No."

"It's because you have two things that are useful to me; your obedience, and your anger," Edward replied. "That rage needs an *outlet* . . . and I intend to provide one."

Edward offered Cross his hand. Cross took it and rose shakily to his feet, only to have Edward punch him in the stomach without warning. Cross dropped like a stone, and anger flared inside him. He kept it bottled up.

"It doesn't have to be this way, Cross," Edward continued. "You don't have to suffer, helpless, as you've been doing your whole life."

"I haven't—"

"But of course you have," Edward sneered. "Don't you want to taste what it'd be like to be the bully for once? Or will you forever let yourself be the bullied?"

Cross glared up at Edward. "You're the one beating me right now."

"Then get even with me, Cross." Edward spread his arms. "I'm right here. What are you waiting for?"

Cross gritted his teeth. "I won't give you what you want."

"Of course." Edward smiled. "You refuse because you think you're at rock bottom and can sink no lower. You think that cruelty is still beneath you."

Edward crouched down and looked Cross in the eye.

"But there's no such thing as a bottom, Cross," he whispered. "No matter how far you've fallen, I can always bring you lower."

Cross looked back into Edward's face, and for the first time he shivered at what he saw.

Cross was jolted from his reverie as a voice whispered from the doorway. "Hey, Captain."

Cross did not turn around. "What do you want, Floe?"

She shifted. "Just wanted to thank you for backing me up there."

"It was nothing."

Floe watched him from the doorway, a silhouette against the firelight.

"*You* remember why I defected, right?"

Of course I do, how could I forget? Cross wanted to say, though he remained silent. His heart was racing again, this time speaking of different instincts than killing. As usual, he fought it down.

"We have a long day ahead of us, Floe," Cross said at last. "You need whatever rest you can get."

With that, he leaned back in his chair, still facing away from her. Through cracks in his eyes he watched her silhouette reflected in the glass. After what seemed like hours, it left.

Relieved to be on his own again, Cross turned his thoughts back to the war. At this rate the fighting would be over soon. Somehow that thought bothered him. The idea of losing the war was bad enough—the possibility of returning to a City at peace was even worse. He knew in his heart that such a City would have no place for him.

As time slipped by Cross began to wonder if there was any way left for him to spend his life doing something that mattered.

Umasi knew that Zyid had twice infiltrated City Hall by going right in through the front doors. That was during a time when City Hall was still the seat of power in the City, and no one believed it would ever be attacked. Now, in its waning days, the building was crawling with more guards than an anthill.

Umasi had almost made it to the stairs without being discovered when he turned another corner and abruptly found himself face-to-face with an Enforcer.

"Wha—"

The man went for his gun. Without pausing to think, Umasi drew a sword.

There was a flash of white, and then a splash of red. The gun clattered to the floor, and the man staggered backwards, clutching his bloodied hand. Umasi broke into a run, relieving the man of his radio as he passed by. He didn't bother to knock the guard out; either way, he knew he wouldn't have long before the alarm was raised.

Reaching the stairwell, Umasi took the steps three at a time. By the time he reached the third floor, alarms were ringing throughout the building. A door swung open. Before the Enforcer could realize what was going on, Umasi kicked the door into the man's face, knocking him out. Umasi took off again before his victim hit the ground. More footsteps and shouts echoed from below.

The fifth floor. Umasi opened the door and stepped inside, only to duck back out as a gunshot clipped his windbreaker. *Of course the Mayor would have guards outside his office.*

The footsteps from below were getting louder. Umasi reached into his jacket and pulled out a crude white cube with a match stuck in it. Igniting a lighter, Umasi lit the match and threw the cube through the doorway. The hall began to fill with white smoke.

Umasi burst inside, and in one smooth motion drew both of his ceramic blades. Through the confusion and the smoke he surged down the hallway. Umasi stopped before the doors to the Mayor's office, and all four of the guards slumped against the walls, weapons slipping from their grasps as they clutched various wounds.

Barely stopping to take a breath, Umasi tried the knob and found it unlocked. He opened the door.

"I had a feeling it was you, Umasi."

Umasi froze. He had been expecting that voice, and yet it stopped him in his tracks. All of a sudden thwarting the security of City Hall and taking on its armed guards seemed like nothing compared to the challenge of facing his long-estranged father.

"You should come inside," the Mayor said, holding the door open, "before any of my guards make the mistake of shooting you."

Brought back to reality, Umasi entered just as the sound of the stairwell door slamming closed reached their ears. Heading off the Enforcers, the Mayor stepped out into the hallway.

"Stand down gentlemen," he ordered. "There's been a misunderstanding."

"A misunderstanding?" one of the Enforcers blurted. "Sir, Truants have penetrated the building, and some of them came—"

"Just one, and he's no Truant," the Mayor said. "In fact, this boy has an appointment with me. Are there any injured besides the wonderfully incompetent fools lining the walls?"

"Um . . . yes, sir, we haven't got a full count yet, but—"

"Any dead?"

"Not that we know—"

"Then call an ambulance, if we have any left, and get them out of my sight," the Mayor snapped. "I don't want to be interrupted for the next hour, under any circumstances, understand?"

"Yes, sir."

A moment later the Mayor reentered his office, and Umasi examined him critically from behind his sunglasses.

"You didn't have to treat them so harshly, Mayor," he said. "They were doing their jobs as best they could."

"As were you—but your best was better." The Mayor sighed. "I've been in short supply of patience and competent subordinates these past four years."

"So I've seen."

"You could have called me to let me know you were coming, you know," the Mayor said, sitting down at his desk and regarding Umasi with tired eyes. "It's good to see you again."

"I never expected to return here," Umasi admitted. "But right now there's too much at stake for me not to."

At that, the Mayor smiled. "You have no idea how true that is, Umasi."

"I'm here to try to convince you to end the war," Umasi said. "After the outcome of last night's battle you must realize that your situation is hopeless. The Truancy is willing to negotiate."

"And you're empowered to negotiate on their behalf?"

"I am."

"Does that mean you've picked a side after all?"

"It means I made a promise to my brother," Umasi said, "a promise to the leader of the Truancy. I made it one year ago."

It took a moment for the Mayor to understand the implications of what Umasi had said. When he did, he sat up very slowly.

"You told me," the Mayor said, "that Zen died over three years ago."

"I did not lie," Umasi replied. "By then there was nothing left of my brother. By his own admission, Zen was dead. Zyid was an entirely different creation."

The Mayor immediately recognized the name of the Truancy's mysterious and feared leader—the boy he had hunted for over a year without success until his death had been announced by the Truancy. "Are you telling me . . ."

"That Zyid was once your son?" Umasi finished. "Yes."

The Mayor slumped in his seat, a numb look on his face.

"All that time, I was trying to avenge his death . . ." the Mayor murmured. "All that cruelty, all that violence . . . and it was against him, all along?"

"He wouldn't have wanted you to go easy on him," Umasi said. "He never thought of the conflict being between father and son. For him it was a struggle between the Mayor and Zyid."

"How . . . how did he die?"

Umasi knew why he was asking. The Mayor wanted, *needed* to know if he had caused his own son's death.

"He was not killed by Enforcers," Umasi said, putting that fear to rest. "He died in a duel he had arranged with his own successor. It was his intention to go out that way."

"Were you there?"

"I was. In his final moments." Umasi fingered his windbreaker. "I wear this and his sword in his memory."

For several long minutes the Mayor sat limp, like a puppet without a puppeteer. Umasi was starting to become concerned when the Mayor finally spoke.

"What does the Truancy have to say to me?"

"The war is as good as over. If you are willing to cooperate, the Truancy is willing to incorporate you into the process of reconstruction," Umasi said. "Ideology aside, you know a lot about how to make the City function, and the Truancy recognizes that you'd be valuable in that capacity."

The Mayor paused. What came next surprised Umasi.

"Fine! I surrender! The City is theirs!" The Mayor laughed. "And what then? Has the Truancy given a thought to what they'll do when there's no more Mayor?"

Umasi frowned. "Well, first they would try to rebuild, get utilities working, restore order—"

"If only things were that easy." The Mayor shook his head. "No, Umasi, what's been started here can no longer be ended by me or you. I admit your generation has won, and now you will inherit my burden. It's time that you learned the truth behind this City. It's time for me to tell you about the Government."

Umasi blinked. "Government? Isn't that you?"

The Mayor surveyed Umasi gravely, but just as he was about to speak he was interrupted by a loud beeping. Startled, the Mayor spun around and stared at his monitor.

"Impossible," he whispered. "They haven't made contact in a year."

Sensing that something important was about to happen, Umasi held his silence. With shaking fingers, the Mayor pressed a button on his keyboard. The image of a gray-eyed woman appeared onscreen.

The Mayor blanched. "*You.* I should have known."

"It's been awhile since we last spoke like this, Mr. Mayor. That was nearly four years ago, correct?"

5

HER REVENGE

A single gunshot.

That's all it took to send Sepp, Joe, and Floe from sleeping to pan-icked in the space of a second. The three students were on their feet with eyes wide and hearts pounding before any of them had a conscious thought. That panic quickly turned to ire when all they found was Cross standing in the ashes of the fire, his rifle pointed at the ceiling and a shell casing at his feet.

"What the *hell*?" Joe bellowed.

"I had no time to tiptoe around to each of you and gently shake you awake," Cross said. "As a bonus, you are all already alert."

Sepp sighed and rubbed his eyes. "How long were we asleep?"

"Two hours. It's past noon now. That's precious time we can't afford—for all we know the Truancy has gotten as far as District 2 already."

Floe huffed and smoothed out her skirt.

"I hope you have some kind of plan after waking us up like that," she said. "Otherwise we might as well just sleep in until the Truancy controls the whole City."

In response Cross kicked a pile of clothing stacked neatly next to the bonfire. They were little more than grungy rags, the sort of attire that Truants seemed to love and Students would never be caught dead in.

"I scavenged these from outside," Cross said. "Get changed."

Joe made a face. "Are any of them from dead Truants?"

"Yes," Cross said. "You're welcome to go naked instead."

For a few seconds they stared at the clothing as though weighing the op-tion. Then Floe shrugged and began to change on the spot. The boys averted their eyes as she reached for the only set of female clothing in the stack. Her example got them moving, and in no time they were all dressed like Truants.

"All right then," Floe said. "What's the big plan, Cross?"

"We have no sure way of returning safely to our lines, and we have no time to waste waiting for an opening," Cross said. "There's only one way that we can possibly make a big enough difference at this point.

"We're going to assassinate the leader of the Truancy."

Silence. Sepp began laughing until he finally began to suspect that Cross was serious.

"Are you serious?" Sepp asked.

"Yes."

"Cross, that's crazy!" Floe protested. "You can't really think that the four of us could pull that off. You have no idea what Takan is capable of, where he might be, what his guard is like—"

"But you *do*, and you can help us plan this," Cross pointed out. "Remember all of that destruction last night? That could be happening in District 2 right now. Don't you want to do something about that?"

"Of course I do!" Floe looked scandalized. "I'm just trying to get you to look at this rationally, Cross!"

"I'm not doing it," Joe said flatly. "No diploma is worth dying for, and this right here is suicide."

"Even assuming that we can get close enough to Takan to eliminate him, we're not leaving Truancy City alive," Floe said. "I know you know that. It really *is* suicide. You're asking us to die for the faint chance that we can kill one person."

Cross seemed to struggle with himself for a moment. Then his expression smoothed over as though it had been carved of ice. He said not a word more. This was his way of leaving the decision up to them.

"Screw it," Joe muttered. "I'd rather defect. Get with the winning team while they're still accepting applications. Should've done it a long time ago."

It was Sepp who spoke next. "Joe, if you try it, I'll kill you myself."

Everyone was taken aback by that. This was something new. Sepp, who was normally all smiles and jokes, was suddenly staring Joe down with deadly resolve.

"Takan needs to be stopped. The Truancy needs to be stopped," Sepp continued. "All that stuff that went up in flames last night? That wasn't just scenery. It took decades to build the City to that level—who knows how long it'd take to build again? My family lost their house that way. My father risks his life every day trying to protect what's left. I'm not going to let them down."

Floe hesitated, and then turned to Cross. Her expression was uncertain now. Cross gave her nothing at first, but as the seconds wore by, he cracked and nodded slightly.

"Fine," Floe said bitterly. "I just hope you prove me wrong."

All eyes now turned to Joe. His back to the wall, Joe gritted his teeth and clenched his fists. His eyes darted around as though looking for an escape. Seeing that he had no allies, he seemed to visibly deflate.

"All right!" Joe said. "Just so long as you know I'm not dying for any of you! Just one hint that this is going south and I'm out of there."

"Right." Cross kept his eyes on Floe. "I know you don't want to do this, but we have no hope without you. I need you to tell me everything you know about Takan, starting with where we can find him."

Floe sighed. "He'll probably be in District 15," she said. "After showing himself last night he's going to want to stay far away from the front lines until the final hour of the war. The best bet is that he'll be at headquarters."

"District 15," Cross mused. "We can get there through the subway system in a matter of hours. We can make the entire trip underground. No need to worry about Truancy patrols finding us and asking questions en route."

"That's not a bad idea." Sepp nodded. "Why didn't the Truancy ever think of that?"

"They did," Floe replied. "It's how they got some of their raiding parties so far in before. That's why the Educators sealed off all the lines connected to their territory."

"I've heard that the Mayor has his own private subway that reaches all the way out of the City," Sepp interjected. "I'm betting he kept that one open just for a day like this."

"If we do this right he won't need to use it just yet," Cross said. "Floe, once we're in, how do we take him out?"

"Carefully," Sepp quipped.

"You would want to avoid engaging him at all costs," Floe replied. "Our best shot is to have Sepp take him out from afar. That way we might even stand a chance of surviving afterwards."

Cross thought about that, then nodded with approval. "That covers all the key bases," he said. "What else do you know about Takan as a person? Anything you can tell us might be useful."

Floe chewed her lip. "I wish I could help you out more there. I don't know him well myself. As a Truant I served mostly under Zyid."

"That was the Truancy's old leader, wasn't it? The one whose message played on the City's loudspeakers about a year ago?"

"Yeah." Floe nodded. "I'll admit that I admired him. I know most students think he's a monster, and I'm not saying everything he did was justified, but for his followers—for *us*—he was the embodiment of both our highest aspirations and our darkest wishes."

Sepp tried to make light of what she was saying. "Don't tell me you're turning into a poet now, Floe."

"If you'd known him you would understand," Floe shot back. "After feeling helpless for so long, he empowered us, made us feel like anything was possible."

"You're making him out to be some kind of saint," Joe spat. "If he was all that great, why did you switch sides?"

"Joe." Cross' voice was low and dangerous.

"No, that's fair." Floe looked at Joe. "No one thought that Zyid was a saint. He was brutal to his enemies. I think all of us knew on the inside that he was driven by anger. We followed him because, on the inside, we were all angry too."

"That's not how I remember his last message," Sepp pointed out. "It was like he was trying to make nice with that speech."

"Towards the end Zyid was acting a bit strange. He started to talk about the future and peace, things he never mentioned much before." Floe shrugged. "I don't think anyone will ever understand what he was thinking. He died that night, or so they say."

Cross frowned. "Do you know how it happened?"

To everyone's surprise, Floe laughed at that.

"The story was that he got shot down by the Militia," she explained. "Me, I have my own suspicions."

"Suspicions?" Cross repeated.

"The night he died, Zyid went out on a mission with Takan, who was second in command back then," Floe said darkly. "No one ever saw Zyid again. Takan was the only witness to his death."

Sepp shivered. "You think he offed his own leader so he could take his place? That's cold, even for a Truant."

"Yeah," Floe said, "and I wasn't the only one. There were whispers. A lot of Truants thought that Noni should be the new leader."

"Noni?"

"She was Zyid's second in command for a while," Floe explained. "They said she'd been around since the beginning of the Truancy."

"What happened to that?" Sepp asked.

Floe shrugged. "Not long after Zyid's death, she left the Truancy. No one's sure why, but it did put an end to the whispers. Takan's been the leader ever since."

The students spent a few moments in silence, each of them brooding over the image of their enemy that the story had painted. They were up against a boy who was utterly ruthless, opportunistic, ambitious—and all the more dangerous because of it.

"This still leaves the original question," Cross said at last. "What do you know about Takan himself?"

"Like I said, I never fought under him directly." Floe sighed. "He built his reputation as a fighter, and he wasn't very social. He came off as kind of cold and secretive. There were a lot of unanswered questions about his past. Not the kind of person you can understand. Not the kind of person I'd like to follow."

She shot Cross a look loaded with meaning.

Cross ignored the look and reached for his equipment.

"That much information will have to do," he said. "I want to take him out before he becomes ruler of the whole City. The sooner the better."

Hot summer air blasted Takan's face as he leaned out the back window of an abandoned flower shop. A subordinate standing behind him relayed his report.

"The Educators are offering no resistance so far. Instead they seem to be withdrawing all of their remaining forces back to District 1," the Truant said. "If they still plan to fight, they'll make their last stand there. It might be pretty hard to take the district if it comes to that."

"Only if we waste lives by attacking head-on," Takan said. "Order our forces to stay put. Meanwhile, Aaron can begin preparing the explosives for Plan B. We'll start moving them into position tonight."

"Um, they *have* been avoiding battles since last night. Shouldn't we wait for the Mayor's response before—"

"I want to be ready just in case the answer is no. This has dragged on long enough." Takan gestured towards the distant cloud of dust and smoke. "As you said, they could still put up a fight in District 1. We have to be prepared to act quickly if that turns out to be their plan."

"Gotcha, boss. I'm out."

With that, the Truant hurried out of the unlit flower shop to deliver his message. Takan continued to gaze out of the window, listening to the receding footsteps. For a few moments there was silence. Then there was a sudden movement behind him.

In an instant Takan had drawn his sword and spun around, only to find his white blade blocked by a white knife. A pair of icy blue eyes glinted in the shadows.

"Noni," he breathed.

Takan lowered his sword, and the girl before him did the same with her knife. Even in the gloom, she cut a dashing figure, with long black hair tied into a loose ponytail. A prominent scar ran along the length of her left jaw, giving her a fearsome look. Her black scarf, once used to cover that scar, was now tied around her waist like a sash. She wore a black jacket and blue jeans, and gripped her weapon with a gloved hand.

"How goes the war, leader?" she asked.

"Should've known it was you." Takan sheathed his sword. He wanted to hug her, but her glare told him that now wasn't the time. "There aren't a lot of people who could sneak up on me like that. It's good to see you again."

Noni turned away and began inspecting documents on a table. "Finding you here was coincidence. I expected you to still be out on the front."

"It's not time for me to make another appearance just yet," Takan said. "Have you had any luck with your search?"

Noni's icy eyes flashed. In one violent motion, she kicked a nearby wooden chair, breaking it in two. Takan gave no reaction, standing calmly as splinters scattered across the floor.

"Obviously not," she replied. "If I had, I wouldn't be chasing down dead-end leads, would I?"

"Don't you ever think that your energy might be better put to use by helping us end the war?" Takan asked. "It's what he would've wanted."

"It's not about what he would've wanted," she snarled. "He's dead. Now it's about what *I* want. The Truancy doesn't need my help, and I don't need the Truancy!"

There was a moment of ringing silence. Takan changed the subject.

"Funny how some people expected a power struggle. I don't think any of them even knew that you and I were . . . you know . . . involved."

Noni's head snapped around. "You think I'd have gone easy on you because of that?"

"Well, I suppose you never went easy on me anyway."

"If I thought you'd murdered him like the rumors said, *you would be dead,*" Noni said. "But I don't believe it of you. You respected him . . . even though you refuse to help me now."

Takan sighed. He knew that the conversation would come to this. "I don't know what you expect, Noni. Should I send Truants to help you investigate?"

"If that's what I wanted I would've recruited some myself," Noni said. "You know what I want. You were the only one there when he died. Tell me who killed him!"

For a moment Takan hesitated, and Noni's eyes narrowed.

"I did not see the face of his attacker," Takan said. "I'm sorry."

"You've said as much before."

"It's the truth."

The two of them stared at each other, unblinking.

"Is it, Takan?" Noni said. "Will you swear?"

Takan met her gaze. "I swear. I'm not lying."

She considered him for a moment, and then shrugged. The tension in the atmosphere seemed to dissipate. "It looks like the Enforcer didn't leave anything useful here. I'll be going now."

Noni walked past Takan as though he weren't even there, making straight for the window.

"You know, you could always come back," Takan offered.

"Revenge first," she replied. "Truancy second."

With that, Noni reached out and gripped the windowsill, preparing to make her exit. Takan hesitated, then spoke again.

"You know, he told me something, the night he died."

Noni paused, her head already out the window.

"He said you might become 'unpredictable' without him," Takan continued. "I'm starting to wonder if he didn't mean 'obsessed' instead."

Noni stiffened, and then she was gone. Takan exhaled. He hadn't lied, exactly, but he knew that was just a flimsy excuse. Deceiving Noni was never pleasant, but Takan couldn't imagine how he would ever explain to her that the face he hadn't seen that night was his own.

Takan shook his head distractedly. He needed a drink.

Cross wasn't sure what he'd been expecting when they had first climbed down onto the tracks, but it wasn't a pitch-black and disgusting series of tunnels.

Their path was lit only by the flashlights that each member of the unit carried, and their footsteps echoed through the vast darkness. They passed station after dead station, all of them deserted with no electricity. It was an eerie sight. Joe seemed especially uncomfortable in the dark, jumping at the slightest disturbances.

"How much longer?" he demanded.

"We're taking the most direct line to District 15." Floe sounded like an irritated mother. "Only four more stations, Joe. If the Truants didn't have vehicles we'd probably beat them there."

"Ah that's right, Truants get to drive," Sepp said. "Do they have designated drivers, or is everyone able to do it?"

"Not *everyone,* but it wasn't like we had adults to do it for us," Floe said. "Back in the day I drove a van during a hideout evacuation. Ran into some Enforcers on the way and led them all the way to one of Zyid's ambushes."

"Well aren't you proud," Joe said.

"Why shouldn't I be?" Floe retorted. "Don't I have a right to be proud of my accomplishments?"

"Not if you throw them away and become a traitor."

Sepp threw his arms up in the air and turned to look at Cross. Fed up, Cross gritted his teeth and did his best to ignore the argument.

"So you would have preferred me stay with the Truancy?" Floe demanded. "Why can't you let this go, Joe? What exactly do you *want*?"

"How about apologizing for being a Truant?"

"In the beginning the Truancy had the right idea, Joe," Floe said. "The system was broken, they just had the wrong approach. Their motives—"

Joe snorted.

"You're such a stupid jerk!" Floe shouted. "What do you know about the Truancy?"

"More than you, obviously!"

By now the argument was turning dangerous. Joe had clearly been holding this in for a long time and looked eager to get into a fight. Floe, for her part, was fingering the knife at her side. Cross was no ambassador, and so he decided to end the argument the only way he knew how.

Before either party could speak again, Cross drew his sidearm and fired once into the tunnel. The deafening sound echoed throughout the tunnel, and all heads turned to gape at him.

"What is with you and shooting that thing to get attention?" Joe demanded. "You're gonna bring the Truants right to us!"

"Any Truant in these tunnels would've known we were here the moment you started shouting," Cross countered. "Your bickering is getting on my nerves *and* giving us away. At least the gunshot doesn't give me a migraine."

He was right, and they knew it. Collectively they now hoped that there *weren't* any Truants in the tunnels.

Floe looked away. "Sorry."

Joe grumbled something inaudible.

Cross sighed and holstered his weapon. Sepp quickly turned to Joe and struck up a conversation, pointedly acting like he hadn't noticed the argument. Joe was already too moody to be very talkative, and only became less so as Sepp cheerfully made morbid observations about the tunnel.

Meanwhile, Cross noticed Floe walking all alone over to the side. He hesitated for a moment, then moved to join her. She tensed at his approach, but he took it as a good sign that she didn't flinch away completely.

"They hate me," Floe said quietly as soon as he was within earshot. "You know they do. You've heard students whispering when they think I can't hear them. Joe doesn't even hide it. Sepp probably hates me too; he's just too polite to say so."

"Joe hates everyone," Cross pointed out. "The other students don't even know you. They're just being students. And I'm not sure that Sepp is even capable of hatred."

"I really don't get it," Floe said. "They don't like me talking about the Truancy, but that's the only thing I'm good for around here!"

"You're as good a shot as any of us," Cross said. "It's just different for you because you've seen both sides. For them, it's irritating to hear you speak about the enemy in such friendly terms when they're doing their best to destroy us."

"So what do you want?" Floe snapped. "Should I lie and pretend to be ashamed of everything in my past? The Educators aren't all good, Cross, and the Truancy isn't all bad. You guys live in your own little black-and-white worlds when reality has color, or at least shades of gray!"

Cross looked away. "You're upset now. If you want to stay behind—"

"Save it," Floe said. "If I don't get self-pity, you don't either. I'm uncomfortable with *them*. But I can deal with it."

"Thanks."

"No problem." Floe looked away.

Understanding that the conversation was over, Cross nodded and turned back towards the front of their procession. Before long another station platform came into sight. Floe spoke up.

"This is our stop."

"Finally," Joe muttered.

With some difficulty, the students managed to climb their way onto the platform. Sunlight filtered down through the ventilation grates. Almost involuntarily all heads turned upwards with trepidation.

"It's 17:12 in the evening." Cross checked his watch. "We don't have a whole lot of daylight left. Sepp is a good shot, but I don't like his chances of nailing Takan in the dark."

Floe nodded. "So how do we do this?"

"First things first, we need to find out where exactly Takan is," Cross said. "Floe, I believe you once mentioned that the Truancy operates a bar near their headquarters?"

6

The Truancy City

Deep in District 15, a little boy wandered down an empty alley. He hummed happily in his head, wishing he could hum aloud. That wasn't possible, of course—he was on an expedition, and it was very important not to be heard on an expedition. Especially not this far from home, where the dangerous kids lived.

Spotting something fluffy sticking out of a pile of rubble ahead, the boy's face split into a wide smile as he ran over to it. It was big and, he was delighted to find, soft to touch as well. He yanked it from the pile, upsetting the rubble as he examined his find. He recognized the stuffed animal as a sheep—big and fluffy. He liked the curly hairs on it.

Then the boy frowned. The sheep also had a lot of dirt on it, and his mother didn't like dirty things. She was probably unhappy right now. The boy knew his mother was always watching him on these expeditions, even though he couldn't see her—and he liked it just fine that way.

The boy held the sheep up by a horn and decided that, though the sheep was dirty, it could maybe be cleaned. Mind made up, he tucked it under his arm and then looked down at his new companion.

"What's your name, sheep?" he asked.

There was a minute or two of silence. Impatient now, the boy decided that the name would, in fact, be Sheep.

"Nice to meet you, Sheep!" the boy said. "My name is Zen."

With that, the boy continued on his way, wondering what other interesting things he might see today.

The Truancy's bar was unlike any Cross had seen before. The atmosphere was more like a carnival than the dim locales he'd frequented in Educator territory. Colorful festive lights were strung from the ceiling, a cotton candy machine sat in one corner, and the walls were decorated with seemingly random paraphernalia. A movie poster hung next to a pink stuffed animal and a dart board. Everywhere there were inane scribbles and carvings, displaying messages like "SCHOOLS OUT" or "5th bomb squad was here!"

The staff and patrons were young people, loud and raucous, with not a single adult. District 15 had long been an abandoned district and center of the Truancy rebellion. This was the belly of the beast.

His heart pounding, Cross made his way towards the main bar. Here he was surrounded by his enemies, and just one mistake would leave him dead or worse. The fear, the very real danger of discovery, made Cross feel more alive than he had in a long time. There was no one to help him either; he had left the rest of his team at the station. Joe hadn't liked that, but a larger group would have attracted far more suspicion.

"What do ya want?" the bartender asked as Cross seated himself.

"Something strong," Cross said. "Impress me."

"You really mean that?" The boy raised an eyebrow. "I reckon we got a couple hours until sundown yet."

Cross considered it. "Just water then. It's hot out there."

The bartender nodded and slammed a bottle down on the counter. As Cross began to drink, he began to look around to see which Truants were already drunk. Hopefully there would be someone he could ply for answers.

"Hell of a battle yesterday, huh?"

Cross jumped. The Truant sitting right next to him had spoken. His face was flushed and his bottle was half empty.

"Sure was," Cross replied.

"Hit the Educators pretty hard, didn't we? Haven't seen action like that in a year."

"Yeah, me neither."

"I don't think I've seen you around before," the Truant said, taking a sip from his drink. "What group are you with?"

Cross' mouth suddenly felt dry. He swallowed more water and made up a suitably vague lie.

"We were carrying out some of Tai   r's special orders."

"Oh, you're with one of Aaron's bomb squads?" the Truant said. "Dunno why you guys think everything you do is so damn secret. It's not like we don't notice things being blown up, you know."

Cross shrugged. "Have to keep up appearances."

"Right, right, appearances." The Truant nodded. "You know, rumor has it that the war might be ending any minute. We might not even have to set foot in District 1. You know Zyid's brother, the one that just showed up after he died?"

Cross blinked. That sounded like trouble, and Floe hadn't mentioned anything like it. "Yeah."

"They say he's got some sort of influence over the Mayor," the Truant said. "Word is that he can get the Mayor to surrender. The battle yesterday should give him enough leverage."

Cross' headache was starting to resurface. He scowled. Influence over the Mayor? What kind of drunken fantasies were these?

"I sure hope it's over soon," the Truant continued. "I gotta say, I'm not eager to be cycled out there again."

"What's Takan think of all this?" Cross asked, taking a sip.

The Truant shrugged. "Who knows what the boss is thinking? He talks more but *says* less than Zyid used to, if you know what I mean."

"Yeah, but after yesterday shouldn't he be celebrating?" Cross asked. "What's he doing today anyway?"

"Beats me," the Truant said. "You know, he does still come in here once in a while. I saw him last week, back when— oh hey, speak of the devil."

No way. Gripped again by the sense that this was all another nightmare, Cross spun around on his stool. He froze. Sure enough, a boy with wild brown hair stood before him, amber eyes narrowed. His brown trench coat was unbuttoned, allowing Cross to see the sword sheathed at his side.

"I happened to spot you while I was getting a drink," Takan said. "Who are you?"

"Excuse me?" Cross felt the eyes of the whole bar upon him.

"I asked for your name," Takan said, reaching for his sword hilt. "Or have the Educators stripped students of those too?"

Dammit, Joe, this isn't a joke!" Floe hissed.

"I don't care what you losers do, I'm sick of doing everything that brat says," Joe said. "If he can have a drink at the bar then I can too!"

The two students were now engaged in a fierce argument in stage whispers as they walked down the street towards the bar. A concerned Sepp followed in their wake, looking unsure of why he was there.

"This is not the time for this crap!" Floe said. "Do you not notice where we are? Do you have any idea how many Truants there are in this district? You're really going to get yourself killed, and us along with you!"

"What about Cross then?" Joe demanded. "Face it, he's just hogging all the good parts for himself!"

"He went alone because it's *dangerous*!" Floe seethed. "Bad enough to have one unfamiliar face asking questions, do you really think we can get away with four?"

"Who said anything about asking questions? I just want a drink," Joe said obstinately. "I'll pretend not to know 'em."

"You guys," Sepp pleaded. "Not so loud, we're getting close!"

"Help me out here, Sepp!" Floe ordered, rounding on him. "Get this complete *idiot* to stop being stupid!"

"Me?" Sepp blinked. "What good do you think I'd do?"

"Yeah, Sepp wants a drink too, don't you Sepp?" Joe grinned. "Things are practically dry back in Educator territory and you know it."

"Look, guys, can't we come up with a compromise?" Sepp pleaded. "Floe, I'm trying to keep the peace here and all you're doing is staring off into—"

"Uh-oh," Floe breathed.

Her attention was fixed upon something far ahead of them. The others followed her gaze just in time to see a brown-haired boy enter the bar.

"That was Takan just now," Floe said urgently. "Cross might be in trouble."

"Takan?" Joe repeated. "The guy we gotta kill?"

"Yeah," Floe said, raising her rifle. "If he hasn't already figured *us* out first. Come on, hurry!"

I'm waiting," Takan said, hand on his hilt.

Cross took another sip from his bottle as he tried to focus. Takan was hesitating, not yet drawing his sword. That meant he wasn't sure. Had his earlier words been a bluff? One false move either way and he was finished. Cross felt a drop of sweat trickle down his neck.

Deciding that his best bet would be to make something up, Cross opened his mouth.

"My name is—"

The glass storefront shattered. Most of the Truants instinctively ducked. Takan kicked a table over and used it as cover as he drew his pistol to return fire. Overwhelmed by the surreal nature of the proceedings, Cross paused for a moment as he pinched himself.

That hesitation cost him a perfect opportunity to shoot Takan in the back. The Truancy leader cast another suspicious glance at him, and then like lightning punched Cross in the forehead. Alert once more, Cross allowed himself to go limp. More gunshots went off, but no further blows came. The ruse appeared to have worked; Takan believed he was unconscious.

Cross opened his eyes a crack. The other Truants were now following their leader's example, firing out the bar window from behind overturned tables. Cross realized that his team must have assumed hidden positions across the street and were now pouring a withering stream of bullets into the bar. Bottles shattered, sending glass and liquid spraying everywhere.

Cross knew the Truants had time on their side and could wait for reinforcements, but to his surprise, Takan didn't seem content to wait.

"Mark, Axel, Johnson, Vanessa, make them keep their heads down," Takan ordered. "Jose, Nix, follow me!"

He knows everyone by name? Cross thought, startled.

"Don't let them escape!" Takan shouted as he exited the bar. "Try to outflank them!"

Realizing that his target was getting away, Cross sprang to his feet. The Truants seemed too preoccupied to notice. The moment he was out the door, he saw one of Floe's illegal firebombs sail towards the bar. The move should have forced the Truants out into the open, but Takan spun around and fired a bullet that caught it in midair.

Flames splattered on the sidewalk in front of the bar, creating a smoke and heat haze that was difficult to aim through. Across the street, the students took the opportunity to withdraw and run for a nearby alley.

The Truancy's leader was now running for an adjacent alley, his two subordinates trailing far behind him. Cross raised his rifle and charged after them, determined to make up for his earlier hesitation.

In that moment a distant shot went off, narrowly missing Takan but striking one of the two Truants behind him. Cross felt his heart soar as he realized that it meant Sepp had found a sniper roost. Takan was drawing close to the alley, but Cross knew Sepp would be able to get off another shot before the Truant escaped. A single bullet could end all of this.

Cross held his breath.

The shot went off, only to strike the sidewalk a moment after Takan vanished safely into the alley.

"Dammit!" Cross swore.

The Truant in front of him turned around to stare, and Cross realized his blunder. Abandoning all attempts at subtlety, Cross drove his fist into the Truant's face. There were shouts, and Cross glanced behind him. More Truants were now pouring out of the bar. They had seen.

"Not good." Cross ran as gunshots rang out behind him.

Takan had already vanished into an alley. The Truancy leader undoubtedly knew the back alleys better than Cross' unit and would have no problem escaping—if he even *wanted* to escape. From everything Cross had seen and heard, he expected Takan to hunt them down himself.

Cross plunged down the alley that his team had vanished into, hoping that he would be able to catch up. Hearing Truants entering the alley behind him, Cross kicked over some garbage cans to make pursuit more difficult. Gunshots rang out just as Cross turned a corner, and he fired a few of his own into the air to intimidate his pursuers.

It didn't work very well. Cross soon reached a point where a narrow side alley split off from the main passage. He paused, unsure of which way to go. Behind him two Truants appeared, weapons bared. Cross was about to pick a random path when suddenly there came a rattle from a fire escape above.

Sepp dropped onto the Truants' heads like a leopard. There was a scuffle and a few gunshots, and then the Truants were down and Sepp was up, breathing heavily, pistol in hand, rifle slung over his back.

"Floe, get him out of here!" he shouted. "I'll draw some of them off!"

Cross felt his arm grasped by a familiar hand, and he allowed himself to be led along down the narrow side alley. There were a few more gunshots and shouts, and then Cross caught a glimpse of Sepp passing by the mouth of the side alley in a blur, a dozen Truants in his wake.

"Is it all right to let him go like that?" Cross wondered.

"He'll be fine," Floe said. "You know how fast he is. You should be more worried about *us*."

Sure enough, even as Cross watched, a Truant turned and ran down the side alley after them. Cross raised his rifle and fired. There was barely enough room to turn around in this passage, making the shot impossible to miss. The Truant screamed and fell to the ground, prompting Cross and Floe to begin running faster.

"Thanks for waiting," Cross said.

"Never mind that," Floe snapped. "What happened in the bar back there?"

Cross shook his head in frustration. He wished he knew the answer to that himself. "Somehow Takan knew I wasn't a Truant. I don't know how. The others were fooled. How could he know just by looking at me?"

"Takan isn't a normal Truant," Floe said grimly. "Speaking of which, let's hope we don't run into him like this. We wouldn't stand a chance."

"So he *is* chasing us?"

Floe laughed. "Of course he is. The Truancy won't risk us getting away alive now."

"So where's Joe?" Cross asked.

"We ran into a little obstacle ahead," Floe said. "I decided to let Joe take care of it while I went back for you."

"What kind of obstacle?"

"You'll see."

The narrow passage ended, opening up into the wall of a larger alley. Cross hesitated at the sound of loud grunting, but Floe didn't seem concerned. She jumped down into the alley and Cross followed suit. There, blocking their way, was a pile of metal barrels stacked three high and two deep. Joe, the source of the grunting, was trying to pull one of the bottom barrels out.

"Come on Joe, we're going to have company soon," Floe said.

"Shut up." Joe gasped as he pulled. "These things are freaking heavy!"

"Need help?" Cross offered, stepping forward.

"Stay outta my way!" Joe snarled.

Joe began backing up, and Cross and Floe moved aside. With a roar, Joe charged at the pile shoulder-first. He slammed into them with tremendous force, enough to knock the middle barrel askew. The whole pile shook for a second, then collapsed.

One of the barrels fell on top of Joe, and for a moment Cross had to suppress a smile as the huge boy groaned beneath the collapsed pile.

"You all right?" Floe asked, moving to help him up.

Joe did not answer, but let out a grunt as Cross and Floe rolled the barrels off him. As Joe got to his feet, the trio became aware of the sound of approaching footsteps coming from farther down the alley.

"The noise got someone's attention," Cross said. "Looks like the Truants have another route to get here."

"Well, which way do we go?" Floe gestured at the path they had cleared.

Cross' heart sank. The alley seemed to split again. One passage led towards what looked like an abandoned warehouse in the distance, and the other twisted off to the left. For a few moments the entire group was seized by indecision. Neither option seemed obvious, and the choice could literally be life or death.

Then, bizarrely, something white and fluffy dropped down from somewhere above and landed right onto the path leading to the warehouse. The students stared at it.

It was a stuffed animal sheep.

The students looked up and saw no one. Cross was the first to speak.

"That's as good a sign as any. Let's go to the warehouse, we can hide out there until things calm down."

"You crazy?" Joe sputtered. "It's got to be a trap!"

Floe shook her head. "No, it's way too obvious for that. Besides, it would've been just as easy to shoot us from above. The wind probably blew it off a rooftop or something."

"I'm in a freaking nuthouse," Joe muttered. "Don't tell me you're actually going to follow the stuffed animal?"

"This is *so* not the time for your testosterone festival, Joe!" Floe snapped.

"When is the time then?" Joe shouted. "We're about to get us killed, like all those other fools that followed this idiot!"

"This isn't a debate!" Cross snapped. "We're going to the warehouse. That's an order!"

Joe seemed to consider that for a moment. Then he swung his fist in a move so sudden that even Cross didn't see it coming. The next thing Cross knew, he was on the ground dazed as Joe ran off as fast as his legs could carry him.

"Joe, you scum!" Floe shouted, reaching for her gun. "Who's the traitor now?"

"Leave him!" Cross grabbed her arm, though his blood pulsed with rage. "He'll distract them. We have to keep moving."

Floe hesitated, then reluctantly lowered her weapon as Joe vanished down the left alley.

"Fine," she seethed. "The Truancy can have him."

Joe ran alone down the alley, thrilled by his escape. Breaking away had been so easy that he wondered why he ever took orders from Cross in the first place. It had felt unbelievably good to finally punch that kid. Joe wished he could've done it some more, but with that vicious harpy around he knew he couldn't get away without getting shot. Those two deserved each other, as far as Joe was concerned.

Not really paying attention to his surroundings, Joe was taken by surprise when the alley opened up into a square space. It was some sort of small yard between buildings that had been fenced off. A dead end. Joe swore, spun around . . .

And found himself face-to-face with Takan.

"Augh!" Joe screamed, jumping backwards.

The Truancy's leader took a step forward and reached for his sword. Confronted by an enemy he couldn't beat, Joe did the only thing that came naturally. He dropped his gun and raised his hands.

"I give up! I wanna switch sides!"

Takan halted at the sound of Joe's voice. His eyes narrowed.

"I know you."

Joe blinked. "Eh?"

"You're Joe, right?" Takan said. "Yeah. Joe, the bully."

"Wh—what are you talking about?

"Don't you remember?" Takan cocked his head. "You chased me into District 19."

It took Joe a moment to process that. Then his jaw dropped. For the first time he looked, *really* looked at the boy called Takan. He saw past the grim expression and the aged face, past the trench coat and sheathed sword. He saw a scrawny boy whom he had tormented years ago, just one among his countless victims.

"You're that little punk, Tack!"

Takan nodded and ran a hand through his messy brown hair.

"Tack! It is you, I don't believe it! Did you think changing your name was cool or something?" Joe laughed. "This is just perfect. I never got a chance to pay you back for my leg, did I?"

Suddenly Joe found Takan's gun pressed against his forehead. He froze. Joe had forgotten that this wasn't a school hallway, that Takan was not a student, but actually the most dangerous Truant alive.

"You . . . you always were too scared to fight me man-to-man!" Joe said, desperately looking for a way out. "You're nothing without your gun!"

To Joe's surprise, Takan paused at that. Then he threw his gun aside. He drew his sword and placed that on the ground as well. Joe felt his confidence return. When it was just fists and mean words, he was a pro. He had been feared at school for a reason.

"So Tack, how come you're alive, anyway?" Joe asked. "I thought you died in that car accident with your little smartass sister. She here too?"

"No," Takan said. "No, she's dead."

"Aww, that's sad," Joe mocked. "But I already paid *her* back anyway. Did she ever tell you that? Me and my buddies got her after school while you were fooling around in District 19. We tried not to leave too many bruises, so I don't know if you noticed."

Joe watched for a reaction, but Takan gave him nothing.

"Put your fists up, Joe," Takan said. "That is, if you want to die fighting."

Joe swung at Takan with what he thought was impressive speed. The blow hit nothing but air. Joe barely had time to blink in surprise before Takan drove his elbow into Joe's chest, and then snapped his forearm up to hit Joe's face with his knuckles.

Dazed, Joe gasped and staggered backwards. Without missing a beat, Takan kicked Joe in the groin, then grabbed his head and slammed it against one knee. Seeing stars, Joe collapsed clutching his privates.

"You bastard," he moaned. "You're like that freak in District 19!"

There was no response. Joe opened his eyes to see Takan approaching him with cool, measured steps. Only now did Takan allow his expression to change. His face was terrifying, a mask of tightly bottled fury.

Takan kicked Joe in the ribs. Once, twice, repeatedly until bones cracked. Joe screamed.

"What was your objective?" Takan demanded. "Tell me!"

"We . . ." Joe gasped. "We were trying to k-kill you."

"So this is how the Student Militia handles defeat, is it?" Takan spat. "How many of you came?"

"Four, just four of us! Three on the g-ground, one sniper too."

"Where are the other three?"

"I don't know, one of them split to draw y-you off—"

"Was that your plan too? Or were you trying to save your own neck?"

"Th-the others, they wanted to hide in some kind of w-warehouse," Joe sobbed. "I thought it was a dumb idea, I . . . I . . ."

Takan's eyes narrowed. "So they're going to the warehouse, huh? Funny, I was going to head there anyway before you guys showed up."

"Please, the one who planned the whole thing is Cross, he's the—"

"Shut up," Takan said, then fished a cell phone from his pocket and began speaking into the receiver. "Aaron, send some troops to the east warehouse." Takan paused, listening to a response. "Yeah, a few students showed up. I'm going to go head them off before they find out what we've been doing. Yes, I *do* know how dangerous the place is, but Plan B is at risk here. I'm out."

Takan shut his cell phone and slipped it back into his pocket. Then he looked back down at Joe. "This little class reunion was fun Joe, but it's about time for us to say good-bye."

"Please, *please*—"

Takan drew a bottle from his jacket and removed the cloth stuffed in its neck.

"You know, I never thanked you for chasing me into District 19," Takan said, crouching down. "That was the start of all this. That's why I'm here now, leader of the Truancy. You never knew it, but you helped create me in a way. Thanks . . ."

Takan poured the contents of the bottle onto Joe, soaking him with the flammable mixture. Joe sputtered, and his eyes widened as he realized what was about to happen.

". . . and good riddance."

Takan switched a lighter on and lightly tossed it.

Joe ignited like a torch, his screams echoing throughout the alleys.

7

Second and Fourth

W hat was *that*?" Floe wondered, looking backwards.

"Screaming." Cross stepped over a broken chair that was part of a collection of debris in their way.

"Well, yeah." Floe pushed aside a wooden plank. "But didn't it sound a bit like Joe?"

"Never mind him," Cross said. "Look, I think we're here."

Indeed, the doors of the warehouse had now come into sight. It was a ramshackle building with rusted walls and holes in its roof, but it was large and could provide sanctuary. Cross and Floe paused for a moment to catch their breath. There were footsteps behind them. They looked at each other wearily.

"Here we go again," Cross said, raising his rifle and turning to defend the narrow passage they had just come from.

"Hold on." Floe reached into her pack for a firebomb, lit it, and then hurled it into the alley. It exploded, setting the debris aflame. "That'll make them keep their distance."

Cross shook his head with admiration even as the shadows of the Truants came into sight. Taking cover behind a wall, he began to fire at the Truants through the flames. Within moments he was caught up again in the full rush of combat. Carefully aiming at a silhouette, Cross pulled the trigger.

The rifle did not fire. Cross angrily tapped the magazine, drew back the charging handle, and tried again. Still nothing. He checked the rifle chamber. A bullet casing had gotten stuck. He swore and ducked lower behind the wall, heart pounding.

"What's wrong?" Floe shouted.

"Rifle jammed up!" Cross pulled the handle back and began shaking his gun.

"That's not how you do it!" Floe scolded as bullets whizzed over their heads. "Lock the bolt back and remove the magazine. Doesn't the Militia teach that?"

In truth, since Edward's death Cross had rarely practiced with his weapon. He could never muster up the motivation; shooting just didn't interest him unless someone was shooting back.

"Forget this." Cross threw the rifle aside and drew his sidearm. He fired five shots through the flames and was rewarded with a cry of pain. The gunshots faded as the Truants seemed to reconsider their approach.

"They'll take another route now," Cross said, "but every Truant in the district is going to be coming with them."

"Joe was a coward, but maybe he had the right idea after all," Floe panted. "We should split up. They won't know which way to chase us."

Cross nodded. "I'll take the warehouse. You go around and take one of the other paths out of here."

Floe frowned. "You're going to trap yourself in the first place they're bound to check?"

"That warehouse is big enough to be as good as a whole maze of alleys." Cross gestured at the massive industrial building. "There's got to be more than one exit. It's probably safer than wherever you're going."

"Don't act a hero, Cross," Floe said severely. "It doesn't suit you."

Through the adrenaline and fear, Cross felt a forgotten emotion flicker inside him. It suddenly occurred to him how alone the two of them were there, in the eye of the storm.

"Thanks for worrying." Cross interrupted her before she could reply. "No, I mean it. About why you switched sides . . . if it's because of what happened way back, we're even now. You've saved me enough times. Go on, get out of here."

Floe opened her mouth, then shut it, a flush on her cheeks. For one mad second Cross felt like they were both children again. She hesitated, then reached into her pack and stuffed a firebomb and a lighter into Cross' hands.

"Take this," she said. "It's my last one. You'll need it."

Without waiting for a response, Floe turned and ran off. Not knowing what to say, Cross watched her go. Once she was safely out of sight, he took a deep breath and stowed the bottle in his pocket.

He was all alone again, just him and his enemies. Cross liked it better that way. He began walking towards the warehouse, firing a few shots into the flames with his pistol. There were more shouts, though Cross had no way of knowing if he had actually hit someone. Cross kicked the warehouse doors open and prepared to slip inside.

Then a familiar voice spoke, and Cross felt his heart lurch with terror and delight.

"Double back and go after the other one, I'll take *him* myself!"

Cross turned and stared as a dark figure leapt off some garbage cans on the other side of the flames. Its feet connected briefly with the wall of the alley, and then with tremendous force propelled it through the smoke. Instinctively, Cross fired at the dark shape until his gun was empty, only to realize a moment later that he'd been shooting at an empty brown trench coat.

The coat's owner landed lightly on the ground, and Cross ducked behind the warehouse door as a series of retaliatory shots flew in his direction.

"Long time no see," Takan called out. "You never gave me your name before. It's Cross, isn't it? I've wanted to meet you for a while now."

Cross slammed a new magazine into his pistol and held his breath as Takan drew closer. His heart was racing faster than ever, the blood thundering in his ears. It was just the two of them, each with no choice but to fight and no desire to do otherwise. A duel to the death with his most dangerous counterpart—Cross couldn't have imagined a better way to go.

"Did you plan to hide here, Cross?" Takan called. "You picked the wrong place."

Takan fired again, and Cross swore as dents appeared in the door. Gritting his teeth, Cross twisted his arm and fired blindly outside. No response. Cross peered out from behind the door and saw nothing but empty space. Cross hesitated for half a second. Then Takan burst from behind the other side of the door with his sword drawn.

Cross' reflexes were just good enough to prevent his head from being skewered, and he leapt backwards into the warehouse. Takan went for his sidearm, and Cross dived for cover behind some nearby metal barrels, exactly like the ones that Joe had earlier cleared from their path. He paused to catch his breath, and that was when Cross noticed his surroundings for the first time.

Blue evening light streamed in through the dirty windows of the warehouse, illuminating row upon row of metal storage drums. Many of the barrels looked old and rusted. All of them looked like they had been placed here recently, for none were as worn as the building itself. For some reason he couldn't place, they made Cross very uneasy.

Takan's footsteps drew closer. His heart pounding, Cross raised his pistol.

"Are you sure you want to do that?" Takan's voice echoed throughout the huge space. "You might hit one of these barrels."

Cross hesitated. "What's in them?"

Takan laughed. "I wish I could give you a proper answer, but I was never any good at science. Aaron tells me that it's a mix of fuel and ammonium, or something like that. It's a powerful explosive. One stray shot and we both die."

Takan halted a few feet away from Cross' hiding place, and doubt began to eat away at Cross. He now had a perfect chance to blow himself up with Takan, fulfilling his mission and going out in a true blaze of glory. And yet he didn't fire.

Grunting with frustration, Cross tossed his pistol aside and drew his knife instead, leaping out to face Takan. "I'll just take you down by hand then!"

Takan smiled, then lifted his pistol and fired. Cross dived back behind the barrels just in time, the bullet glancing off the floor nearby.

"Are you crazy?" Cross shouted.

"No, Cross," Takan said, advancing. "This is just the difference between me and you, between a student and a Truant."

Cross scrambled to get deeper into the warehouse, keeping his head down as he ran from barrel to barrel.

"You're an instrument, used to fight the Educators' battles. They've got you so conditioned you don't even know what *you* want." Takan fired again, narrowly missing Cross. "Me, I'm free. I've got nothing to lose. For us, for the Truancy, all that matters is our cause."

"You *are* crazy!" Cross shouted. "You think you're something great when you're just a fanatic!"

"Better than a coward," Takan shot back. "You could've blown us both to bits, Cross. Why did you hesitate? Did the thought not occur to you? No, you were just scared of dying!"

"Don't pretend to know me!" Cross dashed down the aisles of drums as Takan gave pursuit.

"Then what do you risk your life for, Cross?" Takan demanded. "Why are you here? What are you but a reflection of the ambitions of others?"

That question, a question Cross never dared to ask himself, cut deeply. Sepp and Floe had their reasons. Even Joe, in his own selfish way, knew why he was fighting. Why *was* Cross fighting? Cross clutched his forehead as the image of a faceless man swept through his mind. Somehow, through his jumbled thoughts, Cross heard Takan fire again and eject the empty clip.

Cross turned and lunged while the Truant was reloading. Taken by surprise, Takan blocked Cross' knife with his pistol, but could not stop Cross from knocking the pistol from his grip with a second blow. Cross attempted a stab, but Takan parried it by drawing his sword.

"Is this how you dodge the hard questions?" Takan asked. "You get so lost in your battles that you don't even think about what you're doing?"

Cross recklessly lunged again. Takan swung his sword, forcing Cross to roll aside. The blade clipped his shoulder. Faced with a weapon with a much greater reach, Cross growled and began running again.

By now they had reached the end of the warehouse, and a long ladder led up to a raised platform high above. Cross scrambled upwards with Takan close behind.

"I can see now why we beat the Militia so easily these days," Takan said. "You really are nothing like your predecessor."

Cross glanced down at his enemy. "How did you know who I was?"

"Joe told me you were here before he died," Takan replied. "And I've always known the name of the Student Militia's leader."

Cross shook his head as he climbed. He'd figured that Joe would betray them, and he wasn't sad at all to hear of his death. But something else was bothering him.

"I meant back at the bar!" Cross said. "How did you know I wasn't a Truant?"

Takan laughed at that. "My mentor trained me to tell salt from sugar. Did you really think I couldn't tell a student from one of my own men?"

Cross reached the top platform and took a few steps away from the ladder as he brandished his knife. Takan darted up the last few rungs and paused. The two combatants faced each other.

"You do have a choice, Cross," Takan said. "I don't enjoy killing. If you give up fighting and cooperate with us, I promise you will not be harmed."

"Screw you."

"I expected as much." Takan sighed in resignation. "Then I'll let you in on a secret. Do you know why we've been stockpiling these explosives?"

Cross' heart skipped a beat. "No."

"It's so that we can demolish City Hall, Penance Tower, Enforcer Headquarters, among other targets within District 1," Takan said. "This is my Plan B. I won't wait for a long and drawn-out siege. The Educators will fall in one stroke."

"Impossible." Cross shook his head. "There's no way you can get this much past the front lines without anyone noticing."

"Not past the front lines," Takan corrected. "Under them."

Cross froze.

"Did you know that the subway tunnels run under almost every major landmark?" Takan asked. "Almost every line converges at District 1. We might miss the Mayoral Mansion and Student Militia Headquarters, but everything else will be wiped out."

"You want to rule over a dead City?"

"Don't be melodramatic," Takan said. "If anything this will spare lives. Only those few Educator buildings will be destroyed, leaving us a clean slate to rebuild upon."

"Why are you telling me this?"

"So that you know how completely you have failed," Takan said, raising his sword. "And now that I've told you, I really have no choice but to kill you."

Cross ducked just in time, Takan's sword cleaving the air above his head. Before Cross could even think of counterattacking, Takan struck again, moving so fast that Cross could barely keep up. Despite his best efforts, Cross found himself forced backwards almost to the edge of the platform.

Takan lunged. Cross narrowly managed to dodge. Looking around, Cross saw that there was an open window to his left. He could see another building through it, only about five feet away. Behind him was the edge of the platform, and to his right Takan was preparing another attack.

Instinct took over. Cross drew Floe's firebomb and lighter from his pocket. He lit the cloth just as Takan was about to bring his sword down. The Truant paused, and the two stared at each other. Then Cross dropped the bottle over the edge.

Takan was distracted for just a moment as he watched it fall. It was all Cross needed. His kick caught Takan in the abdomen, knocking him back a few paces. Cross turned and leapt out of the window with all of the strength he could muster.

For a few terrifying, glorious moments Cross sailed through the open air. Then he crashed through the window of the next building, one story down.

Back in the warehouse the bottle burst, sending its fiery contents spewing all over. Explosions rippled through the warehouse, erupting with such force that the blue daylight turned red. Cross shielded his face from the sudden wind and heat. The sheer power of it reminded him of a hurricane of flames, and for a while he lay motionless in awe as it roared.

By the time Cross realized that a second window had shattered nearby, Takan was already there with his sword. Cross struggled to stand, raising his knife, knowing that it was hopeless. The roar subsided, the pale light returning as the two enemies faced each other once more.

"Did you think you'd thwart my plan like that?" Takan was angry now. "That warehouse was just one of several. All this means is fewer explosives beneath Penance Tower. You're still going to die."

Cross said nothing, though he knew Takan was probably right. It wasn't a very auspicious resting place either—the building so cavernous there was an echo, and most of the windows were so caked with filth that it was nearly pitch-black. Rubble was strewn across the floor, and there were no walls that he could see.

The darkness gave Cross an idea. As Takan drew closer, Cross threw his knife at the Truant. Takan knocked the projectile aside with his sword, but not before Cross took off for the cover of the gloom. Takan pursued him, the darkness was absolute. They lost sight of each other, and could only hear echoing footsteps.

Pausing to take a breath, Cross began to realize how much punishment his body had endured. He was bruised all over, there were gashes from the broken glass, and his head still ached. Blood mingled with his sweat, and his lungs felt like they were burning him from the inside. He was tired, so tired that he wanted nothing more than to lie down and collapse.

But the sound of echoing footsteps reminded him that his enemy was still hunting him. Remembering something Floe had mentioned, Cross decided to take a risk.

"You talked about a mentor before!" he called out, the echo masking his location. "Was that Zyid? The guy you betrayed and killed?"

Takan's humorless laughter echoed throughout the space, sending chills down Cross' spine. That wasn't the effect Cross had been looking for.

"You know a lot for a student," Takan replied. "No, Zyid wasn't my mentor. His brother was, a boy named Umasi. I met him back when I was still a student in District 20."

Cross blinked. He'd heard that name before, but his head was going fuzzy and he found it hard to concentrate. "Umasi?"

"Yeah," Takan said. "He was a bit of a loner. Supposedly I was only his fourth visitor. Incidentally, your predecessor Edward was the third."

Suddenly Cross remembered. Memories flashed in his mind of Edward hunched over in the dark, muttering to himself, always mentioning one name, never explaining it.

"You and Edward had the same mentor?"

"Funny, isn't it?" Takan's voice was thoughtful now. "We turned out so alike, but so different."

"He was stronger than you."

"How would you know?"

Cross hesitated, then threw caution to the winds. "Because Edward was *my* mentor! He taught me everything!"

There was a moment of silence. Then Takan spoke.

"I see. I'm sorry."

Again, not the effect Cross had been looking for. "Who asked for your pity?" he shouted.

"I don't think you're quite the monster Edward was, but you might become one," Takan said. "I'm not going to enjoy killing you . . . but it's probably for the best."

Takan's footsteps resumed, faster now, and Cross felt true fear. He couldn't see in the dark, but the dark was the only thing keeping him alive. The terror and the hopelessness seemed to suffocate him. Takan had been right—he had no idea why he was even there.

Then Cross felt a gentle hand on his shoulder. He had no strength left to scream, but even his gasp was stifled as another hand clamped down on his mouth. An unfamiliar voice whispered in his ear.

"If you want to live, turn around and run for the light."

Then both hands and voice were gone. Cross spun around, heart pounding, reaching blindly through the darkness. There was nothing. The only footsteps belonged to Takan. It was as if the voice had appeared from and vanished into nothing. For a moment Cross wondered if he had actually gone crazy.

Then he turned his head and saw it—the distant light that the voice had mentioned.

Deciding that he would not sit still and wait to die, Cross latched on to that mad hope and broke out into a run. Behind him, Takan's footsteps sped up as well. Cross knew that he would be clearly visible against the light, but it was too late to turn back. As he got closer and closer, other windows became visible, dirty and cracked, but none of them were as clear as the opening ahead.

When Cross reached it, he saw there was a rope ladder leading down. In his haste, he ignored it and jumped. The fall was high enough to send painful shocks through his legs when he landed, and Cross collapsed with a groan. Crawling forward, he looked around, wondering where he was now.

For a moment Cross imagined that it was the bottom of a canyon. Then he realized that the canyon walls were really taller brick buildings that towered over the rooftop he was on. Leafy green vines crawled up those walls, and all around sat pots filled with delicate-looking flowers. Small trees completed the strange garden, rising up amid the riot of color.

Water gushed from a broken pipe above, sending rivulets streaming into a nearby drain. Pots and pans had been neatly stacked near the flowers. A small bed rested under a large awning, and a fireplace and stove were placed against a wall. The buildings on either side cast long shadows in the evening light. The day was coming to an end.

Under different circumstances, Cross might've found the sight beautiful. Now he only wondered where the promised sanctuary was.

Takan appeared at the entrance. The boy took one look at Cross, then climbed down the rope ladder. Unable to flee, unable even to move, Cross could only watch as Takan approached with his sword drawn.

"I'm impressed," Takan said. "You lasted a long time. You should be proud."

"I told you I don't want your pity."

"It's not pity, Cross," Takan said. "You were stubborn, but you were never a match for someone like me. You can only go so far without a purpose. I'll put you out of your misery."

Takan raised his blade so that it caught the subdued midday glow. Cross turned his head to look at the white ceramic blade, realizing that this was really it, that he was going to die. As the blade came down, Cross took an involuntary breath as all thought abandoned him.

A metallic tinkling filled the air . . .

Takan spun around and thrust his sword upward, blocking a metal ring aimed at his head. Cross stared in confusion. The ring was attached to a chain, which snapped back as Takan deflected the attack.

"Do you really believe that you can judge when someone's life isn't worth living?" a female voice asked. "Or is that how you justify your actions to yourself?"

"Oh?" Takan raised an eyebrow. "And who are you?"

The ring returned to its owner's hand, and as Cross' eyes followed it, he became certain he was hallucinating. The speaker was a girl, ghostly white from her skin to the hair that skirted her jaw. Her eyes appeared a pale blue in the dim light, and she wore a blue headband and matching blue jeans. Her sweatshirt was white, as was the thin sweater she had tied around her waist by the sleeves. She smiled at Takan.

"You numbered Umasi's visitors, didn't you? Well, if you're the fourth, then I'm the second . . ."

Her eyes glinted as she began twirling the end of her chain.

". . . and I don't have a name."

8

Y*ou* were the second?" Takan stared. "I always wondered who it was. He never mentioned it was a girl."

"Surprised?"

"At him, a little," Takan said. "How come you look—"

"Albinism," she replied. "A lack of the pigment that normally gives the body color. I was born with it."

Takan shrugged, apparently unconcerned. Cross, for his part, was relieved to find out that he hadn't been hallucinating, but still felt that the girl's pale appearance was unsettling. He decided to keep that opinion to himself.

"You're not with the Educators, are you?" Takan said. "If you were, I think I'd have heard about it by now."

"No." The girl shook her head. "I have no interest in this war."

"Then why are you protecting him?" Takan asked, gesturing at Cross with his sword.

"He's defeated and helpless," she said. "You've already won. Why sink to murder?"

"He knows things that would endanger the Truancy," Takan replied. "If I let him live, it could mean that a lot of my people will die."

The albino sighed. "This is why war is useless. It makes life and death complicated when they should really be simple."

"If you're not an enemy, I have no reason to fight you," Takan said. "But I can't let this guy go."

"Then we have a problem. I can't allow killing here."

"Is this where you live?" Takan asked. The girl nodded. "Then I'm fine with taking this elsewhere."

"That's thoughtful of you," she said. "But that would be no more morally acceptable to me. I would be enabling murder through inaction."

Takan's expression hardened. "You don't seem interested in compromise. You know that with one call I could have a dozen Truants here in minutes."

"You could," the girl admitted. "But you won't. You're not that kind of person, are you?"

Cross wondered what made her so sure. Takan looked deadly serious, and everything Cross had seen and heard about him indicated that he was a cold, self-serving killer with no conscience. He didn't know who this nameless girl was or why she seemed so confident facing Takan. He could do little but wait and see.

Takan surprised Cross by hesitating. "Have you talked with Umasi? Has he told you about me?"

"I haven't seen that boy in about four years," the girl replied. "I'm just a decent judge of character."

"Then you know that I'm not above beating you myself," Takan said, raising his sword. "I don't mind a fair fight."

She smiled. "I was counting on that."

Takan lunged forward with an intensity that he had never demonstrated against Cross. At the same time, the albino released her chain, launching the weighted ring at Takan. Takan knocked the ring aside with his sword, then surged forward.

The girl darted aside, recovered her chain, and launched it again. Takan raised his sword to defend himself, but the chain wrapped around the blade, trapping it. Takan blinked in surprise, and the girl charged forward. Takan tried to swing his sword, but found it too unwieldy. The albino landed a punch to his chest, but Takan recovered in time to dodge her follow-up blow.

The two began engaging in what looked like a complicated dance. Takan would occasionally add a weighted sword slash, and the girl would use her chain to yank his hand aside. To an awestruck Cross they seemed like two tornados blowing through. He realized now that Takan hadn't even exerted himself in their earlier battle. Now the Truant's entire focus seemed to be on cutting down his pale adversary.

But the albino was matching him move for move, and as Cross watched in astonishment she managed to loop her chain over Takan, pinning his arms to his side. For a moment Cross thought the battle was over, but then Takan landed a devastating kick that knocked the girl onto her back. Takan took the opportunity to free himself and his sword, charging just as the girl returned to her feet.

She blocked his sword with a length of chain held taut between her hands, then pushed the sword behind Takan's back. She slammed her knee into his stomach. He gasped, and she kicked him, forcing him to the ground. As Takan recovered, the albino leapt backwards and swung her chain upwards, wrapping it around a rusted old pipe right above Takan.

Yanking hard with both hands, the girl brought the pipes crashing down. Takan leapt aside just in time, as metal and water pounded the spot where he had just sat. She swung again while Takan was still on one knee, and this time he raised his left arm to shield himself. The chain wrapped around his arm. He grabbed hold of it, and the two found themselves engaged in a deadly game of tug-of-war.

The girl abruptly darted forward, releasing all of the tension on the chain. Takan had been expecting the move, and instead of stumbling back, he thrust his sword as the girl approached. At the last second the albino twisted and backhanded Takan's face. Before he could recover, she looped the chain up and over, bringing it behind his legs. With one end still firmly wrapped around Takan's arm, she pulled, sweeping his legs out from under him.

Takan hit the floor hard, and the albino's foot darted to his throat, though it did not apply any pressure.

"It's over," the girl said gently, kicking Takan's sword away. "Give it up."

Both fighters gasped for air, and even Cross felt a little breathless. Then Takan laughed, his limbs going limp.

"Beaten by Edward," he said, "and now beaten by you. So I was the weakest of us, in the end."

"No." The albino shook her head. "Just the most ordinary. The least twisted. That's something to be proud of."

"At least you're a lot nicer than Edward was," Takan observed as she removed her foot. "You know, we all really did end up different. I wish I could've met number one."

"I had that pleasure once, briefly," the albino said, crouching down. "He looked a bit like you."

"Umasi said that, yeah."

"You're an interesting guy, Four. Someday I'd like to hear your life story."

"Funny, I was thinking the same about you, Two." Takan grinned. "I never introduced myself, did I? My real name is Tack, but you can keep calling me 'Four' if you like."

"Well then, Four," the albino said, standing up. "I wish you good health. I don't agree with what you do, but you're not a bad person. You can rest here as long as you'd like."

"That's nice of you, but I'll be going soon. I suppose you'll be taking the student under your protection?"

Takan gestured over at Cross, who was completely baffled by the behavior of the two former combatants. A minute ago they were doing their best to beat each other down, and now they were chatting like friends.

"For a while," she said. "I know you'd probably hunt him otherwise."

Takan nodded. "It is a war, after all."

The albino was about to say something, but then glanced towards the cavelike building from which Cross and Takan had emerged. She stiffened.

"It's time for us to part," she said.

Before Takan could reply, the albino grabbed Cross by the arm and hauled him to his feet. Her voice was melodic and fostered trust, but Cross was suspicious of someone he knew nothing about. That, and her corpse-pale appearance still disturbed him.

"Come on," she whispered to Cross. "There's someone coming who I'd rather avoid for now."

Too weary to argue, Cross followed her through the flowers and past some ferns that concealed an exit. His head was spinning from everything he had endured and witnessed. Though it was all starting to feel dreamlike again, it was not yet horrible enough to be one of his dreams.

After all, he had survived. He had been saved. And his struggle, at least for now, was over.

Takan sighed as he stood up, rubbing his bruised stomach. He had to admit that this garden was a pleasant place. Despite having lost, despite knowing what was at risk now, he felt no urgency as he examined the potted flowers. It was ironic—he lived in what used to be a flower shop, but he hadn't seen any flowers in a year.

Takan straightened up. His worldly troubles were still out there, but they were nothing to panic over just yet. There was still a chance to catch Cross before he escaped Truancy City, and it would only be a matter of time before District 1 fell regardless.

He was running calculations in his head when something large dropped down behind him. Takan drew his sword and spun around, only to find it blocked by two more identical blades. Unseen eyes gazed at Takan from behind black sunglasses.

"Umasi?" Takan said. "What happened? You're late, and you look—"

"Did you meet her?" Umasi interrupted, sheathing his swords. "She was here just now, wasn't she? I didn't want to intrude uninvited, but the situation—"

"I did meet your old friend, if that's who you mean," Takan said, wondering if she was the reason why Umasi was acting so strangely. "You never told me she was—"

"Never mind that!" Umasi snapped. "Listen, Takan. This little fight between you and the Student Militia, this whole messy war, it's exactly what they wanted, all part of their plan."

"It . . . what?" Takan began to feel uneasy, though he had no idea what Umasi was talking about.

"We're in trouble, Takan," Umasi said. "They're coming."

"*Who* are?"

"The true enemy." Umasi shook his head. "It's too late for City unity. They're already moving. You have to take steps to save the Truants. The only way to do that is to disband immediately and hide in the general population."

"I don't understand," Takan said. "What's going on? Is it the Mayor? The Enforcers?"

"No. It's something bigger. Something worse," Umasi replied. "There's no time. You have to trust me. They might attack at any—"

He was interrupted by a loud roar from above. The two boys looked up just in time to see dark, triangular shapes screech across the dimming sky and out of sight. Moments later, there was a distant flash and a rumbling explosion.

"What was *that*?" Takan gaped. "An airplane designed for war? What's something like that doing here?"

"Dropping bombs," Umasi murmured. "The Mayor was right. We're too late."

Colonel Hines, I'm glad that you could join us for this. We are proceeding on schedule. You're just in time."

The Colonel returned Iris' salute as he walked into the command center. Dozens of technicians worked at their monitors, and on a large screen at the front of the room a live aerial view of the City was displayed.

"I was ordered to keep the War Minister updated about our attack plans," the Colonel said. "I deemed it prudent to wait until the last possible moment."

"I would have to agree," Iris said. "I can't say that I like bureaucrats peering over our shoulder for the whole operation, but if it must be done it might as well be done so as to give them no opportunity to interfere."

"Of course." The Colonel nodded. "I take it that things are already in motion?"

"Bombing of predetermined targets began at sundown as planned," Iris said. "It is safe to assume that the people of that City are now aware of our presence. Ground forces will follow as soon as the potential for resistance is eliminated."

Another soldier ran up to the General, holding a sheaf of papers. He handed her two photographs.

"General, the satellites trained on City Hall caught these photos last night of an individual slipping inside. We think you might be interested in them."

"Why?" Iris asked. "Did you identify him?"

"Well, at first we didn't get anything searching the Educator database, so we ran it through Government files as well."

Iris looked at the pictures. "And?"

"We got a match," the soldier said. "The Mayor must've wiped those files from Educator records. We believe the boy spying on our camp was one of your primary targets."

Iris' gaze intensified. "Are you *sure*?"

"The face matches our file photos and digital estimations. We're roughly eighty percent sure that it's one of the twins. We just can't tell which one it is."

"So, at least one of them is still around." Her face was expressionless. "We now have a slight change of plans. I want a dedicated task force on the ground immediately. Locating our primary objectives is our first priority."

The Colonel shook his head. "It will be difficult to conduct a search while there's still resistance."

"There won't be for long," Iris said. "Bring up the map of the City."

The image on the main screen was replaced by a map of the City and its districts. Most of the districts were colored red, though a good chunk in the center was blue.

"We're starting with the districts held by the Educators," Iris said, pointing at the blue districts. "Paratroopers will secure essential Government buildings and infrastructure. We start with City Hall. With the Mayor out of the way we should be able to quickly assume control of the City's Enforcers."

"What about the districts the locals call Truancy City?" the Colonel asked.

"We'll move in from the docks, force opposition farther inland until they hit the Educators' border," Iris said. "The bridges and tunnels are controlled by the Educators via Penance Tower, so we'll be using our amphibious transports instead. Air support will secure the landing areas."

Technicians and subordinates were already scrambling to carry out Iris' orders. Like a wasp nest roused to action by its queen, it buzzed with activity. The military had enjoyed plenty of time to prepare, and was now able to unleash its full strength at a moment's notice.

"Paratroopers will seize control of communications and power stations. Only areas we control should have either," Iris said. "If a location looks too hot for a drop, bomb it, unless it's of key strategic importance."

Iris turned to the Colonel. A massive number of dots and symbols appeared on the map, each representing a Government force.

"Within forty-eight hours that entire City will be mine," she said. "Now, get me on the line with the Mayor."

Did you hear that?" Cross asked, trying to clear his head. "What was that?"

The nameless albino did not respond, but walked over to an open window as distant flashes went off. The room they were in didn't seem to have electricity, though to Cross it seemed surprisingly clean. There was furniture and carpeting, as well as toys and books scattered around. It suddenly occurred to Cross that this was the girl's home, an indoor extension of the garden.

"Why did you lead me here?" Cross sat down on a chair. "Why did you help me?"

"I dislike killing. As a rule I don't allow murder so long as I can stop it," the girl replied, still looking out the window. "Especially not with my son watching."

Cross blinked, confused. "Your son?"

"Yes. Turn around."

Cross turned, then jumped out of his chair. A small boy stood there, examining him like a fascinating object. He was very young, with dirty blond hair, brown eyes, and skin that looked faintly tan. He showed no sign of fear as he looked Cross up and down.

"Cool hair," the boy said. "Mom, is he safe?"

"Yes," the albino replied. "You don't have to worry about him. His name is Cross."

"He has a name too?"

"Most people do." She smiled. "Cross, meet Zen. He tells me that he helped you earlier today by sending you a stuffed animal. I promised him I'd help you too."

Cross blinked as he remembered the stuffed sheep. So it had come from this kid? Cross grimaced as his headache returned. He'd already felt dazed before, but this whole business, on top of those explosions in the distance, was starting to make him question his sanity again.

"Hi, Cross!" Zen said, smiling.

"Um. Hi." Cross peered again at the boy, then at his mother. "He's not—"

"Like me?" the albino finished. "No. The odds of that were always slim. He's three years old, if you're wondering. Almost four now."

Cross shook his head. "Yeah, but how . . . who . . . what—"

A very loud explosion went off, close enough to shake the house. The flash illuminated the window, and for a moment Cross could have sworn that the girl's eyes had turned red. Then they were blue again, and without a word Zen walked up to his mother and hugged her leg.

"What's that?" Zen asked.

"I'm not sure," the albino replied. "But I think it's dangerous."

"Is that the Truancy?" Cross wondered. "Could they have already planted their explosives?"

"No," the albino said calmly. "I don't think the Truancy has anything like *that*."

She pointed, and Cross walked over to the window just in time to see dark shapes streak across the sky.

"What in the—"

"Planes," the albino replied. "They've been dropping things. I think they were the source of the explosions you heard earlier."

"But that's impossible!" Cross said, hoping that this really was a dream. "Not even the Mayor has weapons like that!"

"*Someone* does," she murmured. "The Truancy City is no longer safe. Against something like that, I'm not sure anywhere in this City is."

Cross' mind reeled at the implications of explosions that came from the sky, with no chance of retaliation. At the same time, the outlandish threat made him want to return to what was familiar. Weariness and doubt fell from his shoulders as he realized where he needed to be.

"Student Militia Headquarters," Cross said, turning to the albino. "It's got to be safe. I'm not sure who's dropping those bombs, but they seem focused only on Truancy City. If I get there, I can find out what's going on."

The albino glanced at him. "You're sure your headquarters aren't a target?"

"No," Cross admitted. "But I'd bet my life on it."

"I see," she replied, then turned to her son. "Zen, what do you think?"

Zen looked up at Cross critically. Then he turned to his mother. "I believe him."

"So do I." She looked at Cross. "Student Militia Headquarters is our destination. Let's go."

PART II

SOLDIER

9

Shattered Enigma

T he Mayor gazed out of the windows of his office, dressed in a new suit, a cigar and glass of whiskey in hand. Outside was a scene of chaos as airplanes streaked overhead, parachutes dappling the sky as explosions blossomed on the ground. The Mayor saw none of it, choosing to reminisce about his accomplishments and the wonderful flow of traffic and lights his City had once been. Despite all the destruction, the Mayor felt at peace.

Behind him, the monitor on his desk flickered on.

"Greetings, Mr. Mayor," Iris' voice called out. "As you can see, we have begun the reacquisition of this City. You have one last opportunity to turn yourself in. Barring that, a paramilitary team will be arriving shortly to take you into custody."

The Mayor puffed on his cigar without turning around.

"So be it," he said. "Is that all you called for?"

"I also thought that I'd inform you that we've located one of the boys already," Iris replied. "Perhaps you'd like to tell me about the other one?"

The Mayor scowled. "Never."

"It's simply a matter of time, Mayor. I will find out sooner or later."

"That may be," the Mayor replied. "But not with my help."

Somewhere in the building an alarm went off, and distant gunshots rang out. The Mayor did not need to look at his security display to know that soldiers had entered the building.

"That should be my men now." Iris smiled. "Sit tight, Mayor. I expect that we'll continue this conversation in person."

The monitor flickered and died, and the Mayor sighed as he turned around. He extinguished his cigar, then sat down at his desk. For the first time in years it was free of papers, and all his pencils were in their mug. His entire office had been carefully cleaned, his files and possessions neatly arranged. His phone had been disconnected, and his mahogany table polished.

On his desk, a photograph of the Mayor and his two sons took center stage. The Mayor looked at it as he emptied his glass.

Iris was wrong. There would be no meeting in person.

The Mayor slammed his glass down on the desk and placed his favorite lighter next to it. He had mixed some poison with the drink, in case his plan failed. Just in case. There was a crash in the hallway, and thundering footsteps approached his office. The Mayor's finger hovered over a button he'd recently had installed on his desk.

The office doors burst open, and a half dozen armed soldiers stormed into the room, rifles raised.

"Good evening, gentlemen," the Mayor said. He pressed the button.

The Mayor, his office, and the soldiers were consumed by a giant fireball as one ton of confiscated Truancy explosives ignited. The Mayor's final thoughts went out to his sons, both the one who had died . . . and the one who still lived to fight.

Run, Umasi. Get out of this City before she finds you.

And then he was gone.

T here they are," Umasi muttered.

Takan stared at the riverside in disbelief. Soon after the airstrikes began, Umasi urged Takan to have the Truancy fortify the docks, the prime landing sites for the military. Takan did as he suggested, then the two of them made for the District 13 docks, the closest site to them.

When they arrived at dusk, a strange and terrifying sight greeted their eyes. Like water beetles on the blue river, strange floating tanks and armored boats surged across by the dozens. The Truants tried to form defenses on the docks, but explosives from above and machine gun fire from the boats pounded their positions to dust. Even as they watched, black helicopters swooped in, each more menacing in appearance than anything the Enforcers had ever used.

"This is impossible!" Takan said, raising his voice over an explosion. "How are we supposed to stop this?"

"You're not," Umasi replied as the boats began unloading soldiers. "You *can't* win against them. Your goal now is to survive—slow their advance as much as possible, give your Truants enough time to disappear. Hide among the general population."

A good distance from the docks, within the cover of a building, Takan growled with frustration and raised his rifle, firing at the advancing soldiers. Other Truants followed suit. The Government soldiers sought cover as they returned fire. Takan ducked his head as the endless snarl of a chain gun rained bullets in his direction.

"Every second we waste means more dead!" Umasi said. "You have to give the order to disband, right now!"

"Are you telling me to just give up?" Takan demanded, glaring at Umasi. "After we've come so close to victory?"

"Not giving up means dying!" Umasi shouted as one of the helicopters began firing at their hiding place. "If you stand your ground against these people, all of you will die for nothing! If you live, there's a chance you can free the City later! *Do as I say, Tack!*"

Another explosion rocked the ground. Umasi's hands were now on the hilts of his swords. Takan shivered. The Truants around them stopped to stare.

"You heard him," Takan said hoarsely. "Get the word out. Tell the Truants inland to get to a living district and hide. If they run into any enemies, try to slow them down so that the others can escape."

"But our phones aren't working!" a Truant protested.

"Then use the radios!" Takan shouted. "Just get that message out!"

Two Truants scrambled away to relay the orders just as a helicopter fired a rocket into the building. Takan, Umasi, and a few others tried to leap clear, but for most there was no time. The blast destroyed the wall and collapsed a good chunk of the ceiling. Coughing from the dust, Takan and Umasi kept their heads down as they retreated.

"The Government must have a way of disabling your phones. I'm assuming land lines are down too," Umasi said. "I bet they're listening in on the radios. They probably know what your orders are as you give them."

"Should we keep running, try to regroup?" Takan asked, still coughing.

"No!" Umasi shook his head. "These moments are critical! If we can slow them here, at the landing zones, it will buy the rest of the City some time!"

More airplanes screeched overhead, and massive explosions demolished buildings to either side. The Truants shielded their faces from falling rubble as more helicopters swooped across the river to cover the advancing soldiers. Takan could hardly see through the smoke, dust, and chaos, but Umasi bent down and picked up a rocket launcher dropped by a fallen Truant. Aiming through the dust, he fired. A rocket streaked through the air, slamming into a passing helicopter.

Fire and smoke sprouted from the side of the chopper, and it began spiraling downwards. Truants dived out of the way to take shelter amidst the rubble as the helicopter crashed and crumpled. By now the soldiers had advanced far enough to shoot at them. Truants hid behind chunks of collapsed buildings as they returned fire. Takan looked astonished as Umasi seized a discarded rifle and joined them.

"Since when do you kill?" Takan demanded.

"Since Edward!" Umasi replied, firing off a burst. "Since it became my responsibility! My brother and I brought *this* on the City!"

Takan had never imagined that he'd see Umasi take to the battlefield, but now that he had, Takan thought they had a chance—not to win, but perhaps to survive. The Truants around them were now being joined by volunteers from other districts, many of them carrying rocket launchers. A little farther out Takan could see more helicopters swooping back towards the river, more cautious now. Takan decided he preferred them that way.

"If you've only got a rifle, help keep those soldiers back!" Takan ordered, seizing a rocket launcher himself. "Everyone with a rocket, aim at the helicopters! Don't waste anything on the ground! Fire with me; three, two, one, NOW!"

A dozen rockets streaked towards the helicopters in one erratic volley. To his disappointment, Takan didn't see any of them go down, though a few had to bank hard to avoid the missiles. All of them now kept their distance, which he regarded as a minor victory. The Government soldiers seemed to dig in and were no longer advancing, though more were landing every second.

It occurred to Takan that maybe they were keeping their distance for a reason. Just then, more planes screeched overhead. Moments later, the earth shook with tremendous force as fire erupted nearby. Takan seized Umasi by the shoulder and forced them both to the ground. The explosion was unlike anything he had experienced before. Even at the warehouse he had not felt such power.

Then it was over, and the soldiers were advancing again. Ears ringing, Takan cursed as he saw the charred bodies of Truants who had been caught too close to the blast. Umasi grabbed him by the shoulder, forcing him to retreat as he fired at an exposed soldier, dropping the man to the ground.

"We can't stay here!" Umasi shouted over the ringing in their ears. "We have to fall back and regroup with reinforcements!"

Takan took heed and retreated. Two years of fighting the Enforcers had taught him to be calm under fire; what he had seen at the docks shook him. He had only half understood Umasi's hasty explanation of who this new enemy was, but all the warnings had left him unprepared for anything like this.

This Government, whomever they were, had struck with lightning speed and devastating power. The Truancy's best efforts had been undone in minutes, and as far as Takan could tell they had inflicted minimal casualties on the enemy. If there had been time to prepare they might have held out longer, but there had been no warning, no chance.

Takan pounded his fist against his knee as he paused to reload. Behind him, the renewed roaring of helicopters made him dive for cover alongside Umasi. The two of them looked up grimly as the dark and menacing shapes headed deeper towards the heart of the City.

"This isn't the end of it!" Takan promised, reaching for his radio. "I'll make them pay for every block!"

General, we just received confirmation," the Colonel said. "It looks like the Mayor blew himself up with his office. The retrieval team did not survive."

Iris brushed her forehead with her knuckles in annoyance. The helicopter nearby started its engines, the rotor blades roaring to life.

"I'm surprised he had the guts," she said, raising her voice over the noise. "No matter, I didn't expect to learn much from that witless fool. What's the situation at the landing zones?"

"All resistance has been eliminated. We're now moving in on schedule," the colonel replied. "We've also secured most of the Educators' former territory. Even so ma'am, don't you think it's a bit premature to go in person?"

"Someone needs to fill the void the Mayor just left," Iris replied. "If I move quickly, I can assume control of the Enforcers and the Educators without firing a single shot. These people crave authority; they *need* someone to tell them what to do. With the Mayor gone they are like sheep running loose towards a cliff."

"But General, the situation is still—"

"I assure you I have no intention of dying, Colonel," Iris said, twirling her staff. "I will be landing in District 1, one of the most secure. The forward command post is nearly set up. I need the City under control so that we can get on with the search, understand?"

"Yes, ma'am."

With a curt nod, Iris shrunk her staff and strapped it across her back. She stepped into the waiting helicopter. It took off immediately, joining two others in the sky before flying across the dark river and towards the City. The sun had fully set now, and the fires and flashes of distant explosions were amplified by the darkness.

As she soared into the heart of chaos, Iris smiled in anticipation. She saw herself as an agent of order, here to set things right at last. It would not happen overnight, but Iris was the type of person who truly enjoyed a challenge.

"I've waited years for this," she muttered to herself. "It's time that I got better acquainted with this City."

With the sun gone the new fires sent shadows dancing in the streets. Under a jet-black sky, Cross, his nameless guide, and her son ducked from alley to alley. Summer nights were normally warm in the City, but this one felt hellishly hot, as if the air itself was alive and hostile.

The flames had a way of stoking the imagination. Cross felt like he was reliving that infamous night a year ago when the Truancy had risen up throughout the City. Sweaty clothes clung to his skin, making him feel like he was covered in ooze.

Each time Cross paused, his every instinct told him that he should be out there in the midst of the violence—that he should be *part* of it. Then the nameless girl would grab his hand to yank him forward and out of his daze, back to lucid reality.

Though her looks still unsettled him, Cross' initial doubts had faded. The girl was an excellent guide. He wasn't sure how she did it, but long before he could even glimpse soldiers, she maneuvered out of their path. Young Zen, apparently more familiar with this routine than Cross, never made a sound. He followed his mother like a shadow, only occasionally holding her hand, always looking around curiously.

It took only several hours of swift and stealthy travel to draw within sight of District 2. Cross was disturbed to see smoke rising from the direction of City Hall, but the area seemed mostly intact.

Helicopters filled the air and soldiers swarmed the streets. The last few blocks were the most difficult, and they were nearly caught when Cross absentmindedly knocked over a garbage can in an alley. Zen promptly kicked him in the shin in admonishment, and the albino seized Cross by the arm and pulled him behind a garbage dump. A soldier came to investigate, but left after a cursory sweep of the alley.

"That was *bad*," Zen whispered in Cross' ear.

Cross did not reply; what response could he have made to that? He was extra careful from then on.

Eventually they reached the safety of a dark alley right across from Student Militia Headquarters. A day ago Cross hadn't expected to see the drab gray concrete building again, so the very sight of it was a relief. But Cross was troubled to find that a number of soldiers in unfamiliar uniform had gathered on the steps outside of the entrance. They were talking with two members of the Student Militia.

"What now?" the albino asked, turning to Cross.

Cross frowned. "I . . . don't know."

"I'm not sure those soldiers are our friends," she said, shutting her eyes and listening carefully. "But your fellows seem to be getting along with them fine."

Cross took a closer look at the scene in front of the headquarters. With a jolt he recognized the two students talking with the soldiers. Sepp and Floe. Sepp was laughing and joking, obviously telling some sort of story while Floe looked on disapprovingly.

"I know those students!" Cross said. "They're part of my team."

The albino opened her eyes. "Then don't you want to go talk to them?"

Cross hesitated. It was true that Sepp and Floe seemed at ease, but the soldiers were still an unknown quantity. Then a hand pushed him forward, and he found himself walking towards the entrance. The soldiers were aware of him immediately and raised their guns. Sepp was the next to notice.

"Cross!" he exclaimed. "Hey man, I thought—"

"You're ALIVE!" Floe shouted. Then she blinked as the albino emerged from the alley behind him. "Who's that?"

"She, ah, helped me out," Cross said. "She—"

"Doesn't go by any name," the albino interjected. "This is my son, Zen. We happened to run into Cross and he was nice enough to suggest that this place would be safe."

Zen walked up to Floe and peered at her. "Your face is red. Why?"

Floe's cheeks, which had been a light pink, now truly did flush red. The soldiers and Sepp laughed.

"She's embarrassed, dear," the albino said, placing her hands on Zen's shoulder. "People blush when they're embarrassed. With strangers it's generally polite to pretend not to notice."

"Oh!" Zen brightened up. "Sorry!"

"Are you all right, ma'am?" one of the soldiers asked, peering at the albino. "Do you need any assistance?"

"No, sir, but thank you for asking," the girl replied.

"Well, your friend was right; this building, and the whole district, is now under Government protection," the soldier said. "You won't find a safer place in the City. If you've been invited by the Militia you're welcome to stay as long as there's space."

"That's very kind of you," the albino said, turning to Zen. "What do you think?"

"I wanna stay," Zen replied.

"I think that's a good idea. This may be the sanctuary we sought after all." The albino smiled and nodded at Cross. "Thanks."

Without another word, the albino and her son vanished like smoke into the building. As they left, the soldiers turned to Cross.

"You must be the Cross that Sepp here was telling us about," one of them said. "You're the leader of the Student Militia?"

Suddenly feeling on edge without really knowing why, Cross nodded.

"There's a new chain of command in place. The Mayor has left the City and yielded control to the Government for the time being," the soldier explained. "We're here to secure the City and restore order. Your part in this fight is over now."

It took Cross several seconds to process those words and their full meaning. He knew that they expected him to be relieved that no more would be asked of him, that he could finally relax. But he didn't relax. For the past four years his world had revolved around the war, the product of Edward's ambitions and his own imagination. Without it, he would be lost. He would drift like a leaf on water—aimless, insignificant, lacking even the slightest control over its own destiny.

It would be like his childhood all over again.

Cross felt his hand twitch as though searching for something to pull himself from his growing sense of madness. There was nothing there this time. Not even Floe seemed to notice.

What are you but a reflection of the ambitions of others?

"No." Cross shook his head to the surprise of everyone present. "The Militia has been fighting this war from the beginning. This is *our* battle, you can't just shut us out—"

"Cross," Floe interrupted. "Don't you think—"

"If you don't want to fight I won't make you," Cross interrupted harshly. "But the Truancy is still out there, their leader is still out there, and if we back down now and let someone else finish it for us then they'll think that they were right all along. I'm not okay with that. We believe in this fight just as strongly as they do!"

Cross' expression was cold and hard. Sepp and Floe took an involuntary step back at the intensity in his eyes.

"Sepp, you said you wanted to protect your family, right?" Cross pressed. "What would it say about our resolve if we packed our bags the moment someone offered to do our job for us?"

Sepp slowly nodded, though he was unusually somber as he eyed Cross with apprehension.

"We've got strict orders to keep you guys from reentering the fight," the soldier said to Cross. "If you'd like to make an appeal, our commanding officer just arrived in the City—"

"Then take me to her." Cross turned his back to his fellow students. "I'll talk to your leader."

"All right." The soldier shrugged. "Let's find out if she'll see you."

10

Fight or Flight

Takan cursed and ducked behind a parked car as enemy soldiers continued their advance. The battle had now spilled over into the nearby District 16, one of the living districts that had fallen under Truancy control when the Educators had withdrawn. In such places life had managed to regain some semblance of normalcy—with children having both more rights and more responsibility. It hadn't been perfect, but in some ways it had been Zyid's dream realized.

Now it had fallen into madness once again.

As Truants and soldiers exchanged fire, civilians ran panicked through the streets. If there was a silver lining to the chaos, it was that the Government seemed reluctant to use airstrikes here. Instead, squads of soldiers filled the streets, backed up by armored vehicles. A gunner protruded from the top of the vehicles, manning a machine gun that forced the Truants to take cover, allowing the soldiers to surge forward.

Across the street from Takan, Umasi took aim with a rocket launcher and fired at one of the vehicles. The hit landed head-on, rocking the vehicle and turning half of it into a smoking wreck. The machine gun fell silent, and Takan sprang from cover, firing a three-round burst at one of the advancing soldiers. The soldier staggered back, then fell, and Takan ducked back behind the car as the other soldiers rained fire down on his position.

Umasi gestured to Takan to retreat again. Gritting his teeth, Takan made a run for it. The soldiers tried to pursue, but Umasi fired another rocket that sent two of them flying. It was overkill, but in a battle like this nothing could be taken for granted. The other soldiers sought cover, and Umasi took the opportunity to run after Takan.

"Check with the others, see how the retreat is going!" Umasi shouted.

Takan took cover in a doorway and reached for his radio. After the initial shock and confusion, the Truancy steadily began to organize its desperate retreat. Divisions all over the City either fought off the advancing Government or hid among civilians in the living districts. They had started with twenty divisions, and each time Takan asked for a report, fewer and fewer responded. He assumed that those that didn't respond had escaped already, or been wiped out. Either way, he didn't need to worry about them anymore.

This time nine divisions responded. Takan was about to relay the information to Umasi when there was a sudden crash behind them. They spun around, and Takan groaned. A huge hulk of metal on treads was now approaching, crushing everything before it as soldiers followed in its wake.

"They've got *tanks*?" Takan said in disbelief.

Umasi grimaced. "So it would seem."

For a kid like Takan, who had spent his whole life in the isolated City, such weapons were an abstract concept, something read about in books. They were certainly not something he ever expected to find himself facing in the streets. The tank's cannon rotated slightly, then fired. The shell slammed into the building next to Takan, exploding and sending debris everywhere. Takan and Umasi ran as the tank adjusted its aim and fired again, blowing up a nearby car.

"How are we supposed to fight—right, we're not." Takan shook his head. "If only we'd had time to set up traps. We have enough explosives stored away to blow up dozens of those things."

"Dozens wouldn't be enough," Umasi said as they regrouped with another party of retreating Truants. "This is just the tip of their power. From the beginning this fight was hopeless, but our goal isn't to win. How goes the retreat?"

"Nine divisions are still active."

"We need more time," Umasi said, heaving his rocket launcher over his shoulder. "We have to try to stop that tank. You take it from the right; I'll take it from the left."

"Got it." Takan nodded, turning to the other Truants. "You guys cover us; make those soldiers keep their distance!"

Takan and Umasi darted forward. The tank did not seem to notice. As he ran, Takan drew a firebomb from inside his jacket and lit the cloth using the flames from a burning car. He hurled the bottle at the tank, and it exploded, spraying liquid fire all over it. The fire caused no apparent damage, but it did catch the tank crew's attention. Its turret began rotating towards Takan.

This gave Umasi a clear shot. He fired a rocket straight at the tank's side. Takan held his breath as the rocket exploded against the armor. The tank paused for a moment, then began spewing machine gun fire as though nothing had happened. Takan cursed as the soldiers behind the tank began firing. He turned and ran along with Umasi as the other Truants fired at the soldiers.

"That thing is invincible!" Takan said to Umasi. "We can't even slow it down!"

Umasi grimaced and said nothing.

The tank rolled onwards, crushing a car in its way as though it were made of cardboard. The Truants had no choice but to pull back as it fired again and again, pulverizing their defenses. Takan fired his rifle at the distant soldiers, but they were using the tank as cover in order to advance.

"Are the students and Enforcers fighting these too?" Takan wondered aloud.

Umasi hesitated. A tank mortar landed nearby, literally blowing a Truant away. Having witnessed the unsuccessful attack on the metal monster, the other Truants panicked and began running. Takan didn't have the heart to stop them—he couldn't ask them to fight an impossible battle. Alone now, Takan and Umasi covered the retreat, firing methodically as they withdrew.

"The Government will probably try to seize control of the Militia and the Enforcers," Umasi said. "For now we're going to have to assume that they're all our enemies."

A familiar roar overhead signaled the arrival of Government attack helicopters. Takan and Umasi broke into a run, darting into a dark alley in order to avoid being spotted. Machine guns snarled as the deadly flying machines hunted down the fleeing Truants.

"So it's just us against the City, huh?" Takan said, panting as he peered around the corner.

"You against the City, Takan. Nothing new for the Truancy." Umasi looked up. "I'm glad I was able to fight alongside you for a while. Now if you'll excuse me, there's something I have to take care of."

Takan blinked and turned around. Umasi was still looking upwards intently. Takan craned his neck but couldn't discern anything up there but a tangled mess of fire escapes and clotheslines. Yet something was clearly bothering Umasi.

"Can't it wait?" Takan asked.

"Trust me, Takan," Umasi said. "It's urgent."

With that, Umasi sprang up to grasp the bottom rung of a fire escape ladder. With some difficulty he lifted himself up and scrambled onto the fire escape, then out of sight.

"What could be more urgent than this?" Takan muttered.

As the tank rumbled by, Takan ran deeper into the alley. He reached for his radio to coordinate one final line of resistance in the abandoned District 15, the Truancy's longtime base. Traps and defenses had already been amassed there over the years in case of an Enforcer attack.

Takan knew it wouldn't be enough to repel the Government, but he hoped it would hold them for a while. When he next asked for a head count, only six divisions replied. All six reported that they were already under attack.

• • •

Water and power has been restored to all Educator districts except District 3. The engineers say it'll be another six hours before they can get that fixed."

"Tell them they have three. How is the medical situation? Can we treat all the injured?"

"All of the City's hospitals, the ones that were still working, are swamped. We've set up first aid stations and temporary clinics in five districts, but we're going to be working at close to capacity pretty soon."

"Bring in more medics and supplies. If you run out, put in a request for more and have them flown in immediately. What's being done about those fires?"

Iris paced around the command post, issuing orders and receiving information like clockwork. The temporary base had been established in the City Square of District 1, not too far away from City Hall, where soldiers were still sweeping for more traps that the Mayor might have left. Right now it was little more than a mess of tents protecting sensitive equipment.

"The City's own firefighters are overwhelmed and a lot of them got drafted into the Enforcers," an officer explained. "We've been doing the best we can with what we've got, but there's just too many small fires spread out all over."

Iris shook her head. "Coordinate with the appropriate agencies and have firefighting helicopters brought in. Identify the firefighters among the Enforcers and put them back to work. Winning is meaningless if we let the City burn down."

The officer saluted and ran off to fulfill her orders. Looking around, Iris discerned that that was the last of them, and calculated that she had five minutes until the next reports came in. She took the opportunity to approach a large monitor that had been set up to display the colored map of the City.

"General." A soldier walked up to Iris. "We've got someone here to see you. One of the locals."

Iris furrowed her brow as she pondered the image on the screen. "Tell whoever it is that it can wait."

"It's the leader of the Student Militia, ma'am," the soldier said. "He's pretty adamant about talking to you. Should I have him leave?"

Iris blinked once, still looking at the screen. Then she smiled.

"One of the Mayor's child soldiers, is it? I can make an exception. Bring him in."

The soldier saluted. A moment later, a redheaded teenager wearing street clothes was led over to her. The boy gave a salute, which she returned.

"My name is Cross," the boy said. "I lead the Student Militia of this City. I've been fighting against the Truancy since they first emerged."

"I'm General Iris. You must have a lot of questions," Iris said. "We only have time for the short explanation. The Government is here to restore—"

"That stuff doesn't matter to me." Cross' eyes were both desperate and dangerous. "You're in charge, right? I want to discuss our role in this war."

Iris narrowed her eyes. This boy was a peculiarity. There was a cold hunger in his eyes that she recognized as battle lust, but his face twitched in ways that suggested he was internally conflicted. She had seen a similar look on substance addicts.

Iris shook her head. It didn't matter—as far as she was concerned his words were those of a dog seeking a master, and she was happy to oblige.

"Yes, I am in charge," she said. "That explanation was short enough. What exactly do you want, Cross?"

"I want my Militia to have the right to fight," Cross said. "We've held the Truancy back for the past year and I think we've earned at least that much. You can't just show up all of a sudden and tell us that we're no longer involved."

Iris' lip curled into a smile. The blueprints of a new plan were swiftly being drawn up in her mind.

"I've been aware of your Militia for a while, Cross. Do you know why I chose not to incorporate you into any part of my strategy?"

Cross hesitated. "No."

"Because by now your entire force has been infiltrated at every level by the Truancy," Iris said. "You probably know the truth of that yourself. I will not rely on soldiers that cannot be trusted. It would put success, and my men, in danger. Your Militia will be disbanded once we're finished."

Cross flinched. But he wasn't done yet.

"Put us all out in one district, away from your men," he suggested. "The risk will be all ours. There's got to be a part of the battlefield we can fill. We'll prove our worth."

"You are clinging to a war that is already won, Cross. Less than twenty percent of the Truancy's forces are still active." Iris turned towards the monitor. "I believe that minority is trying to slow us down while the others escape into the general population. We will not be able to stop them." She rubbed her chin thoughtfully. "It's a surprisingly quick and clearheaded decision on their part, but it also means that they are no longer contesting the City."

Even as Cross looked at the screen, District 16 switched from red to green. Nearly the whole map was green now, with only a few crimson holdouts remaining. Iris wasn't surprised by the astonishment on Cross' face. After all, the Government had accomplished in one night what the Educators, the Enforcers, and students had failed to do in four years.

"Please." Cross looked desperate now. "There's got to be something I can do. It can't end like this!"

Iris nodded to herself. This was exactly the reaction she had been counting on.

"If you are so certain that your Militia can be trusted then perhaps I can offer you a chance to prove it," Iris said. "I must warn you that it will be very dangerous, especially if it turns out that you are wrong."

"What is it?" Cross demanded.

Iris pointed at one of the remaining red zones on the map. "Intercepted radio communications indicate that the remaining Truants are gathering at their headquarters in District 15. I've no doubt that the district is heavily fortified and mined. They're preparing to make a last stand. Before you showed up, I was considering leveling the entire area with airstrikes."

Iris turned around.

"This will be my test for your Militia, Cross. Take over District 15 and you will prove your worth as soldiers."

Cross did not hesitate.

"We'll do it."

Umasi stepped carefully through the dark and empty room. The building appeared to be an office of some sort—rows of desks and computers filled the medium-sized space, and papers were strewn all over the floor. The blinds were drawn over all but one of the windows, casting ominous shadows each time an explosion flashed outside. Umasi made little attempt to conceal his presence. The other person in the room surely knew he was there.

"I'm impressed," Umasi said into the darkness. "Even Takan failed to notice you spying on us."

The voice that responded was even, but frigid.

"Subtlety was never his strong suit."

"You'd be surprised." Umasi smiled. "What do you want, Noni?"

The scarred girl stepped out from the shadows. "Answers."

Umasi tilted his sunglasses up to see better in the gloom. Zyid's former adjutant had changed quite a bit since he had last seen her. Her ponytail was no longer braided, for one thing. For another . . . "I see you've removed your scarf."

"You've changed your wardrobe too," Noni said, glaring at the jacket that had once belonged to Zyid. "How did you get that?"

"I took it off my brother's dead body," Umasi replied. "Why do you ask? I doubt that it would look very good on you."

Noni's eyes were icy as she glared at him. Her hands clenched and unclenched.

"Did you kill him?"

Umasi let his sunglasses fall back down to cover his eyes. "That would be telling."

Noni let out a strangled hiss and drew her knives. Umasi made no motion to go for his swords. He didn't feel that his life was in danger just yet, and he had no desire to fight with this girl.

"I'm not here for games," Noni snarled. "There aren't many in this City who could match Zyid in a fight. You're one of them. Now tell me, *was it you*?"

"If it was, do you intend to fight me with kitchen knives?" Umasi asked. "Think about it, Noni. Whoever killed my brother must have been stronger than him. You would have to be even stronger than that to avenge him like this."

"You," Noni said, "are avoiding the question."

Takan told me she was bothered by his death, but this? Umasi let out a sharp breath. It must have been difficult for Takan, knowing that the girl he loved was being driven crazy by his own actions.

"What will you do when you discover the killer's identity?" Umasi asked.

"I will kill him."

"No matter who he is?"

"No matter who he is."

Umasi shook his head. The situation was more serious than he'd thought. He made his decision. Takan had shared Umasi's responsibility when the Government struck. It was Umasi's turn to share some of Takan's responsibility.

"I see."

Umasi drew one of his swords and lunged at Noni. Noni reacted, parrying the stab with one knife while thrusting with the other. Umasi twisted aside, then slashed again. Noni leaped backwards onto a desk. Her knives lacked the reach to take advantage of the high ground, but as Umasi lunged again Noni kicked a lamp off the desk and into his face.

Umasi staggered backwards, his sunglasses knocked askew. Hearing something swoop towards his head, Umasi raised his sword, only to feel something unfamiliar wrap around it. It was Noni's scarf. She had added a weight of some sort to one end, and was now using it as a weapon. His sword trapped, Umasi could only duck and weave as Noni leapt down and began stabbing furiously, holding the end of the scarf in one hand and a knife in the other.

"I've seen a technique like that before," Umasi said, narrowly avoiding being gutted. "But it was a chain, not a scarf. Did someone inspire you?"

Noni said nothing. She yanked on her scarf, tipping Umasi slightly off balance. She lunged. With no chance of blocking and no time to dodge, Umasi went for his last option.

Umasi's second sword came swinging out of its sheath, and Noni aborted her lunge just in time. As she drew back into a defensive crouch, Umasi held the scarf taut, then stabbed with his free blade. There was a ripping sound, and Umasi tore his first sword free. Noni's eyes widened, and then narrowed to slits as she lunged again, brandishing both knives.

As Umasi fended off her attacks with alternating swipes of his swords, he began to worry. His original intention was to beat some sense into her, but at this rate he was really going to have to hurt her. A flash went off outside, illuminating Noni's icy eyes, and Umasi was reminded of a small and frail girl who had placed herself between him and his brother long ago. Then he remembered the words he had once exchanged with that brother.

"*You underestimate her. Who's to say that she mightn't have hurt you?*"
"*Someday, perhaps. But she is not ready now.*"

Umasi shut his eyes. It was ironic that it had been Zyid's death that pushed her to her full potential, but Umasi didn't have time to appreciate it. He understood now that his own life was in danger, and that he would have to fight with everything he had.

In one swift motion Umasi tore his jacket from around his neck and flung it at Noni. Engulfed by the black material, Noni flailed about for a second, enough time for Umasi to stab through it. The jacket sagged, empty. Realizing he'd missed, Umasi brought his other sword up, prepared to parry a lunge. But Noni remained a good distance away. As she lifted her knives Umasi realized what she was about to do.

Noni hurled one knife, then the second, and with a flick of each sword Umasi deflected both. For a moment Umasi thought it was over, but then Noni seized a keyboard from a nearby desk and brutally swung it at him. It was not the sort of attack that Umasi could have blocked with his sword, and he had no choice but to back up to avoid it.

Noni threw the keyboard at him. As he knocked it aside, she picked up a monitor and hurled that as well. Umasi staggered backwards from the blow. Relentless, Noni picked up an entire computer and heaved it with a violent yell. Dropping his swords, Umasi caught the heavy object, but could not stop its force from sending him crashing to the ground.

This was not a technique. There was nothing elegant about it. It was just sheer, focused determination to crush the enemy.

As Umasi shoved the computer off of him, Noni lunged. Umasi raised his arms and legs fast enough to meet her, and for a few moments they grappled down the aisle, neither able to get the upper hand until they bumped against the window. Pinned to the floor, Umasi struggled to keep Noni's hands off his throat.

"Your devotion to Zyid is admirable. I envy you for it," Umasi said through gritted teeth. "But if you haven't noticed, there are more important things to worry about right now."

"This whole City can burn for all I care," Noni snarled. "As long as I have my revenge first."

Umasi sighed, then tossed his head to relieve himself of his sunglasses. He looked Noni straight in the eye.

"Then if you survive this, return to Takan and tell him I think you deserve the whole truth."

With that, Umasi shoved with all his strength, sending Noni crashing through the window. He rose to his feet and brushed glass from his shoulders as warm air rushed in from outside. They were only on the second floor, so the fall probably wouldn't kill her. He made no effort to look out the window. He didn't know what Noni would do now, and he didn't want to know. He had done all he could—the rest was Takan's burden to bear.

Retrieving his ripped windbreaker, Umasi decided that now was the time to begin making his way back towards the center of the City. The Government would win this battle. When they did, there would be an enemy that Umasi knew he was destined to face alone.

11

Floe found the nameless girl on a bench in a lonely hallway of the fourth floor, her son fast asleep using his mother's lap as a pillow. It hadn't been easy to locate the pair—they seemed to vanish like smoke and no one had been sure where they went. Floe had spent some time wandering around the building, carrying a plastic tray.

The lockers in the former school had been converted into arsenals, the classrooms into dorms, but the cafeteria, at least, was still a cafeteria. Floe had piled the tray high with whatever food could be gotten there.

"I thought you might be hungry, so I brought you this," Floe whispered so as not to disturb the sleeping child. "It's not much, but we've been short on supplies lately."

"Thank you," the albino said, accepting the tray. "It's been a long day."

"Tell me about it." Floe sighed, sitting down at the foot of the bench. "Things just seem so crazy now."

The albino picked up a plastic fork and began eating immediately. If the strange girl was bothered by the pungent cafeteria food, she gave no sign of it.

"You're handling things well," the albino said between bites. "I heard you had a mission today. You were with Cross?"

"Yeah."

Floe didn't elaborate, nor did the other girl seem to expect her to. Not for the first time Floe wondered who she was and where she had come from. Before she could ask, the nameless girl spoke again.

"May I ask why you're in the Student Militia?"

Floe tensed. Was the girl a Truant spy? Floe dismissed the idea as swiftly as it had come. The albino didn't seem like a Truant at all.

"I used to know Cross a long time ago," Floe answered carefully. "I believe in him."

The albino seemed to consider that for a moment.

"What does that mean?" she asked.

Floe laughed. "I'm not really sure myself. I guess I just think he's a good person and that he'll do the right thing when he has to."

The albino nodded.

"That's as good a reason as any," she said. "I just think the whole situation is lamentable. The Truancy was born with a legitimate purpose, but they were lost the minute they accepted what they'd have to do to achieve it."

Floe smiled. "It would have been better if we could've negotiated a peaceful compromise, wouldn't it?"

The albino shrugged. "A force for change will always find opposition."

"So will a force of violence."

The nameless girl did not disagree. Indeed, she smiled and looked at Floe with twinkling eyes.

"You've got an interesting spirit," she said. "But you don't sound like you're well suited for the grisly business of a soldier."

Floe didn't know how to respond to that. A few moments of awkward silence passed. Taking the hint, the albino changed the subject.

"You must be exhausted," she said. "Have you eaten yet yourself?"

"Yeah, in the basement cafeteria," Floe replied, glad to return to a more mundane topic. "I know that I should feel tired, but there's just so much going on that I can't even think about lying down. I didn't want to feel idle so I decided to check on you two."

"I appreciate it. I didn't know where to find the food," the albino confessed. "This is my first time being inside a school building."

Floe looked at the other girl quizzically. "How old are you?"

The albino paused. "Nineteen, I believe," she replied after a moment of consideration. "I may be wrong."

Floe wasn't sure what she was expecting, but that answer surprised her enough to make her forget all about the other girl's schooling. She turned to stare at Zen, still slumbering at his mother's side.

"B-But . . ." Floe sputtered. "How . . . how old is your son?"

"He's three," the other girl said, stroking Zen's hair. "Yes, I was young."

"Was . . . did you . . . did you mean to—"

"I knew what I was doing," the albino said simply. "I knew what the consequences could be, and I accepted them."

Floe found herself at a loss. A thousand questions jammed up in her mind, and before she could settle on any of them, the school bell rang twice. It was the signal for an emergency meeting. Floe shot to her feet.

"Excuse me," she said to the albino as Zen stirred.

"Of course."

Floe ran for the auditorium on the second floor, where all the common briefings were given. Even sliding down the banisters, she knew she would be late. By the time she got there, Cross was already onstage and in the middle of explaining the current situation. Government soldiers watched in silence from the back of the room.

Floe found a seat next to Sepp. Her confusion turned to horror as she realized what was going on.

"Right now the Truants have withdrawn into District 15 and are holed up in there like rats. The Government is offering us a great honor," Cross said. "To prove that we can be trusted, to have some say in what comes next, we're going to go in first. We were there for the start of this chaos, and now we can finish it.

"You all know that it's going to be dangerous, but yesterday we were prepared to stand and die just to lose the war. Right now I tell you that we can stand and die to win it. This is the only chance we'll get to end the war on *our* terms."

Floe looked around. Sepp's expression was unreadable, but most of the others present seemed to be reacting positively to Cross' speech. Like kids in a classroom, the poor students heard the lecture—but they didn't understand what it really meant.

The Government is trying to draw out the Truancy's infiltrators. It'll probably work too. Floe thought bitterly. *How neat. When the bloodbath is over they can move in easily over our dead bodies.*

Floe stared grimly up at the stage as her leader proceeded with his briefing.

I am not *ordering* any of you to do anything." Cross looked out into a sea of unfamiliar faces. "I do not feel that I should order you to do anything. I never wanted to be the leader of the Student Militia, and I'm sure most of you have noticed that I've been running from that responsibility."

A boy heckled from the back row. "Got that right!"

Cross ignored him.

"I've never really spoken to you all like this, and I should have," Cross admitted. "For more than a year now the Student Militia has been my entire life—serving was my only purpose. I won't pretend to be Edward, who had a vision for this City. I have no great ambition, no extraordinary perspective."

The audience was murmuring now, and yet their eyes remained fixed upon Cross. Cross found that the words spilled easily from his mouth when he told the truth. Perhaps he had never given a speech before because it was hard to sell one full of lies.

"If Edward were here he would probably remind you that it has to be us students who defeat the Truancy. He would say that we're fighting to have a voice, to say that no one else speaks for us, to make our own choices and stand for them."

Cross took a deep breath.

"Maybe that's how we got started, and maybe that's why some of you still fight. But as far as I'm concerned, I just *want* to fight. The Student

Militia gives me a purpose and in return I offer it everything I have. That's why I'm going to District 15."

Cross hesitated, then continued.

"As I said, I'm not ordering you to do anything, least of all imitate me. I know that my reasons are pretty bad. The reason I'm asking for volunteers is because I know there are better reasons in this auditorium. I know some of you want to protect your families. I know some of you want to punish the Truancy for all they've done. I know some of you want to win benefits for yourselves.

"All of those are better reasons than mine, and I'm still heading out there. What I really mean to say is this—if my bad reason is good enough to fight for, then what is *yours* good for?"

Cross stepped away from the microphone. His heart pounded as he stared out at the audience. Then the students burst into applause. A few of them even raised weapons into the air and shouted their enthusiasm.

Cross felt a smile tug at his lips. He had done it.

The auditorium emptied quickly as students ran for their lockers. Cross descended from the stage and walked down the aisle, elated. All of his weariness and confusion vanished, swept away by anticipation of the coming battle.

Cross found it easy now to embrace his lack of purpose and ambition. He could live with devoting everything to the war that had been the reason for the Student Militia's existence, and which had become the reason for his own.

Floe and Sepp were already waiting in the aisle. Cross ignored the looks on their faces as he approached.

"You two, hurry up and get your gear," Cross said. "We're—"

"Are you out of your mind?"

Floe's shrill words caught Cross completely off guard. This was the last reaction that he had expected from her.

"What are you screaming about all of a sudden?" Cross demanded.

"What am I screaming about?" Floe looked at him in a way he had never seen before, as though she could not recognize him. "What do you *think* I'm screaming about? We just lost a member of our team, you just admitted to being some kind of adrenaline junkie, and as if that wasn't enough, you want to waste more lives attacking District 15?"

Cross staggered back a step. The words were like a physical blow. They hurt more than he imagined words could.

"Cross, even you must be able to see that all we can hope to accomplish is clearing a bunch of mines with our bodies!" Floe continued. "This is suicide—"

"You said that about our mission against Takan!" Cross felt his anger rising. "We're still here, aren't we?"

"Barely, and Joe *isn't!*" Floe said scathingly. "And we *failed* that mission, if you haven't noticed!"

"I meant every word I said up on that podium." Cross spoke with hard conviction. "There will be consequences beyond this one battle. The Militia has only this one chance to prove itself. That General believes that we're infested with Truancy spies—"

"Then she's not wrong, Cross!" Floe insisted. "I know you meant what you said, but don't let your emotions blind you! The Truancy has tons of spies in the Militia, you *know* that! You're walking into a death trap!"

"I'm with Floe on this one." Sepp looked uncomfortable. "Cross, I was touched by your speech, but there's no *need* for us to fight. We're safe now, man. You saw what the Government's got out there. Why not let them handle it?"

"You don't know what it's like to watch you do this, Cross!" Floe's eyes were full of tears now. "I'm watching you lose yourself to a madness you don't even recognize, and I can't save you! Please, I'm trying to save you!"

Cross looked bitterly from one of his friends to the other. Why did they refuse to understand how important this was for him? Other students he didn't even know by name would be fighting by his side, and yet his most trusted companions now saw fit to abandon him. In the one moment when he needed and counted upon their support the most, they had turned on him.

A sudden rage seized hold of Cross.

"Fine!" he shouted. "I only asked for volunteers anyway. If you two want to play it safe and coddle each other here, then be my guest."

Floe whispered, "Cross—"

"Shut up! You got what you wanted," Cross said. "Now leave me alone!"

"She doesn't deserve that, Cross." Sepp glared.

"Of course you take her side!" Cross ranted. "I bet you guys blame me for our failure of a mission, right? You've probably been whispering to everybody about what a terrible leader I make. Well you know what? You're right! ARE YOU HAPPY NOW?"

Cross spun around and kicked an auditorium chair so hard that the armrest broke off. Punctuating each blow with a roar, Cross drove his foot into the seat again and again until it was nothing but a pile of splinters on the ground. Behind him Floe collapsed into sobs.

Cross slung his rifle over his shoulder and stormed out of the auditorium, kicking another seat into the upright position just for good measure. Some small part of him felt sick on the inside, but he knew that the battle would make it better. Battle always did.

Floe had never known physical pain that hurt like this.

It was as though the image in her mind that she had labeled and cherished as Cross had suddenly removed a mask to reveal something ugly and monstrous beneath. She couldn't recognize him. The boy who had just flown into a violent rage showed not a trace of the person she had thought she'd known so well.

Sepp laid a sympathetic hand on her shoulder, but she shrugged it off. Wiping her tears away, Floe mumbled an excuse and ran out of the auditorium. She sought out and found an unlit and empty hallway, and there she slumped against a window, a lonely silhouette against the light of a streetlamp outside.

"It's tearing him up inside, you know."

Floe nearly choked on her tears as she spun around. In a shadowy corner of her own, the nameless albino stood serenely, holding hands with a sleepy-looking Zen.

"You . . ." Floe swallowed, regaining her composure. "You heard him?"

"I think the whole building did," the albino said. "That boy has experienced a lot of pain in his life, I think, and he has trouble recognizing his friends from his enemies. He cares about you a lot. His anger at your disapproval proves that. He's just having trouble understanding who he is."

"If he doesn't understand," Floe said, "then what good is it?"

"That, I suspect, may be up to you."

She gave Floe a reassuring smile, then turned and began to lead Zen off in the direction of the cafeteria. Speechless, Floe watched her go.

Then, almost against her will, she turned to gaze out the window at the students heading off in the familiar black vans.

How many left?"

"Just two divisions, Aaron. One all the way out in District 48, and us."

A warm wind rustled their hair as Takan and Aaron stood high atop the roof of the abandoned office building that the Truancy had long used as their main headquarters. It was long past midnight, and the clouds had lifted, allowing the bright and faintly bluish moonlight to cast its tint over the City. With electricity out and most of the fires subdued, the City itself was now almost totally dark.

"The airplanes have been quiet for a while now," Aaron remarked. "Can't we just scatter into the neighboring districts?"

"Not a good idea." Takan shook his head. "For one thing, as long as their attention is on us, the other division will be able to get away. For another, they've surrounded the whole district. They probably know we've set traps here. They're holding back."

"Well, isn't that a good thing?"

"You would think so," Takan muttered, his eyes scanning the horizon. "But the enemy being as powerful as they are, I'm wondering if they're just waiting for something worse to come along. How are the tunnels going?"

"Just about done. We've blasted tunnels in five places all over the district. Plus we've got the subway and manholes," Aaron said. "It's not gonna be clean, but we can be gone at a moment's notice."

"Then we'd better get back down to ground level," Takan said. "It looks like we've got trouble coming."

In the distance dark shapes were approaching from all over the City. The Truants recognized them immediately as the black vans that the Student Militia had taken to using as transport. Sure enough, as the first of the vans halted at the border of District 15, doors opened and blue-clad figures began pouring out.

"Students?" Aaron said, aghast. "Are they serious?"

Both Truants ran for the stairwell, talking breathlessly as they descended.

"How come the spies didn't warn us?" Aaron wondered aloud, then smacked himself upside the head. "Oh yeah, communications are down."

"Looks like Umasi was right about the students after all," Takan said grimly. "Are they just sucking up to authority as usual? Or maybe the Government threatened them too?"

"Who cares, if they step in here they'll be blown away," Aaron said. "The Militia doesn't have any of that fancy Government stuff. It'll be like meat into a grinder."

Just as Aaron and Takan reached the ground floor, they heard explosions in the distance. They burst out into the open in time to see the first blasts subside. More began to go off, accompanied by distant screaming as the students set off trap after trap.

"Those fools," Aaron gasped. "Are they suicidal? They're dying for nothing out there!"

"Not for nothing," Takan said darkly. "They're clearing our traps with their lives. When they're done dying, the Government will be able to move in easily."

Aaron frowned. "What're we going to do about it?"

"Play our last cards."

Takan reached for one of his two radios. This was the one set to the frequency used by the Truancy.

"Everyone, they're sending students in," Takan said. "You know the drill. Keep them back as long as you can. This is our last stand. Good luck."

More gunfire erupted from all over the district, and the battle began in earnest. Takan and Aaron each raised their own rifles and ran for the front lines.

"They've sent the entire Militia after us, and we don't have many guys left," Aaron pointed out. "If they get through the mines, we won't slow them down much."

"No," Takan admitted, "but this will."

Takan raised the second radio to his mouth. This one had been captured from the Student Militia and was set to their open frequency.

"This is Takan, leader of the Truancy. All sleeper agents, activate *now*!"

12
Government Triumphant

The mechanic paused in the middle of fixing the District 2 School's boiler. He blinked. He turned to stare at the radio, which he had left resting against a pipe. He wondered, not for the first time that day, if he had finally gone insane like they always said he was. Then the sounds of gunfire and shouts came in over the radio, enough to justify the earlier command from Takan.

And if I am crazy, this will just be another act of a madman.

The mechanic licked his lips and put down his tools. He was a teenager, called in to replace the adult mechanic who had been drafted into the Enforcers. He had volunteered to join the Student Militia, but because they could not find a shred of aptitude for fighting in him, and because he had been handy with tools, they took him on as a mechanic instead.

"You better not be messing with my head, radio," the mechanic said, opening his toolbox. "I've been waiting for this for a year now."

The mechanic reached in and withdrew a solid block of explosives and a roll of duck tape. Walking over to a large concrete support pillar, he carefully taped the block to it and returned to his toolbox. He was reaching for more explosives when a voice called out from the open doorway.

"It's Max, isn't it?"

The mechanic froze, then reached for a large wrench. He turned to look at the person standing in the doorway.

"Sepp," Max said. "What's an officer like you doing in a place like this?"

"I heard the message on the radio and thought I'd come admire the view down here," Sepp replied. "You know, these support columns are really relaxing to gaze at when there's a threat of sabotage."

Sepp's eyes flitted to the explosives strapped to the column, and then back to Max. For a moment the two boys stared at each other. Then they both sprang into action. Sepp reached for his sidearm, but with unexpected speed Max struck him upside the head with his wrench. Sepp stumbled, and Max slugged him in the stomach. He seized Sepp by the collar and threw him into the boiler room.

Sepp forced himself to his feet. He ducked another swing of the wrench but was unable to stop Max from kicking him in the chest. The wind knocked from him, his head bleeding, Sepp could do nothing as he was slammed against the support column. Struggling to stay conscious, Sepp abruptly became aware that he was being taped to the concrete.

"You sly bastard." Sepp grinned as he slumped against the column. "You're just a mechanic. Since when could you fight like that?"

"Just a mechanic? I'm one of the *founding members* of the Truancy, Sepp," Max said, finishing the roll of tape. "I even outlived our leader. You tend to pick up a few things along the way."

Sepp laughed, the sound echoing throughout the room.

"I like that. That's good. Irony. You were the officer all along." Sepp shut his eyes. "Are you going to blow up the building?"

"Of course I am." Max strapped more explosives to the support column, right above Sepp's head. "Why do you think I picked this job? No one ever notices the hired help."

"So your mission all along was to make nice with us and then make us go boom."

"That sums it up, yeah," Max said, returning to his toolbox. "Nothing personal, Sepp. From what I could tell, you weren't a bad guy."

"Where're you going now?" Sepp asked.

"To the other columns."

Sepp tilted his head to the side. "Don't you have to kill me first?"

"Nah," Max said. "The explosion will take care of that, along with the rest of the building."

Max shut his toolbox and rose to his feet. Then a new voice piped up.

"Explosions are dangerous!"

Blinking, Max looked down and stared. A small boy with a stuffed animal was tugging at his trousers, a stern expression on his face. Max considered what he was seeing for a moment, and then laughed as he came to the obvious conclusion.

"You're a hallucination," Max informed the child.

"I'm afraid not," a female voice said.

Max spun around. Before he could even see the face of his attacker, there was a swish of white and he had been flipped onto the ground. The impact and the surprise stunned him, and a foot pressing lightly on his back convinced him not to try to rise.

"Mom, what's hallucination?" the child asked.

"It's something you see that's not really there," the girl explained. "Like a dream, but while awake. They're usually seen by crazy people."

"I'm not crazy!" Max shouted, turning his head. Then his jaw dropped. "Impossible."

The albino looked down at him calmly. "What is?"

"You," Max whispered, awestruck. "It's really you. You're real after all. They thought I was nuts. They never trusted me again. They even made me a mechanic, just to get rid of me."

The albino removed her foot and crouched down. "Have we met before?"

"You don't remember?" Max laughed. "*I'll* never forget it. It was just after we got the Truancy started. I was standing watch in an alley, spotted a vagrant running away. I gave chase, and then the next thing I knew . . ." Max brought his fist to his forehead to indicate where the chain had hit.

The nameless girl's eyes flickered with remembrance, and she reached out to pat Max on the head.

"You're right," she said. "You're not crazy. I'm sorry."

"I've been waiting to hear that for four years," Max sighed. Then he let out a bark of laughter. "But it's over now anyway, isn't it? The war, the Truancy, Zyid's dream. It's all over. How many were there when it started? How many are left? I don't even remember." He mimed a gun firing at his temple. "Whatever it is, there'll be one less pretty soon."

"We don't shoot all our prisoners, it's too messy," Sepp said, still attached to the pillar. "Tell you what; I'll overlook the part where you bopped me on the head, but you'll probably do time for the whole 'trying to blow everyone up' thing."

"Bah." Max looked exhausted but relieved, as though a massive weight had just been lifted off him. He rolled over and lay spread-eagled on the ground, moving only when Zen tentatively poked him in the side.

"Are you all right?" the albino asked, turning to examine Sepp. She reached out with one hand, almost but not quite touching his bloodied scalp. "That's a bad head wound. I'll go fetch help."

"Nah, I'm fine," Sepp protested. "I can walk, just get this stuff off me. There's a knife in my belt."

The nameless girl hesitated, then she drew the knife out and quickly cut Sepp free of the duct tape. She helped him up as he winced from his injury.

"Thank you, milady," Sepp said.

The albino looked at him sharply. "I'd prefer it if you didn't call me that."

Sepp blinked, then shrugged. "Sure thing, boss. I'm just glad you were here. It could've been a real mess."

"It still might be," the albino warned as Sepp handcuffed Max. "I'd worry about your friend Cross, if I were you. If they even had spies within the mechanics, imagine how many are out there with him."

Cross ignored the explosions and the screams around him.

Every bit of focus the Student Militia's leader could muster was devoted to the bottles and cans lying in the street that might or might not be deadly bombs. The Militia had long known how creative the Truancy could be in setting their traps, yet never had Cross seen so many, or in such lethal variety. He ducked as a student nearby was blown away by a mine disguised as a car tire.

What bothered Cross the most was that despite the danger he was in, despite the thrill he should be feeling, none of it was having its usual therapeutic effect. Doubt nagged at his conscience as he watched another student fall to shrapnel from a bomb. He pressed forward.

The mines were beginning to thin, and Cross was just beginning to fall back into a rhythm, when a voice came on the radio and fresh hell broke loose.

"This is Takan, leader of the Truancy. All sleeper agents, *activate now!*"

Without warning, students all around turned their weapons on their hapless comrades. Under the bright moonlight Cross watched as the silhouettes of his fellow students crumpled and fell like puppets whose strings had been cut. One silhouette, still standing, turned and took aim at Cross. Instinctively, Cross fired first—without really knowing if it was a friend or a foe.

Now all students were firing, both at their attackers and at one another. Total chaos reigned. The heat made it hard to think. There was a pounding in Cross' head. His headache had returned with a vengeance. This wasn't how things were supposed to go. He had come here in search of purpose, but there was none to be found on this battlefield.

Cross almost found himself radioing for Sepp and Floe before he caught himself. Unfamiliar faces swam all around him, none of which could be trusted. Both enemy and ally wore the same uniform now. What had started as a battle between the Truancy and the Student Militia had turned into a mad free-for-all.

A student hiding behind a car began firing in Cross' direction. Cross dived for the cover of an alley, took a deep breath, then leapt out, aiming for a paint can near the other student. The disguised bomb exploded, sending the student flying and triggering a chain reaction of other mines and explosives. The street filled with flames and shrieks. There *had* to have been allies caught in that blast, but Cross hadn't meant to do that, he hadn't meant any of this—

Gunshots flew at the alley, a bullet clipping Cross' shoulder. Like clockwork, he raised his rifle. Cross no longer knew who his enemies were, and suddenly he didn't care. He began to fire, indiscriminate with his targets. Mechanically he proceeded through the streets and dark shapes fell before him. Some wore street clothes, but most wore blue uniforms like his own. Cross slammed clip after clip into his rifle.

Cross was vaguely aware of shouts and screams. Some sounded like pleas. He ignored them all. A fog had fallen upon his thoughts, and he knew the only way to survive was to attack, attack *everything* before it attacked him.

As he paused to reload once more, a hand flew at his head. Cross ducked and seized the oncoming arm, but before he could break it, a knee slammed into his stomach. Confused, Cross found himself being thrown forcefully to the ground. His gun slid from his grasp as he was dragged into a nearby alley.

Cross slowly began to awaken from his murderous stupor, and found himself limp with shock as he realized what had happened. He could barely twitch as his captor sat him up against the wall. Completely numb, even to the idea of his own death, Cross looked up. Then his eyes widened.

It was Floe, a cold expression on her face as she held a pistol to his forehead.

Terror twisted in Cross' gut. It was not death he feared, but true betrayal. A thousand thoughts ran through his head. Why was Floe here? Had he pushed her too far? Was she punishing him for what he had just done? Had she really been working for the Truancy all along? Had everything been a lie?

Out of the corner of his eye, Cross saw a Truant enter the mouth of the alley. Without even looking, Floe moved her pistol and shot the boy down. Stunned, Cross could only stare up at her in confusion. She crouched down to Cross' level, saying nothing, her features betraying nothing.

Cross swallowed. He had to say something. What could he say?

"Floe . . . I'm . . . I . . ."

Floe slapped him hard across the face. Cross saw the blow coming and did nothing to stop it. The impact stung in more ways than one.

"You don't have to say anything," Floe said. "I know."

An explosive barrel at the mouth of the alley went off, and Floe tackled Cross, shielding him from the force of the blast. He lay limp under her, not wanting to be saved, not deserving to be saved. The enormity of what he'd done finally dawned on him, and he could feel something break inside.

For many minutes Cross lay there, still as a corpse, only murmuring once to tell Floe that yes, he was all right—a lie, and both of them knew it.

The explosions slowly grew less and less frequent as the Truancy's traps were exhausted. The Militia had been decimated and countless numbers of them had vanished with the Truants. Cross stared up at the sky as helicopters roared overhead, blotting out the moon. Armored vehicles rumbled past the alley as Government soldiers swarmed into the district, walking over the bodies of the students.

The battle was over. The Truancy had been put down. Yet Cross could find no joy in any of that, not after what it had cost. And so he just lay there in Floe's arms, feeling like one of the motionless dead himself.

The last red district switched colors, turning the entire screen into one solid mass of green. In less than sixteen hours the Government had secured control of the entire City. Iris smiled and leaned back in her chair.

"I win."

Her plan had been a complete success. Not only had it succeeded in crushing the Truancy with minimal Government casualties, but using the Student Militia had forced the Truancy to reveal their spies and saboteurs. Now that the chaff had been separated, Iris believed that most of the remaining Student Militia could be counted on to comply with her future plans.

Of course, there were probably still some undercover Truants who had not acted for one reason or another—and even students who, given privileges by the Mayor, might protest as the Government reasserted its authority. Things never did go a hundred percent smoothly. But she was ready for that.

Iris smiled as she stood and began walking towards her waiting staff officers. The mere fact that she had been proven correct about the Militia would lend her the credibility and justification she needed to take the next steps towards restoring the Education City. Both the students and the Truants had played their parts perfectly in the last act of their little drama.

"General, the higher-ups are requesting an update," one of the officers said.

"Send them the latest. Detail our successful reacquisition of the City, and mention that the new body armor performed well," Iris said. "Also inform them that I will begin implementing a program immediately to eliminate any dissidence and prove that the philosophy of the City can be salvaged. It should take no more than a few months to see results. Dismissed."

"Yes, ma'am."

The officer saluted and then ran off to relay the message. Iris turned to the others.

"Now that all resistance has been neutralized, our primary objectives must be located," she said. "I want search parties deployed all over the City. Go from district to district. Leave no brick unturned. Do whatever you must."

• • •

In one of the Truancy's escape passages, an abandoned construction tunnel leading out of the district, Takan and Aaron leaned against the dusty walls, sharing a bottle of beer. The battle was long over, the last of the explosions having faded half an hour ago. Most of the Truants had already made it out one way or another. Still, Takan and Aaron waited, drinking in silence as they waited for the Government alert to die down.

"So," Aaron said, passing the bottle to Takan. "This is really it, huh."

"You're taking it well." Takan took a sip. "Four years of fighting this war, coming to the very edge of victory . . . and all of a sudden it's over. You were one of the founding members of the Truancy, weren't you Aaron?"

Aaron scratched his head sheepishly.

"I think I might be the only one left, actually," he said, ticking names off on his fingers. "Ken was shot. Amal died early. Max went crazy. Gabriel got killed by that Edward bastard. Then we lost Zyid himself. I'm glad I was stuck in the workshop rather than out on the battlefield."

"Well, you were there at the beginning of the Truancy," Takan said, passing the bottle back. "I guess it's fitting that you're here to see its end."

"Nah, this isn't the end." Aaron chuckled and took a gulp. "We're just taking a break."

Takan smiled at that. "At least we caused enough trouble to get the Mayor unseated. I'm just worried about what comes next."

"Hey, if these new Government guys turn out to be as bad, you know my number," Aaron said. "If the phones ever get back up, call us back together. We'll sort them out."

Takan shook his head. "The schools are all closed. They'll never get us back in there. In that sense, we've actually won. But we've also lost what we were fighting against. Without a cause to drive us, we're just . . . kids."

"Nah," Aaron said, finishing off the bottle and tossing it aside. "We're past that by now. Takan, it was an honor to fight with the Truancy. I'd do it again anytime."

With that, Aaron straightened up. Takan understood that he was going. One of the first to join, now one of the last to leave. As Aaron began to walk away down the dark tunnel, Takan voiced the question that he had been silently asking himself.

"Where will you go?"

Aaron paused, looking thoughtful for a moment. Then he shrugged.

"Back home, I guess. If it's still there," Aaron said. "I wonder what my parents will have to say when I show up after all these years. What about you?"

At Aaron's mention of home, Takan winced at a surge of bittersweet memories. The silence in the tunnel stretched on for several seconds. Then Takan spoke.

"Maybe I'll do the same."

13

What All Leaders Are

The sun was slowly rising over District 1, sending a pink and orange glow through the dirty hospital windows. Lying on the sickbed of his private ward, Cross stared at his reflection in the glass, his gaze blank and unmoving.

Cross wasn't sure how long it had been since he had been brought from the battlefield. He vaguely remembered doctors examining him, and his arm was still bandaged where they had injected the anesthetic. It felt like a long time ago. He was physically in fine shape, he had been told, but would need some time to recover from the shock.

Cross had said nothing in response.

At one point Cross remembered being wheeled into a room full of other patients. His few waking moments had been haunted by their cries. They were the wounded, the students who had followed Cross blindly into the trap.

Besides the injured there were the traitors, the ones Cross had been warned about but had ignored—in his mind they were everywhere, erasing whatever confidence he had ever had in the Student Militia.

The sun shifted outside and Cross blinked. For a moment it had looked like his reflection had no face. A trick of the light.

The door to the ward opened. A single set of footsteps entered. The door shut again, followed by silence. Cross ignored it. He was in no mood to talk.

"I apologize for such an early morning intrusion, Cross," a familiar voice said. "I know you're not asleep—if you squeezed your eyes shut any tighter I could swear you'd been teargassed."

Cross grimaced. There were many people he did not want to see at the moment, but General Iris was near the top of that list.

"You are acting childish," Iris said. "The Truancy is routed and order has been restored to the City. You should be pleased."

Cross said nothing. The victory, if it could even be called that, was hollow. Fighting had been his only purpose, and now Cross found no satisfaction even in that. The sense of pointlessness was so overwhelming that he felt lost in its depths. With no motivation to do otherwise, he continued to lie there, unresponsive.

That seemed just fine with the General.

"You will be discharged from the hospital today," she informed him. "There isn't enough space to go around, and we've kept you at the expense of other patients with more serious injuries."

Cross nodded mechanically.

"As you might have guessed, we have assumed complete control over this City." Iris placed a hand on her hip. "This has been a resounding military success, and you played your part in it. You have my thanks."

Cross made a small grunt of acknowledgment.

"However, there is still a lot of work to be done before we can say that peace has been established. I was hoping to discuss that with you now, Cross."

Another grunt. It seemed to satisfy the General.

"You must have noticed that the Truancy managed to avoid extermination," Iris said dryly. "Their members are now hiding among the general populace and to put the problem plainly, we have no way of sorting the good from the bad. These Truants represent a continuing threat—they have tasted anarchy, liked it, and are now accustomed to employing violence to get what they want."

Cross was barely listening by now. He found it very hard to give a damn about anything that Iris was saying. The words were like buzzing in his ears.

"Your Student Militia also poses the same problem," Iris continued. "You saw for yourself that my initial concerns were justified. Your Militia has been infiltrated at every level by the Truancy, and there is no telling how many spies yet remain."

Cross turned away from the window. The sun had risen high enough to shine directly into his eyes.

"The fact of the matter is that we cannot simply trust the youth of this City to transition back to an orderly society without some assistance." Iris smiled thinly. "In order to facilitate this, I will disband the Student Militia and have *every* child go through reeducation camps that are currently being built all over the City."

Cross nodded automatically. Then the full meaning of Iris' words finally registered. He sat up.

"What do you mean by 'reeducation?'"

"It's nothing very bad, Cross." Iris turned to look out the window and at the dawn. "Just think of it as summer camp."

Cross creased his brow. Something about this whole proposition struck him as very wrong. Recalling Floe's warnings, Cross realized that this woman was not to be trusted.

"General, I don't think it's fair for the Student Militia to be included in this," Cross said slowly. "We have never defied authority, we did everything that—"

"That is why you must now set an example for everyone else," Iris interrupted. "Do you know what the true purpose of this City was, Cross?"

Cross frowned. He did know. Edward had explained it to him a long time ago, in a dark dormitory as hopeless as his whole life seemed now.

"To control people."

Iris continued staring out the glass. The sun had freed itself from the horizon, its light now pale and yellow, the skies a lovely blue.

"Smart boy. Well informed. I'd ask where you heard that, but it's irrelevant now." Iris turned to look at Cross again. "You're exactly right. Originally it was a very crude system, with all sorts of primitive punishments. Over time, and largely to the late Mayor's credit, it became more sophisticated and subtle. And yet it was still incomplete."

"I don't understand."

"Have you ever stopped to think about what a school is at its heart, Cross?" Iris drummed her fingers. "It plucks children from their homes during the critical years of their development—then it crams them together into a box, enabling whatever twisted social dynamic that pleases them. They are never shown the responsibilities of adulthood. Any real attempt to act like an adult is deemed uppity and met with punishment.

"Meanwhile, a small handful of teachers are set in place at the top as absolute rulers. Rather than encouraging maturity by exposing children to a mature environment, rather than have them work alongside adults, schools instead create this bizarre and unnatural scenario. They are festering cauldrons of social malaise for students to stew in until the system finally deigns to release them, forever altered by their unhealthy ordeal."

Iris paused. Then she shook her head, realizing how far from the original question she had strayed.

"To make a long story short, the Mayor understood all of this, and like an engineer, knew best how to manipulate it to achieve his ends," Iris said. "He intended to reach his ideal system one step at a time. I, however, can now skip straight to the end and prove that this Education City is not beyond salvaging."

Cross shook his head. "The Student Militia has suffered a lot. It would be unfair to lump them in with—"

"I never believed much in the idea of fairness," Iris said thoughtfully. "I believe in results. Ends don't justify the means; they make them irrelevant. There is no other way to ensure that the City will remain safe after I leave."

"How do you expect me to explain this to the others?" Cross demanded. "What am I supposed to tell them?"

"You need to tell them nothing," Iris said. "They already know. Are you aware of how long you've been here, Cross?"

Cross blinked. "No."

"You've been lying there for four days now," Iris said. "I'm here to tell you that I appreciate your help thus far, and why I will need your help going forward. As their leader, your assistance will be invaluable to make sure that the other students accept the transition."

Cross turned to face the General. Iris raised an eyebrow.

"Don't look so glum, Cross," she said. "I know you must be feeling a little disoriented by the sudden end to the fighting. I've been there. This doesn't *have* to be the end, you know—if you do this last job right, I will see about inducting you into the military. I'm sure that you can have a long and distinguished career in our ranks."

Cross nearly scoffed at that, but managed to restrain himself. He merely nodded. Her mind already elsewhere, Iris gave a curt salute and left the room, her face impassive.

Cross creased his brow. The great General wasn't as astute as she thought she was. Iris believed that he still wanted to fight, and perhaps a week ago he would have been delighted by her offer. Now he couldn't even imagine accepting it. After what his last reckless rampage had wrought, Cross didn't care to hold a weapon ever again.

Cross sighed and plunked back down onto his cot. If only he could figure out what he *did* care about. Everything was so pointless.

Takan walked cautiously through the familiar corridor, as though afraid of waking sleeping ghosts. It was mostly dark now—the power was still out in this section of District 20—but a little morning light crept in through a window at the end of the hall. The paint was peeling from the rough wooden doors to either side, more so than he remembered. But as he walked, drawn by an invisible force, the only door that retained his attention was at the end of the hall.

Takan stopped in front of the door. It had not been an easy trip from District 15, especially with soldiers swarming all over the nearby District 19. It had taken him three days on foot, but he was finally here. He reached out and tried the doorknob. It was unlocked. That was unusual. Takan pushed the door open silently, and then stepped into his past.

For a moment Takan wondered if he had the wrong place after all. The apartment as he remembered it was neat, orderly, almost boring and un-remarkable. Now it was a mess. Dishes were piled in the sink, filthy car-pets rolled up and shoved in a corner. Papers, pens, and clothes were strewn everywhere. His father's shoes were by the door, but of his moth-er's things he saw nothing.

As though in a dream, Takan stepped deeper into the apartment. He picked up a document lying on the dining table, and felt his heart skip a beat as he read it.

> Agent 207549627,
>
> The emergency message you sent months ago has been received. There was some difficulty verifying its authenticity, as we had not heard from you in quite awhile. Both your claims and your iden-tity have since been confirmed through investigation.
>
> The situation you described is being given our utmost atten-tion, and already there is a discussion about possible military ac-tion. Until a decision is made, we urge you to keep a low profile so as not to arouse the suspicions of the Mayor. Your continued cor-respondence may yet prove useful as most of our other contacts have fallen silent.
>
> You have our sincere condolences concerning the deaths of your children. We appreciate that you were willing to risk con-tacting us in a time of personal difficulty. Should you wish it, your children will be entered into our records with full honors as Gov-ernment citizens.
>
> Regards,
> XXXX

Takan stared, confused, not understanding. It was a message from the Government to one of its spies. What was it doing here? Had his family moved out, and a Government spy moved in? But it was his father's shoes at the door, his father's pants draped over the sofa. And yet, impossibly, this note was here. Could it mean—

Takan ducked. A golf club whooshed over his head, skimming his hair. Takan had sensed the other presence just in time. He'd allowed himself to get distracted by the note, not paying attention to his surroundings. And his attacker was very quiet.

Takan spun around and caught the man in the face with a left hook. The man staggered backwards and tried to swing the golf club again. Takan caught the handle of the club, punched its owner in the chest, and then wrested the club from his grasp. The man was already off-balance, and now Takan swung the club at his legs. The man fell to the ground and Takan was on him in an instant, pinning him there. He had questions that needed answers.

The man had stopped fighting now, and seemed to be talking madly to himself.

"Miserable Truants! Killed my kids, and now you'll kill me too? Is that it?" The man laughed. "Go ahead! The Government will have you all in the end, just watch!"

Takan froze. He knew that voice. He reexamined the man's face, almost afraid of what he'd find. The beard was new, but under all that facial hair . . . The man finally seemed to notice Takan's hesitation. He looked up, and recognition flickered in his amber eyes.

"Tack?" he whispered. "Is that you? Is it—is it really you?"

Takan felt a lump grow in his throat. He was suddenly very conscious about how he must look—grim, tired, clothed in a ragged trenchcoat with his hair a complete mess. His father had always said his hair was too messy.

"Yeah, it's me," he said.

The man pulled Takan into a tight embrace.

"My son, oh, my son, my son."

Takan tried so hard to bring the word "father" to his lips, but it wouldn't come. It stuck in his throat, feeling fake and forced. The letter he had discovered had been addressed to a person Takan had never known. Was it the same person who now embraced him?

Then for the first time in Takan's memory, the man began crying. The word came easily to Takan's lips now. This was not the father that he had known. But it was one he was willing to get to know.

So, what do you think about the camps?"

Floe sighed at the question. The mood at Student Militia headquarters was somber. The battle had been won, but at too great a cost to celebrate. It seemed that everyone had lost a friend or had watched one turn on them. Then the mourning had been interrupted by news of the reintegration program, and suddenly it seemed as if people were talking about nothing else.

Floe and Sepp met up in front of the door to the classroom their unit used for meetings. In the aftermath of the mass betrayal, even Sepp was unusually businesslike. Being hit on the head had diminished his sense of humor, Floe decided as she glanced at his bandages. She'd have to remember that.

"I don't like it," Floe said bluntly. "It sounds to me like they're trying to force us all into school or worse all over again. What do *you* think?"

"I don't know." Sepp shrugged. "I guess it seems reasonable. Just spend a year or so in there and then everything can go back to normal."

"You're just going to take their word for that?" Floe raised an eyebrow. "Don't you think it's a little unfair that we're being treated like criminals after what we just sacrificed?"

"The timing is a little insensitive, sure," Sepp allowed. "I just don't know if it's worth getting upset over."

"You're pretty much the only one who's so calm about it," Floe countered. "We were promised graduation by the Mayor when we first joined—we were supposed to be treated like heroes! If the Government won't honor that promise, how can you trust them to honor any others?"

"Okay, you have a point there. But what else can we do?"

Floe frowned. "Organize a formal protest?"

"That'd be up to Cross, if he were here." Sepp shrugged again. "I wonder if they've broken the news to him yet. Speaking of which, you saw him last, didn't you? How was he doing?"

Floe winced.

"Not good," she said. "He was like a corpse when they took him."

Sepp frowned. "Were his injuries that bad?"

"No, I got to him before that, thank goodness. But there is something wrong in his head." Floe bit her lip hesitantly. "When the confusion started . . . I think he was shooting everyone in sight. He wasn't himself. I think he hurt a lot of our own people."

"Harsh," Sepp observed. "Good thing you went after him."

"Sorry to leave without telling you," Floe said. "I heard you had some trouble back here too."

"It could've been a lot worse than it was," Sepp said. "We were lucky. We had our guardian angel around."

Sepp nodded to the side. Floe turned and looked. At the end of the hallway, the nameless albino was sitting on a bench, reading a book to her son by the window. Floe could see where Sepp's analogy had come from—under the pale light from the window, the girl did appear almost otherworldly.

"She's something else, isn't she?" Floe whispered.

"Tell me about it. Floored that Truant like it was nothing. Mind you, we're talking about the guy who gave me this." Sepp gestured at his head wound. "From what he said, I think she's got a bit of a reputation with some of the Truants."

"I wish I knew who she was." Floe shook her head. "She's friendly enough, but she's kind of . . . odd."

Sepp shrugged. "Seems obvious to me. She doesn't have a bar code." Sepp twisted his arm to display the tattoo on his forearm. "That means she was never a student. And *that* means she was probably a vagrant."

Floe glanced at the albino again. The girl didn't look like any vagrant Floe had ever heard of, most of whom had gone on to join the Truancy. "Do you think it'd be rude to just ask her?"

"Point-blank?" Sepp scratched the back of his neck. "Probably."

Floe sighed. "Well, at least the war is over now," she said. "You know, I can barely remember what things were like before all of this happened."

"Boring, I think." Sepp chuckled. "Oh well, at least I'm looking forward to seeing all my family. There'll be time for at least that before the camps, I'm sure. What about you?"

Floe shifted uncomfortably. "I was a Truant, remember? I'm not exactly on speaking terms with my parents." She looked away. "The way things are going, I guess I'll be heading straight for the camps."

"Well, if you want, you're welcome to visit at my place first."

Floe turned to Sepp and raised an eyebrow.

Sepp laughed. "Hey, it was worth a try."

Floe shook her head in annoyance. Before she could come up with a retort, she suddenly became aware of another person approaching. Sepp and Floe looked down the other end of the hallway and saw Cross walking mechanically towards the door, as though unaware of their presence. Floe's greeting stuck in her throat as she saw the blank expression on his face.

Cross passed by without even sparing them a glance. As he reached for the doorknob, Floe put her hand on his shoulder. He grimaced, and she quickly withdrew. Cross pushed the door open, stepped inside, and then shut it behind him.

A few uncomfortable moments followed as Sepp and Floe stared at the closed door.

"You were right," Sepp said at last. "Heck, he even creeps me out a bit. Think we should talk to him?"

"No." Floe shook her head. "Give him some space. He needs some time alone."

Floe believed that. Cross would heal, she was sure. Things would work out. She had a brief vision of a peaceful City a few years from now, rebuilt to its former glory as all of them made new lives for themselves. With that hope in her mind, she turned and followed Sepp away from the room.

Meanwhile, at the end of the hall, the nameless albino finished reading the book. She closed it, handed it to Zen, and then turned to look thoughtfully at the door that Cross had vanished into.

As he shut the door behind him, Cross didn't even bother to turn the lights on. He sat down at a desk, his head swirling. He was tired. In the darkness he was free to imagine a phantom classroom with students just as faceless and purposeless as he. All that was missing was for Edward to step out of the shadows.

Cross thought about Floe and Sepp, talking with each other out in the hallway, probably about him, behind his back. He clenched his fists.

He knew he should say something to them, to everyone, that it was his responsibility to do so. But Cross now dreaded facing the Militia more than anything his father had ever done to him. He had asked them to follow him on his mad whim and they had come, only to die.

He was tired. A little light seeped in through a tiny square window cut into the door. He could make out a paint splotch on the desk—Cross didn't like paint, it brought back bad memories. He was *so* tired. He shut his eyes.

Hey, you! What are you doing in here? Wake up!"

Cross groaned and opened his eyes. He had been sleeping on the floor in a classroom at school. His nights fighting with Edward left him exhausted, and he was always trying to catch up on sleep during his free periods.

Today he had taken refuge in a room on the fourth floor, trying his best to go unnoticed. Evidently, it hadn't worked. A pair of roaming female security guards had spotted him.

The school guards were technically Enforcers, though they were the very lowest in the ranks. Underpaid and unskilled, they were ironically drawn from the dregs of the Educators' own system, unsuited for anything more difficult than bullying already downtrodden students. Most of the ones in the District 18 School consisted of ugly, short women. The students quietly called them the hallway hags.

The two guards stepped forward into the room, angry at Cross' lack of a response.

"I said, what are you doing in here, kid?" the first guard screeched, like nails on a chalkboard. "Students aren't allowed to be unsupervised in rooms!"

Cross blinked sleep from his eyes.

"Mr. Gregory said I could be here," he mumbled. "He said he didn't want to see kids sleeping in the hallways."

The guards glowered, somehow managing to twist their faces into even more hideous shapes. These women reveled in the power they had on school grounds, eager to wield it at any petty excuse or none. Cross had given them such an excuse.

"You are not allowed to be unsupervised," the first guard repeated. "There is no teacher here. You are not allowed to be here."

"But Mr. Gregory said—"

"Show us your arm!"

Cross hesitated. "But—"

"NOW!"

Cross rolled up his sleeve and presented his arm upon which his student bar code had been tattooed. The guard held up a scanner and swept it over the number.

"A Disciplinary Officer will be seeing you later today," the second guard said. "Now, get out of this room."

Fuming, Cross allowed himself to be pulled from the room and shoved into the hallway. The guards locked the classroom behind them.

With nothing else to do, Cross sighed and sat down on the floor again, leaning against the wall. He still felt very groggy, and was nearly asleep again when he heard footsteps coming down the hall.

"What are you doing out here again, Cross?"

Cross' eyes snapped open.

"Mr. Gregory, sir, I—"

"I thought I told you I didn't want to see kids sleeping out in the hallways!"

"Some of the security guards came here and—"

"I was nice enough to let you use my room!" Mr. Gregory shouted. "I didn't write you up before when I saw you lying around, but I'm going to be writing you up now!"

"Sir, please, the guards—"

"Out of my sight! I'm writing you up! A Disciplinary Officer will set you straight!"

Cross felt a surge of anger, and for a moment he thought about shouting at the man. But that would have been suicidal. Instead, Cross turned and stormed off.

Cross made it to the stairwell and stumbled down some steps, not really sure where he was going. He felt exhausted, wronged, and angry. He paid little attention to his surroundings. It came as a surprise when he found himself abruptly cornered by three older boys.

Cross groaned. What now?

"Hey kid," the first boy said. "Heard you've been causing trouble for our friend Edward."

Cross blinked in confusion. Then he felt cold fear as he understood.
"I haven't done anything," Cross said quickly. "Edward is just—"
The second boy punched him in the stomach.
"Shut up!" the boy snarled. "We've got something to show you, isn't
that right guys?"
"Yeah," the third boy said. "We heard you were *real* proud of this!"
The boy reached into a plastic bag, and then held up a ruined painting.
The paper was soggy and dripping, the colors had run, and yet still Cross
could recognize the flowing landscape of a playground—his most trea-
sured accomplishment.

That painting had hung for years in a display case on the first floor. To
Cross it meant more than his own body.

"We put it in the toilet," the first boy explained, "where it belonged."

In that moment, all Cross saw was red.

Then he snapped.

Cross woke again with a jolt. The dream was already fading from memory, but some of the emotion still lingered. Taking a deep breath, Cross
forced himself to sit up. There was something white in the corner, something that hadn't been there before. He rubbed his eyes and focused on
the strange whiteness.

It had a face. It was still white. Too white.

Cross leapt to his feet, his heart suddenly pounding, his chair toppling
and skidding across the floor.

"What do you want?" Cross demanded.

The nameless girl cocked her head. "To help."

"I don't need any help," Cross lied. He didn't trust *anyone* right now,
and this girl, with her ashen skin and silent comings and goings, thoroughly unnerved him.

To his surprise, she didn't argue. She merely nodded and went for the
exit.

Taken aback, Cross spoke again. "Wait!"

The albino paused, halfway out the door. "Yes?"

Cross hesitated. If nothing else, the eerie girl was not a student, not
someone who he had let down. He could speak to the albino without responsibility clouding his thinking. He was ready to try anything to escape the confusion he found himself in.

"What would *you* do if you'd put a lot of people in danger?"

The albino blinked, then slowly stepped back into the room and shut
the door behind her. "I would try to save them."

"Why?" Cross pressed. "What if you didn't care about the people at all and made bad decisions as their leader?"

The albino regarded him carefully.

"You seem to care now."

Cross blinked. Then he sat up straight. It was true and he hadn't even noticed. It was *guilt* that he had been feeling over the disastrous attack on District 15. He cared that the rest of the students were being sent to camps they didn't deserve. He cared about the outburst he'd had in front of Sepp and Floe.

He wanted to make it right.

"How can I do it?" Cross demanded. "I'm not a leader and everyone knows it. No one is going to follow me if I ask them to defy the Government. They don't think I really give a damn. They won't trust me now."

"If your current image is not enough, find a different one. Put on a new face." The nameless girl stepped closer. "There was once a time when I survived only because I could make others believe I was something I wasn't. Project an illusion. That's what all leaders are, Cross; illusions made greater in the minds of their followers."

"That's just talk." Cross shook his head. "There's no way to just flick a switch and *do* something like that."

The albino tilted her head.

"If your need is great enough, you'll find your switch. When *my* need was great enough, I became a ghost." She placed a hand on Cross' shoulder. "If you believe strongly enough in a lie, then it becomes the truth."

Cross breathed deep and leaned back in his chair. After so long not knowing what he believed in, he was ready to believe anything. The albino withdrew her hand.

Cross shut his eyes and concentrated on the Student Militia. At first it was difficult; images of the previous night's battle swam into focus, followed by flashes from his childhood. He relived again his argument with Sepp and Floe. He went over every mistake he could remember, and thought about all the comrades he had hurt. Instead of denying the guilt he embraced it—the intensity of the emotion made him gasp.

When Cross opened his eyes they were wet with tears. He knew what must be done. The Student Militia had been a mistake from the start. And it was his duty to correct it. He clung to that purpose like a buoy in a sea of doubt.

Cross looked up at the albino, his voice hoarse.

"Is this always what it feels like to be motivated?"

The albino inclined her head. "It's usually better than the alternative."

Cross stood up, determined to work quickly. He wasn't sure how long his newfound conviction would last, and his great fear now was that at any minute he might slip back into aimless apathy.

"One last question." Cross switched on the lights. "I'm going to try to save the students from the camps. What happens if I go back to the way I was? Why would I help them if I don't care?"

The albino smiled. "If you don't care, then why *not*?"

A whole day passed before Cross emerged again from the classroom, and even in his absence unrest was brewing. The hallways were buzzing with conversation. Everyone had an opinion, and very few were pleased. No one seemed willing to stop the discussion, which was starting to border on talk of mutiny.

Where was the just reward that the students had earned? Where was the respect they had won through their sweat and blood? Had they risked everything fighting the Truancy only to be treated like Truants themselves? These questions were asked and repeated until the atmosphere simmered with anger.

That state of affairs suited Cross just fine. Iris had told him of her plans with the expectation that he would help quell the unrest. Instead, Cross planned to put it into overdrive. He knew he had to act quickly—if the Government got the slightest hint of what he was planning then it was all over.

Cross figured he would have a matter of hours at most between the time he briefed the Student Militia and the time it reached Iris' ears. Their escape would have to be well underway by then.

As Cross headed for the cafeteria, conversation ceased and students stared openly. He had been absent for days now, and everyone was wondering what he was thinking, what he would do. The stares reminded Cross of how unfamiliar he was with fellow students, and briefly he recalled Takan and how the Truancy leader had known each of his subordinates by name.

There was a time when that disparity would only have driven Cross to stubbornly isolate himself further. That path was no longer open to him.

In the cafeteria Cross waited in line with everyone else and took his serving of chopped chicken and unrecognizable vegetables. There were bones in the chicken and the vegetables were foul, but Cross ate without complaint. At the tables all around him the dissatisfied murmurs persisted.

As difficult as their lives as soldiers were, every member of the Student Militia remembered what the old schools were like. Now, faced with the prospect of returning to something that promised to be just as bad, no one seemed willing. No matter their age, they had outgrown the classrooms.

Cross smiled. They were too much like real people to make proper students again.

As he put away his lunch tray, Cross reflected on his conversation with Iris, and irritation flared. Her final offer to him was what bothered him most at that moment. Iris had been so confident that she had the measure of his character that it obviously never occurred to her that Cross might disobey.

In fairness, if that last battle had gone differently Cross knew that Iris' confidence might well have been justified. As it was now—

"I have a real reason to fight," Cross muttered to himself.

Cross still possessed no great ambition of his own. If it was just his fate at stake he would have been content to continue dangling it recklessly in the wind. But it was not just his fate that was threatened now. The Militia he'd been entrusted with, and all of the students that had joined it, were in danger.

Those students were dissatisfied with their lot, yet the idea to flee from it and to defy authority would never occur to them on their own. They were too used to the system to imagine a life beyond it.

This was why Cross had spent so many sleepless and hungry hours ensconced in that classroom. It was up to him to let the Militia be free to decide its own destiny.

"Hey, Cross! What do *you* think about the camps?"

Cross glanced at the student who had addressed him.

"I think we deserve better."

The student smiled in response. Cross tried to smile back but the motion felt too unfamiliar to him. He simply nodded instead.

Cross stood up and headed for the nearest group of students. He had to spread word of a secret meeting to be held immediately.

Sepp walked into the gymnasium and paused, surprised to find that the lights were not on. Another student bumped into him from behind, and he took that as a cue to keep moving. Though Sepp had yet to see Cross for himself, news of the meeting had reached him, and he was curious. A group of students had been instructed to stay with the Government soldiers at the front doors to keep them busy, so whatever Cross wanted to talk about had to be important.

With the light from the open doorway, Sepp managed to pick out Floe in the front row of the bleachers. He wandered over and sat down next to her as the students around them sought seats of their own. In the center of the gymnasium Cross stood, barely visible as more than a shadow. There was something about him, something in his posture that struck Sepp as different.

Floe leaned over to whisper in Sepp's ear. "Do you know what this is about?"

"No," Sepp whispered back. "Do you?"

Floe shook her head. "He didn't tell me anything. Just said it was important."

Floe shifted agitatedly, as though she had an itch she could not scratch. Sepp blinked. Something about *her* behavior seemed odd too.

"Something bothering you?" Sepp asked.

"Yeah," Floe said, tossing her head. "*She's* here."

Sepp turned to look at what Floe had gestured at. It was the nameless girl, leaning against the wall in a corner with her son standing beside her.

"Well, shouldn't she be?" Sepp said reasonably. "I mean, she's not part of the Militia, but she's still—"

"I saw her coming out of the clubhouse yesterday," Floe said darkly. "They were *alone* in there."

It took Sepp a moment to understand. Then he clapped a hand over his mouth to prevent himself from laughing aloud. Here they were, hiding a secret and probably illegal meeting from the most dangerous people the City had ever seen, and Floe was worried about—oh, that was *too* funny.

Floe glared at him. "Is something funny?" she demanded.

"No." Sepp lied. "Nothing!"

Before Floe could press him further, Cross cleared his throat. All heads turned towards him. The bleachers were mostly filled now. The meeting was starting.

"Before I begin I want to establish one thing," Cross said. "If time runs out before I finish, or if you don't stay quiet and end up attracting attention, then every one of us is probably as good as dead."

A student called out. "What's the big deal?"

"I think you know already what the big deal is, but I have things to say about it that you guys might want to hear."

Sepp raised his eyebrows, and not just at the ominous warning. Cross was being unusually direct and personal, something that was even more peculiar considering how cold and detached he had been the previous day.

"First of all, I owe you an apology for the disaster in District 15. I wish I had more time to explain how I made the mistakes I did." Cross glanced at Floe. "For now let's just say that I blew it. I was stupid and reckless and I dragged a lot of you along with me into a battle that should never have been fought."

The students stirred in their seats. Sepp was nearly dumbstruck. He had never known Cross to apologize for *anything* before, let alone make a public mea culpa like this. What was going on?

"The reason I'm telling you that right off the bat is because I want you to know that I'm not going to make the same mistake again," Cross said. "I was visited yesterday by General Iris, who is in command of the new Government. She asked me to help sell the idea of the camps to you."

There were angry murmurs among the students. Cross ignored them.

"I'm not going to do it," Cross promised. "I will not lead you into a trap a second time. I'm through carrying out the Government's plans. I know a lot of you already have your own objections to the camps. I can add another— Iris told me herself that the end result will be a system harsher than anything the Mayor ever ran, and she wanted me to help sell that to you."

The murmurs grew louder now. Sepp bit his lip and turned to look at Floe. Her eyes were wide.

"I'm not going to do what she wants," Cross continued. "If it seems like we're being treated no better than Truants, then that's because we aren't. The General believes that we've been infiltrated so deeply that there's no difference between—"

"That's impossible!" a student cried. "They saw what happened out there, the traitors already turned on us!"

"Tell it to the Truants when you find yourself locked up with them in the same camps. Iris claims it's all necessary to restore the peace. I don't think she cares how many of us have to suffer for it. All she sees when she looks at us is a threat."

The simmering anger was now starting to boil over. The students had enough sense to keep their voices down, but they could no longer contain their outrage. Sepp himself was stunned. After years of sacrifice, this was how their loyalty would be rewarded? They would be rounded up with the *Truants*?

Then to everyone's surprise, Cross smiled. A rare sight.

"I'm glad that you already feel that way," he said. "To be honest, I was a little worried. I didn't want to twist anyone's arm to get them to see things the way I do. I don't want to go to camp, and if none of you want to either, then none of us have to. We have can give the Government a different answer.

"We can defy them."

A fresh wave of murmuring broke out, but not as much as Sepp expected. Sepp had seen the suggestion coming—the thought had crossed his mind too—but he was sure many others had not. The quiet was in deference to Cross, he realized. Somehow their leader was really connecting with his audience.

"The Truancy has managed to escape by scattering into the general population," Cross said. "Anything they can do, we can do better. Most of you have something the Truancy does not—family and friends you can count on to hide you."

Sepp nodded at that. Floe, however, spoke up.

"What about those who don't?"

Cross looked back at her. "Then you'll be like me, able to make your own choices. Here's mine: I'm staying behind to hold the Government's attention here for as long as possible." Cross returned his gaze to the crowd. "If you have families, I recommend you leave immediately in staggered bunches. I've already sent messengers with similar instructions to all the smaller Militia bases in the City.

"Remember, we have to do this quickly and quietly. I trust all of you not to speak, but word is bound to get out sooner or later, and when it does the Government is going to be here in force. We have hours at most. Get moving, everyone. Now."

At his command, the students began pouring from the bleachers, not orderly, but not quite as a mob. Most of them headed straight for the doors, though a good number crowded around Cross, asking how they could help. Sepp hesitated for a moment, unsure of which group to join.

Floe stood up and glanced down at him. "I suppose you'll be going off to visit your family after all then?"

Sepp looked at her, then at Cross. He quickly made his decision.

"Nah." He grinned. "They can wait. If I left now, who'd be the savior for the rest of you?"

Floe giggled at that, and together they went to join their leader as he began to explain his plan.

The soldiers were building something.

Hammers fell and walls rose. Concrete oozed and drills roared. Bulldozers demolished obstacles, tossing their crumbling remnants aside.

Umasi watched it all as he leaned against an alley wall, wrapped in his windbreaker. Concealed by the shadows and a pile of trash bags, Umasi tried to discern what it was that the Government was doing to what had been a war-torn parking lot in District 2. They had taken over some buildings around the area and were renovating them, but the barbed wire fences and tall concrete walls were new. It all struck Umasi as ominous. Perhaps a military base of operations?

A group of soldiers began walking in his direction, and though they were a good distance off Umasi ducked behind the trash bags. He adjusted his windbreaker, trying to cover more of his body. The black jacket had been overlarge when Zyid had first worn it, but now it fit Umasi almost too perfectly.

Minutes passed by, and soon so did the soldiers. Umasi released the breath he'd been holding. The fear of being discovered was both familiar and unpleasant. How long had it been since he had felt like this? Hunted, afraid, vulnerable.

Over the past three years, respected by both the Truancy and the Educators, Umasi had gotten used to the City being his domain. Now things were back to the way they had been the winter he had run away. He was finding it harder to evade his pursuers this time. His intended trip to District 1 had run into a snag when he found it impossible to move any further without running into soldiers. To proceed, he would need the cover of darkness.

"You're getting old," Umasi told himself. "Old, complacent, sentimental, and tired."

A roar of engines as armored vehicles passed by. More soldiers on patrol. Umasi decided to move deeper into the alley. He was being a bit unfair to himself, Umasi decided as he crept along. Iris had more resources and more strategic prowess than the Mayor or his crony Rothenberg had when they were the ones hunting Umasi.

Umasi sighed as he crouched down in his new hiding place behind a garbage dump. He missed his brother, he missed *Zyid*—and not for the usual reasons. With Zyid's help he was certain that they would be able to overcome Iris. As things stood now, he felt like half of a solution. It didn't feel right or fair that he was the only one left to face their enemy.

Umasi laughed quietly. At age nineteen he really was getting old, allowing the memory of the Truancy's founder to become inflated in his mind. He knew better than anyone that Zyid was a human with more flaws than most. And so was Iris. And so was he.

With that sobering thought, Umasi looked up at the sky. The sun would be setting soon. It was time to move. With a swish of his windbreaker, he stood up and began walking deeper into the heart of the City.

Behind him, hammers fell and walls rose.

The soldiers were building something.

Floe stood in the entrance hallway of the school as another group of students went out the doors and into the evening air. Her rifle was slung loosely over her shoulder, her posture relaxed, though in truth she was very carefully watching the two soldiers stationed outside. Cross had agreed that too many students in the hall would arouse suspicion, and so Floe had volunteered for the lonely work. If something went wrong, she was the first line of defense.

So far everything had gone smoothly. Hundreds of students had left already in small groups at random intervals. A few stopped to chat with the soldiers outside. The soldiers were friendly, and so were the students. Floe was even starting to wonder if they might all get out before the Government suspected anything.

There was a movement behind her, and Floe turned to see the nameless girl leaning against the wall, her eyes shut as though listening to soundless music. Floe ignored her. Another group went out the door. The girl didn't move. Floe frowned, then against her better judgment approached the albino.

"Hey," she said. "Mind if I ask why you're not leaving with the others?"

The albino opened her eyes and gestured at the open doorway, where the sun was only just beginning to set, sending ruby streaks through the azure sky.

"Too much light," she explained. "It hurts my skin and it's not easy to get around in. Zen and I tend to stick out. We'll be hiding somewhere safe when the action starts."

"I see," Floe said, pausing for a moment. "What exactly is your interest in Cross?"

Floe had meant to unnerve the other girl with that question. The albino, however, merely rubbed her chin thoughtfully.

"Curiosity, more than anything. He's in a very precarious state, and I'd like to help him." She glanced at Floe. "Don't worry. My affections are reserved for someone else. You shouldn't consider me competition."

Now Floe was the one who was unnerved. "I . . . I have no idea what you're talking about," she sputtered.

"You're a poor liar, girl." The albino smiled. "You know, if you want something you should go ahead and reach for it. Boys can be clueless. If you wait for him to catch on, you might wait forever."

Speechless, Floe felt her cheeks redden. A voice issued forth below her.

"I'm not noticing!"

Floe looked down, and her embarrassment doubled. Zen was standing there, pointing up at her face. Like his mother, the boy seemed capable of being unusually quiet when he wanted to. Floe hadn't noticed his approach at all.

Completely unabashed, Zen walked over to his mother, who placed a firm hand on his head.

"Zen," she said, crouching down. "Pretending not to notice something means acting like it's not there."

"Oh," Zen said, turning around. "Sorry, Floe!"

"That's better," the albino smiled. "Now, was there something you wanted?"

"I wanna leave too," Zen said, pointing at a pair of students going out the door. "I don't like it here."

"Really? But Cross is staying," the albino crouched down. "You know, it'll be easier to move at night. Maybe we should leave then."

Floe shook her head and turned away from the conversation between mother and child. The latest pair of students were almost out of sight. Floe noticed that something was wrong. The soldiers were watching their every step. Floe did not change her demeanor, but inside she felt uncomfortable. Sure enough, one of the soldiers approached her.

"Hey, you," the soldier said to Floe, "where's your leader?"

"Why, is something wrong?"

"There've been an awful lot of students going out today," the man said. "But I haven't seen any coming back."

Floe cursed silently. Why hadn't they thought of that? They should have sent some of the defenders out temporarily so that they could make a show of returning. Now it was too late.

"Everyone just wants to enjoy their last days off," Floe said innocently. "I mean, wouldn't you?"

The soldier seemed to consider that. He didn't appear satisfied.

"I think it'd be best to stop the sightseeing for today," he said. "It's getting dark."

"Oh, come on, sir, it's not curfew yet," Floe said. "Why make a big deal out of nothing?"

The man hesitated. As if sensing what was about to happen, the albino and her son quietly vanished down a nearby hallway.

"I'll ask my superior." The soldier reached for his radio. "Hold on a second."

In a flash Floe drew a silenced pistol. She fired once, killing the man before he knew what hit him. The other soldier spun around. She fired again, and the second soldier dropped as well. Floe felt a twinge of guilt— the men had been nice enough, and it felt wrong to take them by surprise.

"Sorry guys." Floe muttered, then turned to yell down the hallway. "Cross, we've got trouble!"

Cross was already running towards her at the head of a large number of students in plain clothes. These were the rest of the students who were evacuating, all of them armed despite their lack of uniform.

"I heard!" Cross said, catching up to her. "Let's do this part right, if nothing else. Ring the alarm!"

As planned, the remaining evacuating students stormed out the front doors en masse. The two Government sentries had been killed quietly, but if the fleeing students ran into trouble there were enough to fight their way out. The school bell began ringing shrilly as the last of them went out the door.

Cross and Floe shut the doors and then barred them with metal poles. Other students came carrying tools and materials from the metalworking shop, along with bookshelves, desks, and other heavy objects to pile in front of the door.

"Forget the Truancy, forget the Militia," Cross said as he heaved a bench into place. "This will be the *real* Student Rebellion."

ris switched the lights on as she entered the room. It was large, had two beds, with neatly stacked toys and belongings that teenage boys might be expected to own. There was a dartboard on one wall, alongside a largely empty desk. On the other side of the room there was a second desk, piled with study materials. A large dresser seemed to divide the room in half. Next to the door were several jacket pegs.

Iris stepped over a fallen baseball bat as she continued to look around. There was a layer of dust over everything—clearly the maids had been forbidden to enter this particular room. It was as if the place had been frozen in time, a perfect snapshot of how things were before its inhabitants left.

Iris tapped her shoulder with her staff. So this, then, had been the room used by her brothers. The two clearly had different personalities. She suspected that they'd eventually gone separate ways, but without one to balance the other how did that turn out? She shook her head and left the room, shutting the door behind her. Such speculation was irrelevant—at least one of them was still out there, and she had to track him down.

So far there wasn't much new on that front. Days had already gone by since Iris had ordered the sweep of the City. The search had turned up nothing but an abandoned dwelling in District 19. Iris frowned at that. Could the boy have slipped by the search parties? Probably. After all, he did know the City better than her men. She would have to divert resources to a more thorough effort, occupying every district and offering incentives for local cooperation.

Iris walked upstairs and pushed open a large mahogany door. City Hall, a massive building with little privacy, was fine for a command post. But for her personal headquarters, Iris preferred the Mayoral Mansion. As she stepped into what had once been the Mayor's study, she decided that for all the man's faults, he had a decent sense of décor.

Iris sat down at the meticulously clean desk, surrounded by monitors. Behind her, military maps and charts had been pinned up on a bulletin board. On one screen was a progress report about the camp construction. The camps were an unfortunate measure, she'd decided, but necessary to prove that the system could be made to work again. It was her policy to never doubt and never regret what was necessary.

Just then, a red light began flashing on one of the monitors. Iris' eyes narrowed as she studied the data. Some of her soldiers were firing their weapons in District 2; more than a dozen. That was strange. A false reading? Had some Truancy remnants attacked? Or was it—

Right on cue, there was a knock on the door. Iris smiled. Twenty-three seconds. Impressive response time.

"Enter," she said.

A slightly breathless officer burst into the room and saluted. "General, we've just got word from District 2. Apparently significant elements of the Student Militia have mutinied. They've barricaded their headquarters, and some have been spotted on the streets, probably trying to escape."

Iris rubbed her knuckles against her forehead.

"Well. *That* is unexpected," she said. "I wouldn't have thought that their leader had the inclination or the initiative to start a revolt by himself. I must remember not to count on capricious figureheads like that."

The officer coughed. "Orders, General?"

"Quarantine District 2. See if we can catch most of them before they escape." The orders came like clockwork. "Put out a general alert to arrest any children found walking the street, even if they're students—*especially* if they're students. Investigate the other student bases, though I suspect that those have been evacuated by now."

"And the students barricaded in the District 2 school?"

"Probably a distraction. Is it a problem?"

"Word is they're holed up pretty tightly in there, ma'am," the man said. "The Mayor had that building fortified when they started using it as headquarters. Short of blasting it with artillery or calling in an airstrike, breaking in might take awhile."

"Those are our last resorts," Iris said, standing up. "I want that building intact and I want most of our resources devoted to catching the escapees. Get me a vehicle. I'll handle the holdouts."

The officer blinked. "General, are you sure that—"

"I did not anticipate this move," Iris interrupted. "I made a mistake. I will correct that mistake personally."

Floe adjusted the crosshairs on her sniper rifle and pulled the trigger. A couple hundred yards away, a dark figure stumbled but did not fall. Floe cursed under her breath and ejected the spent casing.

"Did you get one?" Sepp called.

"I think I *winged* one," Floe responded. "This is supposed to be your job. You should be having a field day."

The two of them ducked as retaliatory fire came whizzing through the shattered windows and clanging off the bars. The District 2 School had bars on the windows even before the Militia started to use it as headquarters, and afterwards the Mayor had ordered the building reinforced with an extra layer of metal and concrete. So far the extra protection was holding up against everything the Government had thrown at it.

"Why are they holding back?" Floe wondered as she took aim again. "Shouldn't they be dropping bombs on our heads or something by now?"

"Don't sound too eager," Sepp advised, pulling the trigger on his own rifle. "Hey, I think I got one! Let the field day begin."

Before Floe could congratulate him, a return shot flew through the window and caught Sepp in the shoulder. He let out a yelp of surprise and fell to the floor. Worried, Floe dropped her weapon and rushed over to him.

"I'm okay," Sepp insisted. "Just grazed my shoulder, nothing serious."

Sighing in relief, Floe removed a roll of gauze and some cotton from her hip sack and staunched the bleeding.

"Where are they even shooting from?" Floe said. "It's not the soldiers on the ground, and it's too dark to see farther than that. Where are they hiding?"

Sepp glanced up at the window as Floe finished treating his wound. The sky was indeed a very dark blue, matching their uniforms. The Government had cut the power awhile ago, and everything inside the school was shrouded in darkness.

"Maybe they have a way of seeing in the dark," Sepp suggested. "Maybe they have better guns than us. And *maybe* us being here isn't such a good idea anymore."

As if to punctuate the point, the snarl of endless, automatic fire issued forth from outside, and a hail of bullets clanged off the bars and into the room. Floe hauled Sepp to his feet and the two of them ran for it. They were on the fourth floor—their job had been to keep the soldiers at a distance and off the front doors. Now it was just survival.

The bars over the windows cast eerie shadows that seemed to dance as Sepp and Floe ran for the stairway. On the second floor they found Cross coordinating the bulk of the defenders. If the wounded and dead lying in the hallways were any indication, they weren't having much better luck either.

"What's wrong?" Cross asked as they approached.

"Their snipers are better than ours, and Sepp thinks they can see in the dark," Floe said. "They started to hit our windows with machine guns, so we got out of there."

"Hey Cross, what're those?" Sepp asked, his attention fixed on a bunch of large tubes the students were now pointing through the bars.

"Stuff we set up in the science labs," Cross said. "Do you remember how we learned to launch bottles? Well, we're about to launch a few bottles."

Floe frowned. "What do you mea—"

There were a series of loud *whump* noises, and a barrage of bottle rockets shot out from the windows, trailing white foam. At the end of each rocket was a flaming container. The contents soon ignited, bursting and sending liquid fire raining down on the soldiers outside.

A cheer went up from the students, but Floe did not join in. She had a bad feeling that they had just bitten off more than they could chew. As if in response, there was a loud noise from outside. An explosion burst through the window, ripping the bars from their frame, its sheer force sending Cross, Sepp, and Floe tumbling backwards. The students who had been closer to the window were not so lucky.

Head spinning, Floe forced herself to sit up. She wasn't sure what the Government had hit them with, but it proved that they could crush the students with brute force on a whim. She couldn't imagine why they were holding back.

Cross rose to his feet and reached for a rocket launcher that the Student Militia had captured from the Truancy. With the bars gone from the windows, Cross took aim and fired. As the rocket's ignition illuminated Cross' face, Floe thought that his face was grimmer, less eager than he normally looked in combat. Then the rocket slammed into one of the Government's armored vehicles outside, and Cross was moving again.

Cross seized Sepp and Floe by the arms and pulled them deeper into the building. A moment later, another shell flew in through the gaping window and exploded, demolishing a good chunk of the hallway and collapsing the ceiling.

"We can't buy much more time like this," Floe said, staring at the destruction. "They could wipe us out in an instant if they wanted to."

"Well, they haven't yet," Cross said, pausing to load another rocket. "I consider that a good sign. They probably want to take us alive."

"There's a happy thought," Sepp said. "What do we do next, boss?"

"Trying to shoot at them is getting us killed." Cross turned to look out into the dusk. "But unless they're willing to collapse the first floor, they can't get inside. We've got a stalemate for now. It's their move."

"Cease fire."

The soldiers spun around to see who had given the order. Stepping out of an armored vehicle, dressed in full combat gear, Iris marched towards the soldiers amassed two blocks away from the District 2 School, completely unfazed as a rocket shot from the school and blew up an armored vehicle nearby.

"General Iris, ma'am," one of the soldiers saluted. "What are—"

"I'm here to take charge," Iris said, reaching their position behind a building. "First things first: no heavy ordnance. I want that building in as few pieces as possible, it could contain valuable intel. Someone get me a speakerphone."

A speakerphone was quickly produced, and Iris brought it to her mouth. Her amplified voice boomed through the streets.

"This is General Iris," she announced. "The Government is willing to accept your surrender. Lay down your weapons immediately and you will not be killed."

There was a moment of silence. Then, in response, another rocket shot from the school. Iris and the other soldiers ducked to avoid the blast as Government snipers in the surrounding buildings returned fire.

"How tedious." Iris sighed, rising to her feet and dusting herself off. "Looks like we'll have to do this the hard way."

"They've barricaded the front doors," a soldier said. "We could blow some holes in the walls if we had to."

"Ignore the first floor. It's easy to defend and difficult to approach," Iris said. "That building has a complete blind spot on the left side. We'll get onto the roof from the adjacent building and get in without risking enemy fire."

"Can't we just get up there with a chopper?"

Iris shook her head. "All available helicopters are helping to hunt down the escapees. They're also too noisy for this. We have more than enough resources here to take care of this petty distraction. Divide into three groups. I will lead the first."

"You personally, ma'am?"

Iris smiled. It violated all sorts of regulation and procedure, but her father had always approved of her willingness to get hands-on. Her detractors had nicknamed her the *Spoiled Princess* because of whims like these. Most of those detractors had been silenced when her operational record proved to be nearly flawless.

"Yes, me personally," Iris said. "I believe I counted five snipers just now, correct? They will cover us when we go in."

"One of the snipers is reporting that his night vision is malfunctioning."

"He'll have to do without," Iris said coolly. "Let's get going. Oh, and fire a few shots at the front doors, just to make some noise. They'll think it odd if we don't."

"Yes, ma'am!"

• • •

Cross grimaced as another round of bullets clanged against the front door like a hailstorm. He and most of the remaining students had gathered by the entrance, helpless to do anything but watch as the machine guns pounded away at the metal doors. Dents now pockmarked almost ever inch of their surface, but so far they held. The doors remained shut, bolstered by the piles of junk the students had used to reinforce it.

"I think they've fired enough metal at us to make a new door," Sepp said, clutching his wounded shoulder. "You'd think that if it really were their General out there, she'd be more creative than this."

"It's her," Cross said. "I recognized her voice."

"Pity you missed with that rocket, then," Floe said. "She's probably planning a way to get in here right now."

"Well, she won't do it like this," Cross said. "Even if they shoot the doors off the hinges, we've got too much junk welded to them. It's going to take something bigger than—"

An explosion rocked the doors, and several students screamed. The metal shuddered from the blast, bent out of shape, but did not give way. Every eye now seemed fixed on the doors, unblinking.

They knew that all that stood between them and the unstoppable forces out to kill them was the fragile junk that they had piled up. The atmosphere was tense, and everyone was scared. Though Cross couldn't see their faces in the gloom, he could guess how they felt. His own heart was pounding, but he took it as a good sign that none of his prior madness had yet shown any hint of resurfacing.

Another blast hit the doors. This time no one screamed. It was almost better than the tension of waiting. Everyone was ready to get it over with now. Cross held his breath, bracing himself for the next hit. Then a voice came in on the radio.

"Cross, we've got a problem up he—"

The voice dissolved to static. Everyone stared at his radio, the doors momentarily forgotten. Cross stared along with them; he had ordered the lookouts on the higher floors not to use the radios except in case of an emergency. What could possibly—

"They're coming in through the windows!"

"—the roof, man, they're on the roof!"

"They're here! Argh—"

More voices came in on the radios as the other sentries all began to report in. There were gunshots, followed by static and screams. Cross stared up at the ceiling, cold dread filling his stomach. Some of those noises hadn't come from the radio.

"Dammit, it was a distraction!" Cross leapt to his feet, and the other students followed suit. "Get to the stairways, right now! GO!"

The students dashed for the stairways in groups of three to five. With a sickening feeling Cross knew that it wouldn't be enough, that they were probably all going to die. Sepp and Floe ran beside him as he dashed for the nearest staircase. They kicked open the doors and ran inside, where they could already hear descending footsteps.

Cross aimed upwards and fired a three-round burst. A uniformed soldier toppled and fell, screaming on his way down. Retaliatory fire immediately began raining down on them, and the three had to back out of the way. Floe drew a firebomb from her hip sack and hurled it upwards. It detonated against the railing, spraying fiery liquid onto the floor above.

As if in response, one of the soldiers dropped a grenade onto their floor. It bounced against the ground, and there was a blinding flash and a deafening noise. Completely disoriented, Cross stumbled around, unable to hear anything over the ringing in his ears. He didn't know what kind of grenade it was, but it was far more debilitating than a little fire and smoke.

Just as Cross started to wonder if he would ever see or hear again, his vision began to clear, and he lunged for the open door. Sepp and Floe were nowhere to be found—had they left him behind, or had they stumbled out on their own? As the descending soldiers behind him began to fire, Cross shut the door and ran for it.

The ringing began to subside, and Cross became aware of distant gunshots. With a sinking feeling, he realized that the battle for the other floors must already have been lost. The soldiers were storming the first floor.

Cross ducked down a side hallway in the hopes that the soldiers coming from behind wouldn't notice. As he ran, a dark shape appeared ahead at the end of the hall, too large to be a student. Cross fired, and the shape crumpled. Another shape appeared, more cautious than the last, and Cross ducked into a classroom doorway as bullets flew at him.

The gunfire ceased, and Cross quietly shut the door, thinking to hide inside. Then he heard hinges squeak open behind him, and he realized his mistake. The classroom had two entrances.

Cross dived for the floor as three soldiers entered the room, all firing. His rifle slipped from his hands, and bullets clanged above him as he crawled for the safety of the teacher's desk. The soldiers stopped wasting their ammo and began cautiously approaching his hiding place. His heart pounding like it was ready to stop at any moment, Cross resolved to go out fighting.

Cross drew his knife and crept forward, keeping his head below the desks. A soldier came into sight, and Cross lunged, aiming to plunge his knife into the man's neck. Instead, his momentum carried the blade into the soldier's body armor, failing to pierce it.

Cross and the soldier hit the ground, and as the other soldiers approached, shoving desks out of their way, Cross knew that he was dead. He was glad, at least, that he would die for something that had meaning— the intensity and excitement was there as usual, but they brought him no satisfaction. His mind remained clear.

Then a chain shot through the air, a metal ring striking one of the soldiers in the face. The others turned to see what had happened, and Cross seized his chance. He plunged his knife into the nearest soldier's armpit, a vulnerable spot in their armor.

At the same time, a specter swept into the classroom, clutching the metal ring like a brass knuckle and knocking a soldier out with it. A second soldier tried to bring his rifle around, but she deftly seized his arm, grabbed him by the armor, and then hurled him into a pile of desks.

As the three soldiers stirred, disarmed and disoriented, the nameless albino advanced upon Cross. She had found a blue Student Militia jacket somewhere and now wore it unbuttoned, blending better into the gloom. She kicked the knife out of Cross' hand, grabbed his arm, and then pulled him up so that they were face-to-face.

"That's enough killing," she said, finality in her voice. "The battle is over. There's a service exit in the kitchen—it's the only way out."

She looked both more and less unsettling in the shadows, Cross thought. Her appearance was less like a weird human and more like the stories of a typical phantom. In that moment Cross felt he knew exactly what she had meant when she spoke of becoming a ghost.

"All right," he said. "Let's get out of here."

At the head of her squad, Iris preferred to do the dirtiest work herself and let her subordinates cover her. She fired a burst on full automatic, forcing the students at the bottom of the stairs to scramble for cover. With the coast clear, Iris stormed down the stairs before the students even saw her coming. The nearest boy's eyes widened as Iris fired again on full automatic, then he toppled and fell down the stairs into his comrades.

Knowing that her weapon was empty, Iris didn't bother to reload. Instead she tossed her rifle aside and unhitched her staff from her back, pressing a button to extend it to full length. With a leap she was upon the students, and with two quick movements she had struck one in the belly and the other in the face. Each time her staff made contact, Iris pressed a button on it to discharge an electrical shock.

The staff flitted through the darkness with incredible speed and precision. Several more times there was a crackle of electricity, accompanied by cries of pain. Within seconds all the students had fallen, paralyzed. There was a thunder of footsteps as Iris' troops descended and began to handcuff the students.

Iris shrunk her staff and slung it across her back once more. Drawing her radio, she checked in with the other squads.

"Report."

"Stairwell B is secure."

"Stairwell C, secure!"

Iris nodded. As far as she could tell, the raid had gone exactly as planned. They had started from the top down, eliminating all resistance along the way. All the floors from the first to the sixth were now under control, and yet . . . something seemed off. They'd encountered less resistance than she had expected.

As her soldiers fanned out around her, Iris drew out her handheld GPS and examined their location. In an instant she noticed it—a service entrance that connected the basement cafeteria to an alley behind the school. She had assumed that every exit was covered by Government snipers. A careless error. The second in as many days. She was slipping.

Iris replaced the GPS and made a quick calculation. Her troops had saved the basement for last, and any students hiding there were probably making a run for it at that very moment. There was no way she could catch up, and trying to would be foolish. She reached for her radio.

"Blow the front doors," she said, then turned to her squad. "Follow me."

Everyone knew better than to ask questions. They quickly exited out onto the first floor, just in time to see the front doors and the junk piled behind them blasted away, large pieces rebounding off the ceiling and walls. Iris stepped through the smoldering wreckage, her squad following behind her. Now out in the night air, Iris broke into a sprint, heading around the building and towards the back alley where any escaping students would have to pass through.

As they headed for their inevitable confrontation, no one—not the students, not the soldiers, not even Iris herself—noticed that there was a boy watching from an empty building nearby. The unseen spectator adjusted his sunglasses. Then he wrapped himself in the darkness of his windbreaker, and waited.

16
Brother Against Sister

I t was a grim bunch of students that gathered in the cafeteria kitchen. Barely more than a dozen of them were left now, all others presumed dead or captured. Cross was relieved to see that Sepp and Floe were among the survivors, but the others he had failed weighed on his mind. Cross supposed that came with having a conscience.

"Good to see you again, boss," Sepp said. "For a while there I thought it'd be just us and the local roach infestation."

"When the soldiers dropped . . . whatever it was, Sepp and I managed to get downstairs," Floe said shakily. "We were really worried when we found out you weren't with us."

"At least we made it." Cross shook his head. "A lot of the others didn't."

Cross felt a familiar hand on his shoulder. He didn't have to look to know that it was the albino.

"We don't have much time," she said. "The Government may already have figured out what we're up to."

The words were sobering, and Cross forced himself to stand and think straight. He glanced at the albino, finding it ironic that she was the only one still wearing a Student Militia jacket. Then something occurred to him.

"Where is your son?" Cross asked. "Shouldn't he—"

"I got him to a safe place awhile ago," she replied. "Shortly after you began barricading the building."

"Will he be all right on his own?" Floe asked.

"I expect so," the nameless girl said. "It's not the first time I've had to leave him alone for a while. He takes good care of himself."

"Okay then." Cross took a deep breath. "It's time for us to say our good-byes. Everyone did well. I wish it hadn't come to this. You deserve better. If you have families, pay them a visit. Either way, try not to get caught. The sewers and subways are our best bets at this point. Good luck."

With that, he walked over to the back of the kitchen and pulled open a small door that led out into the night. In a glum procession, the students began filing out of the room. Their expressions, some sad, some even accusatory, did little to improve Cross' mood. As Floe reached him, she paused for a moment as their gazes met.

"Are you all right, Cross?" she asked gently.

"No." Cross shook his head. "I'm a mess and I'll be lucky to ever get my head on straight. Get out of here, Floe."

"We're still alive, aren't we?" Floe smiled. "Don't be too hard on your-self."

Cross felt a sudden urge to say something else, but it was too late. She stepped outside and was lost from view. Cross cursed himself. Why hadn't he asked to go with her? Feeling fresh regret gnaw at his insides, Cross reached out and put a hand on Sepp's shoulder to stop the boy.

"Sepp."

Sepp looked apprehensive. "Yeah, boss?"

"My last orders to you," Cross said. "Forget about splitting up, follow Floe. Take good care of her. Don't tell her I sent you."

Sepp blinked in surprise, then saluted. "Got it. And thanks."

For what? Cross wondered as he watched Sepp go.

The rest of the students swiftly made their exit. Soon Cross was the only one left in the dark kitchen, alone with his thoughts. Then there was movement behind him, and he realized that he *wasn't* alone. The girl with no name walked forward and looked at him expectantly.

"Well then," she said. "Shall we go?"

Cross glared at her. "What do you mean, 'we?'"

"You'll need a guide, Cross," she said, entering the doorway. "Other-wise you'll just end up losing yourself again."

Cross hesitated for a moment, wondering what exactly she meant. Then as though drawn in her wake, he followed her outside. The night air was oppressive and humid, but the darkness afforded him some comfort. It seemed like the Government really hadn't known about this exit.

Soon the silent procession of students reached the beginning of a tan-gled maze of back alleys, and Cross felt ready to relax.

At that exact moment, soldiers appeared from around a corner. At their head, Iris smiled coldly. Without a word they opened fire.

Umasi waited patiently as the gunshots rang out. Resting atop the rusted fire escape, he could hear panicked orders to scatter, followed by other orders to pursue. One of those voices was familiar—now getting closer. Good.

Umasi's plans to continue on to District 1 had again been rendered impossible, this time by the sudden commotion in District 2. However, the disturbance had also aroused his curiosity. In lieu of other options, he'd decided to investigate, and there at the District 2 School he had seen and heard Iris identify herself. In a stroke of luck or misfortune, his en-emy had come to him.

Umasi frowned as muzzle flashes lit up the darkened alleyways. He had been surprised to find the students rebelling against the Government, especially after the war had ended. The students' efforts had been valiant but suicidal, and Umasi couldn't imagine what it was that had driven them to such desperate action. Had the Mayor left secret instructions for them before the Government's invasion? That seemed far-fetched, for he knew the Mayor had avoided doing the same with the Enforcers for fear of being thought insane.

Gunshots and cries of pain echoed up from the tangled alleys below. Umasi averted his gaze, though his ears could not drown out the noise. He had learned to steel himself against such sounds—as much as he wanted to help, there was no way for him to save everyone, and sometimes saving any would put everything at risk.

Umasi refocused on his goal, his purpose for being here. He had definitely picked out Iris' voice among the dozens of others, and he was fairly sure that she was heading his way. A pair of dark shapes came into view in the alley below, and as he braced himself for the coming confrontation Umasi felt a tinge of apprehension. This was the best opportunity he could imagine for confronting his sister, but this was an enemy who'd hated and watched him since he was born—an enemy he knew nothing about.

There were more flashes of gunfire, and suddenly Umasi's heart skipped a beat. One of the fleeing students down there was *not* a student. Even in the dark he could tell that she was white like paper. It was impossible . . . but there she was. As Umasi struggled with this realization, a third shape entered the alley below. The pursuer. Iris.

He did not have to think now—his course of action was clear. Drawing a sword, Umasi leapt into the darkness below.

In a moment of clarity, Cross wondered why he was running. Maybe it was because of Iris' rank and the authority it carried with it. Maybe it was the way she had calmly shot two students in the head before any of them could retaliate. Maybe it was because the nameless girl beside him hadn't even tried to fight, perhaps sensing an enemy she could not match.

Whatever the reason, it was not excitement or logic that now ruled his actions, but instinct. Fear. Of course Iris had come after him herself, leaving her subordinates to chase down the others. She was fast, and her aim precise. Cross knew that he and the albino had only survived this long because of the winding alleyway and sheer luck.

Bullets struck the wall next to Cross, and he ducked his head. As they rounded a corner, he pointed backwards with his sidearm and fired blindly. The move did not seem to impress Iris. The general responded with a shot that bounced off the wall and grazed his hand. Cross let out a curse and dropped his gun, clutching his wound.

She was gaining, Cross realized. At any moment she would be able to get a clean shot. Cross had become almost numb to the idea of death, having narrowly escaped it so many times already. It was the anticipation that irritated him now; knowing what would happen but being unable to prevent it.

Then without warning, something black, something *huge* fell from above. Cross had a vision of massive wings, and a series of irrational thoughts ran through his head. He heard Iris halt, and no more gunshots came. Though Cross was surprised, he did not turn around to see what had saved them. His nameless companion, however, did. Whatever she saw seemed to have an impact on her.

"Him!" she cried. For the first time Cross heard shock in her voice.

Cross didn't know who "him" referred to, but his curiosity had been piqued. He himself was relieved that they'd been saved, and yet the albino now seemed more agitated if anything. Cross glanced at her.

"Should we—"

"Keep running." The albino had her eyes shut. "He's trying to buy us time."

"Who is?" Cross pressed. "Do you know whatever that was back there?"

Just then the albino made a turn, so abruptly that Cross almost overshot her. She darted down some old stairs and into the subways. Inside the operator booth Cross could see Zen waiting for them.

Looking relieved, the albino scooped the boy up in her arms and slipped over the turnstiles. Cross, still feeling tense, followed behind as they climbed down from the platform and onto the dark tracks.

"To answer your question," the albino said at last, looking at Zen rather than Cross, "I do know who saved us back there."

The moment she detected movement above, Iris raised her rifle and fired. It was dark, too dark to see anything amidst the tangle of iron and brick. She clucked her tongue in disappointment as she realized that her bullets were piercing an empty windbreaker jacket. Visual misdirection, she realized as her rifle was knocked from her hands by her descending foe. Clever.

The enemy thrust a sword at her neck. That was strange—a primitive weapon, but admittedly dangerous in such close quarters. Iris sidestepped the thrust and drove her knee into her assailant's belly. The boy stumbled backwards, but recovered surprisingly well. That's when Iris saw his face. She froze, her full attention focused upon the boy.

"Zen?" she said.

"No," came the cold reply. "Umasi."

As miraculous as this encounter was, Iris swiftly suppressed any emotion. This was no time to lose her head. It was still a dangerous situation, and she would need her wits about her if she was to emerge with the desired outcome.

"I've been waiting years for this," Iris said softly, unhitching her staff from her back. "I never expected it to be so sudden. The best things in life really are surprises."

"So are the worst," Umasi said, lunging forward.

Iris jabbed her staff forward and pressed a button, extending it right into a surprised Umasi's chest. Knocked off balance, Umasi stumbled for a moment, long enough for Iris to swing her staff around and hit him in the legs. Umasi fell to the ground, and like lightning Iris brought her staff down upon him. With impressive speed Umasi raised his sword to block the attack, supporting the blade with his flattened palm. Iris smiled, then pressed the second button on her staff.

Nothing happened. No current traveled down the white blade, and no cry of pain escaped Umasi's lips. Instead, he lashed out with his feet, catching Iris by surprise. The General stepped backwards to keep her balance, and Umasi leapt to his feet.

"Not metal, then?" Iris said, glancing at the sword. "Ceramic, I suppose. I recall that we had a research lab in this City. Such facilities produce the ceramics used in our body armor."

"I suppose I should thank you then," Umasi said, lunging forward. "Otherwise I might've been armed with plain metal."

"You might have been better off that way." Iris smiled, dodging the sword stroke. "Ceramic knives were never approved for the military. Do you know why?"

Umasi aimed at her unprotected waist. "Enlighten me."

Iris twisted her body to avoid the thrust, and then her hand shot out, pinning the white blade to the alley wall.

"While ceramic can indeed be harder than steel," Iris explained, "it is also far more brittle."

With that, Iris shrunk her staff and brought its weighted end crashing down on the end of the sword. The ceramic blade cracked, its tip broken off, and Iris released it, allowing a shocked Umasi to recover his weapon and stare at the damage.

"Give it up," Iris said. "You might as well be fighting with glass."

Gripping his broken sword tightly, Umasi's expression hardened. "Where is the Mayor?"

Iris tilted her head, surprised by the change of subject. "Dead, of course."

Without a word, Umasi drew his second blade. Iris sighed at the futile display and extended her staff once again. But Umasi did something unexpected; he speared a rag on the alley floor, and with one flick tossed it at Iris' head. Reflexively Iris knocked the cloth aside with her staff. Umasi seized the opening, lunging forward with both blades. Iris knew she had blundered, but her reactions were still fast; she dived to the right, avoiding the first sword's thrust—

Only to realize that it was the one with no tip.

Blood splattered onto the alley wall as Umasi's long blade cut a gash across Iris' arm. Ignoring the pain, Iris calmly recognized that the cut was shallow. Her arm would remain functional long enough to win the fight.

By now she'd seen enough to understand Umasi's fighting ability; his strengths were quick reflexes and good instincts, combined with creative feints. He was not afraid, but he was reckless, to a degree that she could exploit.

Umasi's next attack also drew blood, this time from her hand, but it also left him wide open. Many combatants would not have had the clarity to take advantage of the momentary vulnerability, but Iris did not hesitate. Wielding her staff with her injured arm, Iris slammed it down on Umasi's shoulder, pressing a button as she did so.

Umasi let out a shout of pain, falling to the ground. Before he could react, Iris slammed her foot down on his shorter blade, trapping it beneath her heel. She brought her staff down, and he moved his long sword to block it.

Iris had been expecting that, and before the weapons made contact she pressed the button on her staff to shrink it. Umasi's blade passed through thin air, and he was left completely exposed. Iris extended her staff again, then pressed the other button. Umasi seemed to writhe for a moment from the shock, releasing his broken sword.

Iris stepped back. Umasi seemed to shrug off the pain, managing to pull himself to his feet. Iris was impressed. One zap was usually enough to keep someone down. There was cold, flat determination as he reached into his pocket—a hidden gun? No, a knife this time. He threw it at her in one smooth motion. Iris almost casually knocked the projectile aside, even as Umasi lunged forward.

Iris decked him with her staff before he could get within range. She followed up with two quick blows to his elbow and his knee. With the last blow, she released another jolt. Umasi's sword flew from his hand as he fell onto his uninjured knee. His sunglasses fell from his face, and he stared up at Iris with dark, unyielding eyes. He'd been beaten, but did not give in to hysterics or useless acts of desperation. Iris admired that.

Umasi, for his part, was calm. He had always known his odds would be poor in this fight. He had never underestimated Iris—she had simply been too powerful. Zyid was gone, the Mayor was gone, and now he was ready to join them. Having lived life by his own rules, with his death he would buy time for others to escape. And so Umasi was calm, free of regret, facing the woman who'd been his oldest enemy. She moved, an unreadable expression on her face, and Umasi waited for death.

Then Iris did something Umasi would never have imagined.

She dropped to her knees, and pulled him into a warm embrace.

"You've grown up strong," she whispered. "I'm so glad."

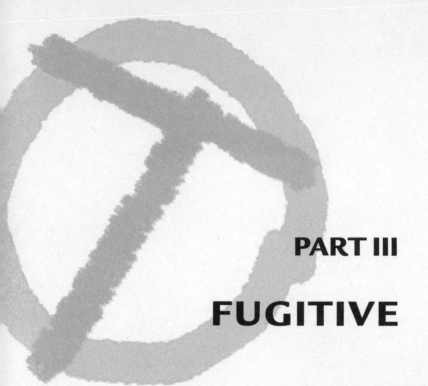

PART III

FUGITIVE

I t was the greatest regret of my life."

Umasi did not look at Iris as she spoke, but he could discern no deception in her voice. Umasi had just finished explaining what had happened to Zyid. As he described his brother's fall, a momentary look of agony had passed across Iris' face, too fleeting and too raw to be rehearsed. If she was faking, Umasi thought it was the best act he'd seen since Edward—no, better than that.

They were in the Mayoral Mansion now, inside the bedroom Umasi had once shared with his brother. It was not a place he had ever thought he'd return to, and certainly not a place he ever imagined holding a conversation with his estranged sister. She had suggested they might find privacy here, and so Umasi had come, listening to Iris explain herself as he examined the objects left in his old room.

"You have to believe me, Umasi," Iris continued. "I didn't know what would happen. I thought you and your brother would be safe here."

Umasi shook his head as he picked up one of his old test papers. Despite her earnestness, he still found Iris' claims difficult to reconcile with what he knew of her. His anger over the Mayor's death had yet to fade completely.

"Why did you do it in the first place?" Umasi demanded, turning around to face Iris. "What kind of threat did you think that Zen and I posed?"

"Threat?" Iris looked genuinely surprised. "Umasi, what exactly did the Mayor tell you about me?"

"He said that you were trying to get rid of us," Umasi replied. "That you thought we were in your way. That you tried and failed to have us killed."

Iris' gray eyes widened, then narrowed to slits.

"That *man*!" she said coldly. "I should never have trusted the dimwitted fool."

Umasi waited for her to explain herself.

"Umasi, the Mayor was wrong." Iris rubbed her knuckles against her forehead. "He might have believed what he told you, but he had it the other way around."

Umasi frowned, suddenly feeling uneasy. "What do you mean?"

Iris looked him in the eyes. "It wasn't me who wanted you out of the way; it was my—our father. *I* fought to have you placed with the leader of a City, where I thought you could be safe and happy."

As the words registered, Umasi felt his heart nearly freeze from the shock. His test paper crumpled in his hands. A wave of nausea washed over him as the full magnitude of the implications dawned upon him.

"Why?" he whispered.

"Politics. Your presence would have complicated my father's situation. Furthermore, he does not fully trust his own children and had no desire for more," Iris explained. "He thought it would be most expedient to have you separated and raised in anonymous poverty so that you would never rise to prominence." Iris sighed. "Since he was set on disposing of you, I wanted him to do it properly. After many angry arguments, I was able to have you sent into a more comfortable exile. It was the solution your mother would have fought for, had she not died in childbirth."

"You did it for my mother?"

"Partly. She was a good woman. But I did it more for you. I saw you two as my siblings. I still do," Iris said. "My father, clearly, did not, and I never forgave him for it. I think he blamed you for her death. In her place, I decided to keep an eye on you. All these years, it's been me watching from afar."

Umasi swallowed, still trying to take everything in. "What do you mean by 'watching?'"

"Whenever I could, I tried to make sure you were all right. It was I who noticed the money your brother was spending four years ago." Iris took a deep breath. "My father, fearing that the truth would be exposed, refused to allow an official investigation. I did the best I could, on my own." Iris' jaw clenched with anger. "But no matter how hard I tried, that wretched Mayor thwarted every attempt to gain proof."

Umasi shook his head. In spite of everything, he still felt some affection for his dead adoptive father. "The Mayor was a good man," Umasi insisted. "He did his best as a father."

"He placed his position, his authority, above your safety," Iris said coldly. "I was wrong to ever put faith in him."

"That's not true. He was torn between us and the City." Umasi blinked back tears, glad that they were hidden behind his sunglasses. "Trust me Iris, he cared."

Iris looked at him strangely, then shrugged. "Even if he meant well, he made things difficult for me," she said. "When it became obvious that there was a problem in the City, I had to fight long and hard to have the military intervene. My father still feared his old indiscretions. By the time I got here . . ." Iris shook her head sadly. "I'm sorry that I could not save Zen."

She really meant it, Umasi thought in amazement. His own emotions were overridden by his surprise, and he felt a sudden urge to comfort her, let her know that Zen's fate had not been her fault. Then he remembered the things that Iris *was* responsible for, and he forced himself to swallow his words.

"If I accept what you say at face value," Umasi said, "then where do we go from here? You've captured the City, won the war, yet thousands of your enemies have escaped you. What is your plan for them?"

Iris blinked, apparently surprised by the change of subject.

"When I gained approval for this intervention, I was given a deadline," she explained. "Within three months I must demonstrate that I'm on my way towards eliminating all resistance in this City. I've already begun. Have you heard about the reeducation program?"

Umasi didn't like the sound of that. "No."

Iris explained her plans for the reeducation camps, and Umasi listened with growing distaste as she described the methods behind it. He understood now that she only meant well for the City, and, by the end of her explanation, even admitted to himself that it might work. But it was the very embodiment of everything that had driven Zyid to his fatal rebellion, and Umasi told Iris so in forceful terms.

"Umasi, if you can think of another way to pacify a rebellious City within three months, I'm willing to listen," Iris said. "As things stand, I believe that this is the only way to do it in time and do it right. I try to do things in the least wasteful, most humane way I can. But when it comes down to it, I have to do what needs to be done."

"I don't understand that," Umasi admitted, shaking his head. "There's always a choice."

"Is there?" Iris said softly. "When your brother was on the verge of destroying himself and the City, you said you stood against him, didn't you? If you had gone all the way, he would've been spared much grief, and the City would've been spared a war."

The words hurt, and Umasi resented Iris for saying them. And yet at the same time he knew they were true, for he had whispered them to himself. He understood the great burden that had been placed on Iris' shoulders.

But unlike him, she could handle that burden because she did what *must* be done, without hesitation or doubt.

And it's my mess she's cleaning up, Umasi realized. Slowly but surely he was arriving now at what he knew would be a life-changing decision. He was drawn to Iris. In many ways she resembled both him and Zyid—and he wanted, so desperately, to have a family again.

"Promise that you won't execute anyone," Umasi said. "Promise that these will be reeducation camps, not death camps."

"I promise," Iris replied. "I am neither wasteful nor sadistic. Every precaution will be taken so that the detainees remain physically healthy."

Umasi took a deep breath, his mind made up.

"All right then, sister." He tilted his sunglasses up to look at her. "The war is over, time to make the best of it. I'll do my part. Let us bring a lasting peace to the City."

Somehow, the dark and lonely subway tunnels seemed far more unsettling the second time around. Neither the albino nor her son had spoken during the journey, and while that was probably wise, it made Cross feel like he was traveling with phantoms. He was not yet crazy enough to speak aloud to himself, but his mind wandered—mostly to the other students and what might have become of them.

By the time they emerged from a station deep within District 11 it was nearly dawn, and a faint glow bloomed on the horizon. Due to the curfew the street was blessedly free of civilians. After a quick glance around, the albino settled on an empty nursery across the street from the station.

Entering the building did not prove to be a problem. The door was already ajar, sparing them the trouble of breaking in. As they entered the narrow foyer, the albino paused and shut her eyes, listening. Zen stopped and did the same, and Cross wondered if the three-year-old's hearing really was sharp or if he was just mimicking his mother.

Detecting no immediate dangers, the nameless girl opened her eyes and continued up the stairs, Zen and Cross trailing behind. They pushed a creaky door open, and emerged into a small gymnasium with a polished wooden floor and a wall of mirrors. Enormous windows overlooked the street, though they were too dirty to see in or out of.

Zen quickly made himself at home, inspecting a hula hoop that had been left on the floor. Meanwhile, the albino checked the other rooms for any sign of other people. After a few minutes she seemed satisfied, and had even discovered a kitchen.

"I know we're all tired," she said, "but it's probably best that we eat before resting so that we'll be ready to move by nightfall."

Zen didn't seem to care much either way, and busied himself playing with his hoop. Meanwhile the girl opened her pack and lit the stove. Cross donned a dirty apron hanging from the kitchen door. The albino looked at him in surprise as he pried open a can of tuna fish and began to stir the contents with vegetable oil.

"You cook?"

"I used to," Cross replied. "My father was . . . well, at home I had to take care of myself."

The albino looked at him strangely and said nothing to that, but allowed him to heat some bouillon for a soup. It was not difficult to work with what few resources they had, and in no time at all they were sitting down at a small table and eating. Zen dug into his tuna with a spoon, while his mother used crackers for the same purpose. Cross merely nibbled at his portion, finding that despite his exhaustion he wasn't very hungry.

How many of the students had escaped? Could they elude capture for long, hunted by an enemy like Iris? Had he only made things worse by trying to resist? Cross' mind assumed the worst. He was no good at leading. Cross wished that he'd had the courage to refuse his promotion long ago; that he'd never become the leader of the Student Militia.

That wish triggered a fresh wave of guilt. Cross clenched his spoon so tight that it hurt. He had reminded himself that there was a reason he hadn't refused the promotion.

'm impressed," Edward said. "I wasn't sure you had it in you."

Cross said nothing. It was nighttime. The two of them were sitting in the darkness of their dormitory again. Cross was bandaged up from several wounds, his chest bare.

"You should thank me, Cross," Edward continued. "The drawing was a regrettable loss, but your focus would be better spent on more ambitious endeavors. Plus I vouched for you, so you'll get off easy for putting those three boys in the hospital."

Cross shook his head. "Those guys were your friends."

"Oh, I don't really have friends," Edward said. "They were just instruments—no, more like currency, things to be earned and spent as needed."

Cross remained silent.

"Don't feel bad, Cross. This is a turning point for you," Edward said. "You now have a reputation as an angry, violent, antisocial lunatic. The other kids will probably leave you well alone. That's what you wanted, wasn't it?"

Cross continued to sulk. Edward was right. Word had spread quickly. The other students hated him, laughed at him, saw him as dangerous. Edward had not orchestrated their cruel response. They had been eager to make him an outcast.

Cross blinked back tears. He hadn't wanted this, he hadn't deserved this. The world had been unfair to him, but fighting back had only made it worse. Cross understood now that there would never be a place for him among his peers. They deserved the fate Edward had planned for them.

Cross balled his fists. "I'll do it."

Edward raised his thin eyebrows. "Do what?"

Cross looked up at Edward with blazing eyes.

"I'll help you take over the City. I'll help you destroy them." Cross shook with anger. "I hate them. I hate them all, everyone."

Edward smirked.

"Good," he said. "When the time comes, I'm sure you'll make a useful ally on the battlefield. But you know where I want to begin for now. Let us discuss ways to destroy the Truancy, and make me the obvious successor to the Mayor."

Cross clenched his fist. He was prepared for this. Edward's ambitions had planted the seeds of a dark idea in Cross' mind, but this would be the first time he ever allowed it to bloom.

"If you want to take down the Truancy," Cross said, "you'd have to cut them off from their base of support."

"The students." Edward grinned. "That much is obvious. But how to do it?"

"Make the Truants fight the students." Cross pictured his tormentors being blown apart on the battlefield. "Start recruiting students into the Enforcers, or even better, create a new organization for them."

Edward leaned forward. "You propose an entire militia of students."

"Yeah. A Student Militia."

A re you going to eat your food, or just play with it?"

Startled out of his trance, Cross looked up. Zen's bowl was already empty, and the little boy had curled up in a chair to sleep. The albino had also finished, and she was now looking at Cross with mild reproach. Embarrassed, Cross picked up his spoon and began eating.

"Sorry," Cross said. "I was just thinking about—"

"The other students?" the girl finished.

Cross could not bring himself to tell the whole story. He nodded instead.

"Are you worried about them?"

"Yes."

The albino shrugged off her blue militia jacket and laid it over the sleeping Zen. "Then what do you plan to do about it?"

"Plan?" Cross put his spoon down. "There's nothing *to* plan. The plan is to avoid getting caught for as long as possible."

"Is that all you aspire to do?" she asked. "Run away?"

"What else am I supposed to do?"

The albino looked at him as though it were obvious. "Try to help your friends."

"Help?" Cross nearly laughed. "Every time I try to help it just ends up helping the enemy. The Government *won*. The rest of us lost, and now there's nothing to do but wait until they catch every one of us."

"If you're still free, then you haven't given up yet," the albino pointed out. "The City is not beyond hope."

"Yes it is," Cross said. "Even if we weren't scattered, the Student Militia would never have a hope of taking on the Government. You've seen their power. We're kids with toys compared to them."

"Didn't the Truancy successfully resist the Enforcers for years, despite being outmatched by the Enforcers' tools and numbers?"

That observation, while true, irked Cross. "Well then it's too bad that the Truancy can't give us some advice," he said sarcastically.

"Maybe you should go and ask them for some."

Cross stared at the albino. She seemed serious as always, her eyes an honest blue in the faint light. Still, Cross was not convinced that she hadn't been joking.

"That's impossible," Cross said flatly. "The Truancy is scattered now, and even if they weren't, working with them is—"

"Necessary," the albino said. "If you want to save your comrades, if you believe that they're not yet dead, then your path is clear. Do you feel no responsibility for the Student Militia?"

The question cut deep. Cross had never wanted that responsibility, but he could not bring himself to deny it.

"Why do you care?" he demanded. "What does it matter to you what we or the Truants do?"

The albino gestured over at where Zen slept. "I don't know what kind of City he will grow up in," she explained, "but I don't want it to be one ruled by terror."

Cross swallowed, remembering what it was like as a child, to live day to day in constant fear, without hope or succor. He took a deep breath.

"How would we even contact the Truancy?" Cross asked. "They're all in hiding, like us."

"I don't have any easy answers," the albino said. "It may take awhile to find them, but that might be for the better. As things are now, you're not ready to negotiate with the Truancy."

Cross frowned. "What do you mean?"

"If you want to deal with their leader, you should appear to be his equal," the albino explained. "Right now, I don't think you can pull it off."

Cross hesitated, then turned to look at one of the great mirrors on the wall. He looked thin and haggard, his face gaunt, black rings forming under his eyes. He resembled a corpse that had been dragged through the sewer. She had a point.

"So what am I supposed to do?" Cross asked. "Appearances can be changed, but there's more to it than that. I can't match Takan in a fight and everyone knows it."

The albino's chain clinked as she unfolded her arms. Outside the sun steadily climbed higher into the sky, its bright morning rays spilling into the street. As the fresh light diffused through the windows, the girl's eyes seemed to glow red, and for a moment Cross felt very small before her.

"Train with me," she said simply. "If I can teach you anything useful, I will. For as long as our journey lasts, you will be my pupil."

quish, squish, squish.
   "Sepp, this is gross."
"I totally agree. Hopefully the Government does too."
Squish, squish, squish.
"Do you think they suspect some of us are hiding in the sewers?"
"Hide in the sewers? Who would do something crazy like that?"
Squish, squi—
"Sepp."
"Something wrong?"
"I need to stop for a bit. I think I cut myself on something sharp."
"Oh, that sounds bad. Here, let me kiss it to make it better."
"Sepp!"

Sepp smiled at the squeal of outrage. He always found that noise endearing. Too bad Floe didn't seem to think the same about his jokes.

"Guess not," he said. "Well I see a little light up ahead. Maybe we can take a break there."

The light turned out to be barely a ray flowing down through a street drain from the dusk outside. Grateful for both the illumination and the fresh air, Sepp and Floe sat down and rested in a nearby alcove, surrounded by heaps of decomposing litter that had fallen into the gutter over the years. Sepp could definitely think of more romantic settings than this. He glanced at Floe, who was now bandaging her cut with gauze from her fanny pack. She caught him looking, and frowned.

"What are you even doing here, Sepp?" she demanded, tying off the end of her bandage.

"Most recently?" Sepp scratched his head. "Thinking about how nicely your hair offsets all this charming garbage."

"Shut up!" Floe flushed red. "You know what I mean! Why did you follow me?"

"'Cause," Sepp said, leaning back, "I love being interrogated about my motives."

Floe let out a strange sound as though she were trying to laugh and be angry at the same time. Sepp grinned. That was a new reaction.

"Sepp, we're running for our lives here, with no clue where to go, and an entire army out to kill us!" Floe said. "Can't you be serious for one moment?"

"I am serious, this is how I handle serious!" Sepp held his hands up. "I prefer laughing and joking to tense and moody, but if you'd prefer the latter . . ." He hunched over and made a grimacing face like the one Cross often wore.

Floe almost giggled, but caught herself in time. She swiftly rearranged her features into a neutral expression.

"Seriously, Sepp, what are we going to do?"

"Remember when I said you were welcome at my place?"

"Sepp, I'm trying to be *serious* here—"

"So am I," Sepp said. "Look, Cross ordered us to hide with our families. He had a good idea. Mine has room for you."

Floe blinked. "You said it was a one-room apartment. Where would we hide if the Government came looking for us? We can't endanger your family like that."

"Hm, you have a point there," Sepp said. "Guess we'll just have to squeeze in the cupboard if the worst happens."

"Sepp!" Floe looked ready to slap him.

"Not a joke, not a joke!" Sepp said hastily. "It's pretty big, it'd fit the both of us. Anyway, it's not like we have any other options. I mean, I don't think we're going to find any hotels down here."

Floe looked away, biting her lip.

"Will your parents take me?" she asked. "It's a big risk for someone they don't know."

Sepp shrugged. "I think they will. I'll just tell them you're my—"

Sepp caught himself before he said the word *girlfriend*. He had intended it as a joke, but for some reason the word had sobered him. Now that they were alone, he found himself considering for the first time the possibility that his attraction might go beyond simple teasing. Remembering Cross, Sepp felt guilty.

"Your what?" Floe asked.

"Uh, comrade," Sepp said quickly. "You've saved my life plenty of times, they'll appreciate that. And besides, we're technically following orders, aren't we?"

"You mean to hide with our families?"

"Er, yeah, those orders."

Sepp had no idea what Cross had intended when he'd told Sepp to follow Floe. Rumors about Cross and Floe's relationship had circulated among the Militia—it was Cross, after all, who had recruited her from the Truancy—but Sepp's attentive eye had never caught any evidence of Cross making a move on her. They definitely had *some* sort of history, but whatever it was, Sepp decided, it probably wasn't romantic.

That worked for him. If Cross wasn't interested, it was every man for himself.

"All right then." Floe stood up, accepting that Sepp's house might be better than sleeping in sewage. "Where is your house?"

"It's in District 9," Sepp said. "I'm not an expert on sewer navigation, but given the two options I'd say going forward makes the most sense."

Floe rolled her eyes. "Forward it is. Come on, let's go."

With that, Sepp and Floe resumed their trek through the dark tunnels. As she walked along, Floe's hair caught the light from the drain, and Sepp found himself smiling. He'd been joking at the time, but those light brown curls really did strike a nice contrast with their surroundings. And that wasn't the only part of her that was nice.

Squish, squish, squish.

"Sepp, what are you staring at?"

"Nothing!"

18

WAKING NIGHTMARES

What are you up to now, Iris?"

Iris smiled faintly and shut the folder she had been perusing. She'd only barely detected the newcomer coming up the stairs, but had known exactly who it was—the only other person allowed to enter and leave the Mayor's study at will.

"I was browsing through the Mayor's old files," Iris said, looking up. "Or at least what could be salvaged of them. He was quite thorough, but it turns out that he forgot to wipe his Enforcer profiles."

Umasi adjusted his sunglasses. "What could possibly interest you there?"

Iris set the folder aside. When he was not talking with her, Umasi spent most of his time trying to acclimate himself to his new environment. She could tell that he felt out of place among the uniformed soldiers, and so he had been living mostly out of his old bedroom in the mansion. It still felt a bit awkward to talk with him, but they had steadily begun to build a polite rapport.

Really, in Iris' opinion they thought a lot alike. She believed him when he said he wanted to help, and she knew there was a lot he could do towards that end. Iris looked forward to seeing what he could do. But she wasn't ready to share *everything* with him just yet.

"I was trying to determine which of the Enforcers might prove useful," she said. "Did you have something you wanted to discuss?"

Umasi nodded, though Iris could tell that he hadn't entirely bought her explanation.

"The City is secure, for now," he said. "But I'm worried about a few loose ends."

"Which in particular?"

"For one, the leader of the Truancy is still at large," Umasi pointed out. "As is my brother's former lieutenant, who I actually consider to be the more pressing threat. She's been unpredictable and dangerous ever since Zen died."

Iris drummed her fingers on the desk. "Do you believe the Truants might rally around her?"

"That possibility exists," Umasi allowed. "But I find it more likely that in her confusion and anger, Noni will end up targeting important people. With one success she could throw the City into chaos."

Iris considered that, then looked sideways at Umasi.

"Do you think you or I are in danger?"

Umasi laughed.

"If she had a chance to kill me, she probably would," he said. "As for you, I can only guess. It depends whether or not she ends up directing her anger towards the Government. Either way, I would feel more at ease if we were able to detain her."

"I'll put an alert out for her description," Iris promised, "though it sounds like she's just as likely to be her own undoing. But what about the Truancy's current leader? You mentioned that you once tutored him."

Indeed, the information that Umasi had been able to provide the Government had been extensive and invaluable. Iris was surprised to learn that Umasi knew, directly or indirectly, almost all the major figures in the Truancy. He had provided the names and backgrounds of all of them. But even where Umasi was an aid, the Mayor proved to be a hindrance from beyond the grave. Among the records he had destroyed was the entire City's student database, making cross-referencing impossible. So, for now, Iris was left to rely on Umasi's information and opinions alone.

The boy shook his head.

"As things stand now, I don't believe that Tack is an immediate threat," Umasi explained. "He's more stable than Noni. I believe he'll do the sensible thing and try to lie low for a while. Given time, I might even be able to convince him to come quietly."

"That would be a very happy outcome for all involved," Iris said. "If the Truancy leadership could be convinced to cooperate, we'd be well on our way towards reconstruction. Is that all that was bothering you?"

Umasi hesitated. That was unusual for him, Iris noted.

"The new leader of the Student Militia did cross my mind," Umasi said after a moment. "I know very little about him. He may try to rally his Militia against us. It could turn out to be a big problem."

Iris nodded.

"I agree. His unexpected rebellion proved that he's not to be underestimated again." She tapped the folder on her desk. "But you needn't worry about that, Umasi. I've been doing some research on this very subject, and I believe I know how to deal with him."

A familiar hissing filled the air. Acting on instinct, Cross raised his knife to deflect the chain, successfully knocking it aside. Even as the chain fell, it began to slide back towards its master. But Cross was already moving. He lunged at his pale opponent, only to have her twist out of the way like a wraith. The next thing he knew, his knife arm had been tangled up in the chain. The albino looked at him, and then calmly slammed her elbow into his forehead.

Cross saw stars and tried to stumble backwards, but his arm was still trapped and the movement sent him crashing to the ground instead. It was a familiar position for him.

"Your speed isn't the problem, Cross. You alternate between hesitation and recklessness."

The albino looked down at Cross, offering her hand. The sunset had reached its apex, and the girl looked otherworldly in the red light that bled through the dirty windows. Remembering how Edward would punish him after helping him up, Cross tensed as the albino pulled him to his feet. No punishment came.

They had a couple of hours before it would be dark enough for them to travel. Having slept through the day, they'd decided to start his training while they waited. So far it hadn't gone well.

"I didn't think I was hesitating at all," Cross said. "You're just too fast."

"You *were* hesitating, but not for my sake, I think," she replied. "It was like you were trying to reign in your own power. You need to trust yourself to be in control of every movement."

Remembering his unthinking rampage through District 15, Cross grimaced. The albino had a point.

"Do you think that's my only problem?"

"No." Her eyes were red in the setting sun. "Your technique is all wrong. Your moves rely too much on power." She looked thoughtful for a moment. "Who taught you to use a knife?"

Cross frowned. "Edward."

In fact, it was because of his tutelage under Edward that Cross had initially been skeptical that training would help. Neither Rothenberg nor Edward had been particularly constructive in their guidance.

Despite her unsettling appearance, however, the albino had been different. She proved to be no softer than she should, and no harsher than was necessary.

"Edward probably meant to handicap you, then," she said. "Your knife lacks the range and length of a sword, and it is less practical for blocking. The advantage is that once you get close enough you have more options, and you can move faster with it."

Cross nodded, trying to absorb what she was saying while at the same time tuning out the unpleasant memories their training had evoked.

"Flexibility and accuracy should be your priorities, Cross, not power, which you have plenty of." She glanced at him. "Are you all right? You look a little distracted."

"I'm fine," Cross said. "Maybe we should take a break."

The albino nodded. "Sure. I'll go see what Zen is up to."

With that, she carefully wrapped her chain around her arm again and headed towards the kitchen. Cross remained where he was for a few more minutes, brooding. Irritated by the red light from the windows, Cross finally slunk off down a hallway he hadn't explored before, searching for somewhere darker and more private.

Coming across a wooden door, Cross turned the handle and pushed lightly. The door creaked as it swung open. Cross was disappointed to find that there were windows here too. He was about to leave when his eyes fell upon something resting against the wall. It was a child's easel and a set of paint.

All at once Cross felt like he was six again, entering a nursery, discovering paint for the first time. He would smear the colors on his fingertips, delighted, and then press them to the paper, watching forms and shapes come to life beneath his touch. Those moments would be bliss, and he would be happy until he brought his creation home to show his father.

His father, who would call it disgusting and tear it up as Cross cried. His father, who would crush it beneath his feet and laugh.

Cross did not realize at first that he was screaming, or that the hot rivulets on his face were tears. Then a door slammed open and the next thing Cross knew was *cold,* cold and wet. The shock made Cross gasp and open his eyes. The pale girl stood above him, holding an empty water bottle.

"What's wrong?" she asked.

"I . . ." Cross swallowed, trying to focus on the present. "Bad memories."

The albino sat down beside him and hugged her knees to her chest. "Why don't you tell me about them?"

For a moment Cross considered refusing—he knew that she would accept that. But the girl radiated such a sense of calm that he relented. He'd gone so long without talking to anyone that he'd forgotten how much he wanted to.

"I used to like painting." Cross gestured towards the easel without looking at it. "The Mayor himself once complimented me when he visited our school."

"That must have been quite an honor."

"It was but . . ." Cross shook his head. "My father didn't think much of it. He made me hate it. He would tell me it looked like crap."

The girl frowned. "Why would he do that?"

Cross laughed.

"How should I know?" he demanded. "I always wondered why, why, *why*? For a lot of things. I never got any answers. You wouldn't ask if you knew Rothenberg. You don't know him, you don't know what it was like!"

Cross was ranting now, wildly talking half to himself and half to his companion.

"I wanted to paint!" Cross let out something between a roar and a moan. "I wanted to create! Not destroy, *not* destroy!"

The albino laid a hand on his shoulder. "You're not a destroyer, Cross. You're a protector."

"No I'm not!" Cross laughed again. "Look at everything I've done! And why? I don't know why! Takan was right—I didn't even have a *reason* to do what I was doing. The only reason I ever did anything was because . . . because . . ."

"Someone told you to?"

"Yes!" Cross shouted. "That was all the reason I needed to kill! I was doing what I was told to do! And *enjoying* it! Isn't that *funny*?"

The albino didn't laugh. She looked at Cross with pity.

"I think I understand now," she said slowly. "You needed your father. No matter how bad he was, you needed guidance, and Rothenberg was all you had. Then he was gone . . . and Edward was there to fill the void." The girl stopped, seemingly unsettled.

Cross could tell what was bothering her, and his hysterics quickly faded.

"You're not like them," he said.

"Aren't I?" she asked, tilting her head. "I'm just one more person trying to impose my will upon you."

"No." Cross shook his head. "They . . . the others . . . they all wanted to break me. You're the only one who ever tried to fix me."

The sun had now fully set, and the windows were dark now, only faint streetlight pooling on the floors. The albino turned to look at Cross with blue eyes, and suddenly, in a move as swift as it was unexpected, enveloped him in a warm hug. Cross froze for a moment, then relaxed.

Was this what it was like to have a mother? Cross had no way of knowing, but he could only imagine that it felt something like this. He envied Zen, who had always had a mother, and no father to terrorize him.

"Why don't you have a name?" Cross asked.

The albino shifted. "I had one once, a long time ago," she replied. "It became part of a past that lost its meaning. I neither need nor want one now."

"Why?"

"Sometimes we're better off forgetting our history, Cross," she said. "Do you think you can try that? To disarm your nightmares?"

Cross nodded. The albino smiled at that. She stood up again as though nothing had happened, dusted herself off, and then offered Cross her hand. This time he felt no apprehension as he took it.

"You need to let the past go, Cross. Otherwise it can consume you," the albino warned as they left the room. "Agonizing over what's done can only lead to suffering—for everyone around you, and especially for yourself."

Iris frowned as she walked through the hospital hallway, tapping her staff against the linoleum-tiled floor. It had been four days now since the end of major combat operations, and still the facility was overloaded with the injured. The place was a flurry of activity, with medics from both the City and the military rushing through the halls. Most of them knew who she was, but so urgent were their tasks that they paid her little attention. As was proper.

The one exception was the annoyingly cowed hospital chief whose business it was to escort her through the halls. The squat man panted as he tried to keep up with her brisk pace, lecturing as he dodged doctors and trolleys.

"The thing you have to understand, ma'am, is that we had strict orders *never* to discharge him," he said. "He's very dangerous, and one of our psychologists told me that if he were ever let loose—"

"I read his profile, and I know what your orders were," Iris said. "I am now countermanding those orders. That would be his room at the end of the hall, correct?"

The man looked at the door she was pointing at. It was large and metallic with no handle and only a small square window cut into it. A number pad beside the door provided the only access. The room, Iris knew, was both prison and infirmary, designed to hold patients who were threats to themselves and others.

The hospital chief fidgeted. "Yes, ma'am, but we don't like letting people go in there alone. You see, he's very irritable. He still goes into fits every now and then and he's, uh, injured a few of the orderlies that way."

"I think you'll find that I'm a bit harder to injure than your orderlies," Iris said, glancing back at him. "But you may remain outside if you wish. Open the door."

The chief hesitated, then pressed a combination on the keypad. The door slid open. As Iris entered the room, the man ducked away out of sight. A moment later, the door slid shut behind her.

Unconcerned, Iris looked around. The fluorescent lighting was a bit dim, and the tiled walls were a sterile green. To one side there was a large mirror, behind which Iris knew a soldier was watching, just in case. On the other side there was a set of weights. And on the far side of the room, directly opposite Iris, there rested a lone hospital bed and a wheelchair.

A lump on the bed stirred. Iris waited as it yawned. Then the sheets shifted to reveal a truly large man with graying red hair and a thick mustache.

Iris smiled.

"Wake up, Mr. Rothenberg."

The man opened his eyes and sat up. Iris noted that while his upper body and arms were muscled and powerful, his legs remained unnaturally still beneath the covers.

"Who are you, the new nurse?" Rothenberg demanded as he regarded Iris. "Dinner isn't supposed to be for another two hours."

Iris hid her distaste as Rothenberg stretched his arms. The Mayor had been a fool to ever place faith in the man's abilities. Fortunately, for Iris' purposes, Rothenberg did not require any extraordinary talent. If she was right, then merely setting him loose would be enough.

"I am not your nurse, Mr. Rothenberg," Iris said. "You might not have heard, but there's been a change of leadership in the City. I am General Iris, and if you play your cards right, I am your ticket out of this prison."

Rothenberg stared at her. Seeing that she was serious, his entire demeanor changed in an instant.

"Well then, General Iris, what can I do for you?" he asked.

Iris inclined her head. "You can tell me what you know about your son Cross."

"Cross?" he repeated. "What *don't* I know about him?"

Iris narrowed her eyes but said nothing. Taking the hint, Rothenberg elaborated.

"As far as I'm concerned I raised that boy right—or would've if they hadn't locked me up in here," Rothenberg said. "I can't say how he's grown up since, but when *I* had him I taught him to be independent. I let him do things for himself, and I never let him slack off. No matter what I did he never grew a spine though. I never could cure him of that."

Iris tilted her head. "It may surprise you then to know that he ascended to the leadership of the Student Militia and subsequently plotted a mutiny against me. His behavior indicates recklessness, not cowardice," she said pointedly. "Perhaps you are allowing personal bias to cloud your objectivity?"

"Of course not," Rothenberg said. "If he rebelled against anything you can bet it was someone else's idea. Cross doesn't know how to say 'no.' I must've tested him a thousand times and he never so much as batted an eye."

"And how, exactly, did you test him?"

"I'm sure you've read my record." Rothenberg looked Iris in the eye. "You've heard what they say about me. Well, it's all true. People these days don't understand that sometimes the only solution is to use force—beat them into proper shape or you end up with a useless lump. I was trying to make him *strong*, and the ignorant bastards condemned me for it. I can't say Cross was ever properly thankful either."

The man really believed what he was saying, Iris realized. He had convinced himself that he was a perfect father, casting himself as a victim. Iris looked around the sterile green room once again. The years had clearly left him with plenty of time to twist his memories to suit himself. The man was truly unhinged.

"If you were to be released from this hospital," Iris said, "do you believe that you could locate and apprehend Cross?"

Rothenberg gestured at his legs. "Not without these I can't."

"That is not a problem," Iris said. "The Mayor could have had your legs fixed, but chose not to. My surgeons are better than his. I can have you walking again within days. I'm offering you the chance of a lifetime, Rothenberg—a second chance."

"In return for what, exactly?" Rothenberg demanded.

"Finding your son, and delivering him to our custody."

"What, are you planning to execute him?" Rothenberg snorted. "It's not my fault he's done whatever he did. Do your own dirty work."

"You may bring him in alive," Iris said. "If you wish, you may even take charge of his captivity. My *only* requirement is that he no longer pose a threat to the security of this City."

Rothenberg considered that, his expression dark. Iris saw him glance at his useless legs. A few more moments passed, and his attention seemed drawn somewhere far off. Then a slow smile spread across his face. With only a few visible teeth framed by his unkempt mustache, the grin seemed disturbingly ratlike.

"You have yourself a deal," Rothenberg said briskly. "Fix my legs and I'll find my boy. I'm interested in seeing how he's grown up without me— I'll probably have my work cut out for me setting him straight again."

Rothenberg offered his hand, but Iris did not shake it. She crossed her hands over her chest and looked down at him sternly.

"I understand that the Mayor once gave you a *similar* assignment regarding his own children," she said. "I do not intend to repeat his mistakes, Rothenberg, so be sure you do not repeat yours. I believe you may enjoy greater success with Cross, so long as you do not underestimate him."

Rothenberg laughed at that. "Girl, with Cross there *is* nothing to underestimate."

Iris moved, and suddenly Rothenberg felt an intense pain shoot through his body. He screamed as though every nerve in his body were on fire. Then it was over. Panting, he glared as Iris withdrew her staff and reattached it to her back.

"I am not the Mayor, Mr. Rothenberg," Iris said. "I have no patience for disrespect or incompetence. Should you demonstrate either again, I will dispose of you and move on to other options. Do remember that."

Iris nodded curtly at the mirror, and the door to the room slid open. Iris turned and left the room as medics entered to sedate him.

"You'd do well not to hinder them, Rothenberg," Iris called over her shoulder. "If something goes wrong with the anesthesia you might wake up during your surgery. Or perhaps not at all."

The door slid close again and Iris was gone from sight. Rothenberg twitched, but did not struggle as a needle was inserted into his forearm. He had no reason to believe that Iris was lying. He swore to repay her for this humiliation, but for now he was content to cooperate long enough to earn his freedom.

Rothenberg licked his lips as the chemical drowsiness took hold. For years he'd been an animal inside a cage, cut off from the outside world, with only the barest rumors of war reaching his ears. He'd heard of the Student Militia, but not that his son was part of it. So many things must have changed.

What was the world like now, beyond the confines of this wretched ward? Was it still ripe with opportunity, waiting for a determined individual like himself to make his mark? And had his son grown strong as the Iris woman had claimed—or was he still the meek and sniveling brat that Rothenberg remembered?

For four long years Rothenberg had yearned to walk the streets again, to know the answer to those questions. As unconsciousness took him, Rothenberg's last waking thought was that he would finally be able to see the truth for himself.

19

W ere it not for the barbed wire, Umasi thought that the facility would look rather unremarkable. There was a courtyard and a large brick building for classes. A dormitory was also located on the grounds. Of course the windows had bars over them, but so had many of the City's schools. Walls, too, were nothing new—though the concrete bulwark that separated the camp from the rest of the City was larger than any the Mayor had built.

And, of course, there was the barbed wire.

"It's mostly to deter escape attempts rather than to stop them," Iris explained, pointing with her staff. "The walls are tall and sheer enough to defeat any climber, but the wire looks intimidating. This way they'll give up before they begin."

Umasi nodded reluctantly. From their perch on top of one of the watchtowers, he and Iris were observing the first of the new "students" being moved in. The kids had all been provided with new uniforms—gray like the old ones. Most seemed resigned to their fate, but some looked defiant.

That defiance worried Umasi. He'd come to accept as a fact that the less trouble there was, the faster the City could return to something resembling normalcy.

"And if there are escape attempts?" Umasi said. "Or other disturbances?"

Iris shrugged. "We have methods to encourage compliance, special programs for difficult cases. Students will repeat their courses if they must."

"I don't believe half of those kids down there are actually subversive," Umasi remarked. "They don't all deserve this."

"And what if we let half of them go?" Iris asked. "How many hidden Truants will then be free to do mischief? We don't have the luxury of giving the benefit of the doubt. If we are serious about restoring order we have to be prepared to do whatever it takes."

Umasi frowned. Iris' words had reminded him of something else that he'd discovered that morning.

"On that note," Umasi said. "I had a chat with the District 1 Hospital Chief. I hear that you had a certain patient released a few days ago."

Iris closed her eyes. "I knew that couldn't stay secret for long. What of it?"

"You let him loose to hunt down his own son."

"I did."

Umasi drew in a sharp breath. "Iris—"

"You're about to tell me that I've done a foolish thing, that Rothenberg is an unstable and untrustworthy man, and that he could end up being as great a threat as those he's meant to neutralize," Iris said. "Am I correct?"

Umasi hesitated.

"Yes, I read the man's file," Iris continued. "He was born to a pair of teachers, both accused of abusing their students in violation of City regulations. Mayoral inquiries pushed them to commit suicide, leaving their son orphaned at the age of thirteen.

"He had a troubled record in school, including a series of altercations with other students. He graduated with mediocre grades and joined the Enforcers. After the end of his troubled marriage, he became known for extraordinary brutality on the job. Rothenberg maintained no known close relationships with anyone from that point on. The man is a true sociopath."

Umasi shook his head. "If you knew all that, then why did you do it?"

"Because I believe it will work," Iris said. "Cross is a dangerous wild card who lives for war—I know his kind, he *needs* it, and as leader of the Student Militia he might have the clout to get it. Rothenberg is uniquely suited to neutralize him, and if he succeeds then the method becomes irrelevant."

"But Rothenberg himself—"

"Has been defanged, of course," Iris said. "During his surgery I had a tracking device implanted under his skin. I also have a trusted officer keeping an eye on him. He's no threat to us."

Umasi frowned but said nothing.

"If he gets out of hand we'll rein him in," Iris promised. "I have no illusions about the man's character. I merely intend to use him towards a noble goal."

"And if he succeeds?" Umasi pressed. "What will you do with him then?"

"Lock him up again, of course." Iris looked genuinely surprised. "It wouldn't do to have someone like him running loose forever, would it?"

Umasi was deeply conflicted. The decisions Iris had made rubbed him the wrong way, and yet all of her words contained a certain ruthless logic.

A shrill cry from the camp rang out, followed by hysterical shouting. Umasi's eyes were not good enough to see who was making the noise, but it sounded like a young girl. He could make out the shapes of soldiers rushing towards the site, and moments later the crying ceased.

"It's an ugly business," Umasi said. "This whole thing is an ugly business. There has to be a better way than this."

"We just went over this, didn't we?" Iris said. "I like it no better than you, but think of it like this—we are making sure that they can go back to a functional society. We're *saving* these kids, Umasi."

"They don't see it that way."

"This isn't about perspective. There are hard truths that guide our actions." Iris gestured towards the City at large. "Days ago there was open warfare in these streets. After years of bloodshed we've brought peace to this City. Is that not an achievement worth protecting?"

Umasi sighed. "At times like these," he muttered, "I think I understand the dilemma the Mayor must have faced."

"The Mayor?" Iris repeated, a chill entering her voice. "I find it hard to believe that he was ever conflicted about anything. It always seemed to me that he was only interested in saving his own hide."

"You did not know him personally, Iris," Umasi said. "He had good intentions, and his philosophy was not much different than yours."

Iris considered that. "And perhaps yours as well?"

With only the barest hesitation, Umasi nodded.

"I'm glad that we are on the same wavelength," Iris said. "Incidentally, I have something to ask of you, Umasi."

Umasi turned to look at her. "Yes?"

"We've lifted the blockade and there are now Government transports regularly coming and going from this City," Iris said. "I would like you to board the next one this evening. I appreciate your assistance thus far, but there's no need for you to stay for this whole unpleasant process."

"That's kind of you, but I'll have to decline." Umasi looked down at the camp. "This is my City. This is where I belong."

"I had a feeling you would say that." Iris sighed. "But even if you're determined to get your hands dirty, I'm not sure there's a place for you here. You're not one of my soldiers, Umasi, and it's not within my power to pretend that you are."

"I know I don't fit in with your military," Umasi said. "Put me where I belong. Surely there's a civilian position that I can take."

Iris brushed her forehead with her knuckles. "That could be arranged, perhaps. . . . I'll have to give the idea some thought." She glanced at Umasi. "If you change your mind, the transports will always be ready for you."

"My mind is made up," Umasi said firmly. "It's not just because I love this City, you know."

"Oh?" Iris looked surprised.

Umasi lifted his sunglasses and looked at her. "It's also because you're the only family I have left."

For a moment Iris was rendered speechless, her tough façade melting away to reveal a sensitivity that Umasi had never seen before.

"I-I see," she stammered, struggling to regain her composure.

Umasi let his sunglasses fall back over his eyes as he turned to look out at the City once more.

So, he thought, *in the end even she feels lonely.*

"My hair is yellow," Zen said, patting his head. "Yours is red. Did you know that if you put them together you'd get orange?"

"I don't think there are any orange-haired people." Cross bit off the end of a granola bar.

"Why is that?"

Cross shrugged, passing the bar to Zen. "Maybe so we wouldn't mistake their heads for traffic cones."

"What if someone mistakes yours for an apple?" Zen took a bite.

"Then they'd probably think yours is a banana," Cross retorted.

Zen giggled—not too loudly, for they were outdoors. Cross cracked a smile himself. The two of them sat alone under a pedestrian bridge. The albino had gone on ahead to scout out their next path, as she always did before they moved, and in the meantime the boys were left to wait for her return.

Over the past four days they had slipped in and out of the subways, with painstaking stealth and patience, searching for any trace of the Truancy. So far they had found nothing. They would search at night, through back alleys and narrow streets, and return underground by sunrise. Then they would sleep, wake up late in the day, and train for a few hours before moving again.

Cross flexed his arm as Zen devoured the rest of the granola bar. He already felt faster and sharper, and his nameless tutor had provided a lot of good advice—about fighting, about survival, about the City and the Truancy. But perhaps even more important to Cross were the normal conversations he was now able to have with both the albino and her son.

"That was good." Zen licked his lips. "I wonder when Mom will be back."

"I'm sure she'll be back soon," Cross said. "She sometimes takes awhile."

Zen made a face. "Not *this* long."

Cross hesitated. The kid had a point, didn't he? It had to have been at least an hour since they last saw the albino. Cross began to feel a little uneasy—it normally didn't take more than twenty minutes to do her scouting. It was probably nothing . . . but if it *was* something . . . Cross shook his head. He didn't want to think about that.

He stood up.

"I'm going to go look for her real quick," Cross told Zen. "Stay right where you are, okay? Don't let anyone see you."

Zen made another face. "I know that."

Cross smiled, then turned and ran for the alley where they'd last seen the albino. It was probably nothing, he told himself again.

Fate was a funny thing, Aaron thought as he lugged the plastic garbage bag along. After all the victories he had contributed to, and after all his time spent as a respected veteran of the Truancy, he was back to taking out the trash.

"Oh well." He sighed to himself. "Could've been worse."

That much was true. When he turned up on their doorstep his parents had seemed more pleased to find him alive than anything else, and they'd asked no awkward questions so far. Things in the house had since settled into an old routine, though Aaron knew that everything left unsaid would have to come out sooner or later.

"Preferably later," he muttered to himself, navigating the maze of back alleys that concealed the entrance to his house.

He wasn't sure how they would take the news that he'd been behind nearly every major explosion the Truancy had ever set off. They were steadfast believers in education, though ever since the Government had replaced the Educators even they had developed doubts about the authorities.

News of the Mayor's resignation had been met with shock, and while everyone was glad that the fighting was over, no one knew what to think about the new Government. Aaron had been worried when he heard about the camps at first, but no Government soldiers had come to pick him up yet.

Reaching the mouth of the alley, Aaron opened a Dumpster and tossed the trash inside. Now that things had calmed down, garbage collections had started up again. Aaron reached for the lid.

"Your house is well hidden," a voice said. "Took me a few days to find it back there. Is that why the Government hasn't come calling yet?"

Aaron slammed the lid shut and spun around, heart pounding. The alley appeared empty, but he knew that voice and what its owner was capable of.

"Show yourself, Noni," he said. "Friends shouldn't be trying to scare each other."

In response, there came a cold chuckle that sent shivers up his spine.

"Friends?" Noni repeated. "I guess that's what we were, once, when we both served Zyid. But he's gone, Aaron. Gone. What's that make us now, I wonder?"

So the rumors were true. She's gone nuts. Aaron reached for his right pocket, where he kept a very special remote. His family would've had a fit if they'd known about his mines, but he now felt fully justified in planting them.

"What do you want, Noni?" Aaron asked with bated breath.

This time the voice was directly behind him. "Answers."

Aaron spun around, but Noni was too fast. The blow hit his solar plexus, knocking him backwards and leaving him short of breath. There was a black blur, and then his arm was being pinned painfully behind him, unable to reach the remote. Noni relieved him of the device, and then threw it against the wall, shattering it.

"Did you think I hadn't checked for traps before dealing with you?" Noni whispered in his ear as she pressed a kitchen knife to his throat. "I know you, Aaron, I watched you work for years. Didn't you notice little me in the workshop, hiding under the tables? The Truancy could never kill me . . . *if* the Truancy is my enemy. Are you my enemy, Aaron?"

Aaron gulped. This wasn't good; she was even crazier than he'd heard.

"Why would I be?" he said. "Listen to me Noni, you're not right in the head. Everyone misses Zyid, but—"

"*Do not speak his name!*" she hissed. "You don't deserve to. You're not worthy. He gave you everything, everything, and you—you *betrayed* him!"

"I—*what*? Noni, I didn't—"

"Then tell me!" She removed her knife and shoved, knocking Aaron to the ground. "Tell me where he is! Tell me where I can find Takan!"

Uh-oh, she's after the boss. Aaron rolled over and looked up at her, and then all thought fled his mind.

Noni's appearance had changed. In addition to her fully exposed scar, a number of smaller wounds now covered her face, the scabs giving her a truly fearsome appearance. Her clothes were bloody and torn in places— even her trademark scarf was ripped. There were dozens of knives strung from her belt. Her hair was no longer braided, and she'd made no effort to brush loose strands from her face.

It was as if a vision of madness itself stood before him.

Aaron's mind raced. Noni had clearly gone completely insane, and now was after Takan, their leader, the only hope of ever reestablishing the Truancy. If she killed him, it was all over. And even if she didn't, it would kill Takan to have to kill her. There was no way he could allow them to meet.

His thoughts were interrupted by a sharp kick to his ribs.

"Answer me!" Noni shouted, her voice deep and terrible. "If you do not answer me, I will hit you again, harder!"

"Then you'll have to keep going until you kill me," Aaron said. "Takan disappeared like the rest of the Truants. I don't know anything, and even if I did," he added with more bravado than he felt, "I wouldn't tell you."

Noni's pitiless blue eyes narrowed, and her next words were cold as ice. "I'll have to pay your family a visit before I believe that."

Aaron felt a surge of anger. "Don't you da—"

Noni kicked him in the face, and he toppled backwards.

"I'll get some answers out of you," she snarled, "one way or another."

Noni watched in satisfaction as Aaron twitched, unable to rise. He had never had much physical endurance—at some point during those long hours spent sequestered in the workshop, he had put on weight. Noni hauled the boy up by his collar and began dragging him farther into the alley.

Then a new voice spoke behind her.

"What's going on here?"

Without even a glance at the speaker, Noni threw one of her knives backwards. She knew her aim was true, but to her surprise there came no cry of pain. Instead, there was a sound of rustling metal, and Noni's blade clattered to the ground.

Noni released Aaron and drew two more knives, turning to face her challenger. Then she froze. It was a girl with impossiby white hair and skin. She had on a white shirt, blue jeans, and a worn-looking and unbuttoned Student Militia jacket.

A memory flashed into Noni's mind, of a bridge and a battle, stinging hail and a warm hug. The first time she'd ever had her hair braided.

"I know you," the girl said. "Your name is . . . Noni, isn't it?"

"That's right."

The girl looked sad. "So this is how you turned out," she murmured. "That's unfortunate. I'd hoped for better."

"Save the lecture," Noni snarled, the memory vanishing. "I remember you're pretty strong. Maybe strong enough to kill Zyid. Do you know anything about that?"

"I don't." The albino shook her head. "What happened to your face?"

Noni smiled coldly. A year ago she would have been ashamed of her scars, unwilling to discuss them or even allow them to be seen. Not anymore.

"I got the big scar when I was tortured by an Enforcer named Rothenberg—you probably know him, he was famous back then." Sure enough, the albino seemed startled by that. "The rest are recent. I got them while hunting down Zyid's killer."

"And is that him?" the albino asked, nodding at Aaron.

"No," Noni said. "He's just someone I need information from."

The albino looked her in the eye. "What are you going to do to—"

"That's none of your business," Noni interrupted. "I'm a lot stronger now, you know. Get out of here and stay out of my way if you know what's good for you."

The albino glanced at Aaron, then back at Noni.

"No," she said simply.

Noni thought about it for a moment. A fight would probably take a lot of time. Then again, it'd probably be faster than a debate. She shrugged, and without warning hurled one of her knives at the albino.

The pale girl sidestepped the projectile, and Noni drew another knife and ran straight for her opponent. Without room to swing her chain in the alley, the albino gripped the metal ring at the end like an iron knuckle and met Noni head-on. She deflected one knife with the ring, and blocked the second with the chain wrapped around her left arm. Then she kicked Noni, sending her staggering back a few steps.

Noni lunged again, keeping one knife behind her as she drove the other at the albino's neck. The albino ducked the first strike, and as the second knife came around she used her arm to block Noni's—then she rapped Noni on the forehead with the metal ring and leapt backwards.

Noni recovered quickly. Her opponent's elegant and defensive style gave her an idea. She charged again, but this time Noni twisted her shoulder forward and slammed into the albino with full force. They crashed to the ground together. Straddling her foe, Noni raised her knives for the kill.

"*Teacher!*"

Noni turned her head and saw a red-haired boy running down the alley towards them. Reflexively she threw a knife at him, and was surprised to see him deflect it with his own. Then he lunged, and Noni was forced to leap to her feet and out of the way. From the corner of her eye, Noni could see the albino rising, and then the boy was upon her.

Noni jumped backwards in time to avoid having her neck slit. She raised her own knife as the boy sized her up, his expression furious. The two of them began circling each other, each looking for an opening.

"Cross, don't interfere!" the albino was saying.

The boy frowned. "Sorry, teacher, that's an order I can't obey."

Then Noni growled as she realized something.

"Cross—leader of the Student Militia?" She turned to glare at the albino and her jacket. "So, you went over to *their* side."

But the albino did not reply. She looked distressed now, staring at Cross and Noni, her eyes flitting from one to the other. Then she spoke.

"He's Rothenberg's son, Noni."

Noni froze, nearly dropping her knife.

"What did you say?" she snarled, turning to look at Cross again.

"He's not like his father!" the albino said quickly. "He's as much a victim as you were—more so, even. Just think! Imagine how it must have been to grow up under that man."

Noni and Cross looked at each other again as though seeing each other for the first time. She could see his green eyes tracing her scar.

"Please, I can't stand watching you two fight," the albino pleaded. "That man tried to ruin both of your lives. Don't let him succeed, not like this!"

Noni hesitated. Then she lowered her knife, and Cross followed suit. She turned to face the albino.

"That boy, Umasi. You know him," Noni said. "Tell me where he is."

"I last saw him confronting the leader of the new Government in District 2," the albino replied. "I know nothing else."

"If you're lying—"

"I am not."

"Well, *if you are*, then I'll find you and kill you," Noni said stubbornly, then turned away. "It seems that only the Government has the answers I need."

With that she tucked her knife into her clothing once more and ran deeper into the alleyways. Behind her she could hear the boy's heavy breathing, and one word from the albino, softly spoken:

"Farewell."

Rothenberg took a step.

It was amazing how easy it was to take such a thing for granted, he thought. For four years he had been trapped inside that damned hospital, his prison. Now, finally, he had taken his first step outside that building and on the sidewalk. Rothenberg inhaled deeply, enjoying the zest of fresh night air. With a grunt of satisfaction, he glanced down at his legs and took another step.

With just one day of surgery, Iris' doctors had repaired his knees and legs. He spent a day recovering, and then a couple more in therapy. Throughout the whole painful, humiliating ordeal, Rothenberg had kept going with only one thought on his mind—getting back out onto the streets.

Now, though he was not yet able to run, and though his steps were slow and awkward, Rothenberg could finally walk again on his own feet. He insisted on being discharged as soon as possible, against the doctors' wishes. Iris approved it, and so here he was. A free man.

Rothenberg was pleased to find that a military car was already waiting for him in front of the hospital. A single soldier leaned against the hood.

"Evening, Mr. Rothenberg," the soldier said. "I'm Colonel Hines. General's orders; we'll be riding together during your search."

Rothenberg grinned. So, he had his own chauffeur—or was the man a spy, sent to keep tabs on him? It didn't matter really; Rothenberg knew what he had to do, and it made little difference if Iris knew how he was doing it.

"That's generous of the General," Rothenberg said. "Are there any limits to where you can go?"

"Parts of the City are still off-limits for safety," Hines replied. "Except for those, you name it and we'll see it."

Rothenberg turned to gaze out at the ruined cityscape. Once-great skyscrapers now loomed dead and lightless, shadows against a black sky. The evidence of war was everywhere.

"The City has changed a lot since I last saw it," Rothenberg said. "I think I'll begin my search somewhere familiar."

"Where's that?"

Rothenberg smiled. "Get me a map and I'll show you."

Colonel Hines reached into a compartment and produced a detailed map of the City. Rothenberg slammed a pudgy finger down onto a section of District 2.

"This is where your General said that she lost sight of my boy," Rothenberg said. "As you can see, there's an old train station right nearby."

Hines shook his head. "Even if he took that tunnel he could be anywhere in the City by now."

"Let me finish!" Rothenberg moved his finger. "That particular train line runs straight under here, District 18. That's where we used to live. If my son passed through that area I'll bet anything he stopped by. It's the first place I'd look to find his trail."

While all of that was true, Rothenberg had other reasons to want to return to his apartment. He had never particularly liked staying there before his imprisonment, but years on a stiff hospital cot made him miss his old bed.

Colonel Hines nodded and folded the map before sliding behind the wheel of the car. "Makes sense to me," he said. "There's a ton of debris and checkpoints blocking the road, so don't be surprised if we're not there by dawn."

With only a little discomfort in his legs, Rothenberg managed to climb into the passenger's seat. "I've been away for four years now," he muttered. "A day is nothing."

"We can layover in District 12," the Colonel said. "We'll be passing right through and they're building a big camp there, so it should be comfortable enough."

"Just get moving."

Colonel Hines shrugged and started the engine.

So, who was that girl, exactly?" Cross asked as he pulled the boy they'd rescued to his feet.

The albino paused in the middle of dusting her jacket off.

"An old acquaintance," she said. "She was a deeply troubled child when I met her four years ago. I pitied her."

The other boy spoke.

"That was Noni. She used to be one of our heroes—before she went crazy," he said, coughing. "I take it that you guys aren't Truants."

Now that the boy mentioned it, Cross did remember that Floe had told his team about Noni. Realizing that the boy must be a Truant, Cross felt both wary and excited. Even with the war over he wasn't sure if the Truancy considered him an enemy, but here was a chance for them to make contact.

"I'm Aaron, by the way. Thanks for the help." The Truant peered at the albino and her chain. "Hey, am I crazy, or are you the vagrant ghost?"

The albino smiled. "I haven't heard that term in a long time."

"So it *was* you," Aaron breathed. "I always thought that there must be a rational explanation—albinism, I take it?"

She nodded.

"Well, that just goes to show that stupidity and superstition go hand in hand," Aaron said. "Man, we owe Max an apology."

Cross was beginning to feel left out when Aaron finally turned to him.

"So, *you're* the leader of the Student Militia, eh?" he said, sounding amused. "I heard you guys went Truant on us. What happened?"

"The Government told us about the camps and we had a change of heart," Cross said. "Listen, we need to find Takan. We want to form an alliance. We want to take back our City."

"An alliance?" Aaron blinked. "With us? Are you for real?"

"Yes."

Aaron considered that, evaluating Cross. Then he shrugged.

"Well, you did just save my life. And I don't think you're lying—no offense, but we never pegged you as the cunning type." He grinned. "Noni is going after Takan too, for who knows what reason. All things considered, I'd rather you two find him first."

"So you *do* know where he is?"

Aaron shook his head.

"Sorry, I don't have any specifics. All I know is that he said he was going home."

Cross' jaw nearly dropped at that—*he* knew where Takan's home was. Takan had mentioned it in their duel.

"*. . . when I was still a student in District 20.*"

District 20! Cross turned to see the albino giving him a meaningful look, and he could tell that she remembered as well. Cross decided to keep his mouth shut about this revelation.

"Listen, I appreciate what you guys did for me and I'd love to stay and talk," Aaron said, "but I've been out here too long already. My parents are going to come looking, and that's going to mean awkward questions."

The albino nodded. "It's about time that we got going too," she said, then glanced at Cross. "Did you leave Zen behind?"

Cross nodded. "I thought it might be more dangerous to bring him along."

"You were probably right." She turned back to Aaron. "Thank you for your help."

"Hey, no problem," Aaron said. "Good luck, you two!"

Cross and his teacher watched as he left.

"Takan was going home. When you were running from him—"

"Yeah, he said that was in District 20."

"But *where* in District 20?"

"That's the problem; it's not exactly a small area."

"It's still easier to search a district than a whole city."

"Back to the subway, then?"

"Agreed."

20

OLD WOUNDS

This is it, Mr. Rothenberg—the District 12 Reeducation Camp. Get some rest now if you want it, won't be another chance until our destination."

Rothenberg let out an exaggerated yawn as he stepped out of the car and stretched. It felt good to be able to flex his legs again, even if they weren't strong enough to sprint anymore.

"This is it?" Rothenberg snorted as he stared out at the camp. "I think I might be better off napping on the sidewalk like a vagrant."

"You can do that too if you like."

Rothenberg did not bother to conceal his disappointment. The camp was clearly a work in progress. It was little more than a large parking lot surrounded by war-torn buildings, many of which had been demolished by the engineers at the site. The place was bristling with construction equipment, and there wasn't a student in sight.

"Why is it not done yet?" Rothenberg demanded. "Where am I supposed to get a proper meal and bed in this place? And where are all the prisoners?"

Colonel Hines leaned against the hood of the car.

"I didn't promise a luxury hotel, Rothenberg. This is gonna be one of our main camps, a regional headquarters," he said. "We're expanding it from one of the City's old prisons. The students are being kept there until we're done."

Rothenberg glared. "I hope you don't expect me to sleep in a jail cell after just getting released from that miserable hospital."

Hines grinned. "There are temporary facilities in the surrounding buildings. If those don't suit you, the sidewalk is right under your feet."

Tired and irritated, Rothenberg growled in frustration. The colonel seemed utterly unconcerned, and Rothenberg felt a sudden urge to be free of the man and his maddeningly indifferent attitude.

"Fine then," Rothenberg snapped. "Go make sure that bed and food is ready—I'm going to take a look around this place. Alone."

"Knock yourself out," Hines said. "But if you're going to be by yourself you're going to have to wear some body armor."

Hines gestured at a spare set inside the Jeep.

"I'm not going to wear that ridiculous thing," Rothenberg said. "I thought you people had this whole district locked down."

Hines folded his arms. "I don't make the rules."

Seeing that the soldier wasn't going to budge, Rothenberg grudgingly allowed the armor to be strapped onto him. Feeling stuffy and absurd, he turned to the colonel.

"It's all safe *now*, I suppose?" he asked, voice laden with sarcasm.

The soldier replied with a thumbs-up.

Scowling, Rothenberg turned and limped through the half-finished gates, trying to adjust to his awkward gait. Even now, despite his improved fortunes, the world seemed determined to deny him the fair treatment he had earned. All his life he had worked hard and suffered to do things right, so why was no one ever grateful for it? It wasn't right, he told himself. He deserved better.

Rothenberg spotted the main prison building. It seemed to have taken some damage during the conflict, and parts of it were still cracked. The Government had mounted a large crane on one of the upper levels to bring up materials for repairs, though no one was manning it at the moment.

Rothenberg found himself wondering what had become of the Truants now in captivity. Would they still be so unreasonable and disrespectful when locked behind bars? Curious, Rothenberg entered the prison, where he was waved in by soldiers who had apparently been told to expect him. Stumbling into a cell block, he found that it was constructed with three stories of cells with various levels of security.

Prior to the Truancy rebellion, the City hadn't had much need for prisons. This one, Rothenberg saw, hadn't changed much since he was with the Enforcers. What were new were the sounds, the young cries and wails of despair. The cells with bars instead of doors allowed the unfiltered noise to wash over Rothenberg, and he stood there for a moment, finding that it delighted him.

The imprisoned children would now have as hard and miserable a life as Rothenberg had endured in the hospital, day after day of monotony and humiliation, the boredom more crippling than any injuries. This struck Rothenberg as a small measure of justice, of balance. Finally, the Truancy would have a taste of what they had put him through.

Nearby prisoners shouted pleas or insults at Rothenberg. Rothenberg was tempted to torment them in return, but stopped. He spotted something odd through a door window on one of the higher floors. It was a dark shape, fleeting and hard to make out from a distance, but Rothenberg could tell immediately that it was the wrong size and dress for a soldier.

Intrigued, Rothenberg looked around for anything that could be used as a weapon. Spotting a two-handed construction hammer, he picked it up and began to hobble towards the door as fast as he could.

• • •

Teacher, I was wondering something."

"Yes?"

"Why do you refuse to kill?"

The albino smiled faintly. "So, you noticed."

Though Cross knew it was morning outside, it was eerily dark down here in the subway, the only light coming from a few flickering campfires. Cross, Zen, and the albino had reentered the underground as had been their habit—except now that they had a clear destination they could also use the tunnels to get closer to District 20.

They hadn't gotten far before they found an abandoned station that had long ago been sealed off from the surface. Other kids, other fugitives, had sought shelter here. They too had stopped to rest.

"I thought it was a coincidence until yesterday," Cross said, heating up a can of beans over their fire. "Noni was fighting to kill, but you weren't. That's why you lost, right?"

The albino merely nodded.

"Teacher, that's—"

"My choice," she interrupted gently. "It wasn't *just* a difference in intentions, actually. My chain is poorly suited for countering knives in a tight space."

Cross didn't let her change the subject. "You're really willing to be killed in a random fight?"

Her expression turned serious as she gazed into the fire.

"I think that if it ever came to the point where I had to murder, I would prefer to die myself," she said. "There's enough death in this City without me contributing to it."

Cross had no reply for that. It struck him in that moment how incredibly different the girl was from Edward, who had taught him to kill without question. He helped finish preparing their meal in silence. Soon they were wolfing down beans, beef jerky, and crackers. To Cross it felt like a feast after the stress and exertion of the previous night.

"Three crackers!" Zen said happily, stacking three of the crusty wafers together.

"Very good." The albino smiled, giving him one of hers. "Now how many do you have?"

"Four!"

Cross gave Zen three of his own. "And now?"

Zen looked at Cross slyly. "Seven."

"Smart kid."

Cross smiled in spite of himself as Zen abruptly munched down the crackers all at once. The boy had a purity, an innocence, a *freedom* that Cross had never enjoyed as a child. The effect was almost therapeutic.

But as Cross looked around, he was brought back to grim reality. The other fugitives on the platform were huddled around their own fires, ragged, desperate. From the conversations Cross could overhear, the prevailing opinion seemed to be that the Government's camps were actually execution grounds. Some spoke of terrifying nighttime raids on homes suspected of hiding students. A few even claimed that dissatisfaction was beginning to build among the adults of the City who resented the radical changes the new Government was proposing.

Most, however, just cried or stared listlessly off into space.

Cross felt an intense bitterness as he averted his gaze. It was as if the platform encapsulated the spirit of the entire City—broken. He scraped the bottom of his can.

"It's ironic," the albino said, "how things have come full circle for children in this City."

"What do you mean?" Cross asked.

"I've seen faces like these before." She gestured at the other fugitives. "Back when vagrants were common in the City. They were also hunted and shunned. They had the same look."

"I remember being scared of vagrants when I was a kid."

"As you should have been," the albino said. "They were desperate people . . . frustrated . . . violent . . ."

The sound of a scuffle, followed by crying interrupted her reminiscences. Cross turned his head. Three boys close to his age had cornered a younger girl on the platform. The terror on her face bothered him, bringing back memories of childhood. He glanced over at the albino.

"Do you think we should get involved?" he asked.

She frowned. With a gesture that Cross should remain seated, the albino stood up and walked over to the three boys.

"Excuse me," she said, "what's going on here?"

One of the boys, probably the leader, turned to look at her. Seeing her pale face he took a step back, then looked her up and down, repulsed by her appearance.

"What are you, some kind of freak?" he demanded.

Cross was instantly angered by that, but then remembered that he had once had a similar reaction himself. Feeling guilty, he kept his mouth shut and watched. The albino, for her part, seemed to be immune to such comments.

"What's going on here?" she repeated, more firmly this time.

The boy laughed. "You wanna know? Well, this girl here is trying to steal our food, isn't she?" He held up a can of soup. The other boys made noises of agreement.

The albino looked at the girl questioningly. She was scrawny and trembling, her clothes relatively clean—the look of someone who had not been out on the streets for long. The girl looked at the can and burst into tears.

"I-It's mine," she sobbed, turning to the albino with pleading eyes. "The Government kept r-raiding our h-house so my p-parents gave me f-food to flee."

"Yeah, well you dropped it, didn't you?" the leader of the boys said. "It's finder's keepers, isn't it? Trying to take it back from us is stealing!"

The albino looked sadly at the small can. Cross could guess what she was thinking; it was a stark sign of the times that such a thing was worth fighting over.

"I'll trade you for it," the albino told the boys. "I'll give you a bigger can."

The leader seemed to consider it. Then he smiled. "Deal."

The albino returned to the fireside. Trusting that she knew what she was doing, Cross reached into their pack and handed her the can. She brought it back to the boys and then held her hand out expectantly. The leader took the can. Then he shoved her, laughing.

"Looks like you dropped yours too, freak!" he mocked. "I guess we'll be keeping both, then."

The albino's face was unreadable. The boy laughed some more, and the scrawny girl began crying. He turned to aim a kick at her—

The albino's chain hissed like a snake, the blow so swift that even Cross couldn't see it. The weighted ring dangled from her arm as the boy collapsed, the cans rolling out of his limp hands.

Cross leapt to his feet, drawing his knife. The other boys took a step backwards, shocked, but looking like they were prepared to fight. The whole platform went silent; all eyes were on them. Tense moments passed. The boys looked at the albino, then at Cross. They finally seemed to understand that they were outmatched.

"C'mon," one of them muttered. "They're not worth it."

The two boys turned and left to sulk by their fire, not even bothering to drag their unconscious friend with them. The albino calmly picked up the cans, and then gave both of them to the girl, who was now staring at her with something that resembled hero-worship.

"You're not yet ready for this environment," the albino told her. "Be strong—and until you are, avoid gatherings like this if you can help it."

With that she returned to the fireside, and Cross understood from her posture that it was time to leave. Feeling a renewed admiration for his teacher, he began packing their bag. Heaving it over his shoulder, he followed the albino and Zen down onto the tracks as they resumed their march into the dark.

"We drew too much attention to ourselves," the albino said. "We'll walk to the next station and sleep somewhere more private."

"As you wish," Cross said. "You know, at this rate we can reach District 20 within a day."

She shook her head. "This line will only take us as far as District 18 before veering off in another direction. We're going to have to resurface."

District 18. Cross felt a sudden tightness in his chest, but then relaxed. He had nothing to fear from that place anymore.

"That's fine," he said. "The apartment where I used to live is in District 18. We can take shelter there, I still have the keys."

Noni gave one last look around for any soldiers that might be patrolling this part of the prison. Finding none, she entered the dark room and was pleased to find it empty. A number of computers and monitors were lying around—probably an administrative office. It appeared to be recently used. Perfect.

Her heart beating with excitement, Noni accessed a system. She knew that this was a risky move, but she was now after information that only the Government could provide. She had guessed, correctly, that because the camp was still under construction it might have some security gaps. The building had been adequately repaired on the inside, but most of the repairs were made to prevent escape, not entry.

Noni frowned as several monitors flickered to life, showing live feeds of prisoners in the cells. She tried to ignore the terror and hopelessness on their faces. On her way here she had seen some of the students in person. Their pleading and sobbing had stirred old sympathies inside her, which were quickly quashed—the prisoners had nothing to do with her objective, and there was nothing she could do for them anyway.

Noni drew up the rosters for the entire camp system. This was what she was looking for; data on prisoners that the Government had processed. She searched and found nothing on Takan, which was expected—she'd had faith that he'd evade capture. Then she found that there was nothing on Umasi either. *That* was a surprise. The albino had sworn he had confronted the Government's leader. If not captured, had he been killed, then? Surely he couldn't have won.

Noni slammed her fist on the desk. All her efforts were getting her no closer to the truth. Grunting in frustration, Noni switched the system off and then rose to leave. She had barely gotten three steps out of the room when a nearby door swung open. Bracing herself for a fight, Noni quickly drew two knives.

Then a man emerged from the door, and the knives dropped from her hands.

He had a red mustache, a massive frame, and a grin both predatory and cruel. He wore body armor and grasped an enormous hammer. There was no mistaking him. This was Rothenberg, the Enforcer, the terror of Noni's childhood.

The shock of recognition hit Noni like a physical blow. Ghostly pain from a phantom knife traced itself across her face. She trembled. This was nothing like meeting the albino again—this time Noni felt that she had stepped into an old nightmare.

"What have we here?" Rothenberg whispered. "A little rat running around."

With that, Noni realized it wasn't a nightmare. She really was standing before this monster again, so many years after he had terrorized her in an alley and left a mark she could never erase. She managed to choke out a single accusatory word.

"You."

Rothenberg looked surprised. "You know me, brat?"

Noni stared in disbelief. "You—you don't even remember?"

"Remember what, *kid*?"

Anger surged in Noni, erasing her shock.

"Four years ago you found me in an alley and gave me *this*!" she seethed, pointing at her scar. "You were going to kill me, until *he* sorted you out."

For a moment Rothenberg looked at her as though she was crazy. Then something seemed to click, and he remembered. Out of the sea of his countless victims, Rothenberg drew her out of the depths of his memory. And he laughed.

"The girl with the apple!" Rothenberg roared with delight. "Even more ragged and pathetic than before."

Noni drew a fresh knife.

"I am going to kill you."

"I don't think so." Rothenberg waved a finger. "Haven't you heard? The Mayor's brat is dead now. Who's going to help you this time?"

Noni exploded with rage, her vision clouded with fury. She lunged blindly with her knife and felt the impact of an unyielding surface. Then a heavy blow stuck her stomach. Noni was flung backwards. As her vision cleared she realized that Rothenberg had driven the hammer into her belly.

Rothenberg advanced upon her with slow, deliberate steps.

"You're just like all the other worthless Truants I've faced," he breathed. "You're pretending to be adults and you're in over your head. Children like you have no place in this City—I'm going to finish what I started and split your empty head open!"

Noni hurled a knife at him, but it bounced off his body armor. Rothenberg laughed. Noni dodged aside just in time as he slammed the hammer down. Drawing one of her few remaining knives, Noni lunged again, aiming for his throat. Rothenberg grabbed her by the arm and hurled her body down the hall.

Bruised from the fall, Noni scrambled to her feet. Rothenberg was advancing again, still with those slow, heavy steps. Breathing heavily, Noni looked around. She knew that she couldn't drag this fight out indoors with soldiers in the building. Spotting an unfinished window, she climbed out of it and onto the rooftop.

She gained some distance from the window and paused to catch her breath. A large crane was positioned nearby, its arm slanting downwards. Noni heard a thud behind her, and spun around to see that Rothenberg had followed her. His grinning visage renewed her anger.

Noni charged head-on, ducking as he swung his heavy hammer. Taking advantage of the opening, she leapt and slashed at his unprotected shoulder. She felt a surge of triumph as Rothenberg roared in pain and outrage. He dropped the hammer and punched her full on in the face. Noni staggered backwards, stunned.

Rothenberg took two heavy strides forward, then seized her and threw her off the edge of the roof.

There was a loopy feeling in her stomach as she fell. Noni reached out and grabbed the nearby crane. The abrupt stop felt like it would tear her arm off, but she did not let go. Slowly, she began to pull herself up.

Peering over the edge, Rothenberg scowled. As he looked at the crane, a twisted idea came to mind. He hobbled over to the cockpit and crawled inside. Turning the machine on, he jammed one of the control sticks as far to the right as he could.

Lying on top of the crane arm, Noni felt a tinge of fear as she realized she was moving. She braced herself and shut her eyes as the crane swung and crashed into a taller neighboring building. There was a terrible noise; bricks and glass fell all around her. It was like the whole world was collapsing.

Then Noni heard laughter, Rothenberg's laughter, and she remembered what had transpired in the alley all those years ago. She felt again the cool knife on her face. She remembered the years of pain and shame, the scars that had sent her down this self-destructive path in the first place. Feeling all fear evaporate, Noni burst from the debris and glass and began running full speed up the crane.

She could see Rothenberg's smiling face in the cockpit, and relished how his expression quickly turned to fear. Noni was dimly aware of other persons spilling out onto the roof, but none of that mattered now. Her one goal in that moment was to end the life of the man who had destroyed hers.

Noni dropped from the crane and ran for the cockpit, rewarded by Rothenberg falling out of his seat in his haste to escape. He was close now. He couldn't get away. Noni drew her last knife, preparing to drive it home—

Something slammed into her hard from behind. Noni was knocked to the ground, a heavy weight pinning her down. She had been tackled by a soldier.

"NOOOOOO!" she howled, realizing now that she would never reach her target.

More soldiers came, seizing her limbs, dragging her back. Rothenberg climbed to his feet and smiled. His face filled Noni's vision, and she struggled harder in vain.

"NOOOOO!" Her voice was anguished. "NOOOOOOO!"

Rothenberg laughed.

"I told you you're no better than the others!" he taunted. "Uglier perhaps, but you all go down the same!"

Furious tears flowing down her face, Noni made one last, vain attempt to reach the focus of her hatred. Through sheer force of will she nearly broke free, and the soldiers holding her had to redouble their efforts.

One of them struck her on the head with the butt of his rifle. Then Noni's world went black.

21
FULL CIRCLE

The next day, well-rested, Rothenberg leaned back in the car, enjoying the wind on his face. He was finally nearing the comfort of his home, which he had been assured was still standing, and the Government had granted his request to use it as his base of operations. The vehicle had been stocked with plenty of nonperishable supplies. Life was good.

"The General was really pleased. Don't see that very often," Colonel Hines said, steering around some fallen debris. "Turns out we've been looking for that Truant you caught yesterday."

"It was nothing, really," Rothenberg said. "She was hardly any trouble at all."

"Right." Hines smiled. "So, how's your shoulder doing?"

Rothenberg scowled. The cut hadn't been deep, but the medical treatment had brought back unpleasant memories of the hospital.

"Just a scratch," Rothenberg said. "It's not like a little girl could do me any real harm."

"Whatever you say." The colonel sounded amused. "I gotta admit, though, that was impressive—defending yourself with that clunky thing."

Rothenberg glanced at the large construction hammer that was propped up next to him. He had brought it along as memorabilia.

"It just takes strength," Rothenberg said. "For years I could only exercise my upper body. This thing feels like a toothpick in my hands."

"Even so, I'd carry a gun if I were hunting rebels."

"That's what you're here for, isn't it?" Rothenberg snorted. "Me, I've always preferred to feel things break when I hit them."

"I'll let you know the next time I need a jar opened."

Rothenberg laughed.

"You're spying on me for Iris, aren't you," Rothenberg said suddenly.

"Of course I am," Hines replied, not missing a beat. "Took you this long to figure that much out?"

"You are shameless."

Hines snorted. "You know, I read your file—"

"All lies the Mayor made up."

"—and you didn't like the last guy sent to spy on you either."

It took Rothenberg a minute to recall who Hines was talking about.

"Jack?" he said. "That man was a glorified clerk who never had the guts to get his hands dirty. I doubt anything ever made him happy other than writing reports."

"Guess the Mayor had a bit of honesty in him after all," Hines said. "By the way, we're here."

The car came to a halt, and Rothenberg lurched forward in his seat. There it was, the unassuming brownstone building that had been his home before his imprisonment, before unruly children had ruined his life.

"This entire neighborhood was vacated after the Truants took over," Hines said, getting out of the car. "You'll be alone while conducting your investigation. You have a radio, so let us know if there's any trouble."

"There won't be any." Rothenberg put his feet onto the pavement. "I have no intention of getting injured again just yet. I've had enough of maniacs in white coats trying to stick things in me."

Together Rothenberg and Hines moved all of the supplies from the car onto the doorstep of the building. Finished, the colonel climbed back into the car.

"You've got all day to see what you can find, Rothenberg. I'll be back to pick you up again tomorrow." He gave a salute. "Oh, and don't think that we're not keeping track of you when I'm not around—trust me, we are."

Rothenberg grunted as Hines drove off. He idly wondered if the man was bluffing. Either way it didn't matter; Rothenberg didn't expect his stay here to be eventful. He turned to look at the door to the building. It was a little older, a little more worn than he remembered.

Rothenberg reached into his pocket and fished out a set of keys. He smiled as he picked one out and slid it neatly into the lock. It had been too long since his last visit, and he was looking forward to finding out if Cross had finished the chores he'd been assigned all those years ago.

As the stars twinkled overhead, Cross and his two companions poked their heads out of a subway entrance deep within District 18. They had waited until night to make their move on the surface.

Finding the entire neighborhood blessedly unoccupied, the three of them made their way towards Cross' old home. They were heartened by the fact that District 20 was so close now—they could even see its buildings in the distance. Little Zen walked ahead of his mother, a skip in his step.

"The fastest path would be through District 19." Cross glanced in that direction. "But I've never been there before. It was sealed off when I was a kid."

"I've been in District 19," the albino said. "I know it pretty well, actually. If it's clear, I can probably get us through in less than a day."

"You seem very familiar with the City."

"When I was younger, fences and district borders were nothing," she said. "I could watch the Truancy sprout up around me. I even knew more about their founder than they did."

Cross blinked. "You mean Zyid?"

"That was not his original name, but yes."

"How could you possibly—"

"Edward probably knew a great deal of what I do," she said. "We had a mutual friend. He lived in District 19."

Cross now remembered more of what Takan had said during their duel in the dark. Umasi, that mysterious character he had never met, who had befriended so many extraordinary people, had also been Zyid's brother. And he had lived in District 19. It felt odd now to think of all the times Cross had passed the fence between Districts 18 and 19, never suspecting that anything interesting could lie on the other side. He wondered how his life might have been different if he had ever thought to climb over that fence.

Walking at a brisk pace they soon reached Cross' old neighborhood, still recognizable even with empty streets and vacant buildings. Cross felt a brief moment of nostalgia as he spotted a fire hydrant that he'd played with as a kid. There were still no soldiers around.

"They must not have enough soldiers to patrol every block of every district," the albino mused. "At this rate we really might reach District 20 soon."

Cross finally allowed himself to believe it. Their journey was almost over. It had only been a week since the Militia had disbanded, but to Cross it felt like a year on the run, a hunted man.

"What exactly should I do when I meet him?" Cross wondered. "We were enemies last time we met. He nearly killed me."

"Well, first things first—*relax*," the albino replied. "Keep your shoulders straight and hold your head high. Just be confident and speak from the heart, you're much more persuasive that way. You do want a free City, yes?"

"Of course I do," Cross said. "Maybe I didn't really believe that at first, but after meeting Noni and seeing those kids down in the subway . . . I know that things shouldn't be like that." Cross watched Zen skipping happily up the street. "Things don't *have* to be like that."

The albino was silent for a moment. "Well said," she said at last. "You've grown a lot in a short time. I'm proud of you."

Cross felt a twinge of embarrassment. He quickly changed the subject. "That's my house over there," he said, pointing at a plain-looking brownstone. "I was the only one who ever took care of it, so I'm sure it's filthy by now, but it's better than the subways."

The albino frowned. "Did your father ever do anything?"

Cross shook his head. "Just me. He was always out, doing work for the Enforcers. Whenever he did come home"—Cross grimaced as he recalled bruising pain—"it was like a monster breaking in."

"I was separated from my family when I was six," the albino said. "The Educators evaluated my 'condition' and decided I could never be a normal student. At that point I think my parents were glad to be rid of me."

Reaching the building, Cross glanced up at the door. It was a little older, a little more worn than he remembered.

"Did *you* ever consider going back home?" he asked. "After all that happened?"

She smiled. "It never crossed my mind."

Cross reached into his pocket and fished out a single key. With one final glance around to make sure that the street was empty, he slid the key into the lock. It still fit. Cross felt a moment of trepidation as he turned the knob, as though he were disturbing an old tomb haunted by its past.

The door creaked open, and they entered.

Iris and Umasi were having dinner in her office, their neat table surrounded by monitors and classified documents. It was an informal affair, but something they had taken to doing regularly. It gave them an opportunity to swap advice and discuss news of the City. For Umasi, it felt reminiscent of meals he used to have with the Mayor and Zen. Then, as now, he gave his sibling his undivided attention. Matters of great importance could be decided over a dinner table.

"The relief effort is finally underway, though not robustly as I'd hoped." Iris poured herself a glass of wine. "We've resumed commercial shipments, so goods are now flowing into District 1 and the surrounding area."

"So where does the problem lie?" Umasi asked.

"With nearly the rest of the entire City," Iris replied, taking a sip. "While the civilians around here are relatively feasting, the situation is desperate elsewhere. Many roads still need to be cleared, and to make matters worse, we only have one commercial harbor active right now."

"Perhaps supplies can be airlifted for distribution in the other districts?"

"That would be at best a temporary and expensive measure." Iris shook her head. "It might not even be possible. Protocol forbids civilians from working in an active war zone—which most of the City is still classified as. My soldiers can't carry out that kind of operation on their own."

Umasi poked at his main dish, pasta in some kind of clam sauce, thinking about the refugees and civilians starving in some forgotten corner of the City. He had known hunger himself when he'd lived among the vagrants. He knew the weakness, the desperation, the shame that came with it.

"Chin up," Iris said, seeing his face. "You needn't worry. Aside from that hiccup with the Student Militia, the camp program is proceeding on schedule. The results will open up the rest of the city to our relief effort."

Umasi shook his head. "A large number of renegades are still evading the camps. We're not making enough progress on that front."

Iris brushed her forehead with her knuckles.

"That is true, unfortunately," she admitted. "There are rumors circulating among the civilians. Parents are hiding their children. People don't believe that we won't seek retribution for slain soldiers."

"And they're wrong, of course."

"Of course," Iris said. "The only problem is getting them to believe it."

Umasi thought about that. Not too long ago even he had been convinced that Iris was his enemy, and that the Government could not be trusted. His experiences since then had convinced him otherwise, but how could they spread that understanding to the rest of the City? Umasi blinked. A possibility had just occurred to him.

"Allow me to explain the situation to them," Umasi told Iris. "I am known to the Truancy, among others in the City. I can be the public face of the program. If you can get me that civilian post we discussed—"

"That post isn't mine to give, Umasi," Iris interrupted. "And to be a spokesperson for the camps might be dangerous. From what you've told me, the Truants are stubborn. They might turn on you."

"That would be better than lounging around here, useless," Umasi said. "The kids in this City will never listen to an outsider. At the very least they will hear me out. Iris, there must be *something* I can do."

Iris sighed, setting her glass down. She took a moment to collect her thoughts.

"Very well," she said at last. "For now I can have you mediate for the squads that are conducting raids. It's not a very dangerous job. Just go in after the fact and explain everything to the children and their families." Iris smiled. "And while you're doing that, I'll try to pull some strings to get you the post you want."

Umasi smiled back, relieved to have something constructive to do. Iris finally seemed to understand how restless, how powerless he'd felt ever since the end of the conflict.

"Thank you," he said. "Can you pass the wine?"

Iris did, and the two drank a quick toast to new beginnings, then resumed eating. The food was quite good, prepared by a City chef in the kitchens of the Mayoral Mansion. It wasn't until they had turned to their dessert course, a chocolate soufflé, that Iris dropped another surprise on Umasi.

"By the way," she said, pointing her spoon at him, "it appears that the Rothenberg gamble has already started to yield results."

Umasi blinked.

"Surely he can't have already found—"

"No, not Cross. Not yet, anyway." Iris shook her head. "Yesterday by chance he helped apprehend a girl named Noni. That former Truant you were so worried about."

That was a surprise. Feeling a combination of shock, relief, and a little guilt, Umasi put down his napkin.

"Is she all right?" he asked.

"She did sustain some injures. She's being treated as we speak."

Umasi exhaled. "I would like to talk to her, as soon as she's well."

Iris shrugged, digging her spoon back into her soufflé. "That can be arranged."

"I appreciate it," Umasi said, turning his attention back to his meal. "So, where is Rothenberg now?"

"He had a hunch that his son might have passed through District 18." Iris glanced at her watch. "If his driver hasn't run into any delays, he should be in his old apartment right now."

Cross and the albino entered the old apartment first, with Zen right behind them. It was hard to see in the gloom, and they didn't dare to try the lights. Still, it was clear that the place was pretty dusty, the furniture left exactly as Cross remembered leaving it years ago.

"The bathroom is at the end of the hall," Cross said, pointing. "The kitchen is to the left. That's the living room to the right. My . . . father's room is over there, and my old room is next to it."

"I'm tired," Zen complained.

"Me too, love," the albino told him. "Why don't we go get cleaned up and then get some rest?"

"M'kay."

The albino nodded at Cross and led Zen off down the hall. Cross watched them go, taking in his surroundings. It was a strange feeling to step back into a place that was so familiar, frozen in time, filled with memories. Bad memories.

Cross shook his head. He had work to do. Slinging their bag over his shoulder, he entered the kitchen. Their supplies were still adequate, bolstered during their journey by anything they could rummage out of old stores or markets. Even so, he began opening drawers looking for anything he'd left behind that might be useful.

Cross collected some silverware, sharp knives, a corkscrew, and cooking utensils. Stuffing them into his bag, he opened a cupboard and found it full of canned goods. He paused. That wasn't right. It took him a moment to remember, but then he was sure. He hadn't used this cupboard for cans.

Cross seized a can and checked it—the date was recent.

A primal fear took root in the pit of his stomach. Cross noticed that the refrigerator had power. He flung it open. The light flickered on, revealing shelves stuffed with food and beer. His heart racing, it occurred to Cross that the kitchen was not as dusty as it should be.

Cross ran out of the kitchen. There was a noise in the hall. He turned to warn the albino.

"Teacher, I think we're in troub—"

Cross froze. A massive shadow stood in the hallway. It stepped forward, and Cross gasped. Rothenberg glowered back at him, a large hammer clutched in his hands.

You woke me up, boy," Rothenberg whispered. "You know that means a beating."

Rothenberg felt a twinge of disappointment as Cross stood dumbstruck before him. The boy's jaw was slack, his eyes wide with horror. After four years, it seemed that Cross hadn't grown up at all—could this spineless wimp really be his son? Rothenberg shoved Cross to the ground with one mighty push.

Cross looked up from the floor as Rothenberg towered over him, a familiar position for both of them. Rothenberg had thought that Cross might have already passed through the apartment, but he had never expected to actually catch him there.

His cleverness surprised even himself.

"This house is filthy, Cross!" Rothenberg roared. "Didn't I tell you to keep it neat while I was gone? Before I drag you back to the Government, I'm going to make you clean this whole mess!"

Rothenberg dropped the hammer. It fell with a thud beside Cross' head. Rothenberg seized him by the scruff of his neck, then slammed him against the wall. Cross seemed to be trying to babble out some sort of an apology, but Rothenberg was having none of it.

"I hear you've caused a lot of trouble, boy," Rothenberg said. "You're lucky it was me who found you—Iris would've had you skinned alive. You see how I'm always looking out for you, Cross? You'd better show some gratitude this time!"

Cross cringed, and Rothenberg laughed in delight. Things had gone better than he'd ever hoped. With this success he would earn the lasting thanks of the Government, and he would also be able to resume rearing Cross as he pleased, to correct whatever damage had been done while he was gone. It was almost too good to be true!

A metallic tinkling filled the air, and Rothenberg saw Cross' expression turn from alarm to relief.

Before Rothenberg could twitch, something metal struck him squarely on the side of the head. He saw stars, and with a shout of surprise released his grip. Cross slid down the wall. Rothenberg staggered back from the blow, but did not fall. He turned to see what had hit him, a scowl on his face.

Then Rothenberg's face went as pale as his attacker.

"It can't be," he whispered.

The ghost drew her chain back, a cold expression on her face, the same face that had haunted Rothenberg years ago. If there was anything positive to be said about his captivity, it was that he had been untroubled by this phantom. Remembering his encounters with her on the streets and in his dreams, Rothenberg began to shake. The ghost had finally come for him.

The ghost began twirling her chain again. Rothenberg let out a terrified roar, then seized his hammer from the floor, desperately charging down the hallway like a bull.

The ghost released the chain with casual ease, and the ring struck him square on the forehead. There was pain, stars, and then Rothenberg hit the floor.

The ghost advanced upon him, her chain tinkling as it swayed. Cross watched the encounter from a corner, a look of dumb shock on his face. Rothenberg scrambled to get back up, to flee, to somehow escape this spirit of vengeance.

"Stay back!" He pointed a trembling finger at the ghost. "You're not real!"

She halted in front of him, and Rothenberg felt as though he were shrinking before her.

"This isn't the first time we've met, is it?" the ghost said. "I know your face. You were so easy to scare off that I never even suspected that you were Rothenberg. I expected someone less cowardly."

Rothenberg stared. The ghost had never spoken before. Something clicked in his head, and for the first time Rothenberg dared to look closer at his attacker. It was the same figure, certainly, but older now, and dressed differently. Did ghosts age and change clothes? As the truth finally dawned on him, a slow smile spread across Rothenberg's face.

As if seeing the smile and knowing what it must mean, Cross slid his knife from his sheath and lunged. Rothenberg twisted to face the new threat.

"Cross, no!"

The girl's voice seemed to affect Cross like a dog whistle, and the boy froze, knife inches from Rothenberg's throat. Rothenberg looked down at the hand that held the blade. It was shaking. Pathetic.

Cross looked into his father's eyes, and Rothenberg glared back. There was only hatred and contempt between them.

Rothenberg sneered. "Do it, boy. If you have the guts."

Cross' hand twitched. The girl placed her hand on his shoulder.

"Don't listen to him, Cross," she said. "Don't become him. He wants you to do it. You're better than that. You're your own person."

Cross wavered, and for a moment appeared to entertain the idea of disobeying. Then he exhaled, and the tension in his muscles eased. The girl patted him on the shoulder, and Rothenberg let out a derisive snort.

As the girl began to bind Rothenberg's hands and feet with rope, Cross continued to hold the knife to his father's throat. Rothenberg did not struggle, but he was no longer frightened either. Understanding now that he had been deceived, he glared at the pale girl with muted anger.

"Should we gag him?" Cross asked once they were done.

The girl shook her head. "No need. There's no one around to hear him anyway."

"Then we should leave right now."

"I agree. We'll go straight through District 19, as fast as possible. Coming here was a mistake."

Rothenberg watched from the floor as the pair ransacked the house for anything useful. They emptied all of the canned goods from the cupboard, and took drinks from the refrigerator. They discovered Rothenberg's radio in the bedroom and took that as well. It was enough to fill another bag, and so they retrieved one of Cross' old school backpacks from a closet in his room.

Then, after fetching Zen from inside the locked bathroom, they headed for the door. Rothenberg grinned as Cross couldn't help but cast another glance at him.

"You better run, boy," he said. "You've crossed the line now. When I catch up to you, it's not going to end with the usual beating."

A dark look flitted across Cross' face, and he slammed his fist against the wall, denting it. Then he turned away and stormed out the door. The girl watched him go, then ushered Zen out the door. She paused for a moment.

Her eyes met Rothenberg's through the gloom.

"He was your *son*," she said finally. "How could you?"

"Don't run your mouth about what you don't understand," Rothenberg spat. "You'll regret making a fool of me, you paper-skinned freak."

For a moment it seemed as though the girl's eyes blazed even in the darkness. Rothenberg smiled at having provoked a human emotion from her. Making a small noise of disgust, the girl turned to leave.

"I don't know what you are, little monster!" Rothenberg called. "But now I know you're no ghost. That means you can die."

The girl did not turn around.

"There is a monster in this room," she said. "And it will still be here when I'm gone."

Then the door shut behind her, leaving Rothenberg alone in the darkness.

22
For Your Own Good

U masi peered through the glass viewing port and into the sterile ward. His attention was focused on a girl with black hair strapped down to a gurney. It was unmistakably Noni, her chest rising and falling in regular rhythm, though otherwise she was motionless.

"She's healthy enough to talk, then?" Umasi asked, turning to the doctor next to him.

The doctor nodded. "Her injuries weren't life threatening. She'll be fine."

Inside the ward, Noni began to stir, her mouth moving. If she was speaking, Umasi couldn't hear the words from out here.

"She looks delirious," he said.

"We've had to anesthetize her to keep her from struggling," the doctor explained. "I've never had such an uncooperative patient in my life. It was like trying to treat a tiger."

"But she can talk?" Umasi was dubious as Noni went still again.

"Oh, yeah. She might seem a *little* out of it, but at least she won't try to take a bite out of you. Though I would stay back anyway, just in case."

The doctor smiled wryly. Umasi wasn't amused—there was something sad about seeing such a fierce individual reduced to this. Still, it was probably for the best. With a sigh, he opened the door to the ward and stepped inside.

"Go away," Noni mumbled, not even opening her eyes.

Umasi ignored her and walked over to the side of her gurney. She was strapped down tight, the medical staff evidently having taken no chances that she might get loose. She looked different this way, dressed only in a white hospital gown, her shiny black hair splayed beneath her. With her eyes closed she looked almost peaceful.

"Noni," he said, "can you hear me?"

Noni seemed to spasm at the sound of his voice, straining against her bonds again. Slowly her eyes slid open, struggling to focus. Then she recognized him, and her eyes shut.

"I hate you."

Umasi had not expected those to be her first words. He watched as a single tear slid out from under her eyelids. Umasi struggled to understand how Noni must be feeling—defeated, humiliated, restrained in body and spirit by bindings and medication.

He steeled himself. This was going to be harder than he thought.

"Hate me or not, Noni, I need to talk to you," Umasi said. "I need you to understand why all of this is necessary."

Her face twitched. "You're with them. With the Government."

"Yes."

Noni began thrashing against her bonds so violently that Umasi took a step back. She screamed in frustration, and her icy blue eyes snapped open to glare accusingly at him.

"You lied!" she seethed. "It was you all along!"

There was pure loathing in that gaze, and Umasi felt his heart sink. She wasn't right in the head, he told himself. The drugs were confusing her on top of everything else.

"I did not kill Zyid, if that's what you're saying," Umasi said. "Noni, trust me, you would be happier if you could let go of the past."

Noni's eyes glazed over, and she slumped back down onto the gurney, exhausted.

"Release me, Umasi," she mumbled, "and I swear I'll give you a quick death."

"That strikes me as a poor trade," Umasi said. "Listen, Noni, this is for your own good. You have deeper problems than my brother's death, and we can help you—"

"I *will* kill you!" Noni's words were both a scream and a sob. "I'll kill *all of you*!"

"Noni, be reasonable—"

"I'll kill you!"

Umasi sighed and turned his back on her, leaving her to sob angrily on the gurney. He beckoned the doctor over.

"It seems I'm only making things worse," he said. "Treat her well. Make sure she recovers in full. If she calms down, reward her. Then send her off to one of the camps—put her in an intensive program, under extra security. I'm sure we can rehabilitate her."

"I'll kill you!" Noni screeched her new refrain. *"I'll kill you!"*

A soldier entered the room and walked up to Umasi, completely ignoring the wailing prisoner on the gurney.

"Sir, one of our teams is preparing to conduct a predawn raid nearby," he said. "It's a sensitive matter. One of the parents is an Enforcer. We want to handle this in a way that won't make the community any more upset. Your presence is requested."

"—*kill you, kill you, kill you, kill you, kill you—*"

"I'll come immediately," Umasi replied. "Let's not waste time."

"—KILL YOU! KILL YOU! KILL YOU!—"

The doctor rubbed his temple and reached for a radio. "All right, that's enough, let's get her sedated."

As Umasi slipped out of the ward behind the soldier, he was passed by two men and a nurse carrying a syringe. Noni screamed louder as they entered.

Then the door swung shut, and all was silent once again.

As the dawn broke, a depressed and exhausted trio found themselves slogging their way through District 19. Even the normally patient Zen had begun to grumble, and neither the albino nor Cross had the heart to tell him to be quiet—they had, after all, been on the move now for more than twelve hours straight. Both of them were just as tired as he was.

The sky was cloudless as the dawn light began spilling onto the streets, but it brought no joy for the travelers. The sun brought heat, and light meant that they were vulnerable, easy to spot. They hadn't encountered any soldiers yet, but all it would take was one to raise an alarm.

"They've been here." Cross gestured at the road. "The Government."

There were fresh vehicle tracks in the street. The crumbling buildings and unmaintained streets of District 19 had allowed a lot of dust to accumulate, and there hadn't been any rain recently. It was like walking through a desert.

"They must've done some scouting here," the albino said. "I don't think that they would set up a base after they realized no one lives here."

"Mom, I'm thirsty," Zen whined.

The albino reached into her pack and drew out a bottle of water. Zen drank eagerly. As they continued down the street, a warm wind kicked up dust, which mingled with the orange rays of the dawn.

The subject of Rothenberg had not come up since they'd left the apartment, and neither of them seemed to want to broach the subject. Still, his presence seemed to loom over them like a shadow. Cross wondered a lot of things—how Rothenberg got free, what his connection to Iris was, and most of all, how long their ropes would hold him.

Somehow he did not regret leaving the man alive. In the moment when he had held the knife to his father's throat, he thought that he could see his own face staring back at him. The albino had been right after all.

Following the nameless girl, Cross turned a corner and went down a new street. Halfway down the block, she paused for a moment, looking at a certain spot.

"What's wrong?" Cross asked.

She shook her head. "Nothing. It's just . . . there used to be a lemonade stand here. I miss it."

Cross didn't know what to make of that strange pronouncement, and so he kept his mouth shut as they resumed moving. It didn't take them long to reach the fence bordering District 20. Exhausted, Cross and Zen slumped against it. The albino rested her hands on her knees, her breath coming in small pants. Cross realized with some guilt that for the whole journey she had been working the hardest.

"District 20 is on the other side," Cross said, craning his neck up so he could see the top of the fence. "Any ideas where we can take refuge?"

The albino shook her head. "Not unless we stay here in District 19."

"Look for cover here, then?"

"That would seem to be our best option."

The albino straightened up, but Cross could see by the droop of her eyes that she was as tired as he felt. Little Zen was now sitting down, his back against the fence, eyes shut. Suddenly the albino tensed and she spun around, the first to detect a stranger standing silhouetted against the rising sun.

What now? Cross wondered.

A vaguely familiar voice addressed them.

"You've been searching for a long time. May I ask what you're looking for?"

Cross blinked as his eyes adjusted to the light. He hoped this was not a dream. Framed by the sun's rays, Takan stood in the middle of the street, hands inside his brown trench coat. The leader of the Truancy nodded at them.

"Yeah, we've been looking for *you*." Cross smiled back. "You bastard—how long were you watching us?"

"I caught sight of you awhile ago from a rooftop," Takan said. "It was a bit careless of you to be out in the open like that, you know."

"And were you just waiting there in case we came along?"

"'Course not." Takan scratched the back of his head. "I've been coming here a lot recently. It gives me a good view of the area, and I kind of hoped that I might run into Umasi. Fond memories." The boy spared a glance back in the direction the lemonade stand had once stood.

"It's a pleasure to see you again, Four." The albino curtseyed. "It wasn't easy to find you."

Takan smiled at her. "I'd love to hear how you did, actually."

"There will be time for that later, I'm sure."

"Indeed. It's good to see that you're well, Two." Takan glanced at Zen, who was now awake and hugging his mother's leg. "You and . . ."

"My son, Zen."

Takan blinked. "Zen? As in—"

"We've been traveling a long time without rest," the albino said, cutting him off. "Do you know of any place we can stay?"

Cross thought that something unsaid passed between them in that moment. Whatever it was, it was gone in an instant. Takan made a bow.

"Of course, where are my manners?" he said. "Come on, I'll show you the way to my house. It's easy to dodge the soldiers in District 20—they have predictable patrol routes, you'll see."

Cross was sharp enough to tell that Umasi's two disciples had kept something from him, but he wasn't sharp enough to know what. At any rate he was too tired to care. He helped boost Zen over the fence. Immense relief spread through his body. The darkness, and Rothenberg, felt a long way behind.

Floe rolled over on the bed, looking up through the small window that offered a glimpse of the faintly lightening night sky. Next to her, Sepp pulled on his pants. They were alone in the small bedroom they shared inside Sepp's house. Floe smiled in contentment. Then she glanced at Sepp. He seemed distracted—funny, considering what they'd just finished doing.

Floe sighed. "Okay, what's wrong?"

"Nothing!" Sepp said quickly. Too quickly.

"Men." Floe snorted. "Why do you always save the regrets for afterwards?"

"Why do you think? Hey—no, that was a joke!" Sepp held his hands up in surrender as Floe raised her fist. "Floe, seriously, this was the best night of my life."

Floe sighed again, this time vexed at herself, and let her arm drop back down onto the bed.

"Something's bothering you," she insisted. "Spit it out."

Sepp frowned and began buttoning his pants.

"It's nothing to do with you," he said. Floe made a small noise of disbelief. "No really, it's not! I was just thinking about . . . well, Cross."

Floe raised her eyebrows. "Don't tell me you were cheating on him with me."

Sepp laughed. "No, definitely not. I was just wondering—everyone in the Militia was wondering, really—what exactly is the relationship between you two?"

Floe closed her eyes. She'd expected that question to come up sooner or later. She just hadn't expected it to be this soon.

"He was a childhood friend."

Sepp glanced at her. "*Just* a friend?"

"Okay, and maybe a mutual crush too," Floe admitted. "But it never got further than that, Sepp. I didn't see him for many years, until we met again in battle."

Understanding dawned. "You were still a Truant then?"

Floe nodded.

"That's the reason you defected, isn't it?"

Floe nodded again.

Sepp whistled. "Sheesh, now I really feel guilty."

Floe rolled her eyes and threw her pillow at him.

"Sepp, you're *too* much of a nice guy sometimes," she said. "The Cross we know is not the same kid I used to like—a lot changed in the years we were apart. Anyway, I'm attracted to you, we're here together, so why deny ourselves anything?"

Floe shifted underneath the covers. Sepp looked at her, all other distractions forgotten, and bent down for a kiss. Floe let her eyes flutter shut. The kiss was soft and undemanding, an almost teasing pressure that set her heart racing. She could feel the warmth from his bare chest. In that moment Floe felt that things were perfect, she would have liked nothing more than it to endure forever.

Then she heard the front door crash in. Loud footsteps stormed into the house. Sepp and Floe sprang apart, and as the door to their room burst open they realized that their safety had been a lie all along.

With one last jerk of his teeth, the thin ropes binding Rothenberg's hands finally fell away. Rothenberg spit some stray fibers from his mouth, took a deep shuddering breath, and then began untying the ropes binding his legs. With his hands bound behind him it had taken him hours to get loose—he had pressed his knees to his chest, then painfully worked his arms under his backside and legs until he had them in front of him.

Loose once more, Rothenberg staggered to his feet. Far from tiring him out, his struggle for freedom had only made him more determined to make good on his word. Seeing Cross with his own eyes had given him new life. Rothenberg went for the door only to find that the kids had jammed it shut. Chest heaving, he glanced around. His hammer lay nearby.

Picking it up, Rothenberg charged at the door to the apartment. With a single swing the old and brittle wood of the door gave way. Staggering through the hole he'd made, Rothenberg stepped over the splinters and down the stairs. Without even testing the knob, he smashed open the front door. Rothenberg relished the shock traveling down his arm.

Rothenberg stepped outside into the morning light, blinking as his eyes adjusted. There was no sign of Colonel Hines. Rothenberg staggered down the street. Ever since he was a child he had relied on no one but himself—he had no intention of waiting for help now.

Rothenberg urged his legs to move faster. A madness had taken hold of him, lending him unnatural energy. Rothenberg had endured many indignities as a child, as he knew all children of the City were meant to, but he was an adult now. He had earned respect, and he was determined to have it from his own son, if no one else.

"District 19, eh?" he muttered as he stormed down the street. "You'll never learn, boy. You shouldn't have talked about your plans in front of me. I'm coming, Cross, I'm coming!"

Rothenberg reached the fence that divided Districts 18 and 19. His legs useless for climbing, Rothenberg swung his hammer instead. The impact smashed a few boards loose, and Rothenberg swung three more times until the gap was big enough for him to slip through.

Stepping into District 19, Rothenberg paused to catch his breath. He grimaced in disgust. The whole district seemed to be full of dust and litter and other muck from the ruins. He looked down and saw that his boots left prints in the dust.

A thought occurred to him. Could those kids possibly have been so careless?

Rothenberg glanced all around him. Then he spotted it, only a block down—a faint but distinct trail of footprints leading deeper into the district. Rothenberg grinned in triumph.

"I've got you now, boy."

Like a hound on the scent, Rothenberg hobbled towards the trail as fast as he could. This was not the first time a trail had led him into District 19. Rothenberg had a memory of prints in snow, leading him to a lemonade stand and terror. Those were events from a lifetime ago, when he still believed in ghosts.

Rothenberg grimaced as he began to follow the tracks. This time would be different. The nature of all his enemies had been laid bare to him, and now there would be nothing to get between him and his wayward son.

23
FATHERS AND SONS

ross took his place at the dining table. A bowl of canned soup sat steaming before him, alongside toasted bread and a protein bar.

"About as good a lunch as can be found in the City these days," Jack—Takan's father—said as he ladled soup into his own bowl. "I'm glad you lot were willing to share your supplies. I only receive government rations for one person, and it's pretty nasty stuff."

Takan smiled in agreement, taking a bite out of his protein bar. The Truancy's leader was sitting straight across from Cross, dressed in a plain shirt, his trench coat draped over his chair. He looked so ordinary now, Cross didn't know what to make of it. He'd always known Takan as a ruthless warrior and tactician. Finding out that he was actually on speaking terms with his father had been a bit of a shock.

Cross began eating. He felt refreshed after a comfortable nap in a guest room. He had to admit that Takan had so far been a friendly host, but there was obvious tension in the air. Takan didn't quite trust him yet, either, hand never straying too far from his sword.

The albino was a different story—she and Takan got along famously. After some banter about their respective pasts, she related the purpose of their journey, and Takan seemed receptive to the idea of a united resistance.

"Actually, my father and I were already thinking about ways to start up a new resistance," Takan said. "The camps were the last straw for us, as they were for the Student Militia." He nodded at Cross.

"How easily do you think you can rally the Truants again?" Cross asked.

"It can probably be done very quickly, on a small scale," Takan replied. "We've had to be very careful, but my father tells me that the Government can't monitor all communications all the time. When the phones went back up I started to form an informal network of sorts, like what I understand Zyid did in the early days of the Truancy." He looked at Cross. "What about you? Can you gather up the Militia?"

Cross kept chewing to stall for time. He actually hadn't thought about that. Over the past week his attention had been fixed on survival and their destination. Cross felt the albino's eyes on him. He swallowed.

"The Militia was forced to scatter very quickly. There was no time to collect contact info," Cross admitted. "But that doesn't mean we can't be useful. There are students all over the City now, in the general population and in the camps. If they're motivated, they can cause all sorts of trouble while we work to reach them."

Takan thought about that. He turned to Jack. "The idea has merit."

"I agree." Jack nodded. "A straight fight would never work against the government's equipment and resources. However, a guerrilla war might have great success. There are fifty-seven districts in the City covering an enormous area, with millions of people. There are only twenty thousand soldiers under Iris' command. That's a drop in an ocean."

Cross saw a problem with this.

"The Militia at its peak only had around ten thousand members ready to fight at any one time," he said. "I'm not sure what the Truancy had, exactly—"

"Our numbers were similar," Takan said.

"—but that's still not enough to kick the Government out. The weapons they have are far beyond us, and even if our casualties are one for one, we'll all be wiped out in the end."

Jack shook his head. "You're thinking in terms of the old conflict, Cross. This can be different."

Cross blinked. Takan also looked puzzled. The albino looked on impassively.

"Can you explain that?" Cross asked.

"This isn't just a matter of freedom for students anymore, Cross," Jack said. "I've been hearing that a lot of adults are starting to protest the Government's occupation and policies—they don't trust change, and they increasingly view Iris and her regime as alien and unwelcome. This presents you with an extraordinary opportunity."

Cross and Takan looked at each other. Neither of them had considered the idea that adults might back their side. The albino said nothing, but stood up as if satisfied. She quietly excused herself from the table.

"Look, I've kept Tack here hidden for this long, and it's not been easy with supplies being what they are," Jack said. "But now that Cross is here, he provides a missing piece. Together the two of you can call for united resistance throughout the City. Once it starts, I guarantee it will snowball from there."

"Where should we start, though?" Cross asked. "The Government has control of all the broadcasts. Ever since Zyid infiltrated Penance Tower they moved those controls to City Hall."

"You won't need the broadcasts," Jack said. "Start from the bottom up. Head into the deep City, to the districts where people are the hungriest and most disaffected. You will find only allies there."

Takan nodded, and Cross began to feel a sense of elation. They had a real plan now, one that stood a chance of working. A united City, Truants and students fighting alongside each other, no longer seemed like an abstract concept.

"When should we leave?" Takan asked. "There's no point to staying here for long. I can call for some Truants from the deep City to meet us."

"How about this evening, right before sundown?" Cross suggested. "The sooner the better. The Government is looking for us both."

Takan nodded in agreement, then turned to Jack. Father and son looked at each other.

"You don't plan to come, do you dad?"

Jack smiled. "Sharp as always, my Tack. No, I'll be more useful to you here. I can stay behind and spy on the Government—they still believe me to be one of their loyal agents in the population."

"You were a Government agent?" Cross blurted.

Jack nodded. "For many years my job was to keep tabs on the Mayor. You could even say that it was one of my reports that brought Iris to this City."

Takan looked away, an unreadable expression on his face. Cross frowned.

"What made you change sides?" he asked.

"My son," Jack said simply. "When he returned from the dead, came back to me, I realized what I'd done in my grief. Now I'm trying to undo it." He sighed and looked down at his plate. "Being trusted by the Government has its uses. I still get occasional briefings, and I'm friendly with the local garrison. Before you leave I can provide you with all sorts of information about troop deployment, camp locations, things like that."

Cross sat in silence, trying to absorb all of that. Despite Jack's shocking admission, what had surprised him most of all was that he had so readily turned on the Government for his son's sake. Rothenberg would have thrown him to the wolves without hesitation.

Cross was so caught up in his thoughts that he barely noticed it when the albino emerged with Zen, placed a hand on his shoulder, and whispered a single word into his ear.

"Good-bye."

Cross distractedly waved a hand in farewell. A moment later, the front door slammed shut. Cross noticed that both Takan and Jack were looking at him curiously. Then he realized what had just happened.

"Excuse me," he said, jumping to his feet.

Cross ran out the door and found the albino walking leisurely down the empty street, hand in hand with Zen.

"Wait!" Cross called.

They paused, then turned around, looking at Cross expectantly.

"Where are you going?" Cross demanded. "Were you going to leave just like that? I thought you wanted to see the City free!"

"That's a lot of questions at once." The albino smiled, a warm breeze rustling her white hair. "We're going off to find somewhere we can settle down again. Zen and I enjoyed meeting you, but there's a war coming now, and that is something we cannot follow you into."

Zen nodded vigorously at that. Cross felt a lump in his throat. This was too sudden. In the time that they'd been together Cross had come to rely on the albino's strength, her wisdom, her presence. He had begun to take those things for granted.

Cross swallowed. "But the City's freedom—"

"Has a chance now," the albino said. "We've given it that chance."

"I'm still your student, there's still a lot I can learn that might be useful!"

"You're now well equipped to learn those lessons yourself." She smiled. "I told you Cross, that you would be my student as long as our journey lasted. Well, now it's over. Go forth and do as you will."

This was it. She was really leaving. Cross felt a pain he'd only ever felt once before—the pain of parting with someone dear. Cross found himself blinking away tears. The albino stepped forward and wrapped him in an embrace that was gentle and familiar, but this time it had a touch of finality.

"Thank you," Cross said. "For everything. You were a lot of things I'd never had before; a guardian, a mentor, a friend . . ."

"What about me?" Zen complained.

Cross laughed, then withdrew and hugged Zen too.

"You're a good kid," Cross said. "You can have the life I never could. I'm going to fight so everyone can have that life."

Zen looked at Cross seriously—with Cross kneeling they were almost the same height—and nodded. "Someday I'll fight too."

The albino looked a little sad at that, but said nothing. She took Zen's hand, gave one last glance at Cross, and turned to leave. Cross watched them go until they turned a corner and vanished from sight. Then he returned to the house. There were still plans to be made.

Iris stepped into the apartment and found a lot of commotion packed into the tiny space. Soldiers were still going over every inch of it, checking for hidden compartments, loose floorboards, or anywhere else that a teenager might be hidden. They had only expected to find one fugitive here—the discovery of a second warranted a thorough search. Iris returned the soldiers' salutes as she passed them by, heading straight for a door that was slightly ajar.

Inside the bedroom, things were much calmer. There was only one boy, dressed in black, sitting on the floor against the wall. His broken ceramic sword was propped upright as he loosely held it by the handle. He had his sunglasses off, Iris realized. She wasn't used to seeing his eyes, even when they were closed, as they were now.

"Congratulations, Umasi."

Umasi raised a lazy hand in greeting. "Good evening to you too."

Iris smiled. "I heard you helped resolve a little problem."

"There were two fugitives in this room," he said. "The boy got the girl out the window. I happened to be outside. Incapacitated her before she got too far."

Iris glanced around the room. The only window was indeed open. Various, seemingly random articles of clothing littered the floor. The bed was clearly ruffled, the sheets scattered.

"Were you interrupting anything, perchance?" she asked.

"Apparently."

"How did they take it?"

"Not well." Umasi shook his head. "They didn't like being separated. The girl calmed down after I explained they weren't going to be killed. The boy was inconsolable when he heard about his parents."

"What about the parents?"

Umasi shrugged. "They'll face a court-martial, obviously. I did my best to reassure them about their son. I think they believed me, for the most part. They're being questioned right now."

He looked tired. It was the lack of sunglasses, Iris thought. Without them he somehow seemed smaller, more human. The regret on his face was easy to read.

"You did a great job, Umasi," Iris said gently. "You should be proud."

Umasi smiled wryly. "Did you come all the way down here just to try to make me feel better?"

Iris shook her head, though she suspected her next words would do exactly that.

"No," she said. "I came because I managed to get you an official position. The one you wanted."

Umasi's eyes snapped open, and he stared up at her in surprise.

"When does it go into effect?"

"Technically, it's already done," Iris said. "If you'd like, I can announce it right now."

Umasi shook his head.

"That should be saved for a more formal occasion," he said. "We need to take our time to make sure it has the maximum impact. Ideally, we might placate some of the angry citizens."

Iris nodded. She had been thinking the same thing herself. The protests from the adult citizenry were becoming an increasing concern as the reeducation program entered full swing.

A soldier entered the room and saluted Iris.

"General, HQ has an urgent message for you," the man said. "It's about Rothenberg."

Iris frowned. Out of the corner of her eye she could see Umasi tense up.

"What is it?" she demanded.

"Colonel Hines arrived at the apartment as scheduled today. He found the front door broken down," the soldier explained. "The apartment looks like it was ransacked. Rothenberg is missing."

Iris brushed her forehead with her knuckles.

"What about the tracking device?"

"We've already checked. It says that he's currently in District 20 and still moving."

Umasi jerked in surprise. He stood up.

"Iris, let me investigate this," he said. "I'll find him."

"Umasi, with the tracking device it'll be child's play to—"

"This is about more than just Rothenberg himself," Umasi insisted, sheathing his sword. "This might be a coincidence, or it might be very important. Please trust me when I say that I need to get to District 20 as soon as possible."

Iris hesitated. "Are you rested enough? You've had quite a day. First the hospital visit, then the raid, now this."

"I've had busier days before."

Iris nodded. She turned to the soldier.

"Get him a helicopter. Take him wherever he wants to go."

As the sky dimmed and the sun began to go down, Takan and Cross stood out on the street, ready to bid a final farewell to Jack. Both of them carried bags stuffed with food and equipment and precious documents. It occurred to Cross that he had only just gotten to know the albino and her son before trading them in for a new companion—one that he knew almost nothing about. Cross was also worried about meeting the Truants that Takan had summoned to join them at the edge of District 20.

Takan, however, seemed to have all of his attention focused on his father. The two bid each other good-bye, promising to see each other again. Cross felt awkward and entirely left out as the two hugged.

His discomfort didn't last long. Soon enough, Takan and Cross were walking together down the street, sticking to the growing shadows whenever they could. The Truancy's leader had his trench coat on again, and Cross could catch glimpses of his sheathed sword at his side. Cross ignored the contrast he made dressed in plain street clothes, armed with just a knife.

Neither of them seemed to be able to think of anything to say, unlike the albino, with whom conversation had come easily. Tired of the heavy silence, Cross decided to break it.

"So, how did you get involved in the Truancy in the first place?"

Takan glanced at Cross. "Revenge," he said simply. "My sister was killed in a crossfire between an Enforcer and a Truant."

"So you joined up so you could fight the Enforcers."

"Something like that."

Takan's expression was blank and utterly unreadable.

Cross grunted. "Floe mentioned you had some secrets in your past."

"Floe?"

Cross felt a fresh pain from somewhere. It took him a few moments to realize that he missed her.

"A girl in my squad," Cross explained. "She was a Truant before she joined us."

"I see." Takan pursed his lips. "Oh, right, I think I remember someone by that name. We thought we lost her in a battle, later heard from our spies that she'd switched sides. So, she ended up in your squad?"

"Yeah," Cross said. "She told us a lot about you."

"Did she?" Takan sounded amused. "What did she say?"

Cross hesitated—was it really a good idea to confront him about this now? Deciding that if they were going to work together he would have to know, Cross plunged head-on.

"She said you killed your predecessor, Zyid."

Silence. Then laughter.

"Well, that rumor did get around." Takan tilted his head down so that his face was cast into shadow. "It's true."

Cross stopped in his tracks. "Takan, why—"

But Takan had stopped as well, suddenly tense. For a moment Cross thought that the Truant was going to attack him. Then he too noticed the dark shape that had staggered its way into the street in front of them. The shape of a massive man with a hammer.

Heart pounding, Cross drew his knife with a shaking hand. Rothenberg roared his challenge.

"I'VE FOUND YOU, BOY!"

Takan winced and glanced at Cross. "Friend of yours?"

Cross grimaced but did not reply. Why did this have to happen now, in front of Takan? Just seeing Rothenberg and hearing his voice evoked childhood terrors. No matter how hard he tried to concentrate his instincts told him to cower and flee.

Takan stared at Cross, then at Rothenberg, and seemed to understand. He lay a hand on Cross' shoulder.

"I can handle this, Cross," Takan said. "Why don't you go on ahead? Get to the rendezvous point. I'll catch up in a bit."

Cross twitched. "But—"

"I can tell that this isn't an enemy you want to fight," Takan said sharply. "Don't worry, I won't take long."

Cross hesitated. Rothenberg roared again and began approaching with heavy steps. In an instant Cross was reminded of the tantrum he had thrown in the auditorium back in District 2. He cringed at the resemblance.

Something clicked then, and Cross turned to flee down a different street. Rothenberg made to follow, but Takan placed himself in the way, drawing his sword, ready to fight.

"Stop!"

Takan and Rothenberg turned to see who had yelled. It was a grown man with brown hair and a mustache, clutching a metal pole from a broken street sign.

"Dad?" Takan blurted. "What are you doing here?"

"I heard this animal all the way from the house and came running," Jack said, gripping the pole tighter. "Keep going, Tack. I'll take care of this."

"I can handle it, dad."

"You don't understand." Jack shook his head. "Look at his body armor. If he's equipped like that, it means the Government is tracking him. They won't be far behind."

Takan glanced at Rothenberg's gear, suddenly indecisive. Rothenberg, for his part, glared at Jack.

"Jack!" he snarled. "I never thought I'd run into you again—and you're this brat's father? A pair of weaklings and failures. I'm going to enjoy killing you both."

Jack ignored him.

"I'm sorry, Tack," he said in a pained voice. "This whole thing is my fault. If only I'd told you the truth . . . if I'd never come to this damned City . . ."

Takan shook his head. "No dad, it's just as much my fault."

"I've suffered your death once already; that was quite enough," Jack said. "Go after Cross. I can afford to be found by the Government. You two can't."

"He'll kill you!" Takan protested.

"I said run! That's an ord—" Jack shook his head. "Tack . . . please. Go. I'm begging you."

Takan wavered for a moment, glanced again at Rothenberg and his Government equipment, then nodded.

"I love you, dad."

"I love you too, Tack. Always did."

With that, Takan sheathed his sword and ran after Cross. Rothenberg growled in frustration as he made to follow, only to find his path blocked again, this time by Jack. Rothenberg glowered.

"Very sweet of you, Jack," he snarled, "but it'll only buy them a minute."

Jack raised his pole. "That'll be enough. Your legs don't seem to be in great shape."

"You know, I always thought that you were an insufferable paper pusher, an example of everything wrong with this City's bureaucracy." Rothenberg spat. "I've wanted to do this for a long time."

"*I* always thought you were an animal." Jack shook his head. "I know your history—you're here to hunt down your own son, aren't you?"

"I'm here to get my son *back,* you dolt. Why are you throwing yours away instead of raising him properly?"

"You're sick," Jack said disgustedly. "You're a sick man. What was it you told me a few years back? That you were beaten as a child?"

Jack realized then that something had changed since they were colleagues. Rather than falling silent as he had before, Rothenberg's face broke into a wide grin.

"My parents did discipline me," Rothenberg said. "They made me strong, strong enough to survive by myself. I overcame every obstacle and clawed my way up to a position of power—I *earned* that power. It's not right that children should be treated so soft these days! IT'S NOT RIGHT!"

"The hospital's made you truly crazy," Jack said. "When the Government finds out how insane you are they'll put you back there for good."

"When the Government finds you," Rothenberg countered, "the only place they'll put you is the morgue."

Rothenberg lunged with surprising force. Jack, who had never had any combat training or experience in his life, jabbed the pole at his enemy. It was like trying to stop an elephant with a toothpick. Rothenberg swatted the pole aside, then slammed his hammer into Jack's chest.

Jack fell backwards onto the ground, coughing.

"Any last words?" Rothenberg spat, raising his weapon.

Jack smiled as the hammer loomed above him. "In spite of all your efforts and all your strength, both of our sons are still free."

Rothenberg scowled. "Not for long. I promise you that."

Then he brought the hammer crashing down.

24

THE NEW MAYOR

Obeita entered the classroom and looked around. The floor was of gray linoleum, the walls painted a sickly green, and the lighting was fluorescent and dull. There were no windows. Her students sat silently at their desks, subdued by the soul-crushing atmosphere and the presence of a soldier at the door. Everything was perfect.

Obeita walked slowly to her desk, letting the students stew in fear, as was proper. She sat down, the chair creaking under her weight. Over her years of service to the Educators she had built a reputation for being able to break tough students. The Government appreciated that record, and so had offered her this job.

"Good evening, class," she said. "My name is Ms. Obeita. From now on, I will be your teacher. As this is our first meeting, let me explain why you are here. This is a class for especially delinquent children. A class for chronic misbehavers, rebels, *Truants*"—she nearly spat that last word—"and the like."

Indeed some of the students, dressed in their gray uniforms, glared at her from the desks to which they had all been handcuffed. Obeita smiled back. They would be broken soon enough.

"Now, as this is just an introduction, we only have time to go over the ground rules," Obeita said. "There will, of course, be no speaking out of turn, no communication at all between students. If any one of you breaks a rule, a punishment will be administered to the entire class. All work must be completed within the allotted time; if it is not, then the entire class will repeat the exercise."

Obeita could see eyes flicking to the soldier and then back. They were students, yes, but also prisoners. None of them seemed willing to provoke her wrath. Obeita smiled and then pointed at a blank board on one wall.

"That board," she announced, "will be your new purpose in life. All students will be ranked up there so the whole class can know who is to blame for the loss of their recess. The top five students will be exempt from all group punishments. The positions, of course, can change at any time.

"You will be rewarded for timely completion of work, your grades; for exposing the bad behavior of your peers, you will earn extra points, and an exemption from the group's punishment."

Obeita smiled at the looks on their faces. They knew what she was doing, and they also knew that they couldn't do anything to stop her. Before long she would have them all hating one another, eager to compete for her favor.

"Finally," Obeita paused for dramatic effect, "You may have noticed that you all have a small device attached to your ankles. It will deliver a small shock as an immediate punishment should any of you misbehave. You are all considered high-risk students, so the shock has, of course, been set unusually high. Now . . ." Obeita stood up and surveyed the class. "Are there any questions before we adjourn?"

One girl with stunning blue eyes and raven hair stood up. Obeita read the name tag clipped to her gray uniform, and smiled. "Yes, Noni?"

"How would you like your guts fed to you after I rip them from your fat, ugly corpse?" Noni asked. "I'm thinking of dicing them before—"

The girl was interrupted as her ankle bracelet came to life. Noni jerked in place for a moment, but Obeita was disappointed to see that she did not scream or fall as expected.

"—before I stuff them down your throat," Noni finished through gritted teeth.

Obeita smiled at Noni, then nodded at the soldier. This time Noni did scream, a cry of pain ripping itself from her throat as the shock sent her crashing to the floor. She began cursing wildly at Obeita, trying to lunge at her, though the handcuff held fast.

Obeita looked at the soldier. "Again."

The other students stared in horrified fascination as Noni began shrieking again, writhing in agony. The soldier would stop, allow Noni to catch her breath, then resume the shocks. Finally, exhausted, Noni slumped silently in her chair.

Obeita walked over to Noni's seat and stood over the defeated girl.

"Now dear," she said, stroking Noni's cheek, "if you don't learn to behave, this will be just the first day of the rest of your life."

Cross kicked off the ground and watched the world whoosh by. He felt a fluttering in his stomach that he hadn't known since childhood. Then, with a creak the swing swung forward, and Cross shut his eyes against the wind.

He was waiting at the rendezvous point, a playground in District 20's Grand Park. Takan was taking longer than Cross had expected, and he was concerned that the Truancy's leader might have underestimated Rothenberg. As the swing came to a rest, Cross remained still, thinking of how poor a start the day had been for their alliance. He'd let secrets come between him and his new ally, and that ally had ended up fighting his father for him.

Cross got to his feet. Just about the only thing that had gone right was getting here. Martial law was in effect throughout the district, and most people were off the streets—certainly none could be found in this part of the Grand Park. It was only upon arrival that Cross had realized that he'd been to this very playground in his childhood. He'd had fun here.

As Cross' mind dwelled on Rothenberg, other more unpleasant memories threatened to surface. He suppressed them, stretching his legs. If Takan couldn't finish off Rothenberg, Cross swore to handle it himself the next time they met, no matter what.

There came a sound of footsteps behind him. Cross tensed, then realized that the steps were not heavy or slow enough to be Rothenberg's. He turned around and saw Takan running towards him, looking almost frantic.

"Takan, what—"

Takan shook his head vigorously and raised a finger to his lips. He seized Cross by the shoulder and dived for a nearby tube tunnel for small kids to crawl in. There was barely enough room to accommodate the teenagers as they hid inside. Irritated, Cross bent his head backwards to glare at the Truant leader.

"Takan, what the hell is going on?"

"You knew that man who attacked us, right?" Takan whispered. "Well he's also working for the Government. My dad stayed behind to buy us time."

"So everything is all right then, isn't it?"

Takan shook his head. "Listen."

Cross fell silent and strained his ears. Coming from somewhere above was the faint drone of a helicopter. Cross glanced at Takan.

"Did it see you?" he demanded.

Takan hesitated. "It *might* have."

The two teenagers waited in silence for many minutes. The air in the tube grew hot and stuffy, and the position Cross had been cramped into quickly became uncomfortable. Shifting around in the small tube, Cross shut his eyes and tried not to think about the Government agents above— there was simply nothing he could do in this situation. The helicopter seemed to grow very loud at one point, and Takan and Cross held their breaths.

Slowly the noise of the helicopter faded away. Cross and Takan waited a few more minutes to be sure, then looked at each other. Nodding, they crawled out into the open. Cross bent over, resting his hands on his knees as he gasped for fresh air. He looked up. The skies seemed to be clear.

"I think it's gone," Cross said.

"Yeah," Takan agreed. "We're still a little early, so give it a little time before our contacts get here. I don't want to risk a call with so much attention in the area."

Cross nodded. Then there was a loud squeak of metal behind them, and both Takan and Cross reached for their weapons. Cross spun around and was surprised to find that the newcomer was an unfamiliar boy in his late teens. His skin had a yellow tinge, and he was dressed all in black, with a matching windbreaker buttoned around his neck like a cape. The boy's hair was dark and shiny, but unkempt, as though it had been neglected for some months.

The stranger carried two sheathed swords, one on either side, and his eyes were concealed by black sunglasses. It was impossible to discern any emotion on that face. Something about the way he moved, the stiff sort of determination in his steps, made Cross very uneasy. This boy, whoever he was, was trouble.

Cross drew his knife, but felt Takan's hand seize his wrist.

"Umasi!" Takan sounded relieved. "It's great to see you again. I was hoping to run into you. You have perfect timing."

"You know this guy?"

"Yeah, Cross, you've heard of him too," Takan said. "Come to think of it, all three of us are here in one place, that's something. Cross, this is Umasi, my former mentor. Umasi, this is Cross, he's the—"

"Former leader of the Student Militia." Umasi's voice was smooth. "His reputation precedes him."

Cross felt a growing sense of unease. Takan was right, Umasi did have perfect timing—*too* perfect. What were the odds that he would appear here right after the Government helicopter departed? And the albino had said it was Umasi who had thrown himself in front of Iris, hadn't she?

Takan still didn't seem to suspect anything, talking animatedly with his mentor. Cross looked again at Umasi. The boy's body was tense, his expression unreadable.

Cross yanked his knife hand free from Takan's grip. Both Umasi and Takan turned to look at him.

"How did you get here?" Cross demanded, glaring at Umasi. "How did you find us?"

Umasi cocked his head. "I got a lift."

"From the Government?"

"Yes," Umasi said calmly, turning to a stunned Takan. "Incidentally, that's what I'm here to talk to you about. General Iris is my half-sister, and it turns out that she's willing to negotiate. She has made a guarantee that no students will be killed. I believe it would be best if we all accepted the offer."

"Your family sounds more screwed up than mine," Cross said. "I've heard a lot about you, Umasi, but I don't know you. I don't trust you."

"Cross, this is my mentor," Takan protested. "I've known him for years, he's a good person."

"I knew you'd be reasonable, Tack." Umasi smiled. "It's time for us to unite and concentrate on recovery. There is nothing to achieve by further struggle against the Government."

Takan shook his head. "That's not true, Umasi! Cross and I are forming a united resistance, we're going to the deep City to rally students and Truants and adults alike to fight the Government! With your help—"

"No."

The utterance seemed to shock Takan. There was a ringing silence, and Cross knew immediately that Takan had made a mistake.

"No, I can't approve of that, my friend," Umasi continued. "The more trouble there is in the deep City, the harder it will be for the Government to help the people there."

"The Government will help them by putting them in camps," Cross said disgustedly. "They don't really care about citizens."

"The people don't *want* the Government's help," Takan agreed. "They want the right to live and die with their dignity. Umasi, we can't accept outsiders just coming in and taking everything over."

Umasi straightened to his full height, and Cross now saw in him the figure that had so impressed Edward, Takan, and the albino.

"You won't have to accept outsiders, Tack. The Government has even appointed a new Mayor. Civilian leadership is returning to this City." Umasi spread his arms. "You two can be part of that leadership. Join us."

"A new Mayor?" Takan blinked. "Umasi, you *know* what that office stands for! This is the same thing all over again! The new Mayor will be just like the last one!"

"Oh, I doubt that."

Cross frowned. "How can you know for sure?"

For the first time, Umasi smiled. The growing unease that Cross had felt abruptly reached its zenith.

"Because," Umasi said, "I *am* the new Mayor."

The silence was absolute. It was as though even the wind had died. Cross felt his body numb with fear as he realized how much trouble they were in. He could think of nothing to say. Cross glanced over at Takan, who looked thunderstruck.

"What—what are you doing, Umasi?" Takan blurted. "How could you betray us like this?"

"Betray you?" Umasi shook his head. "My loyalty has always been to peace, the preservation of life. This City is now my responsibility. I'll do what I must to protect it."

Takan shivered. "This can't be happening."

"Tack, I don't want to kill you," Umasi said. "Don't make me kill you. Give up."

For a moment Cross was worried that Takan would do just that. Then the Truant seemed to steel himself. His ceramic sword came out of its sheath.

"I'm *not* surrendering to the Government."

Umasi sighed. "Very well. If eliminating you two means averting another war and saving thousands . . . then there is no choice."

The new Mayor reached for his weapons. He gripped a ceramic blade tightly in each hand, sizing up his two opponents. Then he attacked.

"Put us down over there!" Iris shouted over the din of the rotor blades.

The pilot complied, and Iris held on as the helicopter descended. The evening air blew cool in her wavy hair, but Iris felt only a warm anger as they touched down near a group of soldiers. Wasting no time, Iris hopped out and walked over to the soldiers, who quickly parted for her.

In their midst sat a disgruntled looking Rothenberg, a bloody hammer at his feet.

"You," Rothenberg said, making a face as Iris approached.

"Me," Iris agreed.

"How did you find me?"

Iris folded her arms. "Mr. Rothenberg, we've been following your movements ever since your surgery. You have a tracking device implanted in you that will allow us to locate you anywhere, at any time."

Rothenberg's face reddened, though he kept himself in check. Good, Iris thought. She was in no mood for his attitude.

"What did you think you were doing, Mr. Rothenberg?" Iris demanded.

Rothenberg glowered. "I was chasing down my son like you wanted, until your soldiers decided to get in my way. What's the meaning of this? I thought we had a deal!"

"Umasi has sent word that he is now in pursuit of your son and another one of our targets," Iris said. "We're sending him backup as we speak."

Rothenberg glowered. "Then get out of my way, and let me join them!"

Iris' eyes narrowed. Before Rothenberg could react, the staff was extended and had already struck him on the head. The massive man toppled to the ground. Iris pressed the staff to his neck. Rothenberg screamed as electricity set his nerves on fire.

Iris lifted her finger from the button. "I told you I had no patience for disrespect or incompetence, Mr. Rothenberg. You have demonstrated both today."

Rothenberg wheezed, his cheeks puffing up like a fish's gills as he gasped for air. "I found my son, I—"

"Let him escape," Iris said icily. "What's more, you managed to kill a Government agent in the process. Unforgivable."

Rothenberg glared. "Jack? He was sheltering the kids! He was helping them!"

"Then he would have made a valuable prisoner," Iris said, "and your failure is even more inexcusable."

Rothenberg went very still as he seethed, staring up at her. Iris merely regarded him as if he were a mess on the sidewalk. Suddenly the man lunged at her, hands outstretched—

Thwak!

Iris' staff caught him in the temple, and Rothenberg crumpled to the ground, unconscious. Disgusted, Iris turned and began walking back to her helicopter.

"Take him into custody," she told the soldiers. "Lock him up again."

Cross ducked as one of Umasi's blades passed over his head, then tried to thrust his knife forward. The attack was parried by Umasi's shorter blade and Cross was forced to leap back to avoid a counterthrust from the longer one. Cross gritted his teeth in frustration. Umasi's style of using the broken blade for defense and the longer one for attack was very effective against his knife.

Cross and Umasi were fighting next to the swings that Cross had played on as a child. From the left Cross could see Takan running to help—he'd been knocked to the ground for a few precious seconds. Before the Truant could get close, Umasi kicked the swing next to him. The swing flew up and struck Takan in the face, knocking him back painfully.

"This isn't you, Umasi!" Takan shouted, clutching his face.

"You've never *really* known me, Tack," Umasi replied. "I always kept you at a distance because of Edward's betrayal."

"You're no better than him!" Cross snarled. "You're just like Edward!"

"Look who's talking—the killer who enjoys it." Umasi lunged at Cross with both swords. "It was I who put Edward down. Did you know that Cross?"

Cross parried one blade and twisted to avoid the other. Umasi followed up with more attacks, so fast and ferocious that Cross had no chance to strike back. The knowledge that he was facing down Edward's killer conflicted him; he had no love for his old master, but anyone who could beat Edward was out of Cross' league.

"Yes, it was me," Umasi said. "I killed him in the belief that doing so would end the violence."

Umasi surged forward, his blades nearly invisible as they cleaved the air. Before such an onslaught Cross had no choice but to turn and run.

"But now I see where I was mistaken!" Umasi continued as he gave chase. "It is impossible to kill once for peace and then wipe your hands clean—the struggle for peace is endless, it is a constant. There is always a new threat!"

Cross chanced a glance backwards. Umasi was still pursuing him, with Takan hurrying to catch up to them from behind.

"I destroyed Edward and you rose in his place, Cross," Umasi called. "Now you too must be put down."

Cross ignored him, looking determinedly forward. He spotted a simple metal carousel. Seized with inspiration, Cross leapt onto it, his momentum causing it to spin. Umasi did not follow suit, but stopped short of the spinning disc. That gave Takan enough time to catch up, and Umasi spun around to cross swords with his former pupil.

As Umasi and Takan exchanged sword strikes, the carousel made a full revolution and Cross came within striking distance. He lashed out with his knife, but without looking Umasi ducked the attack, then kicked backwards with his foot. The blow struck the carousel, causing it to spin even more rapidly, and Cross was thrown off balance.

Umasi thrust his broken sword, surprising Takan, who parried it. He then attacked with his longer blade, and Takan was just barely able to block it. This left him wide open, and Umasi kicked him in the chest, causing Takan to stagger back several paces. Seizing the opportunity, Umasi spun around and met Cross as he came swinging by again.

Umasi's attack sliced Cross' shirt, nearly cutting him open. Cross flinched and drew back, and Umasi jumped onto the carousel, moving to finish the job. Then Takan was there, grabbing a firm hold of the carousel. The sudden stop caused both Umasi and Cross to lurch forward—Umasi landing on his feet, Cross landing on the ground.

Cross scrambled to stand as he saw Umasi come straight for him, clearly considering him to be the weaker link. Cross turned and ran again, this time climbing up a nearby playground tower. The tower was connected to another by a shaky bridge, with a slide at the top. Umasi declined to give Cross the high ground, instead climbing up the connected tower and running across the bridge.

Cross was waiting for him. In a familiar routine he ducked the first sword, parried the second, then punched Umasi in the belly. Umasi staggered backwards into the center of the bridge, just as Takan came from behind. Takan's two-handed swing was so powerful that it knocked Umasi's long sword from his grip. For a moment Cross thought they had won. Then, with all three of them on the bridge, Umasi jumped.

The bridge began shaking as though it were made of jelly. Takan and Cross were caught by surprise, and Umasi was able to slash Takan across the collarbone with his short blade, missing his neck but drawing blood. Takan let out a yelp, and Umasi followed up by kicking him down.

By now Cross had regained his footing and lunged. Umasi greeted him with a punch to the face, knocking Cross back. He advanced on Cross, short blade raised. Glancing at the injured Takan, Cross backed up off the bridge and onto the small platform of the tower. As if he were waiting for this all along, Umasi promptly hurled his remaining sword at Cross.

Acting on instinct, Cross leaped backwards as the pointless sword bounced off his chest. His feet did not land on a flat surface. The next thing he knew he was falling backwards down the slide, headfirst, until he came to a disoriented rest at the bottom. Now unarmed, Umasi turned around to face a recovered Takan. His former pupil glared at him, shirt stained with blood.

"You once told me," Takan said, "that violence would only lead to chaos and destruction. You told me you wouldn't tip the scales!"

"I told you that our best hope for change would be to *become* the Educators!" Umasi countered. "It's no longer an idealistic hope, Tack! It's happening now!"

"In the worst way!"

Takan lunged with a powerful downwards slash. Umasi simply sidestepped it, then seized Takan by the collar and waist. At the bottom, Cross was now on his feet again. Umasi hurled Takan down the slide just as Cross began to run up it. Takan and Cross collided, tumbling to the ground in a tangled heap.

Thoroughly battered and worn, Takan and Cross struggled to extricate themselves from each other and get to their feet. Meanwhile, Umasi quickly retrieved both of his blades, and then slid down after them. They were able to jump out of the way just in time. Side by side, breathing heavily, Takan and Cross faced their enemy.

"You can't win, Mr. Mayor," Cross spat. "We have allies on the way."

"That's fair," Umasi said. "I do as well."

Then they noticed it—black dots against the blue sky. More helicopters heading fast towards their position. Cross felt a sinking feeling in his stomach. There was no way they could possibly fight off the soldiers that were surely on their way. Sensing their defeat, Umasi turned to address Takan.

"Tack, you're making a mistake. I've always looked out for you," Umasi said earnestly. "I've even taken care of Noni for you."

Takan looked uncertain. "What did you do?"

"I kept your secret. I protected you from her," Umasi replied. "She's now safely in our care, undergoing reeducation in one of our camps."

Takan clenched his fists. "Damn you."

"Wouldn't you like to see her again?" Umasi said softly. "Explain to her what you did and why? Tell her about your dear sister? Rebuild your relationship?"

Takan went silent. Cross thought he could hear the helicopters now in the distance. He had no idea what relationship existed between Takan and the scarred girl he'd met in that alley, but whatever it was appeared to be enough to make the Truant pause. Then Takan leaned towards Cross.

"Hey," he whispered. "Give me your knife."

"*What?*"

"Just do it!"

Cross thought about it. Then he lightly tossed the knife to Takan. Takan caught it by the handle, then threw it. Umasi did not seem to expect this. The projectile struck the new Mayor in the leg, and he let out a cry of pain.

Takan and Cross ran for it, making for the playground exit. They opened the gate and dashed through it. Takan lit a firebomb from his pack, then set it down before running again. A few moments later, flames engulfed the gate.

Umasi limped after them, but then a gunshot rang out. Cross' heart soared as he saw teenagers in street clothes with guns appear from the trees. Their escorts had arrived at last. For a moment Umasi seemed to stare at them all through the gate, the flames reflected in his black sunglasses. Then he turned and vanished behind the rising smoke.

As the drone of helicopters grew louder, Cross and Takan and the Truants all fled. All Cross could think about was the fact that it had been two against one, and they'd still barely escaped—Umasi was surely the most dangerous foe he'd ever encountered, worthy of his reputation. As he ran, Cross glanced at Takan. The Truant still seemed to be in shock.

"Are you all right?" Cross asked.

Takan shook his head.

"I can't believe he's our enemy," he said. "I just can't believe it."

● ● ●

The albino lay down on the sofa and sighed, wrapping her coat snugly around her. Traveling under daylight hadn't been easy. To avoid Government patrols, she and Zen had been forced to pass through neighborhoods still populated with civilians. Martial law kept most people indoors, and while she knew many eyes watched them from behind curtained windows, no one had been bold enough to say anything.

They were now safely resting in the lobby of an abandoned building in District 22. The albino guessed it had once been a residence, or perhaps a cheap hotel. Either way it was clear no one had used it for a while—the entire area had once been the scene of a battle between the Enforcers and the Truancy, and evidence of the conflict was everywhere.

Zen was happily playing with bricks from a wall that had a gaping hole blown through it. He banged them together, stacked them up, and then knocked them down, adding sound effects as his imagination reenacted a battle.

Suddenly Zen went quiet, his bricks forgotten on the floor. The albino sat up, knowing that meant he had a question on his mind.

"Mom," Zen said, looking at her. "Will Cross be okay?"

The albino smiled. "I'm sure he will. He's strong."

"Mmm." Zen picked up a brick with both hands and let it drop. "Cross was interesting."

He certainly was. The albino had never met someone so tortured, yet with so much potential. Their time spent with Cross made her confident that his wounds were starting to heal, that he would eventually be able to become his own person. She had no doubt that he would go on to be a great force for good in the City.

The albino was snapped from her thoughts by the hum of a vehicle outside. She glanced at Zen, and noted with pride that he had already sought cover under a table. Curious, she went to a window and peered out. It was a lone Government Humvee, rolling down the road towards them. That wasn't overly surprising; she'd spotted other vehicles heading in that direction earlier and assumed that there must be a camp there.

Then the albino glanced at the road the Humvee was traveling down, and that's where she saw it—an innocuous-looking two-liter bottle, clearly distinguishable even with her poor eyesight. A leftover from the old battles. In an instant the albino guessed what was about to happen, but could do nothing to stop it.

The albino ducked her head, lying flat on the ground. Zen clapped his hands over his ears and shut his eyes. A moment later there came an explosion that shook the building, dust and bits of rubble coming loose.

The albino stood up and stared out the window. The Humvee had been knocked onto its side, smoke rising from the wreckage. With a glance at Zen that told him he should remain where he was, she rushed out of the building. The blast had created a small crater in the road, and she could already see one soldier's body lying on the ground. Running to it, she checked the pulse—nothing.

The albino found another body with a beating heart and dragged it safely away from the wreckage. She turned and nearly gasped.

A third figure had stumbled from the wreckage, this one too young to be a soldier. His clothes were charred and he was covered in soot and ash. As he toppled to the ground, the albino noticed that his hands were bound behind him. A prisoner, then. She approached him cautiously. Aside from some scrapes and bruises the boy seemed to be fine, though his eyes were wide and bulging as he stared up at the albino.

"You." He gasped, struggling to his knees. "You!"

"Calm down, you're all right," she said, crouching down. "What's your name?"

"I know you!" he insisted. "You're the—you were with Cross!"

The albino blinked in confusion. She studied the boy's dirtied features more carefully. Then it hit her.

"You're that boy Sepp, from the Student Militia!"

But Sepp didn't seem to be listening to her. He let out a cry of pain, his face contorted in exertion. His plastic handcuffs, damaged by the fire, snapped free. There was madness in his eyes, and the albino nearly released her chain on instinct.

"Cross!" Sepp repeated, grabbing the hem of her jacket.

"What about him?" the albino asked.

"I need to talk to Cross!" Sepp bowed his head, and the albino was astonished to hear him sob. "You have to take me to Cross!"

PART IV

CITIZEN

Obeita's first thought upon entering the room was that it looked not un-like some twisted principle's office. The shelves were filled with a vari-ety of pills, syringes, and bottles of medication. The chairs had straps to keep their occupants in place. Armed soldiers stood guard at the door. This was the psychiatric ward that serviced the high-security wing of the camp.

Obeita was approached by a man who wore a doctor's white coat. His name was Ferraro, she remembered. Some hotshot pharmacist or some-thing who used to work for the old Mayor.

"Ms. Obeita, I was hoping you would drop in." Ferraro bowed clumsily.

"Dr. Ferraro." Obeita nodded. "It's been two weeks, so I've come to check on the student I gave you. I want to know what progress you've made, if any."

"Of course." Ferraro sounded delighted. "Right over here, please. I must say, she's made for a really excellent challenge."

Obeita followed Ferraro over to an occupied chair. Obeita looked down at it with interest. Noni had been strapped down to it, blindfolded and gagged, and was now twitching slightly as an assistant administered some kind of injection.

"As you can see, we've been trying on her a combination of chemical treatments," Ferraro said. "I've always been a strong believer that there is a pharmaceutical solution to every behavioral problem. You know, I was working with the old Mayor to make methylphenidate mandatory for all students who—"

"And the *results*?" Obeita asked impatiently. "What are the results?"

"She's responding well to the treatments." Ferraro said, rubbing his hands together. "Like I said, she was a challenge at first, but soon I think she can become my Exhibit A of how the right treatments can turn any-one into a model student."

Obeita let out a bark of laughter. "I'd love to believe that," she said. "You've read about her background, of course?"

"Yes, our new Mayor sent me a copy." Ferraro nodded. "Her history as a high-ranking Truant will only make my success more prestigious."

"*If* you succeed," Obeita said skeptically. "You know, this little tart bit me the last time I passed by her desk. The electric shocks only seemed to encourage her."

"Yes, classical conditioning techniques seem quite ineffective on her," Ferraro said. "But she's come a long way."

"I'd like to see a demonstration."

Ferraro blinked at Obeita. Then he shrugged. "Certainly."

He approached Noni and removed both the white cloth gag and the blindfold.

"Noni," he said. "Can you hear me?"

"Yes," Noni replied in a tiny voice.

Ferraro smiled. "Are you ready to be a good girl, Noni?"

Tears appeared in her eyes. "Yes."

"You won't *ever* disobey a teacher again, right?"

Noni nodded, and a tear ran down her cheek.

"Why don't you smile, Noni?"

Noni complied, smiling up at him, though more tears began to stream down her face. Ferraro smiled back, then replaced the gag and blindfold. Noni did not resist.

"I'm impressed," Obeita said. "But what was all that crying?"

"Oh, it's nothing," Ferraro said dismissively. "Her mind is still trying to resist the treatment, but she'll accept it eventually. You can take her back to class now if you want—as long as you bring her back for daily check-ups!"

Obeita looked down at the girl, rubbing her forearm, which still bore bite marks.

"I'll do that," she decided. "I have a few new students transferring in tonight, and I want little Noni here to be present as an example of what happens to those who disobey."

H ey, old man! Wake up! I got a question!"

Rothenberg groaned as the young voice roused him from his slumber, echoing throughout the prison cell block. This had become his bedtime routine, and there was nothing he hated more.

"Rothenberg! I thought the Mayor got rid of you a long time ago—so why are you here now, eh? Did you blow a second chance? Ha!"

Rothenberg seethed as he sat up on his cot. Two sets of bars separated him and the boy in the cell across from him, preventing Rothenberg from wrapping his hands around the kid's neck. For the past two weeks he'd been longing to do just that. When Rothenberg had first arrived the boy, the only other prisoner in this wing, had delightedly recognized his new captive audience as the former Chief Enforcer.

Since then, as the days dragged on and Rothenberg's patience withered to nothing, the kid only seemed to get more obnoxious.

"Shut up, you brat!" Rothenberg shouted.

"Oh, *scary*," the boy mocked. "I told you the name is Max; you should try using it once in a while. We're gonna be enjoying each other's company for a long time if you ask me."

The boy let out a bark of laughter at the look on Rothenberg's face. Rothenberg slammed his fist against the wall and then dropped back down on his cot, pressing his pillow over his ear while the boy made loud yodeling noises.

After the confrontation in District 20, Rothenberg had awoken to find himself in this miserable place. He had recognized it immediately—the District 1 prison, the main penitentiary of the City in peacetime. During his career as an Enforcer, Rothenberg had sometimes brought criminals to this prison. Now he was the prisoner.

"Rothenberg! Rothenberg, pay attention!"

Along with that insufferable kid.

"Dammit! Shut up you miserable vermin!" Rothenberg shouted, not removing the pillow from his ear. "Shouldn't you be in a camp?"

"Government forgot about me in here, Rothenberg!" Max called. "Just like they'll forget about you too!"

Rothenberg gritted his teeth and did his best to ignore the noise. No crime was worth this punishment. For what seemed to be the millionth time, Rothenberg cursed Iris under his breath. The woman had lied to him, used him. She had let him loose just long enough to find Cross and then discarded him like garbage, leaving him to rot. It seemed that everyone was eager to have his help—but no one wanted to reward him for it.

Rothenberg wondered where Cross was now. Surely the Government wouldn't be able to catch him without Rothenberg's help, unless the boy's battle with Umasi had gone badly. If it had, would Iris have him executed? The thought made Rothenberg bristle. Cross was *his* son. If anyone had the right to end that life it was Rothenberg.

"I'll be free of this place again," Rothenberg promised himself. "No more deals. Next time I'll do it myself."

Max let out a fresh yodel, and Rothenberg groaned. In here the days passed like years, more tedious than his time in the hospital. Bitterness gnawed away at the last vestiges of his reason. Rothenberg no longer saw any difference between the Government, the Truancy, or any other faction laying claim to the City. All of them, he knew, were against him. Everyone was determined to abuse him. He knew better now than to trust their lies.

More than anything, Rothenberg wanted justice. That meant getting his son back and getting revenge not just on Iris, but on the whole City that had betrayed him. If fate gave him another chance, he swore he would take it. Never again would he help someone else only to be betrayed.

For the foreseeable future, however, there was nothing Rothenberg could do but endure Max's yelling and nurse his hatred in the comfort of his tiny cell.

Somehow the stars looked bigger out in the deep City, Cross thought. Using his arms to support his body, he leaned back to better see the night sky. Maybe it was because there weren't so many skyscrapers here, no man-made monoliths to obscure the heavens. Cross liked being able to see the strings of glittering lights hung high.

A warm breeze ruffled his hair, and Cross wrinkled his nose as it carried up the stench of the streets. The building he sat on was only five stories tall, one of the tallest here in the slums of District 47. Cross had never been this deep into the City before. Out here the people had always been poor. Before the war the streets had never been very busy. These days a flood of refugees had made the whole district overcrowded. People here were hungry, desperate, and angry. Fertile ground for a rebellion.

The Government's presence was limited to a small base in nearby District 45. The soldiers couldn't maintain order here, nor did they try to after the new resistance had blown a few of their patrols to pieces. Over the past two weeks that resistance had been formed from whatever Truants they could gather.

A few of them brought their parents, and some adult refugees had joined out of necessity more than anything else. No matter how indoctrinated towards obedience a person was, hunger had a way of bringing out a fighting spirit. Together they struck at the Government whenever they could, however they could. True to Jack's vision, it was a citizen's rebellion, albeit demoralized, outnumbered, and hungry.

Takan and Cross had officially split the responsibilities of leadership, though increasingly Cross found himself doing more of the work. Takan had anxiously waited for word from his father for days before finally accepting that Jack was probably gone. That loss, compounded by his mentor's betrayal, had really affected the Truancy's leader. He spent a lot of his time alone in his room.

Umasi's betrayal itself had nearly ruined them. He had gone public as the City's new Mayor a day after their confrontation. Cross dearly wished that they'd been able to finish him off—his face was plastered everywhere, his speeches broadcast to every corner of the City with functioning radios or televisions. Faced with hopelessness and starvation, many fugitive youths had been persuaded by the Mayor's promises of shelter and safety. Hundreds had turned themselves in to the camps. Cross was sure that many more would follow.

As for Cross himself, all he could do was try to survive and fulfill his responsibilities as well as he could. The glittering sky seemed to wink at him as he stared up at it. Strangely, hardship and responsibility seemed to make him saner. Many of the Truants, once skeptical of the former student, now came to him instead of Takan.

Cross got to his feet as he heard footsteps coming up the stairs. Sure enough, one of the recently arrived Truants stepped out onto the roof and saluted. Cross returned it.

"What now?" Cross asked.

"We could use your help, sir," the boy said. "We're, uh, hearing noises from Takan's room again."

Cross sighed. "That'll be the fifth time this week, right?"

"Yeah."

"All right, let's go see what the problem is this time."

Cross followed the boy down the stairs and into the apartment building, which had become their hideout. The wallpaper was peeling, the floors were stained, and dim illumination was provided by naked lightbulbs. The steps groaned in protest as they descended. Soon they reached the first floor. The Truant halted respectfully as Cross continued on.

Cross walked down a narrow hallway, finally reaching the door to the apartment that Takan had taken as his quarters. He didn't hear anything. He tried knocking. There was no response. Cross frowned, then tried the knob. The door creaked open, revealing a completely dark room.

Cross stepped inside and found Takan slumped over on a sofa in the living room, a bottle of something in his hand.

"You alive?" Cross asked.

Takan nodded.

"You sober?"

Takan shook his head.

"You rarely are these days." Cross frowned. "Well, just so long as you're still breathing."

Cross turned to leave.

"Wait," Takan said.

Surprised, Cross turned around and saw Takan beckoning him over. He complied, walking closer to the Truant leader until he was looking straight down at him.

"You want to know why I killed Zyid, don't you?" Takan whispered. "Let me tell you."

Cross nodded—the question had been bothering him ever since the first time he'd brought it up.

"It was Zyid himself who killed my sister," Takan said. "I joined the Truancy to get revenge on him. It turned out that he knew all along I planned to kill him. He let it happen so that I could take his place, so that he could be free."

Cross blinked. Of all the answers he had imagined, that hadn't been one of them. Zyid had *allowed* himself to be killed?

"Noni loved Zyid," Takan rambled. "Not the same way she loves me, you know. He was her stability. Me, I was selfish. I killed him without thinking what it'd do to her. Now because of me, she . . ." he trailed off. "Well, that's beside the point."

Cross suddenly felt that he really didn't want to hear this. Awkward didn't begin to describe listening to the leader of the Truancy talk about his failed romances.

"Listen, Cross," Takan said. "I know what Zyid felt like now. It sucks. So, I have a request. I haven't murdered your sister, but I would really appreciate it if you would do me the favor of killing me and—"

"You're drunk," Cross said firmly. "I'm not going to kill you."

Takan sighed and dropped his bottle. It clattered to the floor. "Maybe you're right. Sorry for being so pathetic."

Cross couldn't think of anything to say to that, so he patted Takan's shoulder and left him on the sofa. As he exited the apartment he thought he could hear snoring.

Dispirited, Cross decided he needed to take a walk out on the streets, away from the headquarters. He slipped outside through a side door and began wandering through the narrow streets. The air down here was repressive, and the streets stank of human misery. There was garbage everywhere, and then there were the people—the people with nowhere else to go.

Their clothes were tattered, their faces dirty, bodies thin and sometimes emaciated. There were no food shipments to District 47, only what could be obtained through dangerous smuggling or the black market. The people here had come to know Cross, know that his rebellion gave them protection and food whenever possible, and so they did not harass him as he walked.

Was this what it all had come to? Cross wondered. Were they all doomed to rot here in the squalor of the City? Would Cross put up a fight for as long as he could, like Takan and Zyid, only to collapse under the strain? Or would they all be hunted down, one by one, by Iris or the Mayor?

Cross found himself standing in an empty alley. He wasn't even seventeen yet, and he felt that his life had already been exhausted, that he was at the end of his rope. Their resistance had only existed for two weeks and already it seemed to be crumbling from the inside. Cross knew it was only a matter of time before it fell, either to the Government or to itself.

"What are you doing, Cross, looking so defeated?"

Cross jumped, then spun around. He stared, disbelieving. The albino stood before him, smiling, holding hands with Zen. She hadn't changed at all, save perhaps for her Student Militia jacket—the blue fabric was now more worn and frayed than ever.

"That's no proper greeting," she chided. "Do you know how hard it was to find you all the way out here?"

Cross realized that his jaw had dropped open. He shut it, feeling embarrassed. The albino's presence was a welcome delight that he hadn't dared to hope for, and yet it confused him.

"I-I'm happy to see you again, teacher," Cross said. "But why are you here? I thought you weren't going to follow me."

The albino's face turned serious.

"I wasn't," she said. "But things have changed. There's someone here who wants to talk to you."

"Who—"

Then Cross saw him, standing at the mouth of the alley, hunched over. The boy was almost unrecognizable, his hair frayed and unkempt, his face drawn and haggard. Sepp staggered over to Cross and dropped to his knees.

"Cross, I'm sorry," he said. "I'm so sorry. I failed."

"What are you talking about?" Cross asked, mystified.

"Your orders. I failed."

For a few moments Cross wondered what Sepp could possibly be talking about. Then it hit him, and he seized the boy by the shoulders.

"Sepp," he said, trying to keep his voice calm, "where is Floe?"

"She was taken!" Sepp cried, staring up at Cross with moist eyes. "The Government took her—to the camps!"

Floe winced as the handcuffs dug again into her wrists. The soldier dragging her along was none too gentle, and each time he tugged the chain attached to their handcuffs it hurt. She was being escorted down a dimly lit hallway, painted sickly green like the rest of this part of the camp. In front of her there were two boys, both Truants, neither of whom she knew.

Floe had spent the past couple of weeks in general confinement, unassigned to a class while the Government checked her records and decided her fate. They had eventually discovered that she'd been a member of Cross' personal unit *and* a former Truant. That meant an automatic assignment to an intensive reeducation program.

Dressed now in a gray student's uniform not unlike the blue one she had worn during her time in the Student Militia, Floe quietly followed the soldiers into her new classroom. A fat and unpleasant-looking woman stood at the front, presiding over the class. The kids at their desks were all hard at work. No one spoke. No one even looked up from their papers.

The soldier led Floe to a desk of her own. He uncuffed her, then recuffed her to the desk. Floe accepted it all without complaint. She felt like a little girl again, frightened, hating herself for it. The weeks of helplessness, of languishing in her cell, had crushed Floe's spirit.

At the front of the class the teacher was now introducing herself as Ms. Obeita. For the first time the other kids looked up from their work, giving the teacher their undivided attention, but Floe found that she couldn't concentrate as the woman went over the rules of the class. She sadly wondered what camp Sepp had been sent to, and whether or not Cross had managed to evade capture.

"In short, no disobedience of any kind will be tolerated," Obeita was saying. "All of you sit before me because you are former rebels with a history. Let us get one thing out of the way: I don't care where you came from or what you've done. In here, you are all the same."

Floe repressed an urge to scream and cry. She wanted to protest that she didn't belong in this program. She didn't intend to cause any trouble at all. She only wanted to see her old friends, to make new ones. If in that moment she could have relived her life, she would have never joined the Truancy or the Militia.

"As proof," Obeita continued, "I would like you all to turn your attention to the back of the room. There you can see what was once one of the Truancy's highest ranking leaders. She decided to continue being a rebel, and now she serves as an example."

As one, the class turned in their desks to stare at a pitiful figure sitting in a corner. Floe gasped as she recognized Noni, the girl she had so admired as a Truant.

Noni's arms had been locked in a straitjacket, her body completely limp. Her head lolled back to rest against the wall. Her eyes were glazed over, though silent tears flowed steadily from them—the only sign that she was even alive.

Floe felt cold horror grip her. She couldn't even imagine what had to have been done to destroy so strong a spirit.

"The same fate awaits any of you who also wish to continue misbehaving." Obeita smiled. "There is no hope here. Soon enough, every one of you will be broken."

26
MODEL STUDENT

O ur target is here." Cross pointed at a map of the City spread out on a table. "It's a Government reeducation camp built on the docks of District 13."

He stood over a wooden table in a room on the third floor of their hideout. Sitting across from Cross was Takan, who was bleary eyed but completely sober for a change. To his left sat Sepp, who cracked no jokes and looked sullen as he stared at the map. To his right sat the nameless albino, calm as ever, following his words with interest.

Three days had passed since Sepp arrived in District 47 bearing his grim news. The story of the raid on his house, the imprisonment of his family, and the capture of Floe had galvanized Cross and in turn, the rebellion itself. As if taking on his determination, they had become more aggressive in ambushing Government patrols, their headquarters were now a flurry of activity, and recruitment was up.

The presence of the albino and her son had also boosted morale. Some of the Truants had heard of the legendary vagrant ghost, and viewed her support as a good omen. Aside from Cross, who was pleased to have her around again, she had acquired a following of sorts. Many of the boys found her beautiful—which Cross privately thought she *would* be, were it not for her unnatural paleness. Little Zen, meanwhile, had made the base into his playground and could be found romping all over the building.

It was amazing how much of a difference morale made. Things had begun to look up so quickly that Cross felt confident enough to put his bold rescue plan into action.

"Why is it built in District 13?" Takan asked, glancing at the map. "That's an abandoned district. There are no suitable buildings for the Government to use there; they must've constructed it from scratch."

"I think the location was convenient for them because of this." Cross pointed at the river. "The camp can receive shipments of supplies directly from the water."

Takan frowned. "I just don't see it, Cross. It's too deep in Government territory."

"With the right plan, it's possible," Cross insisted. "A strike that close to the heart of the City would be a powerful symbolic victory, and besides . . ." He turned to Sepp.

Sepp nodded glumly. "The soldiers that captured me mentioned Floe was being taken there. I'm sure of it."

Takan sighed. "Look, I know how you two feel about this, but is it really worth risking all of our lives for one girl?"

"You *Truant*, of course it's—"

"Sepp, quiet." Cross hushed his fellow student. "Look, liberating the camps was always on our to-do list. A camp closer to the core will actually probably have *less* security than one of the closer ones."

"We're still talking about over a hundred soldiers stationed on-site, with more reinforcements nearby." Takan shook his head. "Realistically, I don't think we can get more than fifty of ours in that deep without attracting attention."

"Fifty will be enough," Cross said. "I have a plan to create a disturbance within the camps before we attack. In the chaos, the guards will be overwhelmed."

Takan raised an eyebrow. "All right, let's assume that's possible. What are you going to do if the Mayor gets involved?"

Cross clenched his jaw. That was the big question. Memories of him and Takan being thrashed by the newly appointed Mayor were fresh in his mind, and the Mayor was even more dangerous as a symbol than as an opponent. His interference could ruin everything.

"If the Mayor shows up, we'll kill him," Cross said. "If we can't handle him, we'll never have a hope of overcoming the General. Together, I think we have a chance."

"We might have a chance," Takan allowed. "But by no means is it a sure thing. I wouldn't want to risk that fight."

"Isn't it hopeless then?" Cross demanded.

Takan creased his brow. "Quite possibly."

"Well, is there *anyone* who can stop him besides us?"

At that Takan gave Cross a pensive look. His eyes clouded over for a moment, and then a strange look of sadness flitted across his face.

"There is one," Takan said.

Takan turned slowly to look at the albino, who had up until that moment remained silent. She and Takan stared at each other, amber eyes meeting blue. It took Cross a moment to understand what Takan was implying.

"No." Cross shook his head. "She is not a soldier, we can't ask her to—"

"Cross," the albino interrupted. "It's okay. I'll do this."

"But—"

"She's more of a match than we are, Cross," Takan said. "And she knows him better than either of us. It's the obvious choice."

Cross stared at the albino. "Teacher, do you really want to get involved?"

"Where that boy is concerned, I'm already involved." She smiled sadly.

"I won't be fighting your war, Cross. I will come along and deal with Umasi if it comes to that—but *only* with Umasi."

Takan cleared his throat. "You're absolutely sure, Two?"

She nodded.

"I guess that settles it," Cross said reluctantly. He couldn't help but feel that something was going on here that he didn't understand.

Sepp stirred, emerging from his gloom to ask a question. "Cross, you said you had a plan to cause chaos inside the camp?"

"Oh, right. That." Cross smiled. "It's a risky plan, so obviously I'm going to carry it out myself."

Takan raised both eyebrows. "Now you've got me curious."

"Well." Cross straightened up. "It starts with me giving the Government a little of what they want . . ."

Ferraro leaned back in his chair, surveying his favorite project from across his desk.

"I must say, Noni, your progress has been better than I expected," he said. "It's only been a few days since Obeita took you back to class, and already she's praising me to all the other teachers."

Noni smiled, as he had taught her to do. "I'm very glad, sir."

Ferraro smiled, admiring his work. They were meeting in his office for Noni's daily treatment, and the change was truly stunning. Noni now held his gaze without hatred, and there were no bindings on her chair. Her pose was upright and attentive. The gray skirt and jacket of her uniform were immaculate and crisp. Her hair had been combed nicely and tied into a ponytail. Her various wounds had healed, and save for the one permanent scar, she was quite pretty, like a doll.

Ferraro felt an immense satisfaction sweep over him. Noni looked every bit the model student he was making her.

"Now, I was hoping we could pick up where we left off last time." Ferraro picked up a clipboard. "Will you answer a few questions, Noni? For extra credit?"

"Of course. My studies are everything."

"Good, good." Ferraro took a deep breath. "I was hoping that you would, er, tell me about your mother."

Noni stirred, and Ferraro cringed reflexively. That question had always provoked a violent response in the past. This time, however, Noni simply nodded her head.

"Yes, sir," she said. "What would you like to know?"

Ferraro grinned in triumph. "What do you remember about her?"

"She would get angry a lot," Noni replied. "She was often drunk and didn't like cleaning the house. I remember the apartment being filthy."

"Did she ever hit you?"

"Yes, many times," Noni said calmly. "Usually with her hands, though twice she used a belt, three times she used a board, and on ten occasions I can remember she threw various—"

"That's enough, Noni." Ferraro scribbled on his clipboard. "Now, was all of this why you ran away from home?"

"I'm not sure. I think my mother left the door ajar, and I was hungry, so I opened it looking for food," Noni said. "I . . . I remember seeing the hallway for the first time, thinking it was huge. I felt frightened but curious. I started walking and didn't stop."

Ferraro nodded in satisfaction. Noni's composure had held throughout the entire recollection. The expression on her face and her tone of voice had not changed a bit.

"I want you to know that I'm very proud of you, Noni," Ferraro said. "Ms. Obeita tells me that you're number three in her class and climbing. If you keep it up, I'll be able to present you to my peers as a case study."

Noni smiled again, as per her programming. "I'm very glad, sir."

"So," Ferraro set his clipboard aside, "how are *your* studies going, Noni?"

"My studies are everything."

Ferraro smiled. "But I thought you were a rebel?"

"I was wrong," Noni said simply. "I'm sorry for misbehaving—my studies are everything."

"Indeed, they are." Ferraro reached for a syringe. "Now, Noni, don't you think it's time for another dose? You wouldn't want to relapse into old habits."

"Yes, sir," Noni said, holding her arm out compliantly. "Thank you, sir."

Iris stood in front of the bright monitor, trying to control her increasingly dark mood. The lights in her study had been switched off, leaving everything in shadow. There was only her and the elderly man on the screen—her father's War Minister, whose every word was only making her more frustrated.

"Listen to me, Minister," Iris said, losing her patience. "The situation here gets more desperate by the hour, it is our responsibility to take care of the people!"

"The Education City is still considered a combat zone," the Minister said. "I'm sorry, General, but the regulations are clear and my hands are tied. I simply cannot put civilian workers at risk by sending them into a bloodbath!"

"Then just give me the supplies, I'll have my soldiers carry out the effort!"

The Minister raised an eyebrow. "With all due respect, General, do you really have the men to spare for that?"

Iris clenched her fists. She had fought tooth and nail to get every soldier she could for this operation, and had warned she would need more. No one knew that better than this man, and yet he sought to rub in the fact.

"The longer there is discontent in the streets, the stronger the resistance here will become!" Iris said through gritted teeth. "If I cannot have additional troops to break the holdouts, I will need those relief supplies!"

"General." The Minister sighed. "I sympathize, I really do, but you knew the conditions that were set before you accepted this assignment. If you are unable to pacify that City, then your father will—"

"It will *not* come to that!" Iris slammed her fist on the console. "I *will* save this City no matter what it takes; I just need you to *give* me what it takes!"

"You know very well that the bulk of our manpower is already occupied," the Minister said. "It was hard enough to get you the battalions you have."

"Dammit, I— we promised security for these people!" Iris said. "If we cannot deliver on that most basic obligation, we will lose their trust. The resistance will continue, and then . . ."

"I'm sorry, General, that's something you might just have to accept." The War Minister shrugged. "So long as there is fighting on the ground there's nothing I can do to help you. It may well be that there won't be a happy ending for that City."

"I *won't* accept that!" Iris gritted her teeth. "I'll be talking to my father about this."

The Minister shook his head. "Again, with due respect, General, I think you already know what outcome he'd prefer."

With a snarl of frustration, Iris shut off the monitor. The room went completely dark, and she realized she wasn't alone. Scolding herself for not noticing his presence before, Iris turned to address Umasi, who was standing in the doorway.

"What's the latest?" she asked.

She did not ask how long he'd been listening in on her conversation, nor did he act like he ever was. It was an unspoken rule between them that business with the Government would be left to her. Even Iris found it hard to tell what Umasi was thinking behind those sunglasses, but this time she thought she could sense sympathy from him.

"More attacks in the deep City," Umasi said. "This alliance between the Truancy and the Student Militia seems to be gaining traction. There are reports that they've acquired the sympathy of some of those discontented adults."

Iris let out a noise of frustration and plunked down into her chair. "Why, Umasi? Why won't they let me help them?"

Umasi rubbed his leg where the knife wound Takan inflicted had healed over.

"They're stubborn by nature," he said, "and they seem to doubt that you truly intend to help them. I still believe that using Rothenberg was a mistake."

"He served his purpose, he won't be released again." Iris shook her head. "Those children have no idea what they're doing. No one will be helped by their actions—so many might *die* because of them."

"I know their type, Iris," Umasi said quietly. "Our brother was the same way. His stubbornness drove him to destroy himself."

"And now their stubbornness may destroy this City."

Umasi looked like he was about to reply when suddenly he held his hand up to his ear. Iris realized he must be listening to a message coming in through the earpiece that he'd worn ever since assuming the office of Mayor. Whatever he heard seemed to have an effect on him, for he turned to leave Iris' study.

Iris sat up in her chair. "What's happened?"

"Apparently, one of the rebel leaders claims to want to surrender," Umasi said. "I'm going to go see what he has to say. I've met the boy before, I can handle this."

"Umasi." Iris frowned. "Are you sure you want to—"

"I'm just doing what I should've done four years ago," Umasi said. "Don't trouble yourself over this trivial matter, sister. None of this is your fault. If it's anyone's, it's mine."

Cross sat patiently in his chair. Pretty much everyone else had told him this was a bad idea. They might have been right, but he didn't regret going through with it. Floe's capture had affected him more than he would admit.

During his time with the Militia, Cross had been too confused and too isolated to let anything develop between him and Floe. He regretted that, so much that it pained him to think about it. But that wasn't the only reason he was here now. The fact that she had been captured for following his orders made him responsible—and Cross decided that no matter what happened, his fate would be the same as hers.

Overhead the dull lamp creaked as it swayed. Cross frowned and turned to one of the soldiers standing in the corners.

"Will it take much longer?" he asked.

There was no reply but stony silence. Cross sighed. He had turned himself in at the Government base in District 32, far enough from headquarters to throw them off. After a thorough search, they had made him wait in this interrogation room. Two soldiers stood on either side of him, and more, he knew, were watching unseen. His legs and arms had been shackled. The Government was taking no chances with him.

Sepp had volunteered to come too, and sulked when Cross pointed out that it would only arouse suspicion. The boy had become reckless and brooding, and Cross couldn't figure out why. It was almost as though his failure to protect Floe and his family had turned Sepp's personality inside out. Cross sensed there was something that Sepp wasn't telling him, but he couldn't think of how to broach the subject. Cross shook his head. No time for that now.

Finally, the door swung open, and Cross blinked at the light from the hallway. A dark figure stepped inside, its eyes shielded with sunglasses. The door shut with a clang, and the Mayor took a seat in front of Cross.

"Mr. Mayor," Cross greeted. "It's nice to see you again. I'm a little surprised—I requested to see your master Iris instead."

In truth Cross hadn't expected Iris to come herself. At least he was important enough to warrant a visit from her stooge.

"I've got to say," Cross continued, gesturing around with his cuffed hands. "I'm flattered by all this security."

"What do you want, Cross?" Umasi didn't seem interested in small talk.

"To turn myself in."

Umasi looked him up and down from behind those dark glasses. Cross decided that being scrutinized by an unseen gaze definitely had an unsettling effect.

"I can see that," Umasi said. "Why?"

Cross decided to tell the truth.

"I heard that the Government captured a student," Cross said. "Someone I care about very much. More than myself."

His words seemed to have an effect on the Mayor. He stirred.

"If your intention was to negotiate an exchange, I'm afraid it's impossible," Umasi said. "I cannot release a student from the camps for any—"

"I know all that," Cross said. "I'm willing to go to your camps. I don't care what happens to me. I don't care about the war, or the resistance, or the Government—those were all other people's ideas I just went along with."

Cross held his breath. It was crucial that the Mayor accept that lie. He knew that it was consistent with what the Government thought of him.

Umasi nodded.

"What exactly are you asking for, then?" he asked.

"I want to be put in the same camp and class as a student named Floe," Cross said, allowing emotion that was not entirely fake into his voice. "I want to be there for her."

The Mayor sat up straighter in his chair, stroking his chin. Cross could tell he was considering it. There followed several tense moments of silence.

"And what will you do for us in return?" Umasi asked finally.

Cross blinked. "I don't understand."

"If I arrange this for you," Umasi said. "If I have you assigned to the same class as your girlfriend, what will you do for us in return?"

"My surrender isn't enough?"

"Of course not," Umasi replied. "You've already given us that."

Cross felt irked that the Mayor was audacious enough to demand more from him. Fortunately he had come with more cards to play.

"I'll tell you everything I know." Cross feigned reluctance. "All of the rebellion's cells that I know of. Their plans. Everything."

Umasi seemed to size him up for a few more seconds. Then he nodded.

"We have a deal, then," he said, turning to one of the soldiers. "Have him shipped off to District 13 under heavy guard. Take a long route. Place him immediately into the intensive program there."

"As you wish, Mr. Mayor."

"I've upheld my part of our deal." Umasi stood up and looked down at Cross. "Once you arrive and see the truth of that, I expect you to do the same in good faith. I'll be there to see you tomorrow."

Cross nodded in response. As Umasi turned and left the interrogation room, Cross hid a smile. If it wasn't all a trick on Umasi's part, then he had just succeeded in outsmarting the Mayor himself.

27

LIBERATION

Takan took a swig of water from his bottle, grimacing as the harsh taste of minerals washed down his throat, too much like blood.

"Are you thirsty?" Takan asked, looking sideways at his companion.

A few feet away on the edge of the rooftop, the nameless albino turned to smile at him.

"Yes, thank you," she replied.

Takan screwed the cap back on the bottle and tossed it to her. She caught it with both hands, then tilted her head back and took a deep drink.

The two of them waited now on top of an old abandoned apartment building in District 13. The sun was just beginning to set. Takan's brown trench coat lay at his feet—the air was too hot and humid to wear it. The albino had kept her tattered Student Militia jacket, though Takan noted that she now wore it buttoned around her neck like a mantle.

"You don't think Cross will succeed, do you?" she said.

Takan snorted. "I think he's a lovesick fool for even trying it."

"He can be reckless sometimes," she admitted, gazing out off the roof. "But I think he knows what he's doing—whether *he* knows it or not, if that makes any sense."

"I just hope this isn't for nothing," Takan said. "We had a hell of a time just getting in position here."

The albino nodded at that. The military's aerial surveillance had forced them to travel through the old subway systems. They'd arrived in staggered groups to avoid the Government's patrols in the area. The building their fifty fighters had bunked down in was actually a former Truancy hideout. District 13 had been abandoned for as long as Takan could remember, making it an easy place to vanish.

"If you manage to liberate at least some of the students there," the albino said, "this could be a turning point in the war. The other camps will surely hear of it. Hope will return to the City."

"What can I say?" Takan shrugged. "I hope you're right. I just don't share your optimism."

"That doesn't sound like Takan, leader of the Truancy," she teased.

Takan laughed. "You're right. It sounds more like Tack, bitter and jaded student of the City."

"And which are you?" The albino replaced the cap on the bottle and threw it back at him.

Takan caught the water, frowned at it, then took a sip and shuddered.

"I don't know," he admitted. "I never meant for Takan to exist longer than Zyid. Sometimes I wish I'd had just accepted my sister's death. Just turned around and went home rather than coming . . . here." Takan blinked and looked around the dirty rooftop. "Come to think of it, this is the hideout where I first became a member of the Truancy. They found me on the docks when I was at my worst."

The albino looked around with renewed interest. There was soot and what looked like scorch marks on the rooftop, along with some old bullet holes.

"It seems like this place has a lot of history," she remarked. "There were bullet holes in the stairway when we came up here, and the glass on the front doors looked like they'd been deliberately broken."

Takan nodded. "The building was in poor shape when I first came here. I think the Truancy must have evacuated it once before my time."

A warm breeze swept over the rooftop. Takan looked up at the navy blue sky. They were out of earshot of the misery of the camps. From where they sat now, it seemed almost peaceful in District 13.

"How did you first meet Umasi?" the albino asked, still gazing off the roof.

"When I was still a student, I was chased by some bullies into District 19," Takan replied. "I started making regular visits, and he taught me everything I know. What about you?"

"We crossed paths one winter, when we were both kids on the run," she said. "We learned from each other . . . brought warmth into each other's lives. I think we were as close as either of us had ever been."

Takan hesitated. "Do you still love him?"

The albino turned her head away. "Yes."

"Two, if that's true then you should let us—"

"You don't trust me to keep my head?" She smiled, sipping from the bottle. "You misjudge me, Four."

"It's not that." Takan frowned. "The Mayor is not the same boy who mentored me. If he draws his weapon on you, he'll be going for a kill."

"You're probably right," she admitted. "But someone has to take responsibility for him. If anyone can claim to do that, it is me."

Takan sighed in acceptance.

"And what about your son?" he asked, raising the water to his lips.

"Actually, I've been meaning to talk to you about that," the albino said. "If this mission goes all wrong and something happens to me, I would like you to look after Zen."

Takan nearly choked on his mineral water. He sputtered and coughed, sending it spraying out onto the rooftop. The albino regarded him calmly as he pounded his chest.

"Excuse me?" He coughed.

"It's very unlikely that you'll have to," she said with a smile. "But it seems unwise for me not to make sure."

Takan swallowed. "Am I really your first choice for this?"

"To be perfectly honest, you're not," the albino admitted. "But you're the best and most able person available at the moment."

Takan frowned. "All right, you have my word—but please, for my sake now, try not to get killed."

She stifled a laugh. "As you wish."

Takan looked down at his feet where the bottle had fallen. Its contents had spilled into a small puddle around him. He sighed. There was nothing left for him to even drink now. Nothing to do but wait.

There you go, kid, enjoy your stay."

Cross stumbled into the courtyard as the gates clanged shut behind him. The soldiers had taken their time getting to the camp, and it was now almost night.

"What about my friend?" Cross demanded, turning to his escort. "The Mayor promised that I'd be able to see her here."

"You've been assigned to the same class," the soldier replied. "You've got an evening session coming up—if you can't wait until then, just look around and you'll find her."

"Look around where?"

The soldier waved his arm to encompass the courtyard. "Out there!"

Cross glanced at his surroundings. The courtyard was vast, built from a large section of the empty waterfront of District 13. The ground had not been repaired, there were cracks in it, and bits of concrete and asphalt were crumbling from lack of maintenance. As Cross watched, students in gray uniforms swept the ground, collecting the debris and disposing of them in bags. Soldiers watched over everything from the towers surrounding the yard.

Cross turned around. "How am I supposed to find—"

He paused. The soldier was already gone, having joined his comrades in the guardhouse. Cross shook his head and took a step forward into the courtyard. Before arriving he had changed into a student's uniform, and an electric device had been attached to his leg. He'd been told that it would administer a shock in case he misbehaved.

As Cross walked through the courtyard he found that though his uniform blended in, it seemed that he was the only one with nothing to do.

All the other students seemed to be cleaning the grounds, making small chat in whispers as they did. It was a joyless atmosphere. Everyone knew that they were being watched, and both the run-down buildings that served as dormitories as well as the renovated buildings where classes were held served as a reminder of their situation.

Cross paused as he recognized a couple of faces staring at him— members of the Student Militia, he recalled, though he couldn't place their names. He nodded at them, and they averted their eyes.

Cross sighed and continued walking through the courtyard, his hands in his pockets, discreetly looking around for any sign of Floe. Somewhere he could hear the screaming of a student receiving an electric shock. No one looked up from their work. There was no spirit here, Cross realized. The camps were doing their jobs.

A cool breeze from the nearby river swept over Cross, and he spotted a small commotion apparently unnoticed by the guards. In one corner of the courtyard three kids had surrounded another, and by their body language he could tell there was trouble. Cross looked around—no one else seemed to care, either not noticing or deliberately ignoring the confrontation.

Cross removed his hands from his pockets and began walking towards the commotion. When he was a dozen paces away, he paused. The aggressors were jabbing at their victim with broom handles as she curled up in the corner, her arms raised to shield herself. The victim was a girl with brown hair.

His heart pounding, Cross called out to them.

"Hey, you!"

The bullies, two boys and one girl, turned to face him. Their victim wearily turned her head to look at him, and then seemed to freeze. Cross clenched his jaw. It was Floe.

"What do you want, kid?" one of the boys demanded.

Cross pointed at Floe. "What did she do to you?"

"We spotted her chatting up the guards," the female bully replied. "She's been snitching!"

Cross glanced at Floe in surprise. Floe shook her head vigorously, her eyes pleading. Cross turned back to the bullies.

"I don't believe you," he said. "I know her. She wouldn't do something like that."

"Yeah?" The larger boy advanced upon Cross. "Maybe you're a snitch too, then? Are you going to tell the guards on us?"

Cross took a deep breath and swallowed his anger. A month ago he would have fought these three kids without a second thought. He had changed a lot since then, and he knew that a fistfight wouldn't do him or his mission any good.

"If I am a snitch," Cross said calmly, "then attacking me would guarantee I report you. But if I'm telling the truth, then you're bullying an innocent girl. Either way, it'd be best for everyone if you left now."

The three bullies seemed to size up Cross for a moment. Apparently deciding that he wasn't going to be intimidated, they shrugged at one another and walked away. One of them deliberately bumped his shoulder into Cross. He ignored it.

When they were gone, Cross hurried over to Floe and helped her up. She had lost weight—she looked almost pitifully small as she stared up at him. There were dark rings under her eyes, and her normally sleek hair was frazzled and dirty. She took one look at him with haunted hazel eyes. Then she burst into tears.

"Floe!" Cross said, shocked. "What's wrong?"

"I hoped th-that at least y-you'd escape," she sobbed. "But even y-you—"

"It's not what you think." Cross shook her gently. "I wasn't caught. I came here to see you."

"You did what? To see— NO!" Floe cried harder than ever. "Oh no, it's all my fault! All my fault!"

Without thinking, Cross swept her into an embrace, holding her tight. She struggled for a moment, wriggling against him. Then she seemed to relax, crying against his chest. Cross patted her on the back, not knowing what to do or say. He had never been in a situation like this before.

"Listen, Floe," he whispered in her ear. "We are going to escape from here. I have people coming to help; I need to know if there's any way we can start a riot in the courtyard."

To Cross' surprise, Floe jerked backwards, staring at him in dismay.

"You mustn't say things like that!" Floe said urgently. "You can't say things like that! I . . . we're supposed to report things like that . . . you can't . . ."

Cross stared. "Floe, what's gotten into you?"

Floe blinked at him, and he could see terror in her eyes. Then she shook her head, and took a deep rattling breath. She looked at him again, this time with some clarity.

"I'm sorry." Floe shook her head. "The teachers here reward you for reporting other students, I'd gotten so used to it that . . ."

Floe trailed off. Cross clenched his fists. This wasn't like the Floe he knew at all, who had always been spunky and loyal even in the darkest of times.

"Floe," Cross asked gently. "What did they do to you?"

"Not much." Floe's eyes filled again with tears. "I gave up so easily. I wasn't ever strong like Noni was, and even *she* was broken in the end. They pumped her full of chemicals to do it."

"Noni?" Cross blinked. "She's here too?"

Floe laughed bitterly. "Not only was she captured, but she's the star of the class now. You'll see, Cross. You'll see that there's no hope here for—"

Cross couldn't help himself. Realizing how bad the damage was, wanting to do anything to make it better, Cross pulled Floe to him and kissed her. Her eyes flew open, her arms tightened around him, and for the first time that night it seemed to Cross that she looked truly alive. It was like a wildfire had sprung up between them, twisting them both into knots of flame. After a few moments, Floe pulled away, breathless.

"Everything is going to be okay," Cross promised. "I'm here, I understand. It's going to be all right."

The barest hint of a familiar smile tugged at Floe's lips. Then, blaring out over the entire courtyard, the sound of a bell rang out—the signal for the start of evening classes. Cross felt Floe's fingers dig into his arms. She didn't want to leave.

"It's okay," Cross repeated. "I've been assigned to the same class. We'll be together."

Floe looked him in the eyes. "Promise that you'll stay this time."

Was this a dream? It felt like it as Cross gazed back at her. For years Cross had been so repressed that he'd believed he could never be capable of love. But now, in the midst of suffering, here in the wasteland of the courtyard, Cross felt a surge of passion beyond reason, and he realized what he'd been denying himself for years.

"Always," Cross swore.

Obeita yawned as she entered the classroom. She nodded at the soldier standing guard, then moved to her desk where her extra large chair was waiting. The students were already cuffed to their seats, pencils and paper out. They all looked tired, which was how Obeita liked it. By her personal recommendation, the intensive course always met before bed, every day of the week.

Obeita sank into her chair and looked out at her class with pride. She felt entitled to a little pride—after all, they were hers now, every one of them changed permanently by her painstaking tutelage. That feeling of satisfaction, of ownership, had been what attracted her to the teaching profession.

As Obeita surveyed her students, she realized that something was wrong. A redheaded boy that she did not know was cuffed to the desk next to Floe. She scowled.

"Private, who is that boy and what is he doing in my class?" Obeita demanded, turning to the soldier.

The man shrugged. "He's an emergency transfer. I was told that the Mayor informed you of the special circumstances already."

Obeita thought about that. She did remember that a notice had come in from the Mayor's office that evening, but she had been too busy to read it. Obeita shook her head in irritation. She hated it when Mayors interfered with her work.

"Very well," she said, glaring at the newcomer. "What's your name, boy?"

The boy responded in a neutral voice. "Cross."

The name was familiar. It took Obeita a moment before she recognized the name of the former leader of the Student Militia—and an old student of hers from fourth grade. Obeita smiled. She might have to thank the Mayor after all.

"This is a pleasant reunion, Cross," she said. "Do you know the rules here?"

"Yes, Ms. Obeita."

Obeita grinned. Apparently he recognized her as well.

"All right then," she announced. "Everyone, take out your calculus textbooks."

The students hastened to do as ordered. Just then, the door opened again and another soldier entered. Obeita turned to see a handcuffed Noni coming in from her evening chemical treatment. Obeita smiled. The girl looked so compliant as she came through the door, so much so that Obeita felt like showing off.

"Noni," she said. "Come stand up in front of the class, dear."

Obeita nodded at the soldier, and he promptly left, allowing Noni to walk up to the front of the room. Obeita gloated as she saw the eyes of the other students fix upon Noni with hatred—she had after all risen to the top of the class by turning in her classmates. Then Obeita noticed Noni staring at Cross.

Obeita smiled. "Why yes, dear, we do have a new student today. That is Cross, the leader of the Student Militia."

Cross nodded in greeting, though Noni gave no response.

"Cross, this is Noni, the current star of my class," Obeita said sweetly. "You would do well to follow her example—her progress is already making me famous, isn't that right, Noni?"

Noni smiled at her. "I'm very glad, ma'am."

Obeita could see that Cross looked stricken.

"Now, Noni, go take your seat," she ordered.

The girl obediently went to her desk behind Cross, where she allowed the soldier to recuff her to the chair. Obeita nodded, pleased.

"Everyone, to accommodate our new student we're going to begin a fresh session," Obeita announced. "Open your books and start doing problems one through twenty on page four-seventy-nine. You have half an hour."

The students opened their books, took out their pencils, and began scribbling away on their papers. Obeita was happy to see that even Cross went about his work with apparent diligence. She leaned back in her chair with her hands behind her head, totally relaxed as the students toiled away.

Five minutes later, Noni raised her hand. Knowing what that meant, Obeita smiled and nodded at her.

"Ma'am, Cross is scribbling nonsense on his paper instead of doing his work," Noni said, pointing at the offending writing.

Cross looked shocked. Obeita grinned at her old student, then turned to the soldier. The soldier pressed a button on a remote, and Cross let out a cry of pain as he received a moderate zap.

"Just a warning, Cross," Obeita told the boy. "You're new to this class, so we'll let you off easy." She turned to Noni. "Thank you, dear, that means extra points for you."

Obeita could see resentment and what looked like disappointment on Cross' face as he returned to work. It had been a long time since fourth grade. Clearly, her new class hadn't been what Cross was expecting. That pleased Obeita. She now had the chance to redo his education all over again, and it was that learning process that Obeita loved.

A few minutes later, Obeita was surprised to see Noni's hand shoot up again. Obeita sat forward in her chair, leaning over her teacher's desk.

"Yes, Noni, what is it now?" she asked.

"Floe has been neglecting her work, ma'am," Noni said. "She's been glancing over at Cross instead of keeping her eyes on her paper."

Obeita blinked, then glared at Floe, who looked both guilty and frightened. Obeita nodded at the soldier, and Floe let out a whimper just before the shock hit her. She screamed, then slumped onto her desk, face buried in her textbook. Cross looked furious.

"You should know better than that, Floe," Obeita scolded. "Pay attention to your work—you're here to learn, not to socialize!"

Floe mumbled an apology and shakily picked up her pencil again. Cross seethed for a few moments longer, and for a moment Obeita considered giving him another shock as well. Then he took a deep breath and returned to his work.

Another ten minutes passed without disruption. Obeita fanned herself with a notebook. The air was hot and stuffy in here, and none of the classrooms had air conditioning. Noni closed her book and raised her hand. This time almost the entire class glared at her.

Obeita smiled. "Yes, Noni?"

"I've finished my work, ma'am."

Obeita felt another swell of pride. Noni was a smart girl, and it hadn't taken long for Obeita's instruction to bring the best out in her. It occurred to Obeita that it would be a good way to crush Cross' spirit by doting on the successful rival he clearly disliked.

"Private, please uncuff Noni and bring her to the front of the room," Obeita told the soldier. "I would like her to put her answers up on the board for extra credit. The rest of the class could learn well from her example."

The soldier moved over to Noni's desk. He unlocked her handcuffs, and followed her to the front of the class. Like the proper student she was, Noni brought her paper and pencil. Obeita grinned at Cross as he followed Noni with an angry glare. Ignoring him, Noni reached the board, looking down at her paper as she chewed on her pencil eraser.

Then she spun around and plunged her pencil into the soldier's eye.

It was so sudden that Cross almost didn't believe his eyes. After watching Noni betray both him and Floe to Obeita for imaginary points, Cross had been convinced that Floe had been right and the former Truant was totally brainwashed—perhaps irredeemably. The vacant expression on Noni's face and the extent of her robotic subservience had genuinely disappointed him.

Noni wore a look of utmost fury as she drove the pencil deeper into her victim. Cross watched with mingled horror and fascination as she threw the injured man to the ground and jumped on his throat. Obeita seemed dumbstruck, staring at the scene with mouth agape. Noni retrieved the keys and remote from the slain soldier and unlocked the device around her ankle.

Snapping back to her senses, Obeita began waddling frantically towards her desk, where a panic button had been installed. Noni caught her before she took three steps. The teacher opened her mouth to scream, only to have the electric device stuffed into it. Then Noni ruthlessly pressed a button on the soldier's remote.

Cross averted his eyes and saw Floe doing the same as Obeita's muffled shrieks filled the room.

The noise seemed to go on forever. When it finally stopped, Cross turned his head back. Obeita was lying on the floor like a beached whale, unmoving. Noni was breathing heavily, her finger still pressing the button. The look on her face was beyond anger, beyond hatred—it was focused, and had tapped something primal that told Cross that many people were now going to die.

Silence. Then a restrained cheering filled the room. Cross heard a few catcalls ring out as Noni dispassionately pressed another button on the remote, and all the ankle devices in the room unlocked. Cross himself felt no sympathy for the teacher who had been one of his many tormentors as a child.

Satisfied that Obeita was dead, Noni went down the rows of desks, releasing all of their handcuffs. The freed students stood up to stretch, rubbed their wrists, and tried to thank her. She ignored every one of them. Her eyes met Floe's as she came around, and Floe mumbled her thanks. Noni paused and for a moment looked like she might say something. Then she moved on.

When she reached Cross she gave no sign that she'd recognized him, though Cross knew she had by her reaction when she first spotted him.

"I knew you had to be better than that." Cross rubbed his wrist. "How long have you been acting?"

Noni's icy blue eyes seemed to penetrate him for a moment, and in them he could see untold suffering. Then she moved on without saying a word.

Cross watched her go, then turned his attention to Floe. They hesitated, then flew into each other's arms. Cross hugged her tightly, thinking darkly about how powerless he had felt when Obeita had her electrocuted.

Soon all the students were free, though none of them made a move. Perhaps it was part of their conditioning, but they all waited silently at their desks, watching Noni. Noni turned her attention to the dead soldier, stripping him of his weapons and armor, taking them for herself.

As she stood up again, she found the eyes of the entire class on her. For the first time, she spoke, and her voice was no longer monotone and compliant but cold and hard.

"I don't really care about any of you," she informed them. "I'm getting out of here. You can take your chances by yourself, you can try to stop me, or you can follow me. Those are your choices."

Then she donned the soldier's body armor, even though it was too big for her, and lifted his rifle. Without waiting for a reply, she darted out the door.

Another moment of silence. Floe and Cross looked at each other. Then every single person in the room followed Noni out the door as gunshots rang out in the hall.

Well, I've had enough for now," Takan said, standing up and dusting himself off. "Who knows how long we'll be sitting here before something happens."

"Cross did say that we should wait only twenty-four hours before coming to get him," the albino replied. "If only there was a way for us to contact him."

"No use wishing for what we can't have," Takan said. "I'm going inside. If you need me I'll be in the old bar room on the second floor—maybe the Truants missed a few bottles when they left."

The albino waved good-bye as Takan walked towards the stairs. Just then, there came the distant but unmistakable sound of an explosion off in the direction of the camp. Takan froze and the albino shot to her feet. Faint gunshots soon followed. The two teenagers looked at each other.

"You know, I'm starting to get used to being wrong." Takan shook his head. "All right, let's go ask Cross how he did it."

The albino followed Takan down into the old Truancy hideout, where the other rebels had also heard the commotion. They hurried about, loading up on weapons and explosives, marching down the dark stairwell as they prepared to run to the aid of their fellow citizens in the camp.

28
FADE TO BLACK

F rag out!"

Cross ducked behind a column as someone hurled a grenade towards the front doors of the school. A moment later it went off, and the doors flew off their hinges along with a Government soldier. Cross raised his rifle and fired at some of the dark shapes waiting outside. It seemed that the soldiers had been caught off guard, and two of them fell before finding new cover.

"Come on, let's clear the courtyard!" Cross shouted.

The other students roared with approval as they stormed the door. The kids from the Intensive program, armed with weapons from soldiers Noni had slain, had quickly scattered throughout the building and liberated the other classes with lesser security. Not everyone had gone along with the revolt—some were too broken by the system or otherwise cowed. However, enough had joined to overcome the relative handful of soldiers guarding them.

As Cross advanced, he noticed more students running down the hall to join the offensive, all of them armed with guns and armor. Someone must have found a Government weapons cache. Cross let them take the lead, catching his breath against another column. He turned to look at Floe, who had been following him closely.

"You all right?" he asked.

Floe nodded, though she looked shaken. She had only reluctantly donned armor, grenades, and a sidearm at Cross' insistence, and he hadn't seen her fire a single shot yet. Her eyes were wide and kept straying to the bodies of fallen soldiers and students.

"What's wrong?" Cross pressed.

"I-I'm sorry, I can't do it anymore." Floe shook her head vigorously. "I've had enough of war. These soldiers aren't all bad people; some of them were nice to me. Those kids earlier—"

Cross flinched as another grenade blast went off outside.

"—were harassing me because I made friends with a couple of soldiers."

Cross processed her words. Floe had always been the most compassionate of their group, caring even about the Truants they killed. He had thought it was just because they were her old comrades, but now he realized the truth: Floe was by her nature too kind for war. She didn't belong here.

Further blasts and a crescendo of gunfire snapped Cross' attention back to their current situation. He wiped a stray tear from Floe's face with his hand.

"I understand," he told her. "Stay close to me and keep your head down. You don't have to do anything. We'll get out of here."

She smiled faintly at him and nodded.

Cross gave her shoulder a squeeze, and then turned and followed a fresh group of students out the door with Floe right behind him. They burst out into the courtyard and found it in turmoil—the uprising had spread like wildfire. Gray-clad students were everywhere, sheer numbers overwhelming the guards. Mobs of kids beat and stomped on the soldiers with their bare limbs. Others were firing up at the guard towers with stolen weapons.

"Where is Noni?" Floe shouted over the din. "I didn't see her leave!"

That was a good question. Cross hadn't seen their liberator since they'd split up in the school corridors. He glanced around the courtyard and frowned. There was no hope of spotting her in this mess.

"Noni must have her own plan," Cross told Floe. "Don't worry, she's strong, we'll see her later."

Just then one of the students nearby crumpled and fell from a gunshot. Cross looked around wildly for the attacker and then spotted him—a guard standing high atop one of the walls. Cross raised his rifle to fire back, but even as he did an enormous tremor shook the ground, and a huge chunk of the wall blew in as though it were made of sand. The soldier toppled as the section beneath him collapsed.

Cross felt his heart soar as dark shapes emerged from the gap, led by a boy in a trench coat. Takan's reinforcements had arrived. Cheers went up as the Truants closest to the wall recognized their old leader, and for the briefest of moments Cross resented Takan for receiving all the credit. He scolded himself for the thought.

"Come on!" Cross told Floe. "This is our chance! Sepp will be leading another group to blow a different part of the wall, so we should—"

"Sepp?" Floe interrupted, sounding strange. "I thought he was captured."

"He escaped, he was the one who told us you were in trouble," Cross explained quickly. "You'll get to see him later, now let's get out of here!"

Floe did not protest and let Cross lead her along through the crowded courtyard, though there was a troubled expression on her face. Cross' attention was drawn by a group trying to break into the dormitories to release the students still trapped there. Moments later the doors caved in, and many more gray bodies began pouring out into the courtyard.

The excitement in the atmosphere rubbed off on Cross. It was really different when you had something to fight for. He found himself yelling as he fired up at the few remaining guards on the walls. One of them fell forwards, and dozens of angry students surged forward to meet him. Only now did Cross appreciate just how many youths there were in the City. There had to be hundreds and hundreds in this camp alone.

Another enormous blast went off at the other end of the courtyard, collapsing that part of the wall as well.

"That'll be Sepp!" Cross exulted, not noticing how Floe's face went pale. "Nothing can stop us now!"

Indeed the students were now spilling out of the gaps in the walls, climbing over one another in their rush to escape. Cross and Floe elbowed their way through the crowd as they made for the closest exit.

Then Cross became aware of the familiar roar of helicopters, and he and Floe looked up. A dark shape blotted out the moon, and Cross felt his excitement dim. The first Government reinforcements had arrived to investigate the commotion—when they found out that prisoners were escaping, things would get ugly. Ground troops couldn't be far behind.

Cross tugged Floe harder as they scrambled up over broken chunks of the wall. His gaze was held heavenwards, watching the nearest helicopter. As it maneuvered, the light of the moon illuminated the helicopter's occupants. Cross grimaced. He had seen the silhouette of a woman, standing next to a boy dressed in black.

Apprehension settled in as he realized that both the General *and* the Mayor had come for them.

Noni hummed to herself as she strolled down the empty green hallway. After the initial excitement, things had quieted down inside the school. Noni hadn't run into anyone—student or Government—for several minutes. She preferred it that way, it gave her more privacy for what she was going to do. The battle outside could be faintly heard, but Noni ignored it. Her business was here, for now.

Reaching the familiar door to the psychiatric ward, Noni kicked it in, letting the door swing a few times before stepping inside. The room was dark. Still humming to herself, Noni meandered over to the largest desk.

A quivering lump hiding behind the desk gave a yelp of terror and leaped backwards.

Noni smiled. "Hello again, *sir.*"

"Noni," Ferraro licked his lips nervously. "It-it's so good to see you're all right."

Noni calmly raised her rifle. Ferraro stared at the weapon.

"Steady there." Ferraro held his hands up. "Noni, it's clear that you're suffering from a little relapse, but it's nothing I can't fix. I have another dose right around here, just let me—"

Noni lunged at Ferraro, and the man yelped and turned to run. She seized him by the scruff of his neck and threw him into one of his own chairs. Disoriented, Ferraro didn't notice Noni securing his wrists with the built-in restraints until it was too late.

"You, and everyone like you, are the ones that need fixing."

Ferraro gulped as he stared up into Noni's pitiless blue eyes.

"Listen, Noni," Ferraro said. "I know you have some traumatic experiences in your past, but we can work them out! Let's talk!"

But Noni wasn't listening. She continued to hum to herself as she rummaged about the ward. Finding an unused syringe, Noni tested the piston and nodded to herself. Then she turned back to face Ferraro.

"You know, your drugs did work to an extent," Noni said. "I was suggestible at times. I even appreciate the calm focus you gave me. But the programming, the humiliation—not so much."

Noni smiled and began advancing upon Ferraro. Not knowing what else to do, the man smiled back nervously.

"And you know what, doctor? I never stopped hating you for a second," Noni said. "You never changed who I was. Tonight I felt a little more clearheaded than usual, and so . . ."

Noni waved her wrists to show that she was uncuffed. Ferraro looked terrified.

"Obeita is dead," Noni continued. "She had too much respect for your treatments, and too little for me. Same with you."

"Noni, please," Ferraro said in a panicky voice. "Please, I was trying to help—"

"Shut up," Noni snapped. "You're scum. Say it."

Ferraro gulped. "I'm . . . I'm scum."

"Yes, you are," Noni said. "Humiliate yourself like I did. Say that you're a dirty sewage-eating rat, and don't forget to smile."

With obvious difficulty, Ferraro forced a grin. "I-I'm a s-sewage r-rat eating—"

"Close enough." Noni shrugged, satisfied. "Now, I have to get going, so its time for your dose. We wouldn't want you to relapse into old habits."

Noni held up the empty syringe, and Ferraro stared at it. It took him a moment to understand. Then realization and horror dawned on the man's face. Seeing that, Noni plunged the needle into him, injecting a fatal air bubble into his bloodstream.

Then she turned and went to join the battle in the courtyard, leaving a terrified Ferraro strapped to the chair to wait for the inevitable embolism to stop his heart.

Watch out!"

Cross ducked and pushed Floe down as gunfire rained over their heads. They had escaped through the gap in the wall only to be pinned down on the waterfront. A few soldiers from the helicopters had landed to cut off their escape into the district, forcing the escapees to take cover with the water to their backs.

Cross sprung up and fired back at the soldiers, thanking his luck that the moon was full and bright tonight, giving him enough light to discern the enemies. A shot whizzed by dangerously close to his head, and Cross dropped down again. Out of the corner of his eye he could see students still spilling from the gap, taking advantage of the soldiers' distraction as they ran for the cover of the buildings.

"Floe, over there!" Cross pointed at the escaping prisoners. "Go with them, Takan's group will be leaving first so you should—"

"Takan?" Floe repeated. "Isn't he an enemy?"

Cross hesitated, realizing that he hadn't yet told Floe anything about their alliance or Takan's strange history. He shook his head, resolving to explain everything later.

"He's on our side now," Cross said. "Listen, I'll throw some grenades and keep their attention, you have to escape with the—"

"No." Floe looked at him fiercely. "Not without you. We made a promise."

There was no room in her voice for negotiation. Feeling a strange fluttering feeling, Cross closed his mouth and nodded against his better judgment. A roar from above caught their attention, and Cross looked up to see the black shape of a helicopter hovering close by. Cross fired up at it, and the helicopter veered off towards some enormous shipping containers.

Cross gritted his teeth, his heart pounding—not with bloodlust, but with determination to protect the person crouched next to him. More gunfire flew above them, keeping them in place, and he realized that if this kept up then they would both eventually be killed. Then he glanced again at the nearby cargo containers, and a plan came to him.

"Floe, see those containers over there?" Cross gestured with his head. "When I say go, we're going to run for it. The soldiers won't expect it."

Floe simply nodded in agreement.

"All right, hold on."

Cross withdrew two grenades that he'd confiscated from fallen soldiers. He pulled one pin, then the other, and threw both with all of his strength. One of them burst with expected force. To his surprise, the second produced a blinding flash and deafening noise. Even better.

"GO!" Cross roared.

Floe sprang up from her crouch and dashed for the containers. Cross followed as best he could. She was faster than him normally, he had more to carry. As they reached the cover of the containers, Cross breathed a sigh of relief. The containers were bigger than they'd looked from afar, stacked at least two high.

"Hey, look!" Floe was looking back towards the camps. "It's Noni!"

Cross turned around and caught a glimpse of a girl with a familiar black ponytail slipping through the gap and off into the shadows, out of sight.

"I think you're right," Cross said. "But she's gone now."

"If only there were a way to get her attention." Floe bit her lower lip. "She'd be a huge help if she came with us."

Cross shook his head. "Nothing we can do. The way she's going will take her to Sepp's group—we'll probably see her again when we regroup at headquarters."

"I hope so." Floe smiled at Cross. "We should keep going, now. It won't take them long to figure out where we went."

"Yeah." Cross straightened up. "We need to get out somewhere safe and then reach the cover of the buildings."

The two students began running through the spaces between the rows of containers. It was a little like a maze, Cross thought. The metal boxes had been abandoned for so long that they were all rusted, the paint wearing off of most of them. Then a metallic clang echoed throughout the area, and they froze. Someone else was in there with them.

Cross looked at Floe and raised his finger to his lips. She nodded. The two proceeded cautiously, slinking through the shadows without sudden movement or noise. Rusted container after rusted container slipped by. It was nerve-wracking, stalking through the shadows, each row looking like the last.

A soldier appeared from around a corner. Cross fired and the man fell. Cross winced at the noise of the shot. It had surely given away their position.

Abandoning subtlety, Cross and Floe broke into a run, heading towards the safety of District 13's buildings. He tried not to think of how many other soldiers might be hiding behind each container. Cross felt his heart beating in his throat as the noise of a helicopter passed above, and he hoped beyond hope that it hadn't spotted them.

Then they turned a corner, and something huge and black dropped down from a container above. This time Cross knew exactly *who* it was. He raised his gun, but the Mayor fired first, the wild shot grazing Cross' leg. Floe screamed as Cross fell backwards, but he wasn't finished, not yet. Both Cross and the Mayor adjusted their aims—

There was a tinkling sound from above, and then something large and white dropped down between them.

"Teacher?"

Cross stared up at the albino. She had interposed herself between him and the Mayor, her arms spread protectively. Stunned, Cross and Umasi lowered their weapons at the same time. She turned to face Umasi.

"Milady." Umasi bowed his head in greeting.

The albino looked at him gravely, but did not reply. Her next words were addressed to Cross.

"Go," she told him. "I'll handle this."

Cross glanced at Floe, who looked dumbstruck by this latest turn of events. He helped her to her feet and nodded at the girl he considered to be his only true teacher.

"Good luck," he said.

The albino smiled faintly and turned her attention back to Umasi. "Shall we take this somewhere more private?"

Umasi nodded. "Of course."

The two old acquaintances slipped away into the shadows as though they were made of smoke. Alone once more, Cross and Floe glanced at each other. Neither of them knew quite what to say. Cross chalked it up as another thing for them to discuss later.

With the Mayor out of the way, Cross and Floe managed to leave the cover of the containers, emerging very close to the streets. As they reached the cover of the buildings, loud and frequent gunshots indicated a firefight nearby. Cross and Floe dashed down an empty street and turned a corner. A harrowing sight met their eyes.

Takan and a large group of rebels and escapees were pinned down behind large fallen chunks of a building. On the other side of the obstructions, keeping the group in place with a withering storm of gunfire, were two dozen soldiers led by General Iris herself.

Floe crouched down next to Cross as they took cover behind the street corner. Her fingers were clasped around her sidearm, though she had yet to fire it. At this range she knew it'd be no help, yet she hated herself anyway for her uselessness. Cross was risking his life to protect her, firing around the corner at Iris' forces, and she could do nothing to help him.

Floe squeezed the pistol so tight that her knuckles turned white. After

Cross had confessed his love for her she had felt almost like she was floating—even a life in the camps with him hadn't seemed bad. Then the fighting had started, and hard reality returned. Floe wasn't used to being a burden. All her life she had tried to be strong, but now she wasn't even sure what that meant.

Floe couldn't imagine killing as brutally as she had watched Noni do in the classroom. She couldn't imagine pulling off the dignity and grace that the nameless girl possessed so naturally. What then was she capable of?

"Damn, I think they spotted me." Cross breathed heavily as he leaned against the building. "Some of the soldiers broke off from the main group; they're probably coming to flank us."

Gunshots peppered their position, and Cross returned fire. Floe dropped her sidearm, knowing that she wouldn't be using it. It would be all over soon anyway. If the soldiers didn't get to them first, Iris would surely be calling helicopters to wipe them out with deadly fire from above. She was just happy that Cross was standing by her to the end, as he had promised.

Maybe Sepp at least would survive, she thought sadly. Floe felt guilty about that whole affair—she regretted ever burdening Sepp with her presence, regretted sleeping with him, regretted messing with his feelings when she'd always known she didn't love him. He had been loyal to her, bringing Cross to her aid. She wanted so dearly to apologize, but it looked as though that chance would never come.

"Wait, Floe, I think Takan has a plan!" Cross said.

Floe blinked. "What?"

Cross pointed to the middle of the intersection, where an open sewer manhole rested in the middle of the road. Floe remembered now that the Truancy had used the sewers to get around before the subways were vacated. She had never done it herself. But if it was their only hope . . .

"All right, how are we doing it?" Floe asked.

"We're going to get the unarmed out first," Cross said. "Takan will send them in small groups while we hopefully keep the soldiers back. You can go with—"

"No," Floe said firmly. "I'm staying with you."

Cross looked reluctant but nodded. Then he twisted around the corner and fired at the soldiers as a group of gray-clad escapees dashed for the manhole. Floe held her breath as they ran, then let it out in relief as the last one vanished from sight. This happened several times until Floe finally saw Takan slip down the hole behind the rest of his armed compatriots.

Cross continued to provide cover fire until Takan was gone. Then he seized Floe by the arm and pulled her behind him. Floe glanced at the soldiers down the block. They had now realized what was going on and were advancing, but there was no way they would clear the obstacles in time. Floe felt her heart soar, daring for the first time to hope.

Then, just as Cross was a few steps away from the manhole, Floe glanced back the way they came and her blood froze—General Iris was running towards them, ahead of the other soldiers sent to flank Cross. Cross hadn't noticed anything was wrong; he still had his back turned, his focus on the manhole.

Iris raised her rifle at Cross.

Floe realized numbly that Cross was going to die. She was going to lose him after all. Memories of her childhood flashed before her eyes, and Floe saw a sweet boy with red hair who had always helped her. Then she blinked and saw Cross, a determined man doing everything he could to protect her.

In that moment Floe finally realized what she was capable of doing—what she had to do, to repay the debt she had earned and protect what was most important.

Floe reached for her only weapon left, a grenade at her side. Iris noticed immediately, adjusting her aim. Floe pulled the pin from the grenade and prepared to throw it.

Then Iris' bullet caught her straight between the eyes.

Cross spun around when he heard the shot. In the shock of the moment his eyes registered three things: Iris, rifle raised. Floe, shot in the head. Grenade, no pin.

Before Cross' mind had a chance to process what he was looking at, survival instinct kicked in. Cross hurled himself down the open manhole just as Iris' gunfire sailed through the air where he'd been a moment ago. The impact of what he had seen hit him at the same time as the ground.

"No, Floe—"

The grenade went off. Cross saw the explosion as a flash at the mouth of the manhole. Then there was a great crumbling sound, and suddenly it seemed like the sky was falling. Cross rolled aside just as enormous chunks of the road caved in. The streets of District 13 had gone unmaintained for many years, and the blast had been enough to break the ground, sealing the hole.

Lying there amidst the muck and rubble, breathing the dusty sewer air, Cross became aware of pain from his fall—dull, distant, as though it belonged to another person. Worse was the emotional pain. Cross had seen it happen, yet it still hadn't fully sunk in yet.

He and Floe had only just admitted their feelings to each other. He had held her in his arms not even an hour ago. They had so many things left to do, promises to keep, lost time to make up for. She couldn't be dead. Not like this. Not so suddenly.

"Cross! Cross, are you all right?"

For a moment Cross imagined that the voice belonged to Floe. Then with a pang he recognized Takan's voice. He could hear splashing as Takan ran towards him, but he didn't move. It was like there was no energy left in his limbs. Takan cursed as he drew near, clearly thinking that Cross had been injured.

Cross remained perfectly limp as Takan first took his pulse, and then roughly pulled his shirt up. Takan carefully checked for blood or broken bones. Finding nothing serious after several minutes, the Truant let out a noise of puzzlement. Then he noticed that Cross' eyes were open.

"Cross!" Takan shook him. "Where does it hurt?"

Slowly, as though lifted by a puppet string, Cross brought his hand up to point at his heart.

"Here," he whispered.

With that word, the dull ache Cross had been feeling finally burst into the full pain of his loss, pain he had never imagined possible. Cross let out a wail that echoed throughout the sewer, and he cried as he thrashed about, defying Takan's attempts to hold him still. Takan was baffled by the outburst. Then he looked up at where the ground had caved in, and a flickering of realization dawned on his face.

"Cross!" Takan pinned Cross to the ground. "Where is Floe? Did she fall behind? Was she captured again? If so we can still—"

Cross shook his head violently and continued to sob. Then Takan understood the full truth of what must have happened, and the Truant fell silent. Gently, then firmly, he tried to pull Cross to his feet. Cross resisted.

"Leave me alone!" Cross shouted.

Takan shook his head. "Listen, Cross, I know what you feel like—"

"No you don't!"

"Do you think you're the only one who's ever lost someone you care about?" Takan shouted back. "Stop being stupid! We have to get out of here! What about the rest of the City? What would Floe have wanted?"

"I don't care!"

Takan went quiet, looking down at Cross with an unreadable expression. Cross turned his head away, content to lie there forever. Then Takan spoke again.

"What about her killer?" he whispered. "Don't you want to avenge her, Cross? Or do you not care about even that?"

Cross stirred at that. The memory of Iris with her gun raised and Floe dead had been etched into his mind. Slowly, he felt his pain turn to anger—hot, bubbling, destructive anger that gnawed at his insides. Sensing the change in him, Takan reached down and pulled Cross to his feet.

This time Cross did not resist as Takan hooked his arm under Cross' armpit and began dragging him deeper into the darkness of the sewers. Cross had lost a dear friend that night, but now he knew he had also gained a personal enemy.

29
ORDER AND CHAOS

The pale moon lingered overhead, bathing the docks of District 13 in pale light. On the waterfront, two figures that had been running for many minutes finally came to a halt. They turned to face each other. The chaos of the camp had been left far behind, on the other end of the district. The battle was surely over by now, though fires still blazed in the distance—a red scar on the horizon.

Here there was only the lapping of gentle waves against a shattered pier, and the white orb of the moon mirrored on dark waters. The wooden columns that had once supported the pier remained like black pillars stretching out into the river. On either end of that tableau, the albino and Umasi now gazed at each other in silence.

It was the first time they had met in four years. So much between them had gone unsaid in that time. And yet, neither of them now seemed able to find the words.

Finally, the albino broke the silence.

"It's nice to find you in good health," she said. "How have you been, Umasi?"

Umasi inclined his head. "Decent."

"I never got a chance to thank you for protecting me when we were fleeing in District 2," the albino said. "I appreciate it."

"You're welcome."

"It's funny," the albino continued, gazing up at the moon, "I always looked forward to meeting you again. I just never expected it to be like this."

Umasi solemnly removed his sunglasses and placed them in his pocket.

"I don't want to fight you, milady," he told her. "If your intention was merely to get me alone for a chat, then you've succeeded."

The albino smiled. "A chat sounds great. Do you plan to bring me to a camp afterwards?"

"Of course not." Umasi looked stung. "I thought we knew each other better than that. Then again I never expected you of all people to align yourself with this destructive rebellion—what were you thinking, milady?"

"I was going to ask you the same thing," she replied. "I've kept *my* hands clean so far. What about yours?"

Umasi frowned. "If you plan to convince me to abandon my post as Mayor, then I'm afraid you're wasting your time."

"So this General Iris, she really is your sister?"

"The only family I have." Umasi sighed. "I know what it must look like to you, but Iris is doing her best to take care of the citizens. If the rebellion ended today, then supplies would flow into the deep City. Within a few years the students would all be out of the camps. The City would be rebuilt. We would have peace!"

The albino gazed at him thoughtfully for a few moments. Then, to Umasi's surprise, she burst into laughter, like the ringing of small bells.

Umasi creased his brow. "What's so funny?"

"Oh, nothing much." The albino wiped her eyes, suddenly sounding serious. "You really are like your father."

"What?" Umasi blinked. "No."

"It's true," she insisted. "You and your brother were like order and chaos. He tried to fight authority, to change things, and you had to stop him."

"It wasn't like that."

"Wasn't it?" She cocked her head. "You attacked the Truancy, Umasi. You never attacked the Educators, never disrupted their system, never tried to undermine it—your nature wouldn't allow it. You love order."

"I fought with Zen because he was killing people!"

"As if he had any other way to change the City."

Umasi frowned. "Even if I did have a preference, so what? So what if after discovering my father's motivations I agreed with him over Zyid? The Mayor wanted to *save* this City. He gave his *life* for it!"

The albino crossed her arms. "So did your brother."

"Did you think I've forgotten that?" Umasi glared. "I'm the only one left, milady. I'm trying to salvage what's left from their war—a war that would never have happened if Zyid hadn't overreacted!"

"Listen to yourself!" the albino retorted. "You sound just like the old Mayor, and you're making the same mistakes as him too! Umasi, I saw enough of what happens in those camps to make me sick!"

Umasi clenched his fists at that and turned his back on her.

"This conversation is over," he said, taking a step away.

The albino loosened a length of chain from her wrist. The links caught the moonlight, jingling as they glittered.

"I disagree," she said. "I still haven't convinced you to stop."

Umasi went still, his head bowed.

"I don't want to hurt you, milady," he said in a pained voice. "Don't make me do this. Walk away, disappear—I promise I'll forget about you."

"I could never stay hidden forever," the albino whispered. "And besides, I don't want you to forget me."

Umasi seemed to grapple with himself for a moment. Then he straightened up and turned around to face her once again.

"So be it."

The Mayor unbuttoned his windbreaker and allowed it to fall to the ground. The albino did the same with her blue Student Militia jacket. Dressed in black and white they faced each other. Turning towards the columns of the shattered piers, Umasi performed an elegant leap onto the nearest pillar. He continued making short jumps until he was ten columns deep, far out into the river. Only then did he turn around.

"Do you still intend to stop me?" he asked.

The albino smiled. "Of course."

"Then come and get me."

With grace and agility even greater than Umasi's, the nameless girl hopped after him until only three pillars separated them. The moon shone bright above them like a witness, its shimmering light reflecting off the waves. The waters were calm beneath them, and the albino found it all very relaxing as she faced off against Umasi.

"Are you ready?" he asked.

She nodded. Then he drew his white swords, and their duel began.

Umasi charged straight for the albino, bounding across the pillars. She responded by throwing her chain straight out at him. He knocked the ring aside with one blade and then swung forward with the other. The albino flipped sideways, touched down on the adjacent pillar with her hand, with her feet then landing on the pillar after.

Seamlessly she launched her chain again, and as it swung around it skimmed the water surface. Droplets scattered into the air, catching the moonlight—like pearls in the night. Umasi formed a cross at his side with his blades, blocking the metal ring. He prepared to attack again, but the albino was already moving.

Umasi quickly discovered that his opponent was able to jump the pillars faster than he could. Once there were four pillars between them, she abruptly swung the chain around at him—its arc was wide enough to catch him no matter where he jumped. Umasi ducked the attack, the chain whooshing over his head. The albino swung again, and this time Umasi blocked the chain with his broken sword.

The chain wrapped around the short blade, and the albino realized her danger. She jumped straight towards Umasi rather than giving him a chance to pull the chain. As she landed on the pillar in front of him, Umasi slashed upwards, the tip of his sword grazing the river, carving a watery slash through the air.

The albino shocked him by performing a perfect backflip, evading the sword and landing on the pillar behind her. Then she tugged on her chain.

Umasi freed his broken sword just in time to avoid being pulled forward into the river. He jumped forward. Instead of aiming at him, the albino swung her chain low at the pillar next to him. The chain caught onto the pillar, causing the end to swing around.

Before Umasi realized what was happening, the chain struck him from the back just as he landed on the pillar in front of the albino. He stumbled forward, swords outstretched, and the albino reflexively jumped out of the way—but her chain had wrapped fully around the pillar, and when she made her leap she found it had gone taut.

Both combatants plunged into the water. Great splashes followed by ripples disturbed the moon on the black surface. Using her chain, the albino pulled herself up first. She sat atop the pillar, panting, then spotted Umasi still shivering in the river.

The water wasn't that cold, she thought. It seemed almost as though Umasi was reliving something from his past. Smiling now, she lightly tossed him her chain. He looked up at her in surprise, then allowed her to pull him up.

The two old friends soon found themselves sitting back to back on the tiny surface of the pillar, their legs off the side. There was perfect silence between them as they paddled at the water with their feet. The fight, the albino felt, had been more like a dance rather than a serious attempt to kill. Neither of them had really wanted to harm the other.

They remained like that for hours, watching the moon travel through the sky overhead. During that fleeting time, the albino felt at peace with the world and the warmth at her back. Then the first rays of sunrise began to peek over the horizon.

"Now that was the greeting I was looking for," the albino murmured, finding her voice soft with disuse. "It feels like old times again."

"A tie this time—that part is new." Umasi sighed. "You know, I think I was happier back then, living a simple life in District 19. I miss it."

"Why not go back to it?" the albino asked. "Walk away from this conflict. You're not meant to be a warrior, Umasi."

Umasi shook his head sadly.

"I believe in Iris, milady," he told her. "She's the only blood relation I have now."

The albino sighed. She glanced at the sunrise, realizing now that the time had finally come. For four years she had kept this secret. She could now keep it no longer. The albino felt a heavy weight lift from her chest as she spoke.

"That's not quite true," she told him. "You have a son. I named him Zen."

Takan took a sip of beer from his latest bottle—foul stuff, something cheap meant for deli shelves. He was sitting on a large wooden crate that had been used to package the beer he was now working his way through. A small part of Takan's conscience nagged that he was developing a bit of a drinking problem, but he ignored it. After the previous night it was impossible to stay sober.

Takan felt both impossibly tired and unable to rest. The battle and subsequent escape had been exhausting, but no matter how hard he tried, he couldn't take his mind off Cross' loss. Dragging the grieving student through the sewers beneath ten districts had reminded Takan of losing his sister two years earlier. Neither of them had emerged in a good mood.

The bottle empty, Takan tossed it aside. He reached down into the open side of the crate and pulled out another. The beer was warm and pretty bad at that, but he wasn't very picky. His thoughts grew more muddled with each gulp, and all he wanted was to muddle them more.

They had traveled through the sewers and rendezvoused as planned in a hideout in District 29, an old shipping warehouse. Shortly after making sure Cross would be okay, Takan had excused himself. It was in a dark corner of the warehouse that Takan had discovered the providential crate of beer.

He had heard Sepp's group arrive just minutes earlier. Takan knew that was only going to mean more grief. Cross might've been too dense to see it, but Takan could tell by the way Sepp acted that he had also had a thing for Floe. Takan wasn't sure how he would handle two depressed students moping around.

Takan finished his latest bottle and tossed it aside. It hit the wall and shattered. He reached down for another, determined to keep going until he finally passed out.

Through the alcoholic haze he became aware of a dark shape in front of him. In a flash it had knocked the bottle from his hand. Instinctively Takan reached for his sword. Then he looked up and saw her face.

"You're pathetic," Noni said.

Takan blinked up at the girl, who was glaring down at him distastefully.

"This beer is worse than I thought," Takan murmured. "I'm seeing Noni here in a gray uniform. That's pretty wild."

Noni rapped him on the head, hard enough to convince him she was real.

"I was locked up in that camp, Takan," she told him. "I'd wondered if you came for me—guess that was too much to hope for."

Takan massaged his head. "Why are you here, Noni?"

"I just arrived with Sepp's group," Noni replied. "I came to see a boy I thought I liked, but it seems that he's let himself become a mess."

Takan sighed. "Noni, you have no idea what I've gone—"

"No, *you* have no idea what *I've* gone through," Noni snarled. "You don't see me running from my problems like this, do you?"

Takan slumped over on his crate.

"I'm sorry," he said. "I'm glad to see you again. Are you with us now?"

"I suppose." Noni folded her arms. "Your rebellion offers the best chance for me to get my revenge on the Government, on their leader, and on that new Mayor."

Takan stirred at that, remembering how Umasi had told him he'd kept Takan's secret. Feeling a sudden urge to reveal everything, to end the charade and damn the consequences, Takan opened his mouth.

"Noni, the Mayor wasn't the one who killed Zyid—"

"This isn't all about Zyid," Noni interrupted. "There are other things I need to pay the Mayor back for. I'm in this for myself."

Takan watched broodingly as she turned and left. For several moments he lingered on top of the crate, wavering. Then he sighed and reached down for another bottle.

N ot even a body to bury," Sepp rasped.

Cross nodded weakly. He was unable to speak.

For Sepp and Cross it felt like a private funeral, shared just between the two of them. There had never been enough time or much desire to mourn Joe—but with Floe's death they realized they were the last members of their unit left alive. The two survivors sat miserably in the central part of the warehouse, surrounded by enormous metal shelves that were mostly bare.

All around them the other escapees and rebels milled about. They chatted, they ate whatever supplies were on hand, and they rested anywhere they could. Beyond one of the shelves Cross caught a glimpse of Noni pacing around looking restless. For them this was a mild celebration. They were free and alive, and the camp left in pieces.

No one had seen or heard anything from the albino. Cross hoped that she had survived. If she died right after he'd lost Floe, he wasn't sure how he would cope.

Cross blinked hot tears from his eyes. Floe's death was like a physical hole in his chest—at times it felt numb and empty, and at others it burned with so much pain that he imagined death would be preferable. As much as he wanted to keel over and give up, there was no time to break down. Someone had to take charge, and Takan had vanished shortly after their arrival. In the back of his mind Cross was grateful that Takan had brought him this far, but at the same time he wondered if the Truant should've bothered.

Sepp began sobbing, a horrible hiccupping sound. The expression on his face was truly tormented. The boy looked like he was in more pain than Cross himself.

Cross came to a realization. "You loved her too, didn't you?"

Sepp stared at him with red eyes. Then he looked down and nodded.

"I'm sorry, Cross," he said. "I didn't think there was anything between you. We were together, we liked each other . . . things just happened."

Cross' first instinct was to be angry and jealous, to ask what they had done together, to demand to know why Sepp had allowed Floe to be captured. Then he remembered that it had been he who had ordered Sepp to follow her in the first place, and all of his anger turned inwards.

"It's okay, Sepp." Cross shook his head. "This whole mess was all my fault anyway."

There it was, the haunting thought that his mind kept circling around to. The second Floe's death had finally sunk in, the doubt and guilt had begun. If Cross had never loved Floe, she would have gone with the other escapees. If Cross had made her go first, perhaps he would've been the one Iris killed. If Cross had listened to Takan when he warned that the mission was too dangerous, at least she would be alive.

"I hate them." Sepp's eyes were wide. "I've never hated anyone in my life before—I really *hate* them."

"The Government?"

Sepp wasn't listening.

"My parents didn't deserve to be jailed," he continued. "Who's going to take care of my sister? And now they killed Floe." He clenched his fists. "I hate them. I want to destroy the Government. I want to destroy them all!"

Even Cross, in the midst of his own grief, was taken aback by the venom in Sepp's voice. The boy seemed on the verge of madness as he stared at Cross.

"Cross," Sepp said, as though just noticing him. "I've got nothing left. I just want to bring down the Government. Can it be done?"

Cross nodded. He'd been thinking about it all night, as he'd relived the moment of Floe's death over and over. Floe had been innocent, reluctant to escape, refusing to fight. She didn't deserve to die, and yet Iris had shot her down anyway. Iris, a woman Cross barely knew, had become a monster in his mind. The Government, he swore, would pay.

"What are we going to do?" Sepp demanded. "Tell me how we're going to destroy them, Cross."

Cross waved his arm around at all the new recruits in the warehouse.

"We're already started," he replied. "We've got a lot more manpower now. We've found powerful allies. We've liberated a camp, and proven that the Government is not invincible."

"So what's next? Where do we go from here?"

Cross smiled grimly. "First we're going to make sure that word of this escape spreads all over the City and into all the other camps. Then, with our new strength, we're going to become the Government's worst nightmare."

"I'm with you," Sepp said solemnly. "Let's avenge her together."

"The Government will regret ever stepping into our City," Cross agreed. "We're going to finish this once and for all."

The streets of District 13 passed by in a blur as Umasi and the albino walked along. They had no destination in mind, no goal other than to collect their thoughts. Neither of them spoke, and the silence only grew tenser with each step. The albino could sense the anger in Umasi's body language. That was expected—and justified, she knew.

As they crossed an empty intersection Umasi finally spoke. His voice was bitter and harsh.

"I never thought you were capable of cruelty like this, milady."

"I thought you'd like the name. You did mention once that you preferred your brother's name to yours."

"You *know* what I'm talking about. Why didn't you tell me?"

The albino lowered her gaze, a rare display of supplication.

"I admit I . . . may have made a mistake," she conceded. "At the time, I thought it would be a poor thing to do to show up after nine months and surprise you with a burden like that."

"It would've been better than showing up four years later and surprising me with it now!"

"I know, and I regret it." The albino shook her head. "I kept telling myself we would come see you one day, but I was too stubborn, too proud. Would you have wanted to be a part of his life?"

"Of course I would have!" Umasi glared at her. "I would've done everything I could to help. How did you manage anyway, all on your own?"

"I'm surprised you have to ask. You were the one who slipped me that card to an account with an obscene amount of money."

Umasi shut his jaw as he remembered that he had done just that.

"That's the reason why I never gave it back," the albino continued. "I would have returned it otherwise. You know I—"

"*You* betrayed my trust, milady." There was pain in Umasi's voice that tugged at the albino's heart. "I've been living a lie for all these years. Your lie."

Abruptly he took a turn into a dark alley. The albino followed suit. There in the shadows they paused, leaning against the walls as the sun rose in the streets around them. Neither of them was dripping anymore, though both were still damp from the river. They looked at each other, dark eyes meeting pale blue.

"How did it happen, anyway?" Umasi asked.

The albino tilted her head. "You ought to know—or were you really so feverish that you didn't remember anything?"

Umasi frowned. "So it was real after all. I'd convinced myself it wasn't. I thought it must've been a hallucination or a dream."

The albino brought her hand to her mouth and chuckled.

"You're still naïve as ever," she said. "I always liked that about you."

"You won't win my forgiveness with flattery, milady."

"Is that so?" The albino licked her lips. "I've already apologized, Mr. Mayor. How else can I make it up to you?"

Slowly she splayed herself against the wall of the alley, fingers curled, hands pressed to the bricks on either side of her head. Her white garments were translucent from the damp, clinging tightly to her body. Her ivory skin glistened even in the gloom, and wet locks of her white hair stuck to her face. The albino knew that not everyone found her attractive—but for Umasi, who always had, the effect was immediate. She could see his breath quicken as he looked at her.

Umasi let out an exasperated hiss. "You're more manipulative than I ever gave you credit for."

"Oh, I am capable of naughtiness, once in a while." She grinned invitingly. "Shall we make that our secret?"

For a moment Umasi seemed to fight a battle with himself. Then, giving in, he stepped forward and pressed his body against hers. It was difficult and messy, but as passionate as their circumstances allowed. The sun continued to rise overhead until for a few fleeting moments the shadows themselves fled from the alley.

Afterwards, the two rearranged their clothes and sat side by side. Neither of them looked at each other.

Umasi was the first to speak.

"I suppose you'll want me to forgive you now."

The albino blinked as though surprised. "I've never asked for your forgiveness, Umasi."

Umasi sighed. "What *are* you asking for, then?"

"I told you before—I'm here to convince you to stop fighting." The albino turned to glance at him. "I want you to take Zen and leave the City. As Mayor, that much should be within your power."

"I had a feeling you'd say that. I don't seem to have much of a choice, do I?"

"This is your chance to be a father," the albino replied. "This is your chance to do something truly productive with your new power."

"And what will you do?" Umasi asked. "I can probably persuade the Government to make an exception for someone as young as Zen, but they may not look so favorably upon you. They are very serious about their quarantine."

"I had a feeling that would be the case," she said. "But if I know that Zen will be safe, I can be satisfied sharing the fate of the City. If there is any chance that I can make this a place he can return to, I will try."

Umasi sighed and stood up. "Meet me at the docks with Zen one week from now. I will talk to Iris and see what can be done." He glanced down at her. "You win again, milady."

The albino smiled up at him. "You never had a chance."

30

I t was a tumultuous time for the City. A week of destabilizing events once again plunged the streets into chaos.

Despite the best efforts of the Government, rebel agents spread news of the liberation of the District 13 camp all over the City. Riots broke out in three separate camps before being brutally suppressed. With each passing day the supply shortage grew more dire for increasing numbers of citizens, none of whom placed much faith anymore in the Government's promises of food and stability.

Meanwhile, what had come to be known as the Citizens' Rebellion continued to grow in size and support. Government troops could no longer count on the cooperation of the populace. Adults, including former Enforcers, flocked to the rebellion's banner in droves. Forgotten was the old Truancy's symbol of a T within a circle—now there was only the circle, with its bottom right quarter removed to form a C. This new sigil could be found spray painted on streets throughout the City.

Pockets of independent resistance sprouted up everywhere, seemingly overnight. Attacks against Government patrols and even small outposts were now commonplace. Rockets began to fall into military bases on a regular basis. If the City were a living, breathing organism, then it had surely turned against its Government master.

All of the fighting seemed to mirror the chaos in Umasi's mind as he lay on the small bed in the room that had been his as a child. Alone in the gloom, he looked around, his eyes flitting over familiar objects. They paused upon reaching his brother's old bed, empty now. Umasi sighed. There were a lot of memories in this room—leftovers from a simpler time.

"What should I do?" he wondered aloud.

The next day he was scheduled to meet with the albino and his son at the docks, as promised. He was already fully resolved to do what he could for the boy, and had no time to contemplate what meeting him would be like. Right now Umasi was concerned about the fate of the City, newly plunged into war, and about Iris, the sister who even now was struggling to maintain order in the City.

When should he tell her? That was the question. Umasi had managed to put it off until now. A part of him wanted to pick up Zen first and then present him to Iris as his explanation. But no, she deserved better than to be blindsided like that. Iris was a sharp woman, surely she'd have noticed

Umasi's strange behavior lately. Yet she had asked no questions, probably waiting for him to approach her. He did not want to. The prospect of having to tell her he was leaving filled him with guilt.

But that conversation would have to come sooner or later. The new Mayor had learned from the old one's example and mistakes. He would accept the responsibility of fatherhood—and that would mean abandoning his responsibility as Mayor.

Umasi sighed. "Life is so complicated."

He continued to struggle with his thoughts for many more minutes. As time dragged on, the room seemed to swim around him, new worries mingling with old memories. Umasi's eyes were drawn to a bat lying on the floor, and he felt a phantom pain from the past. He groaned almost inaudibly, and then turned his head away.

Finally, after hours in the dark, Umasi shut his eyes and fell into slumber.

W ell, this is a nostalgic moment, isn't it?"
Umasi's eyes snapped open, and then blinked.

White. All he could see was white.

Raising a hand to rub his eyes, Umasi was convinced that he was hallucinating. Opening them again, he creased his brow in frustration.

He knew this feeling. He had experienced this once before. That had been years ago, the last in a series of nightmares long banished. The ceiling, the surroundings, the floor upon which he sat all appeared to be a landscape of white so pure that it was impossible to tell where the ground ended and the sky began.

Looking at himself, Umasi saw that even his garments had turned white, and the two swords at his sides were both unbroken and metal. Just like the ones from his old dreams.

Umasi frowned. "Impossible."

"Well of course it is—that's the point of dreams, isn't it?"

Umasi spun around, looking for whoever had addressed him. There, standing before him was a figure he had nearly forgotten, a phantom he had never imagined meeting again. In body and dress he looked very much like Umasi. However, he wore an olive green jacket that stretched all the way down to his boots, and a hood cast his entire face into shadow.

Umasi pointed at the phantom accusingly. "I got rid of you a long time ago."

The boy seemed to smile beneath his hood.

"I have always been, and will always be a part of you."

Umasi folded his arms. "I haven't been frightened by childish nightmares for years now. I won't play your game."

"That's a shame. We never did get to finish ours."

"What do you mean?"

The boy chuckled. Then, in one swift motion, he lifted his hood. Umasi felt his mind shut down as he found himself looking at a familiar face—a boy with a ponytail.

Zyid smiled. "Long time no see, brother."

"But— But you're dead!"

"Yes, that's correct," Zyid agreed. "Thank you for noticing."

Umasi shut his jaw as he began to think again. Remembering that this was, after all, a dream, some sense of reason began to return to the situation.

"You're not real," Umasi said. "This conversation means nothing."

"I'm exactly as real as you standing right there," Zyid countered. "And on the contrary, I feel that we have plenty of meaningful things to discuss."

Zyid pointed his hand at Umasi's side. Before Umasi realized what was happening, one of his swords flew out of its sheath and into Zyid's waiting grasp.

"Incidentally, thank you for keeping my sword in good shape." Zyid smiled. "It was yours that was broken, wasn't it?"

Umasi drew his remaining blade. "How did you know—"

"Don't be silly, Umasi, I *am* you," Zyid replied. "There's nothing you know that I do not."

As Umasi expected, Zyid charged forward with impossible speed. In an instant he was in front of Umasi, and Umasi barely managed to parry the slash. The force of the impact sent Umasi flying backwards, though somehow he landed safely with his feet planted onto an unseen wall.

"Must we fight like this?" Umasi asked, craning his head to look at Zyid from his awkward perch. "I thought we'd already settled our grudge."

"And that we did. Your mind, however, is still a mess," Zyid replied. "I thought you could use some focus."

With that Zyid threw his sword, and it spun through the air towards Umasi. Umasi leapt aside as the sword passed through the space he had been standing. He landed back on the ground as the sword arced back towards Zyid, who caught it with ease.

"I don't need your help, Zyid." Umasi closed the distance between them with a single step. "I'll figure things out by myself."

"Well then, I offer my humble opinion." Zyid ducked Umasi's slash and sent him flying with a hook kick. "Concerning my new namesake— I'm honored, by the way—I take it that you are already decided?"

Umasi skidded across the unseen ground. "Of course."

"I approve." Zyid smiled. "You always enjoyed the mentoring business more than I did. Honestly, I think you'll end up making a decent father."

"Knowing his uncle, I'd better."

"Worried that he might follow in my footsteps and destroy a city?" Zyid said amusedly. "Ah, well, who knows? It's good for children to dream big."

Umasi hurled his sword like a harpoon. The blade shot towards Zyid with incredible speed, but Zyid simply knocked it aside with his own. Umasi watched as the sword fell through what should have been the floor and vanished as a speck into the infinite whiteness.

"Speaking of our family," Zyid continued. "How about that Iris?"

Umasi frowned. "What about her?"

"She's my kind of lady." Zyid grinned "Of course, if I were still alive I'm sure we would have disliked each other instantly. Strong personalities have a way of clashing like that."

"Would you have continued to rebel against her?"

"Probably." Zyid looked thoughtful. "Personally I think that her camps are an abomination, but that's Takan's problem now."

A faint whistling sound filled the air, and Umasi looked up to see his lost sword falling down towards him. He extended his hand upwards, and seconds later the blade fell into his grasp by its hilt.

"So you're not mad?" Umasi said. "About me becoming the new Mayor?"

"You'll find that death has improved my temper quite a bit," Zyid quipped. "No, I'm not angry. I'm not even surprised, to be frank."

Umasi took a deep breath. "I did try to keep your dying wish—"

"And you did it well enough for long enough." Zyid waved a hand dismissively. "The Truancy is gone. You fulfilled your obligation. Now you have new ones to keep."

The two brothers raised their blades.

"What are you talking about?" Umasi asked.

Zyid flew through the air at Umasi, sword bared. Umasi blocked the onslaught, and for a moment they looked at each other face-to-face. Then the pressure gave way, and both of them were sent free-falling through the air.

"First, you obviously have an obligation to your son," Zyid called, his voice echoing through the white space. "Take care of him as best you can."

"I know that much!" Umasi retorted, landing this time on an invisible ceiling.

"Second, you have an obligation to our sister," Zyid said, landing on the floor far away. "You've sulked and hid for long enough. You owe her a proper explanation. Swallow your fears, she'll understand."

Umasi bizarrely felt as though blood were rushing to his head.

"I can't," he said. "I owe her more than just an explanation. She never complains, but I can tell that the stress is getting to her. To leave her now, when the City is at its worst—"

"I was just getting to that," Zyid interrupted. "You have a third obligation, to this City as its Mayor. You don't have to abandon it just yet, Umasi."

Umasi frowned. "What do you mean?"

"It looks like you're smiling from where I am, did you know that? No, I kid," Zyid laughed. "It's simple, isn't it? Take your son under your protection. Plan your escape for when the time comes, but stay for as long as you can. You can be there for our sister, if indeed you want that so badly."

The suggestion made sense. Suddenly Umasi felt the world shift around him. When he looked up again he was standing on flat ground, facing Zyid. Things felt right once more.

"The war is getting worse by the day," Umasi murmured. "Barring a miracle, we won't be able to stay for long."

Zyid nodded. "It will have to be enough."

"You're right," Umasi said, raising his sword. "I think I feel better now."

Zyid grinned. "Then let's finish this."

Umasi and Zyid ran at each other with swords outstretched. There was no more unnatural speed, no impossible acrobatics, and when they met their swords pierced right through their targets. For several moments the two of them stood there, impaled by each other. Then, finally, they embraced.

Umasi looked down and saw that black smoke seemed to be leaking out from Zyid, flowing up the blade and into him. Umasi's white clothes began to return to the black he had remembered falling asleep in. It was a disconcerting effect, and Umasi knew what it meant.

Umasi looked back up at his brother as the world around him began to dissolve into darkness.

"Is this our final good-bye?" Umasi asked.

"Oh, I doubt it."

Zyid's voice seemed to echo faintly as it too began to fade.

"We can always meet again in dreams."

Noni shook her can of spray-paint, putting the finishing touches on her graffiti. A group of mixed adults and teenagers gazed up at the large purple C up on the wall.

"It'll make a nice marker for the final resting place of those tanks," a former student observed. "I can't wait to blow them up."

"Don't get ahead of yourself," Noni told him. "It could just as easily turn out to be our epitaph. I'm putting this up so that everyone will know we fought here, one way or another."

"So that was the idea behind those damn Truancy symbols?" one of the adults said. "We Enforcers always thought you kids were just making graffiti for the hell of it."

Noni tossed the can of spray-paint aside, and then turned around to face the man.

"Nothing Zyid did was without purpose, Mr. Vito," she told him. "Now get to your position. That goes for everyone. If we survive this, you might learn something."

The rebels saluted and scattered into the surrounding buildings. More were already waiting on the rooftops and upper floors. This operation would be important for morale, and Noni had been chosen to lead it. Their objective was to destroy a pair of Government tanks patrolling the area, to prove that the tanks were not invincible.

Though their insurgency had met a number of successes, some weapons of the Government continued to thwart the Citizens' Rebellion. In particular their tanks were more than just armored weapons of war—they were tools of intimidation. Citizens with memories of encountering the hulking abominations usually did not wish to do so again. So far none of them had ever been destroyed. Noni was determined to break that trend.

Over the past week Noni had volunteered for more missions than anyone, catching a few hours of sleep here and there between battles. While Cross and Takan mostly plotted from behind the front lines, Noni preferred to put herself out in the field every chance she got. This had earned her the respect of her subordinates, even the former Enforcers.

Vito, the man who had spoken earlier, took his position at a window right next to Noni. Together they waited for their prey to approach.

"How long do you think it'll take?" Vito asked.

"Not long," Noni said brusquely. "The scouts said they— wait, listen."

A distant rumble reached their ears, growing steadily louder. Vito glanced at Noni, looking nervous. She did not look back at him. Her attention was completely drawn to the road outside, and the red markers they had placed there.

The enemy came into sight. The tank led the group, followed by a Humvee and a few soldiers on foot. They moved slowly, on the lookout for any danger. The citizens had been extra careful in choosing their hiding places, and this attack was being conducted in the middle of the afternoon—they had long since learned that Government soldiers had equipment to see in the dark.

Noni reached into her pocket and pulled out a detonator as she saw the tank reach the first set of markers. Vito glanced from the detonator to the tank. She ignored him. Thus far no explosives they had attempted had been of any use against the tanks. This time they were trying something a little different.

The tank finally reached the second set of markers, now in the middle of an intersection. The soldiers and Humvee were hanging a little behind, but nothing could be done about that. Noni smiled grimly, then pressed the detonator.

A small earthquake rocked the ground as an enormous explosion went off in the sewers beneath the tank. Vito gaped as the entire intersection collapsed. The tank shuddered and fell into the resulting sinkhole, tipped over onto one side. Its treads began to turn, but had no luck dislodging itself from the pit.

Noni brought a radio to her mouth.

"Fire."

A barrage of rockets shot down from the surrounding buildings, striking the tank from the top. Flames blossomed from the tank, the whole thing reduced to a burning wreck. Noni heard a cheer go up from the buildings. Slowly the rebellion was figuring out which parts of the tanks were more vulnerable.

"It worked!" Vito exclaimed. "No wonder the Truancy did so well against us."

"Don't celebrate yet," Noni snapped, raising her rifle.

Already the soldiers were scattering for cover, and the Humvee's mounted gun fired away at the rebel positions. Noni could hear the roar of the second tank bringing up the rear, and knew that they had precious little time before their hiding places became vulnerable. Noni fired at one of the soldiers out in the open, and was rewarded by seeing him fall.

Another rocket sailed down from above and into the Humvee, and a moment later it too was in flames. Gunfire from the buildings rained down on the survivors, and Noni began moving, followed closely by Vito. The second tank came into sight. It pointed its main gun at the building where most of the citizens were firing from. There was a flash from the barrel, and then a large chunk of the building fragmented. Noni could hear screams on her radio.

"That doesn't look good," Vito said, firing at one of the remaining soldiers. "We should get out while we're still ahead—we've already proved our point."

"We came for two, we're going to get two," Noni insisted. "I'll handle this. Cover me."

Noni reached into her pack and withdrew a thermite grenade. It was a Government weapon, designed to melt and disable equipment. The Government had lately been finding increasingly large gaps in their shipments of weapons.

As ordered, Vito kept firing at whatever soldiers were left outside. Noni was pleased to see that the tank's crew didn't dare open their hatches to man the machine guns for fear of fire from above. This gave her an opening.

Noni darted out into the open, heading straight for the tank. A few bullets flew in her direction, but for the most part the soldiers had other targets to worry about. Noni quickly reached the intimidating war machine, and before its crew could notice her, she leapt up and grabbed the enormous muzzle of its cannon.

Hanging from the cannon by one arm as the battle raged farther down the street, Noni yanked the pin from the thermite grenade using her teeth. Then she shoved it down the barrel of the cannon. Noni dropped from the tank and sprinted away just as the grenade went off. A terrific spray of red sparks poured from the barrel.

Just then the tank fired, and for the first time that evening Noni smiled as the round detonated inside the barrel. The tank shuddered from the explosion, and then began smoking, its barrel a twisted mess. Whether the crew had survived or not, the second tank was out of commission.

Before Noni or any of the other citizens could celebrate, there came a screech of airplanes from above—weapons that the rebellion truly had no counter to. Noni knew that the rebels would be scattering as fast as they could, but there was no time. An enormous explosion simply consumed one of the nearby buildings where a group of rebels had been hiding.

Noni seized her radio. "Everyone, get out of here!"

She didn't need to add that they had accomplished their mission. There was restrained cheering on the radio as the surviving rebels beat a hasty retreat into the surrounding buildings and alleys. In this dense part of the urban jungle, the soldiers would pay dearly for any pursuit.

Another hour, another battle, another success. Noni was beginning to enjoy her work routine. She smiled as she spotted her graffiti, still intact on its wall. The fight was going well.

Sitting on the roof of the Mayoral Mansion, Iris sighed and raised her binoculars to her eyes. More smoke, rising in the distance. Another attack. She mulled the situation over as aircraft streaked overhead. Air support had been scrambled quickly, but Iris knew it wouldn't be fast enough—most of the rebels would have time to get away, as they always did.

The General slammed her fist against her knee. They just didn't understand that this path would end badly for everyone, them and herself alike. Worse, Iris couldn't explain it to them. They would simply dismiss her words as lies or threats.

A flash went off in the distance. The bomber had dropped its ordinance. Iris put her binoculars down and rested her forehead against her knuckles. The situation was only growing worse by the hour. Each misstep she made, each casualty she suffered, each escalation to the conflict only inspired further resistance. This cycle, Iris knew, would only end in one way if she could not find a way to break it.

Iris heard familiar footsteps behind her, and did not bother moving. The footsteps halted, their owner probably seeing her distress. They turned and began walking away.

Iris sighed. "What's the problem, Umasi?"

The footsteps paused again. "It looks like you're busy. I'll give you some privacy and come back later."

Iris smiled grimly. "You were going to tell me that you want to leave the City after all, correct?"

There was a stunned silence. That was enough to tell Iris that she'd been right. She waited for Umasi to explain himself.

"It's hard to hide anything from you," Umasi said at last.

"I'm glad you noticed—perhaps it'll save us some time in the future." Iris turned to look at him. "Why?"

Umasi seemed to hesitate. "This will sound strange and perhaps unbelievable."

"Try me."

"I recently found out that I have a son. His mother informed me a week ago."

Iris raised her eyebrows.

"Are you sure the mother is telling the—"

"She wouldn't outright lie to me," Umasi insisted. "Not over something that big. It's not in her character."

"You're willing to stake your life on that?"

"I am."

Iris let out a deep sigh. "Well then, that does change everything. I'll arrange for your immediate transport."

Umasi seemed startled. "Iris, I want to be here to support you for as long as—"

"You've already done enough, Umasi." Iris waved his protest aside. "Stay a few more days if you want, but I insist that you get out no later than that."

Umasi hesitated again, then he bowed deeply.

"Thank you very much."

Iris did not reply, and Umasi turned and left. Iris sat there alone on the rooftop for many more minutes, staring hard at the horizon where smoke continued to rise. Then she spoke, with only herself to hear.

"I'm glad that you'll be leaving," Iris said. "It's better that you won't be here to see too much of what must come next."

31

S o it's true, then," Takan said.

"No doubt about it," Cross replied. "I've got confirmation from five separate outposts, and they're still coming in. The Government is blockading the deep City and any other districts they deem hostile. Nothing goes in or out."

"Why?" Sepp demanded. "What do they hope to accomplish by this?"

"They say they'll provide supplies if the resistance ceases completely." Cross sighed. "They're offering rewards for our heads, hoping someone turns us in."

The leaders of the Citizens' Rebellion were discussing these developments at a dusty wooden table in the basement of a house in District 26. Takan, Cross, Sepp, and Noni were in attendance. The day after they liberated the camp, their original hideout in District 47 had been wiped out by an airstrike. Ever since, they had kept their headquarters on the move. So far they had managed to stay one step ahead of the Government.

There was no electricity here, the only lighting provided by a series of candles. The tiny flames reflected in the eyes of the rebels. All of them seemed incensed by the news. Cross thought that Noni, who had just returned from a raid, looked especially murderous.

"And what if we don't do what they want?" Takan demanded. "What about the civilians?"

Cross frowned. "Apparently they are expendable in the eyes of the Government."

"Unforgivable," Noni seethed. "There's nothing they won't stoop to."

"The silver lining is that they've pulled their troops completely out of these districts," Cross said. "Of course, those districts will starve soon unless something is done."

Sepp raised his hand. "I've got bad news from the camps too."

Cross glanced at his old colleague. Sepp's responsibilities were mainly to help sow discontent in the camps. He established contact in any way possible, supplied means of resistance, and kept tabs on the situation behind those hated walls.

"They've begun a serious crackdown," Sepp continued. "Drug treatments are being phased in as mandatory. They're taking a zero tolerance policy to riots—anyone who even says the word is subject to harsh punishment."

The other leaders shifted uncomfortably in their seats. Cross turned to Takan, who had been doing some scouting in the central districts.

"What's the latest from the core?" Cross asked.

"About what you'd expect," Takan said wearily. "The Government's cracking down there too. There are constant raids on households suspected of being sympathetic to us. Everyone is scared. Half of my contacts in District 1 have vanished overnight."

There was a grim silence. A candle on the table burned out, sending thin tendrils of smoke coiling into the air. No one seemed to know what to say.

"Look, I know this seems bad, it's also a sign of desperation," Cross spoke at last. "Iris is turning to these measures because she feels she has to. That means we're getting to her."

Noni snorted. "Unfortunately, it looks like she's getting us too."

Sepp clenched his fists. "We can't let this go on. We have to do something."

"The Government's plan is to wear us out," Cross said. "If we just continue on as we've been doing, they will succeed."

"So what are we going to do about it?" Sepp demanded. "We can't just let those people starve!"

"We might have to accept that some starvation is inevitable." Takan shook his head. "There's no way we can break all the blockades in all of the districts. Iris has us by the throat."

"Yes," Cross agreed, "that's why I think it's time for us to try to take Iris herself out of the picture."

The other leaders all turned to look at Cross as though he were crazy.

"When my unit of four was trapped behind enemy lines, we tried to target Takan and nearly succeeded." Cross glanced at the Truancy leader. "Right now I feel we might have better luck working together. If we can manage to cut off the head, the Government is sure to think twice about this invasion."

"A nice fantasy. I'm sure we've all dreamed of it once or twice," Noni said. "Do you have a plan to make it happen?"

Cross smiled at Takan.

"We'll use his old Plan B."

Takan's eyebrows shot up.

"That's right." Cross nodded. "We'll tap into the Truancy's old stockpiles, whatever the Government hasn't gotten to yet."

Cross unfurled a map of the City onto the dusty table.

"We can then get under District 1 using the tunnels," he continued. "Our forces will be positioned as close to the Mayoral Mansion as possible.

When the explosives go off, the whole district will be plunged into chaos. With any luck, this will give us an opening to storm the Mansion."

Takan frowned.

"The slightest error would give Iris a chance to retreat," he said. "It's risky."

"Very," Cross agreed. "What are your opinions?"

"I like it," Noni said.

"I'll lead the charge," Sepp promised. "Any chance to end this war is worth it."

Takan hesitated. "Under the circumstances," he said finally, "I don't think there's any other viable choice."

Cross nodded. "Then it's settled. Takan, can you organize the effort to move the explosives?"

"Of course."

"Great. Noni, Sepp." Cross turned to the pair. "I'd like you each to gather half the forces we have available and get them ready to move out at a moment's notice. Meanwhile, I'll plan our approach."

Everyone nodded in agreement. Cross let out a breath he didn't realize he'd been holding. This was the first time he had ever proposed a plan like this, and he was gratified to see them accept his lead. Their rebellion had so far done well against overwhelming odds, but Cross knew this would be their greatest challenge yet. Iris had forced their hands, and they were betting everything on one final showdown.

"By the way," Cross said, a thought coming to mind. "Have any of you seen my teacher around today? I'd like to explain all this to her."

The other leaders glanced at one another. None of them looked like they had seen her. That was odd. The albino normally attended these meetings, even though she rarely contributed to their discussions. She had returned late after their raid on the District 13 camp, but had told no one what had happened to her. Grateful that she had survived, Cross was content to let that be.

"No idea, Cross." Takan shrugged. "I saw her walking off with Zen early this morning, but that's about it."

Cross sighed. "Well, it's not urgent. She'll be back later, I'm sure."

In the flickering candlelight, no one noticed Noni narrow her eyes in suspicion.

The docks of District 13 were peaceful that day, forgotten by both the Government and the rebellion. The evening sun had set the surface of the river aglitter. The smoke from the camp had long since dissipated, and here no trace remained of the wider conflict that had consumed the City. Umasi thought that it should have made for a relaxing atmosphere.

And yet the Mayor felt nervous as he approached the docks, to an extent he hadn't felt since he was a child. He had no idea what to do or say to his son, let alone what would come after that. None of the mental exercises he had done thus far had adequately prepared him for what he saw when the pier came into sight. The albino was waiting there—along with a young boy who couldn't have been older than five.

The Mayor forced himself to keep walking, and, in an almost dreamlike stupor, he stumbled over to where they stood. For a moment he looked at the albino, who nodded at him, and then he looked down at the boy he was meeting for the first time. Zen was dressed in a small gray sweatshirt over worn blue jeans. His skin was only slightly lighter than Umasi's, complementing his dirty blond hair. Zen seemed just as nervous as Umasi, shifting position every few seconds.

The Mayor found himself inexplicably awestruck by the sight. He was snapped out of his reverie by the rough sound of the clearing of a throat. The Mayor looked up to find the albino smiling at him.

"Zen," she said. "This is your father. I've told you about him."

Umasi forced a grin and waved at Zen. Zen looked at him for a moment, then hid behind his mother's leg. Umasi felt an unfamiliar, vague pain at that.

"I think he senses that you're dangerous," the albino told him gently. "Maybe you should take the sunglasses off."

Realizing that she was right, Umasi took his shades off and slipped them into his pocket. Then he crouched to get down to Zen's eye level.

"Hey," Umasi said tentatively. "It's all right."

The albino glanced down at their son. "He *is* dangerous, Zen—but not to you. You have nothing to worry about."

Zen peeked out from behind his mother's leg, then emerged completely, looking curious now. He stared up at Umasi with brown eyes that seemed to be assessing, analyzing, sizing him up. Yet there was a softness to that gaze, a humanity undoubtedly inherited from his mother.

Zen cocked his head as he looked Umasi in the eyes for the first time. Then he smiled, and Umasi felt his spirits lift. Maybe this wouldn't be so unpleasant after all.

"Hi, Dad," Zen said.

That word sounded strange in Umasi's ears. "Hi, Zen."

The two maintained their eye contact for a few more seconds, until both of them were overcome by nervousness and looked away. Umasi straightened up and turned to the albino. There were things to discuss.

"Milady, I cannot have you evacuated," Umasi said. "However, I can place you under Government protection here. You will be as comfortable and as safe as possible within the City. I think you should consider it."

The albino shut her eyes and shook her head. "Thank you, Umasi, but that's not where my heart is. I wouldn't feel comfortable cooped up like that."

"This is your life we're talking about," Umasi said. "Please don't make a reckless choice."

"Believe it or not, I have given this matter plenty of thought." She smiled wryly. "I've decided I want to have my say when the fate of the City is decided."

"You intend to throw your lot in with the rebellion?"

"I will not bloody my hands," the albino said. "But I will walk with my fellow citizens, where I belong. And when all of this is over I hope to rebuild a City that Zen will want to return to. Then we may see each other again."

The two shared a moment of heavy silence as they looked at each other. Zen looked at them both. It occurred to them now that this was where their paths diverged, perhaps never to cross again. A great sorrow hung in both of their hearts.

"When we last parted," Umasi said, "you said that you'd never loved anyone in your life."

"I was lying." The albino smiled at him, and then at Zen. "Now there are two people I love. But their fates are now different from mine."

Umasi nodded slowly.

"I understand," he said, reciting words from their past. "You and I are too free to be happily bound to each other. We could never remain together. Go and chase your own dreams, whatever they may be."

The albino grinned at that, then she leaned forward. Umasi followed suit, and they heard Zen making icky noises as they shared a final kiss. The albino bent down to hug Zen tightly good-bye.

"Listen to your father," she reminded him. "He's very smart—there's a lot you can learn from him."

Zen looked back at her seriously. "Will I see you again?"

The albino's eyes were wet as she replied. "I hope so."

That seemed enough for Zen, and he went to stand by his father's leg. The albino straightened up again, and she curtseyed.

"Good-bye, Umasi!" she said.

Umasi bowed deeply. "Farewell, milady."

With one backwards glance, the albino turned and began walking away, her footsteps oddly stiff. Zen waved as he and Umasi watched her go. In that moment Umasi felt that he had just lost something that could never be regained, and breathed a sigh of sadness. Then Zen spoke up.

"You look funny—why do you wear your jacket like that?"

Umasi smiled. "It's something my brother used to do."

"Why'd he do that?"

"I don't know, I guess he thought it was cool."

Zen grinned mischievously. "You look like a big bird!"

Umasi laughed at that, and as they walked along the father and son continued to chat, learning to enjoy each other's company. For that short while at least, Umasi felt like he had no worries.

That day the Mayor willingly accepted that an unfamiliar child was his own. He did not know what the future would hold for them, but he knew that whatever that future was, it lay outside of the City.

Iris' face was drawn and haggard as she sat in the darkness of her study. The pale light from the monitor seemed to highlight every line and crease of her face, accentuating the dark rings under her eyes.

"That can't be," she whispered.

The War Minister's face, projected from hundreds of miles away, looked regretful but determined.

"I'm sorry, General," he said. "Your last report didn't go over well at all. These orders come from your father himself."

Iris gritted her teeth. "This is too soon. I was promised more time!"

"If you wish to take the matter up with him—"

"My father won't listen to me anymore, Minister," Iris said. "I need you to convince him to hold off. I *know* that my new measures will crush this uprising if given a chance!"

"I'm sorry, General," the Minister repeated. "I already talked with the Potentate, and he was quite firm on the matter. He wants the troop drawdown to begin immediately—he's ordered a complete pullout within the month."

"That won't happen."

"I think you know what the consequences will be for defying him, General."

Iris glared. "Surely he doesn't intend to go through with—"

"Iris, we both know the answer to that!" the Minister said exasperatedly, abandoning titles. "I'm not happy about this decision either, but to be honest, no one ever expected you to succeed."

"Then why was this operation approved in the first place?" Iris shouted.

"You'd have to ask your father about that." The Minister sighed. "Iris, just let that City go, for your own sake."

The monitor went black, leaving Iris in total darkness. She felt a lump form in her throat. This time there was no Umasi waiting with news, no one left to confide in or share words of support. She had been made a fool of, and soon her failure would be complete.

Iris slammed her fist against her armrest. No, she would not allow it. Her father would not have his way. They all believed that Iris was defeated, but she wasn't done yet. No matter what, the General swore that she wouldn't give up. Even if she was the only soldier left in the City, she could still be a shield between the City and destruction.

"To my last breath," Iris swore. "I will never give up!"

Iris thought about Umasi and his dead brother. This was the City they had loved, and Iris was now its only protector. Its people, their lives, were in her hands. That was a responsibility she would not, could not lay down.

No matter how it would end for her.

As the albino approached the District 28 station through the subway tunnels, she noticed that something new was going on. Her sensitive ears could hear activity in the station—hushed voices, dragging sounds, and the occasional clank of metal. It obviously wasn't Government activity, and so the albino simply shrugged it off and continued to walk alone through the darkness.

Parting with Zen and Umasi had affected her more than she had expected, even though she had been prepared for it. It was like a chunk of herself had been physically left behind. She knew that it was something that had to be done, that it would ensure the safety of both of the people she loved, but that did nothing to ease the ache in her heart.

As she entered the station, she was taken by surprise. Rebel kids and adults alike swarmed over the platform, speaking in whispers as they carried metal barrel after metal barrel down into the subway. Makeshift carts were being fitted onto the tracks so that they could be pushed along the rails, and each of them was loaded up high with explosives. As the albino stared at this unusual sight, the rebels recognized her and gave casual salutes.

The albino tilted her head. "What's going on—"

There was sudden movement from the shadows to her right. The albino reacted immediately, deflecting the knife with the chain wrapped around her left arm. Noni sprang out from her hiding place, catching the albino with a roundhouse kick. The albino stumbled backwards, loosening her chain as she stared at Noni in surprise.

"Traitor," Noni spat.

The albino blinked. "I have no idea what you're talking about."

"Yes, you do." Noni's eyes narrowed. "Where were you?"

"I went for a—"

"You went to see your friend, the Mayor!"

The albino sighed. "You're not wrong but—"

Noni didn't give her a chance to finish that sentence, slamming the other girl against the tunnel wall. The albino did not resist as she looked Noni in the eye. By now a small crowd had gathered to watch from the platform. The observers looked at one another nervously, no one sure of what to do.

"If you wish to kill me, I am ready to die content," the albino said. "But you will be making a big mistake. I haven't betrayed you."

"Explain yourself, then."

"I successfully convinced the Mayor to stay out of this conflict. He won't be fighting you anymore."

"That's not good enough," Noni said. "He's still my enemy. I won't be satisfied until I face him myself."

"What would that possibly achieve?"

"I need to pay him back for some humiliation," Noni snarled. "He also knows who killed Zyid, I'm sure of it. Now tell me—where is he?"

The two girls stared each other down.

"I do not know," the albino replied. "And I would not tell you, even if I did."

Noni let out a sound of inarticulate fury, and in a flash she had drawn a knife. The crowd gasped as she raised the blade. Suddenly Noni found the tip of a white sword at her throat.

"Let her go, Noni," Takan said quietly.

"Leave me alone!" Noni raged. "She's a traitor!"

"You're wrong, she's not that type."

Noni took a deep breath. "Stay out of this, Takan."

"I can't."

Noni wavered for a moment, and to all the witnesses present it seemed as though she were fighting a battle with herself. Her knife hand trembled, then she withdrew, rounding on Takan.

"You were never really loyal to Zyid!" Noni shrieked at him. "I don't know what he saw in you, I don't know why he trusted you! I should never have supported you as leader—*I* should've taken over the Truancy! You know I could have! I didn't!"

Takan looked stunned. "Noni—"

"Why did you never try to help me? Why did you never try to find his killer?" Noni continued. "I thought I understood you! I thought we would be together on this! You let me go on my own! YOU ABANDONED ME!"

"Noni, I never—"

"You called me obsessed, and now you take her side over mine? Who do you think you are? I always supported you! I trusted you! How *dare* you point your sword at me?"

Noni glared at Takan, breathing heavily. For a moment their eyes met, icy blue and warm amber. Then Noni spun around and stalked off into the darkness of the tunnel.

Her last words seemed to be addressed to herself more than him. "If it were anyone but you, Takan . . ."

Takan stood rooted to the ground as though he had been struck by lightning. The onlookers, uncomfortably aware that they were staring, quickly looked away and pretended to not have noticed the conflict. The albino sighed, straightening up and dusting herself off.

"I'm sorry," she said, looking at Takan.

"Don't apologize. It's my own damn fault." Takan shook himself and then glanced at her. "I see you came back alone. Did . . . did you tell Umasi?"

The albino nodded.

Takan smiled. "That must've been a shock for him."

"That's an understatement—he looked like a lost puppy," the albino replied. "But at least both of them are safely out of the way."

Takan nodded. "Speaking of which, you should get out of here before Noni comes back. We're planning something big. I'll fill you in later."

"Thank you."

The albino patted him on the shoulder as she left, climbing up onto the platform and vanishing beyond the turnstiles. Takan did not watch her go, but stayed where he was, brooding in the shadows as the other rebels moved destructive barrels through the station, preparing for their final assault on the Government.

Takan slowly became aware of a new person approaching him from the other side of the tracks. Knowing who it was, he waited.

"Hey." Cross' voice was sympathetic.

Takan cleared his throat. "I take it you were watching."

"Yeah."

"How much did you see?"

"I think the second half of Noni's, ah, speech." Cross coughed. He paused briefly, then continued. "Takan, you should tell her about Zyid. It's obviously eating her up inside."

Takan sighed. "I know. I want to. It's just . . . I don't think this is the right time."

Cross glared at him. "Takan, soon we're all going to be going into a battle we probably won't survive. If not now, when?"

With that, Cross turned and climbed up onto the platform, leaving Takan alone on the bottom of the tracks.

32

Hour of Reckoning

Two days.

Two days of painstaking effort and desperate maneuvers. That was what it had taken to prepare for this moment.

Those days had felt like years, but in hindsight it seemed a small miracle the Citizens' Rebellion had achieved it in that time. The increasing hunger in the deep City had made their efforts more urgent. Further complicating their plans were occasional Government sweeps of the subways—most of those, fortunately, were conducted far from the central districts.

In order to move all the explosives into place the rebellion had been forced to take complicated detours through the tunnels, winding their way under the City until they finally reached District 1. By cart, pulley, and sometimes by hand, the heavy barrels were placed throughout the sewers and subways of the district. Every adult and child in the resistance had chipped in.

Fortunately the Government's own precautions had made one part easy for them—worried about citizen sympathizers, the Government had expelled all civilians from the district and moved them into the surrounding areas. The citizens could wreck as much damage as they wanted without fear of harming their own.

Now the preparations were finally complete, and once again Cross found himself walking through the darkness of the tunnels. Sepp marched just ahead of him, with two hundred armed rebels following in their wake.

Cross watched the back of Sepp's head, wondering what was going through his colleague's mind. The boy had rarely slept, insisting on participating in every part of the preparations. No one except Noni had been more active than him. Cross guessed that Floe's memory still drove him—as it did Cross.

As they walked along, Cross was aware of a pale presence next to him even when he couldn't see it. He was grateful for it. The albino had insisted on accompanying them for this final battle. Cross had made her accept some stolen body armor, but she had refused to take any weapons besides her chain.

That still confused him, and as they marched through the empty tunnel, Cross decided to ask about it.

"Teacher?" he asked quietly, so as not to be overheard.

The albino turned her head. "Yes?"

"I was wondering why you wanted to come along for this. I was under the impression that you didn't like war."

"I don't," she replied. "I just want to see for myself how the fate of this City will be decided. If I can lend you some small help in my own way, then that will be enough."

Cross nodded. "What about Zen? Where is he?"

The albino looked down at her feet. "He's now in a place safer than any I could provide for him."

Cross heard the sadness in her voice, and despite his curiosity decided not to press her too hard on that matter.

"I've said it before, but I'm proud of you, Cross," the albino said. "When I first met you, you seemed like you had no idea what to do with yourself. You've grown up since then. I know you have the strength to succeed."

Cross looked away. "Thank you."

Soon their company reached the first station within District 1 and stopped, climbing up onto the platform. They dared not go any farther than this. The tunnels ahead were likely watched by the Government, and some of the Educators' barriers and traps still remained. The rest of their journey would have to be made on the surface, straight through the heart of the Government occupation.

Cross and Sepp found themselves sitting side by side on one of the platform benches. Cross checked his watch. They had arrived a few minutes early, so there was nothing for them to do but wait. The explosives were set on a timer—Cross could only hope that Takan and Noni's group were already in place.

The momentousness of what was soon to happen hadn't seemed to sink in yet. The rebels on the platform chatted in low voices, joked with one another. It might have been just another routine raid.

"I wish Floe could be here to see this," Sepp said, his head propped up by his arm. "She would've loved to see the City free again."

Cross nodded. "We'll just have to do it in her honor."

"I know what you mean. All I want is to go out in a way that would make her proud," Sepp said. "And my family too, I suppose—assuming the Government hasn't killed them also."

Cross clenched his fists. "All I want is to get a hold of Iris."

"I hope we can do it together," Sepp said. "It'd be like old times in the Student Militia. Doesn't that feel like so long ago."

"Yeah." Cross looked down. "At a time like this I almost miss even Joe."

At that moment Cross' digital watch began beeping, and he quickly silenced it. The numbers on the watch began counting down. The other rebels all turned to look at him, knowing that this was the five-minute warning. Any moment now the battle would begin.

Cross stood up and turned to address the two hundred citizens on the platform. He was not like Edward or the legendary Zyid—he knew from experience that he was uncomfortable with big speeches. And so Cross simply looked out at the troops he led and spoke his mind.

"Everyone, this was a volunteer mission, so if you're here I assume you already know why." Cross smiled. "Just don't lose sight of that when things get tough. Let's do our best."

The rebels all nodded at that, and stood up as they waited. Every one of them was ready to fight, ready to die. Cross felt oddly calm—it felt therapeutic to finally be taking action, to strike at Iris herself. Minutes passed. The numbers on his watch continued to decrease.

Then they hit zero, and the whole City trembled.

An apocalyptic tremor shook the ground as countless explosions rippled throughout District 1. Concrete and asphalt crumbled like sand as the streets caved in, the ground sundered by the tremendous force. Small canyons began to form, taking on a life of their own, ripping their way through the district. Mighty buildings imploded as these fissures ran beneath them, sending enormous dust storms billowing through the streets.

The main street leading straight towards City Hall collapsed utterly, opening up a gaping maw. Moments later, the buildings lining the road began to groan—then one by one they toppled and crushed one another like dominoes. Entire City blocks vanished in an instant. The full destructive power of the Truancy's old Plan B had been realized.

The Government forces stationed in District 1 were caught completely by surprise. Tanks and vehicles and infantry were swallowed up as the ground opened beneath them. Those who survived and were not crushed by falling buildings found themselves stumbling through endless clouds of choking smoke and dust.

It was this chaos that Takan and his troops emerged into as they spilled up through the old subway exits. Even the most battle-hardened among them paused in awe. Nothing in all the years of war the City had seen could have prepared them for this. The dust blotted out their vision, yet the bright sun sent rays streaking through it, creating an almost dreamlike effect.

A few rebels gasped, then coughed—the dust was particles of buildings and concrete and who knows what else. It was toxic.

"Come on!" Takan shouted. "We don't have time to waste!"

Deeper into the awful clouds the rebels plunged. Takan saw Noni running ahead of everyone else, a swift and slender shadow. She had been the first to burst from the ground after the explosions, and she hadn't stopped at all, heading straight in the direction of the Mayoral Mansion. The two of them hadn't spoken since Noni's outburst in the tunnel. Worried, Takan ran after her.

Rebel snipers scattered into the surroundings, looking for somewhere, anywhere they could find a clear shot. Pieces of fallen buildings lay everywhere, and chunks of the torn ground jutted up like massive spikes. As he scrambled down into a newly formed ditch, Takan thought that it was like picking his way through the end of the world.

Then through the dust, Takan saw a dark shape—the first enemy of the day. He fired immediately, and the silhouette crumpled and fell. Takan stepped over the soldier's body and continued running. As he rounded a corner he spotted Noni struggling with a man who must have weighed twice as much as her. She threw the soldier to the ground, then brutally plunged her knife into his neck.

"Noni, wait up!"

Without even pausing to acknowledge Takan, Noni picked up the soldier's rifle and continued running. The look on her face had been cold and feral, devoid of any humanity. Takan felt his heart sink. It was as though Noni had become a different person. Takan uncomfortably remembered the way Noni had attacked the albino.

His attention was drawn by more soldiers, firing down from the intact sidewalks a block down. Takan dove for cover behind a chunk of what had once been the street that was now jutting from the ground. Takan fired back in their direction, but through the thick dust and chaos they were hard to spot at such a long distance.

Then there was a great rumbling sound, and Takan watched in awe as the building over the soldiers finally gave way to the damage its foundations had suffered. The soldiers looked up just in time to see the avalanche of bricks and masonry fall on top of them. The collapse sent a fresh wave of dust rolling over the battlefield, and as Takan continued on through the trenches he found that he felt very small.

A cheer went up and the rebels pressed their advantage. The Government was still disorganized, the explosions having ravaged their forces in this part of the district. Takan encountered only token resistance as he drove farther towards the Mayoral Mansion. For a little while he dared to hope that their mission would be easy.

After several blocks the fissures abruptly ended, the air clearing out. They were deep in the district now, too far to have planted any explosives.

Takan had only pulled himself back onto stable ground when gunfire erupted around him. He ran for cover in a nearby doorway. There he found other rebels who'd also taken shelter. Recognizing him, they saluted.

"What is it?" Takan demanded. "What's blocking our path?"

"Tank!"

That one word made Takan's heart sink. "Do we have any rockets?"

"No, sir!"

Takan peered out from behind the doorway and spotted it—one of the Government's dreaded war machines, parked just two blocks down. The machine guns mounted on top of it were being manned, sending an endless stream of bullets at the rebels in hiding.

Even as Takan watched, an adult rebel in another hiding position managed to shoot one of the gunners despite their protection. The tank swiveled its main cannon, and Takan winced as the rebel and his hiding position was simply blown away. Another rebel, relentless, hurled a grenade at the tank before being cut down by machine gun fire.

The explosion forced the gunners to duck, and for a moment the top of the tank was clear. Takan felt his heart leap into his throat as a familiar dark shape darted out from the shadows and towards the tank. Noni leaped up to grab the cannon, then smoothly slipped a grenade inside. The tank swiveled again, this time aiming at Takan's position. Red sparks began showering from the cannon.

Takan held his breath. The tank fired, and then shuddered as the round exploded inside. The rebels whooped and ran out into the open again as the wrecked tank began smoking.

Takan breathed a sigh of relief—both at the destruction of the tank and Noni's survival. But then he felt a guilt take hold in the pit of his stomach as Noni continued to surge forward, heedless of danger. This was the first time since she had left the Truancy that Takan had seen her in combat. Noni had always been a remarkably tenacious fighter, but never could Takan recall her being so recklessly brutal.

Takan hurried after her, the other rebels all following suit. A couple of blocks down they found more roads had caved in. Takan wasn't sure if they had somehow managed to plant charges here, or if it had just collapsed from the tremors, but he plunged down into the trenches, glad for the cover.

He and all the other rebels were equipped with Government armor, and so when a large soldier dropped down in front of him in the trench, they were both equally surprised. Recovering from his shock first, Takan drew his sword and slashed the man's exposed neck. Experience had taught him the vulnerable parts of the armor.

Just then panicked shouts came in over the radio, and Takan strained to listen. He couldn't discern anything other than that the rebels ahead had run into trouble. Sheathing his sword, Takan dashed forward through the trenches as fast as he could. Scrambling up a chunk of pavement, Takan reached a small two-story building tucked next to taller ones. Several rebels had scaled the fire escape and taken shelter on the roof.

Takan climbed up after them and was relieved to find Noni there with them. They nodded to acknowledge Takan, though their attention was drawn farther down the street. Takan followed their gazes and groaned. They weren't far from the Mayoral Mansion now, but three tanks now stood in their way a couple of blocks down.

"Any ideas, sir?" one of the rebels asked him.

"I think that's too much for us to handle," Takan replied. "No choice—we have to go around them. Try doubling back and taking the Mansion from behind."

The rebels looked relieved. "Yes, sir."

The troops began descending from the rooftop, and Takan was about to follow them when he noticed that Noni hadn't moved. She remained crouched near the edge of the roof, staring at the three tanks. Then she reached into her pack and drew out a thermite grenade. In an instant Takan realized what was going through her head.

"Don't, Noni, you'd never survive it!"

Noni ignored him, standing up and marching purposefully for the fire escape. Takan put himself in her way. She halted, glaring at him angrily, and Takan felt renewed guilt as he looked at her. She was covered in bloodstains, even on her face, and the mad look in her eyes spoke of a willingness to attempt anything to satisfy her vengeance.

Takan knew that look, that feeling. He had felt it control him once years ago on the docks of District 13, on the day that he had sworn to kill Zyid.

Takan swallowed. "Noni, don't do this."

"Why not?" Noni demanded.

Her voice was as cold as her eyes as she glared at him.

"Because I understand now, Noni," Takan said softly. "I know exactly what motivates you. I was the same way once. I needed revenge so badly that it felt like I wouldn't survive without it—that it was the only thing I had to live for."

Noni looked at him strangely, and Takan could see her begin to waver. He had touched a nerve.

"I've been down that lonely path," Takan continued, his throat hoarse. "I know what lies at its end, and there's nothing there but emptiness. It won't bring him back. It won't make you feel better. Noni, the past year since I took my revenge has been one waking nightmare."

Noni blinked. "What are you talking about, Takan?"

In that moment Takan realized that Cross was right—if not now, when? He took a deep breath, and felt an enormous burden lift from his shoulders. At last the charade was over.

"It was me," Takan said. "I was the one who killed Zyid."

Cross kicked a rusted school desk aside as he walked forward, his rifle raised. He swept the area with his eyes. The sounds of gunfire came from all around him, yet he couldn't see the enemy.

The albino and Cross were together making their way through some ruins—not one of the ones recently created, but older wreckage that had once been the redbrick building of the District 1 School. Four years back the Educators had claimed that the building had been demolished. Cross recalled that it was a big deal at the time, especially for the students who had to be bused to schools in the surrounding districts.

Over the years the wreckage had remained there, shrubs and grass slowly beginning to grow over it. From the bullet holes in the bricks, Cross guessed that it must have actually been destroyed by the Truancy. This school had been a battlefield. Now, four years later, it was a battlefield once more.

"Look out!"

Bullets nipped at Cross' feet, and he felt the albino pull him safely behind a pile of old lockers. Cross peered around the corner and spotted the soldier, crouched behind what was left of a brick wall. Cross fired back three times, and the soldier dropped.

Realizing what had happened, three of the soldier's comrades appeared, and Cross was forced to duck again behind the lockers as they fired at his position. Then more gunfire rang out, and Cross heard the soldiers scream. He peeked out again, and saw Sepp waving back at him, leading a small group he had taken ahead.

Cross gave Sepp a thumbs-up. Sepp waved, then turned and continued on out of sight. Cross was about to follow him when the albino grabbed him by the shoulder.

"Wait," she said. "I hear something."

A moment later Cross heard it too—the dreaded roar of helicopters flying low. He and the albino forced some of the lockers open and hid themselves inside just as three helicopters appeared over the hill formed by the ruins.

The helicopter swooped down upon the rebels caught in the open, firing missiles at their positions. Explosions blossomed all throughout the ruins, further pulverizing the remains of the building. Rubble flew through the air, pattering against the lockers. Through the tiny holes of his hiding place, Cross peered up at the sky.

The helicopters came around for another pass, but this time the rebels were ready for them. A volley of rocket-propelled grenades streaked through the air. One of the helicopters was hit, spiraling out of control before smashing into the ground in a burst of flame. The other helicopters broke off, searching for easier prey.

Cross and the albino exited the lockers. They headed up the hill, using chunks of wall and old desks as footholds. Looking up at the top, Cross saw Sepp standing there against the sun, carrying a rocket launcher. He seemed very pleased with himself.

"Nice work, Sepp!" Cross shouted.

Sepp waved back at him, and then vanished down the other side of the hill. Cross blinked as the sun got in his eyes.

"We shouldn't all go the same way," the albino suggested. "Let's go around, they can handle the front."

Cross took her suggestion, and they began running around the mound. They picked their way through rotting textbooks and blackboards and all sorts of other rubbish that had been left forgotten over the years. As they rounded the hill, they saw that the Government had made a stand in the courtyard—two Humvees and some infantry were firing endlessly at the rebels, halting their advance.

Cross crouched behind a corner, firing at the distant soldiers. At this range he couldn't accomplish much, and it was too risky to try to advance any farther this way. He swore under his breath.

Then a rocket shot out and collided with one of the Humvees, the force of the explosion knocking some of the soldiers to the ground. Rebel snipers made quick work of the infantry, and Cross breathed a sigh of relief as the gunfire finally ceased. They had cleared the area. They now had a clear path straight towards the Mayoral Mansion.

Cross looked out at the courtyard where Sepp was now standing with the rest of the troops he had led. He looked almost heroic as he raised his launcher over his head, yelling his triumph to the world. Cross grinned at the sight.

Then there came a screech of aircraft overhead. Cross dove for cover, the albino alongside him. Cross felt a sudden dread twist his insides, but there was nothing they could do. He shut his eyes tight.

There was a flash, an enormous roar, then a wave of heat and pressure. When it was over, Cross staggered to his feet and looked out at the courtyard. Nothing remained of Sepp or his group except a smoldering crater and charred corpses.

Cross felt a lump form in his throat. He had thought he would be numb to loss by now, and yet this one still affected him. It was the impersonal nature of the death. Sepp had been a good person. He had deserved better than to vanish in an anonymous burst of flame. They were supposed to avenge Floe together.

Cross realized that he was the sole remaining survivor of his squad. A strange dizziness gripped him as the faces of the others flashed before his eyes. He took a step forward, and then stumbled.

There were firm hands waiting to grab him. Cross looked up and saw the albino guiding him as she had always done ever since they'd first met. Cross felt strange relief sweep through his body—*she* at least was still alive, still with him. He was not yet all alone.

"Don't lose your focus now, Cross," the albino said, her eyes appearing red in the bright sunlight. "Just look around you."

Cross did as bidden. The area was torn and ravaged by war, but the conflict here was over, moved to other parts of the district. The Government surely thought all the rebels here were dead.

"This will all be for nothing if you break down now," the albino scolded. "You have a clear path to the Mayoral Mansion now. This is your defining moment. What will you do?"

Slowly, Cross nodded. Getting a grip on himself, he returned to his feet. He looked around, then spotted it—one of the Humvees had escaped destruction. It was a little battered but still seemed serviceable.

"Teacher, can you drive?" he asked.

The albino smiled. "I can."

"Good." Cross walked over to the vehicle. "Because I can't."

The albino slipped behind the wheel as Cross took his place in the passenger's seat. There was a hum as the engines started up. Then the two of them were driving on through what was left of the District 1 streets, heading straight for the Mayoral Mansion in the distance.

ood work, Storm Six—now bring your company around and lay down suppressive fire."

Iris pressed the headset against her ear with one hand as she issued orders. Her eyes were glued on the monitor in front of her. The attack had come so suddenly that there had been no time to relocate, and so she was conducting the battle from her study.

Iris was well aware that she wasn't a perfect woman. She had emotional vulnerabilities, as everyone did. As a child, before her father recognized her leadership qualities, she had never been any good at acting polite and ladylike at state events. She was also, as her father often reminded her, needlessly stubborn.

One thing Iris always prided herself on was being calm in a crisis. As situations unfolded and the extent of the damage became obvious, Iris only got cooler and more collected.

"Storm Six, do you have visual on the target?"

"Negative—too much damn dust!"

Iris frowned. The dust clouds were also making it difficult to track the rebel troops via satellite. It was impossible to tell how many there were, though Iris thought that she still had enough forces to hold them back.

Still, Iris was deeply bothered by the extent of the damage to District 1. She hadn't thought that the rebellion had the resources to pull off such a feat, nor did she expect them to become so desperate as to attempt it. Iris knew they must be betting everything on this attack—if she could break them here, there might yet be a chance to regain control of the City.

A flash on the monitor alerted Iris that a squad positioned near the old District 1 School had been wiped out. That was a surprise. Iris calmly ordered an airstrike to level the entire area, then sat back and considered the situation.

The enemy was after the Mayoral Mansion, likely Iris herself. That much was obvious. The naïve rebels probably thought that removing the leadership would end the conflict. The fools.

Iris sighed and checked the screen again. It was still impossible to tell how many rebels remained, but considering the beating they had taken most of them had to have been annihilated. But with the streets in the condition they were in, Iris couldn't bring in reinforcements from other Districts. There were very few forces left to stand between the surviving rebels and the Mayoral Mansion—and inside, there was only her and her personal staff.

A call attempted to come through on the monitor. Iris glanced at it. It was the War Minister trying to contact her for the fifth time that day. The man was probably still wondering what was going on.

As Iris shut down the transmission, she realized that no matter how this battle ended, her struggle with her father had been lost. After this catastrophe the Potentate would never view her operation as anything more than a total failure. That meant a pullout was inevitable.

Iris did not give in to despair at this realization, but instead turned her mind to other concerns. She tapped her headset.

"Colonel Hines, are the Mayor and his son secure?"

"Affirmative. They're in the bunker under the Mansion right now, ready to leave at a moment's notice."

"Tell them to do so immediately."

"Yes, ma'am."

Iris let out a small breath. At the very least Umasi would be safe now, boarding one of the Mayor's private trains out of the City.

The monitor flashed again, and as Iris read the new message her calm composure slipped. Her forces had begun withdrawing from the entire City itself—but not on her orders. Iris slammed her fist on her armrest as she realized that the War Minister must have ordered an emergency pull-out after being unable to reach her.

Iris was about to attempt to countermand the orders when she remembered the soldiers. The casualties her troops had already sustained were horrendous, much more than had been lost in the rest of the conflict combined. Iris knew she had a responsibility not just to protect the City, but to preserve the lives of her troops.

Iris sighed. She had personally sworn to protect the City to the bitter end, but she could not drag her soldiers into that same, potentially suicidal pact.

Iris tapped her headset again, issuing an order for Colonel Hines to cooperate with the withdrawal and evacuate the Mayoral Mansion immediately. In the unlikely event that any of the attacking rebels survived and made it to the Mansion, Iris knew she would be risking her life by staying behind. But she also knew that at this point, the only thing really protecting the City was her presence. Leaving wasn't an option.

Iris leaned back in her chair, eyes glued to the monitor. Her family was safe, and she had done what she could for her subordinates. She had resolved to stay and fight, and she would do just that.

And if by some miracle the rebels managed to reach her, she would stop them herself.

33

For Noni, the earth seemed to tremble more from one sentence than from all the rebellion's explosives combined.

"It was me. I was the one who killed Zyid."

The confession struck Noni like a physical blow. She staggered back, grenade and rifle dropping from her limp hands as she trembled. Her blue eyes were wide as she stared at Takan. The chaos of the battle around them was instantly forgotten.

Noni steadied herself. "That—that *can't* be true."

"It is," Takan said.

"No," Noni choked. "No, you wouldn't. You couldn't. Takan, who are you trying to protect?"

A mixture of emotions twisted Takan's handsome face. There was remorse, guilt, and relief all at once as he spoke.

"All this time, I've been trying to protect myself," he said. "I've even let others sacrifice to protect me. But no more. I'm ready to face what I've done. I killed him."

For a moment Noni stood there, shaking. Then she let out a cry of anguish, drawing her knives.

"Why?" she screamed. "Why did it have to be you? Answer me!"

There was pain in Takan's eyes. "He killed my sister, Noni!"

Noni was stunned at that admission. The final piece fell into place, and suddenly everything made horrible senses. How long, she wondered, had Takan walked among the Truancy intending to take revenge on its leader? How much of it had been an act? Tears began to fall from Noni's eyes, and before she knew what she was doing she had lunged at Takan with knives outstretched.

Takan was shocked—by the tears more than her attack. He drew his sword to defend himself, blocking Noni's blade.

"You don't know what you're doing to me, Tack!" Noni wailed. "Zyid . . . he's gone . . . I've already lost him . . . and now you . . . you're going to have to die too!"

Noni slashed at Takan with her other knife, but with her mind in chaos her aim went askew. Takan easily sidestepped the assault, making no move to counterattack.

"I don't blame you for wanting me dead," Takan said quietly.

"I don't want you dead!" Noni shrieked. "I loved him, Takan . . . and I loved *you* too! I loved you, and now I have to kill you!"

Noni attacked Takan more wildly, with both knives. Takan parried her careless blows, but the action was mechanical. His full attention was on her agonized face and her tears.

Takan swallowed. "If you don't want to, you have a choice, Noni—"

"No!" Noni screamed as she lunged. "I don't have a choice, don't you understand? I made a promise!"

The two Truants locked blades, and their eyes met. Takan did understand. He knew exactly how it felt to be torn between two loyalties. It had been him in her place once, before the cycle had turned. Suddenly, he realized what he had to do.

Takan had taken his revenge. Now it was time for Noni to take hers.

"Then keep your promise, Noni." Takan took a step back. "I won't stop you. It's your turn to carry Zyid's legacy now."

Takan lowered his blade, spreading his arms, silently offering Noni his life. With a shaking hand, Noni raised one of her knives. The two of them looked at each other again, pain and determination on both their faces.

Then Noni burst into tears, collapsing against Takan. Takan swept her up into an embrace, his own eyes too numb to cry. For several minutes the two remained that way even as the sounds of battle roared around them. Had a sudden hurricane swept down upon them the two would not have budged.

As Noni continued to sob into his chest, Takan remembered his duel with Zyid, and how differently that had gone. Finally he understood what the Truancy's old leader had done for him. Zyid had been strong enough to fight Takan to the last—to allow Takan to kill him without guilt.

Takan had never truly defeated Zyid. Zyid had given his life to calm Takan's soul.

And yet Takan had not been as strong as his predecessor, in the end. He had not been able to fight Noni, to allow her to have her revenge. She had spared his life, and now they both faced an uncertain future, the world around them changed.

They continued to embrace even as Government transport helicopters droned overhead, heading away from the district, away from the City. The gunshots and explosions grew steadily fainter—and Noni's sobs along with them. The conflict was dying down.

Finally, Takan pulled away, and Noni did not protest.

"Noni," he said, placing his hands on her shoulders. "I promise we can talk about this more later, and . . . whatever you want in the end, you can have it."

Noni said nothing, but looked away.

"We don't have much time. The Mayoral Mansion isn't far," Takan continued. "Cross will need our help—if you don't want to kill me anymore, that is."

Noni sniffed and stood up, sheathing her knives.

"It's still a possibility," she said.

It was just a house, yet somehow, as they drew closer, the Mayoral Mansion loomed larger than life to Cross. It was an old-fashioned building that took up the entire block, with an empty square left in front of it.

Cross imagined that for a Truant the building would have represented different things; the seat of power in the City, the place where the last Mayor had hatched his schemes to control the populace. For Cross, however, the Mayoral Mansion held a simpler significance: the location of his enemy.

"Look, up there!" the albino said suddenly, taking one hand off the steering wheel to point up at the sky.

Cross peered through the windshield and saw several dark shapes far overhead. Government transport helicopters, probably packed with troops. There was nothing shocking about that, except they seemed to be flying *away* from District 1.

"What are they doing?" Cross wondered.

The albino bit her lip. "If I had to guess, I'd say they were withdrawing."

"Could we be too late?" Cross frowned. "If they're fleeing the district then Iris might be gone already."

"Well, we'll find out soon. The Mayoral Mansion is just ahead." The albino nodded out the windshield. "You should be proud Cross—even if Iris escaped, this is a victory. The Government is fleeing the heart of the City."

Cross shook his head. "It's not a victory yet. The battle is still ongoing, and it'll all have been for nothing if we can't get their General."

As they drove into the empty square in front of the Mayoral Mansion, they could hear explosions and gunshots still going off in other parts of the district, though less intensely than before. The two citizens cautiously slipped out of their stolen vehicle and looked around.

There were sandbags piled up here and there, along with random equipment scattered on the ground. Yet the square was completely deserted. There wasn't a soldier in sight.

"Maybe they all got out already?" Cross wondered. "Or maybe it's a trap—Iris might be plotting something."

"Perhaps we should try asking her ourselves," the albino suggested. "We've come this far. It would be a waste not to check the Mansion."

Cross nodded and raised his rifle. They approached the awning over the front doors to the Mayoral Mansion. In better days Cross imagined that there would have been a doorman waiting there. Now there was no one to greet them.

The foyer was dark, and Cross felt his heart beating in his throat as he stepped into the main antechamber. At any moment he expected to trip a mine or find soldiers surrounding them, but there was nothing. It was inexplicable.

They stepped into a living room and found the lights still on, paraphernalia strewn around the room, as though whoever had evacuated had been in such a hurry that everything had been left as it was. There were monitors and computer equipment set up in here. Cross was about to give up hope and accept that Iris had escaped when the albino spoke up.

"Look!" She pointed at a screen. "Someone is still giving orders from this building."

Sure enough, commands were flashing across the screen and channels of communication seemed to be open. Cross felt his heart beat faster.

"It's Iris."

"Or maybe we're just meant to think that," the albino cautioned. "It could still be a trap."

With that in mind, they proceeded through a series of empty, lavish rooms, some with military equipment scattered throughout. Cross saw no weapons around, though he still had his rifle.

Then they entered a grand dining room with a long banquet table, bare now. At the far end of the room, two staircases on either side curved upwards to reach a balcony where archways provided access to the second floor. Doors on the ground floor indicated rooms yet to be explored.

"Let's split up," the albino suggested in a whisper. "It'll be easier. I'll search the top floors, you handle the ground level."

Cross wanted to protest, but the suggestion made sense. Reluctantly, he nodded.

"Be careful, teacher," Cross said.

The albino smiled and nodded, then headed for the closer stairs. Cross took a deep breath and held his rifle steady as he proceeded farther into the mansion. Somehow, he felt sure that somewhere in this building Iris was waiting for them.

Rothenberg's grin grew wider as yet another explosion rang out in the distance. He was sitting hunched on his cot, excitement pulsing in his veins. He had been eagerly listening to the sounds of the battle ever since the first enormous tremors had shaken him awake.

"What're you so happy about, Rothenberg?"

In the cell across from the former Enforcer, Max was lying on his cot with his hands under his head, looking totally unconcerned by the ongoing chaos outside.

"You little idiot, can't you hear that the City is burning?" Rothenberg laughed. "You see what happens to this world without me around? It was just the same when the Mayor locked me up!"

There was a flash from outside the barred windows, and another blast shook the building. Rothenberg glanced up at the ceiling, where some dust had shaken loose. The prison had held so far, but it was old. Rothenberg hoped it would stay intact long enough for him to see the aftermath of the battle. When the dust settled, he was sure that they would come crawling back to him for help, as they always did.

Max laughed. "Rothenberg, you know you're going to die here."

"I know nothing of the sort," Rothenberg snapped. "But if anyone here has to die I'll make sure *you* go first."

"Great, maybe we can have side-by-side cells in the afterlife too!"

Max laughed again, and Rothenberg tuned the kid out, which he had become good at. Instead, Rothenberg strained to hear each bomb blast, each distant gunshot. He amused himself with thoughts of the Truancy and the Government tearing each other apart. He wondered if Cross was out there with them.

"Don't die just yet, boy," Rothenberg muttered. "We've got unfinished business, you and I."

More flashes went off outside, easily visible through the windows. Rothenberg even thought he could hear the screaming of young voices. How appropriate, he thought, that all his enemies would fight among themselves. They truly deserved each other.

Just then Rothenberg's thoughts were interrupted by another blast, closer than any of the others. There was a crumbling sound. Rothenberg caught a glimpse of falling bricks, and then everything went black.

A light flashed on the monitor once again. Iris spared it a passing glance before turning her chair away. The War Minister was being irritatingly obstinate in his attempts to contact her.

To her surprise she heard a beep as though the call had been accepted. The connection had been forced through. Iris frowned. That should have been impossible. She spun around, ready to scold the man—

"What do you think you are doing, my dear daughter?"

Iris swallowed her surprise. The image on the screen was grainy and full of static, and the face was no more than a silhouette. The voice, however, belonged unmistakably to her father.

"I am trying to carry out my mission," Iris said calmly. "Now perhaps you can tell me why my troops are pulling out of the City without my command?"

The image onscreen inclined its head. "I ordered the withdrawal myself."

Iris clenched her fists.

"Why would you allow me to come here at all if you were just going to sabotage my efforts?" she demanded. "You *know* that I could take control of the situation if I had more time and resources, but at every step you have been completely—"

"Iris, my dearest daughter," the voice interrupted lazily. "You were sent to that City to fail."

Iris shut her mouth. There it was, the obvious conclusion that she had for so long struggled to avoid.

"Why?"

"To teach you a lesson." The image stirred. "You were so childishly obstinate about the matter that it seemed like a good opportunity for you to learn the limits of your own abilities."

"This whole thing was a game for you?"

"Little more than that. I never intended to allow any of my progeny to become a warlord of their own little kingdom. You were naïve to believe otherwise."

Iris glared. "And the City?"

"Is beyond recovery. It is high time that you accepted that fact." The image leaned back. "You will leave the City immediately."

"No."

Silence.

"*What* did you just say to me?"

"I said I refuse." Iris smiled. "If you wish to proceed with this madness, then your daughter will be caught up in it as well."

"Do not be a fool," the Potentate growled. "If you continue to disobey me, you will be disinherit—"

Iris laughed, long and hard. The image onscreen fell silent.

"You've misjudged me, father," Iris said at last. "I've never cared a bit about inheritance. I'm staying right where I am."

The image flickered.

"Enough of this childishness! If you will not come willingly, you will be relieved of command and soldiers will be sent to retrieve you!"

"But as your withdrawal continues, I am left completely unprotected."
Iris spread her arms. "The Mayoral Mansion is already empty. At this
rate, the only thing you'll retrieve is my corpse."

"You dare to test my resolve, daughter? That is a gamble you will lose.
You have gone too far this—"

Iris yanked a cord out of the computer. The monitor went blank, the
connection broken. A line had been crossed. There was no turning back
now. For several moments Iris stood there alone, contemplating the magnitude of what she had just done.

Presently she became aware of soft footsteps outside the study.

The knob turned, and the door creaked open. Without hesitation, Iris
drew her sidearm and fired. The shot struck the thick wooden door, but
did not penetrate. Iris frowned as she heard the footsteps retreating.

Iris calmly got to her feet and stepped into the corridor, pistol raised.
There was no sign of anyone. Her senses alert, Iris descended some stairs
until she reached the second-floor balcony overlooking the dining hall.
Sweeping the area with her eyes, Iris stepped forward.

A gunshot rang out, striking one of the banisters near her. Iris instinctively crouched down behind the banisters for cover. She glanced down at
the dining hall. She could see the boy now, even recognize him. It was
Cross, the old leader of the Student Militia, now one of the leaders of the
Citizens' Rebellion. Good.

Cross raised his rifle again to fire, and Iris ducked. The boy pulled the
trigger, but nothing happened. A rifle jam. In an instant Iris was on her
feet, pistol raised, ready to press her advantage—

There was a tinkling sound from her right. Iris spun around, just as a
metal ring struck her hand, knocking the gun from her grip. The pistol
sailed over the banister and caught on a ledge below, impossible to retrieve.

Iris turned to face her new adversary. It was someone she had never
seen before, a pretty albino girl dressed in white and blue. Iris recognized
the tattered remnants of a Student Militia jacket. There was a grunt from
below, and Iris glanced down. Cross now had the rifle handle drawn back,
unsuccessfully trying to shake a stuck casing loose.

Iris' lips curled into a smile as Cross tossed his rifle aside in frustration,
drawing a combat knife instead. The albino coughed, drawing Iris' attention.

"It's over, General," she said. "Your soldiers are already gone. Call off the
occupation, and leave with them."

"They are withdrawing from the City on my father's orders, not mine,"
Iris said calmly. "*I* intend to stay to the end."

"Why?" Cross demanded, climbing up the stairs. "Why defy even your father? Do you hate us that much?"

Iris laughed. Cross scowled.

"Your type will never understand. Words do not reach you, only violence." Iris detached her staff from her back. "I'm tired of trying to save you, Cross. Your resistance ends here. Die loathing me, if you must."

The albino frowned. "We don't want to fight."

"Speak for yourself, teacher," Cross growled.

Iris pressed a button on her staff, and the weapon extended to full length. The albino immediately lashed out with her chain and Iris blocked the attack, smiling as she allowed the links to wrap around her staff. Then she pressed the second button on her staff, and the albino screamed in pain as the electricity flowed down the chain.

Cross let out a noise of fury, taking the remaining steps two at a time. He charged straight for Iris, who swung her staff to catch the handle of a nearby vase, then hurled it at Cross. Cross caught the vase with one hand, shoving it aside. The decoration fell over the edge of the balcony and shattered on the floor below. Iris took a step towards Cross, but the albino tugged on the chain to prevent her from swinging her staff.

Iris retaliated with another electric shock, and the albino dropped to one knee in pain. Cross seized the opening and lunged forward with his knife, but with the chain now loose Iris struck Cross with the staff upside his head, pressing the button again. Both the albino and Cross received the jolt, and Cross fell backwards from the blow.

Iris glanced at the albino. The girl lay on the ground some distance away, in no apparent shape to fight. Iris freed her staff from the chain, and then advanced on Cross. Cross saw her coming, and made a sudden lunge for her legs. Iris jumped, landing on Cross' arm, and then brought her staff crashing down onto his back. She pressed the button once more, and Cross screamed.

Then there came a terrible creaking sound from above, and Iris looked upwards. The albino's chain was now wrapped around a chandelier directly above them. The albino pulled with all her strength and with a groan the chandelier came free. Iris leaped backwards, and Cross rolled out of the way of the falling ornament.

The chandelier made a terrific crashing sound as it impacted the floor in a shower of crystal. The room grew suddenly darker without its light. As Cross groaned on the floor, Iris turned to face the albino, who was panting slightly.

"I'm impressed," Iris said. "I was sure that I'd shocked you enough to keep you down."

The albino smiled wryly. "I've endured worse in my time."

"I don't know who you are," Iris said, "but it's unfortunate that you've fallen in with the wrong crowd. Are you sure this is what you want?"

"I am."

"Then this fight will be the *last* thing you ever endure."

Behind Iris, Cross had risen to his feet. He lunged just as the albino swung her chain again. Iris knocked the ring aside, and then in the same fluid motion brought her staff behind her to strike Cross on top of his head. Cross stumbled forward. Without hesitation, Iris seized his collar and then hurled him off the balcony.

For a moment Cross felt a strange looping feeling, as though he were a child riding on the swings again. Then there was a sickening crunch beneath him, and Cross found himself lying amid the shattered splinters of what had been a small decorative stand. There was pain everywhere.

"Cross!" His teacher's voice was calling him. "Cross, are you all right?"

Cross realized that he could still move his limbs. Tentatively he began to stir, and a moan escaped his lips. He glanced at his right hand—somehow he had managed to hold onto his knife.

Up on the balcony, Iris looked down at Cross and frowned as he stirred. Ignoring the albino altogether, Iris pressed the button to shrink her staff down to a weighted stick. Then she ran for the stairs and smoothly slid down the banister to the first floor. The albino darted down the stairs after her.

Painfully, Cross managed to climb to his feet. As Iris reached the bottom and began to approach him with determined steps, he realized that they had badly underestimated the General. The two of them weren't strong enough, even together. For the first time Cross considered the possibility that Iris might really kill them both.

"It was a mistake for you to come here," Iris said. "Had you just waited it out, you might have survived a little longer."

Iris charged. Cross backed up, slashing wildly with his knife. It was a panicked attack, and Iris easily avoided the blade. She swung her stick once with precision. The blow caught Cross in the ribs, the stick shorter but heavier than the staff. Iris swung again, this time at his head. Cross narrowly managed to drop to the ground to avoid what he was sure would have been a fatal blow.

As Cross attempted to rise, the albino caught up and desperately swung her chain. Iris extended her staff, one end deflecting the oncoming chain while the other pinned Cross to the floor. Iris held down a button, and Cross' world was engulfed in pain. A scream ripped from his throat as he writhed on the carpet—

Then the main doors to the dining hall slammed open.

"There they are!"

Their fight momentarily forgotten, Iris, Cross, and the albino all turned to look at the door. His body trembling, Cross felt his heart soar as Takan and Noni entered the room, knives and sword drawn.

"Hello," Takan said breathlessly. "Mind if we join in?"

Cross noticed that the two former Truants looked a little strange as they stepped forward. Noni's eyelids were red and puffy, and Takan had an unusually sober look on his face. They also seemed to be avoiding looking at each other.

None of that really mattered to Cross, however—he was just glad that they had arrived when they did.

"Tack, alias Takan, and Noni," Iris greeted. "Of course, you're welcome. I should have expected that individuals of your stature would make it. It's good to see you all in one place. I can now wipe out the entire leadership of the rebellion at once."

Noni narrowed her eyes. "Don't be stupid. There are four of us now."

"You believe that will be enough?" Iris smiled. "Naïve girl. You should have stayed in the camp. In time we might have brought you back to reason."

"This is your last chance, General," Takan warned. "Surrender and withdraw your forces completely. If you don't, you will die here."

"Still you understand nothing of the peril you face!" Iris laughed. "No, there is far too much at stake for me to die now—especially to the likes of you."

Without warning, the albino struck from behind, her chain hissing through the air. Iris swung her staff behind her, deflecting the ring. Cross seized the opportunity to scramble away, climbing back to his feet. Takan and Noni leapt up onto the long banquet table, running side by side towards Iris.

With the wall to her left and the table to her right, Iris drove her staff into Cross' chest while blocking another chain swing from behind. As Takan and Noni drew close, Iris hooked a chair with her staff, and then swung it up at them. The furniture slammed into Takan, who was knocked backwards with a grunt.

Noni managed to get within striking distance, but Iris simply ducked her swipe, and then struck the girl's midsection with her staff, pressing her button as she did. Noni let out a cry of pain and fell backwards, off of the table. Without pausing a second, Iris blocked Cross' knife arm, spun around to deflect the chain, and then leapt up onto the dining table herself.

By now Takan was back on his feet, and he ran down the table towards Iris. The General blocked his sword thrust, and then almost lazily struck his head and leg with either end of the staff in a swift motion. His leg swept from under him, Takan fell painfully off the table. As though without effort, Iris again deflected the albino's chain, and then aimed a staff blow down at Cross, forcing him to keep his distance.

Noni jumped onto the table behind Iris, and Iris swerved around, jabbing her staff into Noni's belly, adding a shock to the blow. From the floor, Takan swung his sword up at Iris's legs. Iris jumped over the attack. Cross rushed forward, attempting to get in a stab, and Iris responded by kicking him hard in the face.

Cross fell to the floor, his head spinning in disbelief. Warm blood trickled from his nostrils. The four of them together were actually losing to Iris. The General was unlike anything any of them had ever seen—her movements were fast and efficient, her awareness and reflexes unmatched.

At this rate, they were going to be defeated.

The albino shot her chain straight out at Iris, and this time Iris snatched the metal ring out of the air and then yanked hard on the chain. Cross could see shock on his teacher's face as she was pulled closer to the table. Iris shortened her staff then slammed the weighted stick hard onto the albino's head.

"Teacher!"

The albino crumpled to the ground, stunned or worse. Cross gasped, the fight forgotten as he crawled over to her. For a few terrible seconds his body was wracked by dread, by the thought that he might have lost her too. Then the albino moaned and stirred, and Cross breathed a sigh of relief.

Meanwhile Iris entered a deadly rhythm. Takan and Noni rushed at her from either ends of the banquet table. Iris extended her staff, hooked another chair, and swung it into an oncoming Noni. Noni swore as she was knocked off the table, the chair shattering into splinters.

Continuing the motion, Iris swept the staff at Takan's legs. Takan jumped, only for Iris to bring the other end of the staff crashing down onto his shoulder. Takan yelped as Iris pressed the button. The Truant stumbled backwards from the shock. Iris ruthlessly followed up with a kick, knocking him farther back.

By now all of the rebels were worn out. Crouched down near his teacher, Cross realized that it was only a matter of time before Iris killed them all, one by one. Anger and frustration clouded his vision, and he slammed his fist against the floor, cursing his powerlessness. He couldn't protect Floe, and now he couldn't even fight against her killer.

Then Cross saw it. Lying on the carpet nearby, where it had been discarded, was his rifle. If only he could use it! The damn thing had jammed up at the worst possible time, and Cross couldn't get the casing free, no matter how hard he shook.

Then Cross remembered something, and Floe's words seemed to filter out of the past and through the haze in his head.

"That's not how you do it! Lock the bolt back and remove the magazine! Doesn't the Militia teach that?"

Trembling on his hands and knees, Cross crawled forward towards the rifle.

Meanwhile, the albino had struggled to her feet.

"Noni!" she shouted, tossing the end of her chain to the other girl.

Understanding immediately, Noni sprang up and caught the ring. The two of them began running on either side of the banquet table, aiming to trip up Iris with the chain. At the same time Takan began charging at Iris from the front. Iris jumped once over the chain, but the girls brought it looping back at her.

As Takan drew close, Iris jumped onto the chain and pinned it to the table with her feet. She blocked Takan's sword with one end of the staff, almost lazily striking him with the other. Then she touched her staff to the chain and pressed a button, smiling as both girls cried out in pain from the shock—

A gunshot went off.

For a split second no one understood what had happened. Then Iris fell backwards, the bullet catching her in her armor, the force of the blow knocking her off her feet. Takan and Noni seized their chance. Their weapons flashed, and Iris let out a small gasp.

Takan's sword had cut her waist, while Noni had driven her knife straight under Iris' armpit, unprotected by the armor. Iris' stormy gray eyes shut, her chest heaving as she understood what had just happened.

"Now . . ." Iris coughed. "My worst fears . . . come true . . ."

Cross rose from his position on the floor, his rifle barrel smoking faintly. The magazine lay discarded nearby. He had cleared the jam and slammed a single bullet into the breech to fire. That single shot had been enough.

As Iris bled out onto the table, the rebels all gathered around her, each of their expressions different. Noni looked satisfied. Takan looked grim. Cross looked triumphant. Then the albino got up and approached Iris, the only sympathetic face of the bunch.

Iris looked up at her. "I didn't want it to end like this."

"There's nothing we can do for those wounds," the albino said quietly, crouching over her. "You fought hard. You should be very proud."

"Proud? No, my life will end now in shame." Iris laughed bitterly. "I've failed everyone. I've failed you."

The albino looked sad. "I know that you were trying to do what you could for the people of this City."

"My brother must have told you that." Iris shook her head. "You're the one he was talking about, then."

"Yes."

"But he couldn't have told you why I decided to stay and fight, even when I knew it would be my death," Iris said. "I never discussed that with him. He never knew about the orders."

Takan blinked. "You were ordered to die here?"

"The opposite." Iris' face seemed to contort with pain. "I was ordered to save myself and withdraw with my troops. By staying behind I openly defied my father."

"Why?" Noni demanded.

"Because." Iris coughed up blood. "Now that my failure is complete, this entire City will be destroyed."

34

ILLUSIONS OF GOOD AND EVIL

The four rebels stood in stunned silence, unsure of what to make of Iris' words. They exchanged confused glances. Then, finally, Cross spoke up.

"What do you mean by destroying the whole City?" he demanded.

Iris opened her eyes.

"My operation here was the Government's last attempt to salvage this City," she said. "They intended all along that if I failed, they would simply wipe the City off the map."

Takan shook his head. "How is that even possible?"

"You do not understand the power possessed by your enemy," Iris said. "The Government could end all life on the planet if it desired. They will use a single explosive powerful enough to destroy the whole City, poisoning the land for years to come."

Iris' voice was hard as steel, though wracked by pain. Moments passed, and the rebels realized that she was serious. Then the implications began to sink in, and the expressions on their faces uniformly turned to horror.

"My father always believed that destroying the City was the prudent choice." Iris sighed. "He did not want to risk the unrest spreading. He argued that it would save more lives in the end."

"Save lives?" Cross repeated. "How would destroying the whole City *save* lives?"

"The first time he faced discontent, the fighting spread far and wide," Iris explained. "The result was a conflict that ended with hundreds of thousands of deaths and untold destruction. Order was restored at a high cost. The Government remembers this—they would do anything to avoid a repeat. The threat of the Education City had to be contained."

"Even if that were true," the albino said, "what about the civilians? The innocents?"

Iris shook her head. "The Government will claim that they are a necessary sacrifice. In truth I don't believe they care about them at all. They're tired of struggling with this City. They want a quick solution to the problem."

"A quick solution?" Noni repeated. "At what cost?"

"They do not see it as a cost!" Iris laughed. "In the world outside this City the Government has rivals and enemies. A demonstration of their power would remind everyone that they are to be feared. It would be a benefit."

"That is a savage doctrine," the albino said quietly.

"It is one perspective among many." Iris shut her eyes again. "I personally did not agree with my father and his Ministers on this. I argued endlessly until they gave me one chance to pacify the City and restore the system upon which it was based."

Horror and understanding finally dawned on the albino's face.

"So that's why you—"

"Stayed behind, yes," Iris said. "I meant to protect this City with my own life. With me still inside, I do not believe that my father would dare to destroy it."

Then the others understood, and the magnitude of their error left them dizzy and breathless. Throughout their struggle they had seen Iris as an outside threat to the City they all called home. In truth, it was Iris who had fought the hardest to save that City, a shield between them and destruction.

And when they thwarted her, Iris had stayed behind to protect the City with her very life. Now she lay before them, bleeding that life away, and the City's true protector had fallen at their hands.

The albino looked at her comrades with watery eyes. "In the end, Iris was a *hero.*"

Cross nodded, swallowing. "Were—were we the bad guys then? Was it our fault, all of this?"

"Maybe it was us, the original Truancy," Takan said wearily. "We started the war in the first place, after all."

"Zyid only rebelled because of the Educators who oppressed him," Noni protested, then hesitated. "But after all, maybe they were just doing their jobs."

Cross frowned in confusion. "So *was* it the Government, for starting this experiment in the first place?"

"Who was right or wrong? Who was good or evil?" The albino shook her head. "All of them and none of them. It's all so meaningless. All it takes is a year of fighting, and people lose sight of how it started . . . and yet it never stops."

"We wanted to save the people of this City." Cross hung his head. "We've doomed them instead. All of them."

"It does not have to be so."

All four of the citizens turned their heads to stare at Iris, who had just spoken. Her words instantly kindled a new hope in their hearts.

"What do you mean?" Takan said quickly. "Can the City be saved somehow?"

Iris shook her head. "There is no way to save the City itself, not anymore. Sooner or later my father will discover what has happened here, and then his vengeance will be swift."

The albino blinked a tear away. "Then—"

"I am not finished," Iris said, grimacing with pain. "There might still be a chance to save the people of the City."

"How?" Cross said, leaning over the table. "What do we have to do?"

Iris looked at him, her gray eyes clear and focused.

"The drawbridges and tunnels leading out of the City have all been raised or blocked off. This is the way the City has been contained for generations," she explained. "Their controls can be accessed from the observation spire at the top of—"

"Penance Tower," Takan finished. "I remember that."

Iris nodded. "Penance Tower is located here in District 1. The building is on emergency power. The elevators probably won't work, so it will be difficult to get up there."

"I will do it," the albino said immediately, resolve clear on her face. "We have no time to waste. I'll leave now."

The albino turned to leave.

"I'm coming with you, teacher!" Cross called.

The albino did not seem to hear him, for she had already walked out of the dining hall. Cross made to follow her, then paused, turning to look hesitantly at Iris. The General looked peaceful now, completely still as she lay bleeding on top of the table. It was almost as though they were attending her wake.

"General," Cross said quietly.

"What is it?" Iris asked. "I cannot move much right now; it will agitate the bleeding, and there are still things for me to do in the minutes I have left."

Cross took a deep breath.

"Iris, I'm sorry for—for shooting you," he said. "I was angry and it wasn't fair, I know that. It wasn't fair."

Iris smiled faintly. "There's no such thing as fairness, Cross. The ends make the means irrelevant."

Somehow the tears snuck up on Cross, and before he knew it he was crying as he supported himself against the table.

"I hated you," Cross sobbed. "You killed someone I loved. When we were fleeing the District 13 camp."

Iris creased her brow for a moment, searching her memories. Then she sighed.

"The girl with the grenade?" Iris glanced at Cross, who nodded. "We buried her properly, if that is any comfort. I once believed that you cared for nothing but violence. I'm sorry. It appears I misjudged you."

"Don't apologize," Cross said, wiping his eyes. "I'm the one doing that."

Then, without another word, Cross turned and ran out of the room after the albino, leaving Takan and Noni alone with the dying General.

The skies of the City had turned a dull gray. As the albino slipped out of the front doors of the Mayoral Mansion, she could feel the change in the weather. Rain was coming; an end to the recent drought the City had suffered.

That knowledge was of no comfort to the nameless girl. What she had done and learned inside the Mansion devastated her. The fatal blows had not been hers in any way, and yet she still felt like a murderer. Whether she knew it at the time or not, whether she meant it or not, the albino was partly responsible for killing a great woman.

And in the process she had doomed the whole City.

The albino let out a quiet moan of anguish. Not since she was a child on the streets, scrabbling through trash cans for the first time had she felt so lost, so confused. It's like her whole world had shattered, as though everything she had ever done, ever tried to be, had been exposed as a lie.

She was guilty now of a crime she could never atone for. There was no redemption for what they had done.

"What would you *do if you'd put a lot of people in danger?"*

"I would try to save them."

The albino tightened her grip on her chain. She would do whatever it took to be true to those words, which had come so naturally and so easily before, but now seemed so difficult. Looking up at the skyline, the albino saw Penance Tower looming ominously in the distance. It was like a great shadow against the clouds.

The albino knew that even if she could get to the top, she might not be able to get out in time. That was okay with her. It was her sacrifice to make. Quickly she walked towards the Humvee that they had ditched before.

"Teacher, wait for me!"

The albino ignored the voice. It came again, louder. Then its owner placed a hand on her shoulder, and she rounded on him, an unfamiliar intensity on her face.

"This is my burden, Cross," she said forcefully. "This is my way of repaying a debt to the City. I need to do this alone."

"Your burden?" Cross blinked. "You can't claim that kind of responsibility for yourself! What about me? I was the one who shot Iris! I was the one who planned this attack, led this rebellion!"

"I don't want to share the risk. We have no idea what might be waiting for us there. I don't think it's going to be easy, Cross."

Cross folded his arms. "All the more reason two of us should go."

The two of them stared each other down, the same determination mirrored on their faces. Finally, the albino looked away and sighed.

"You know that if we go, there's a good chance we won't make it out in time," she said quietly. "You have to assume you won't survive."

Cross blinked. "Teacher, what could we possibly do with our lives that is more important than this?"

The albino smiled grimly at that. Then she nodded. The two of them proceeded together to the Humvee. Moments later, they were driving through the war-torn streets, heading for the great shadow in the distance.

Takan and Noni helped Iris into the chair. By her request, they had brought her back upstairs to her study. They had done their best to staunch her wounds, yet she was still losing a lot of blood, and they all knew it was a matter of time before she died. Takan and Noni looked at her guiltily as she leaned back in her seat, her face pale.

"General," Takan said. "If we can get you to your people, do you think there's any chance that—"

Iris cut him off with a shake of her head.

"If the Government becomes aware of my situation there is a chance that I might be saved," she said. "But it will mean that millions more will die instead."

Noni stepped forward. "Is there anything you want?"

"Yes." Iris pointed at the monitor with her good arm. "Tilt the camera up so that it points only at my face."

Takan hastened to do as she said, carefully manipulating the camera mounted on top of the monitor.

"What are you planning to do?" Noni asked.

"Whatever I can," Iris coughed. "The Government must not find out that I am dying. I will first send them another message saying that I'm going into hiding in the City. Then I will order whatever soldiers that will listen to help evacuate the civilians."

"Is there anything that Noni and I can do to help?" Takan asked.

Iris nodded. "The people of the City must know. They must be told to evacuate, that the bridges and tunnels will be available."

"How can we do that?" Noni asked.

Iris' voice grew steadily weaker as she explained.

"About a year ago the Mayor had the Citywide broadcast controls re-routed to City Hall," she said. "Those controls are off right now. You must go to City Hall and reactivate them. It shouldn't be hard, with the military gone."

Noni nodded. "We'll do our best."

"Yeah," Takan said. "And Iris—I'm sorry, for everything."

Iris smiled at them, and for the first time they saw the youth in her face, drawn and pale though it was.

"I can tell you've both endured a lot of suffering in your time," Iris whispered. "Too much, for kids your age. You should live to see some happiness, after all of this. Take that." Iris nodded at a folder on her desk. "It contains maps and documents you can use to get out of this City. I recommend you leave via what's left of the District 8 overpass; it will take you to an old rail bridge, abandoned now."

Noni and Takan looked at each other, and then away. Takan took the folder and tucked it under his arm.

"Is that all?" Takan asked.

Iris sighed and closed her eyes. "If someday you ever run into my brother, tell him that I'm sorry, but that I did all I could."

Takan nodded gravely. "I will. Thank you for everything."

"Good luck, boy."

With that, Takan turned and walked out of the study. Noni lingered a moment, studying the older woman as she rested in her chair. Iris looked back at her, knowing that this would be the last time she ever saw the face of another person. Then Noni bowed her head and left the room, shutting the door behind her.

Now all alone in the gloom of her study, Iris sat up straight with whatever strength she had left to muster. The General pressed a few buttons on her keyboard, preparing to send some final orders to the soldiers still loyal to her and their consciences.

Rothenberg opened his eyes and groaned. He could see nothing but blackness. There was a heavy pressure on his chest, restricting his breathing, and the air itself was dusty and foul. His head was pounding, and he found it difficult to think.

Rothenberg stirred a little, and felt something yield at his movement. He pushed harder, and was rewarded with a crumbling sound. Then Rothenberg shoved with all of his considerable might, and the chunk of wall that had fallen on top of him finally gave way. He gasped as the pressure on his chest eased, his lungs filling with fresh air.

Rothenberg sat up, brushing tiny bits of rubble out of his hair and mustache. His legs were still trapped, but his vision was now clear, allowing him to examine his surroundings. He gaped as he saw the state of the prison.

The entire wing of the building had collapsed, probably destroyed by a bomb. Rothenberg wasn't sure which side had done it, nor did he care. He glanced over to his right, past the twisted remnants of what had once been the bars to his cell. There, half buried under some bricks, was Max's body, twisted in impossible ways. Clearly the boy had not survived.

Rothenberg laughed at that, long and hard, until he coughed from some stray dust in the air. He had been right, in the end. Too bad Max would never know it.

Something wet fell onto Rothenberg's forehead, and he looked up to see a cloudy sky through the shattered roof, so different from the sunny day he remembered. He wondered how long he had been unconscious—hours? Days?

Rothenberg attempted to stand but found it impossible. He looked down and saw his legs trapped under more rubble. Painfully, with difficulty, Rothenberg managed to extricate himself from the bricks, grunting as he finally pulled free. Breathing heavily, he glanced outside.

The streets were strewn with junk. There were bodies lying around, citizens and soldiers alike. Not a living thing seemed to be moving. It was surreal, as though the City had been utterly forsaken.

Rothenberg rose to his feet and stumbled out of the broken wall that had until recently held him prisoner. He gazed all around with a feeling of awe, the wrecked streets and collapsed buildings evidence that the City was suffering as he had suffered. And he, Rothenberg, had survived it all.

For a few quiet moments Rothenberg wondered what to do. His thoughts turned again to Cross—did he still live? Rothenberg shook his head. There was no way to find out now. Either the boy was strong enough to survive or he was not.

Then out of the corner of his eye Rothenberg glimpsed an enormous dark shape, and turned to stare up at the massive figure of the nearby Penance Tower, the nerve center to nearly the entire City. It was only a few blocks away. For a few moments Rothenberg entertained visions of himself as Mayor, using the controls at Penance Tower to secure the obedience of all citizens.

Then Rothenberg laughed. Why did it have to stay a fantasy? The Government and the rebels were both clearly in ruins; evidence of that was all around him. This was a perfect opportunity for a man like Rothenberg to take the initiative. He *would* be Mayor—no, he would be King!

Armed with his new purpose, Rothenberg staggered over to a dead soldier nearby, pulling a pistol off the man's body. Then he turned and began making his way towards Penance Tower. As the rain began to fall, Rothenberg imagined what he would do when finally the City was his to rule.

35

PENANCE TOWER

I n times of peace, Penance Tower had been a symbol of pride for the City. One hundred and one stories tall, it soared over a thousand feet above the street. From its place at the very center of the City, the tower was visible from almost every district, dwarfing all competition on the skyline. A hulking monolith of concrete, steel, and glass, Penance Tower was said to have been built long before the Educators ever ruled the City.

It was a true marvel of engineering, a relic of a bygone era of City peace and prosperity. Before the war, many had regarded the building as the very beating heart of the City.

Now, as Cross and the albino parked their vehicle in front of the building, Penance Tower stood lifeless, its thousands of windows dark. The only traces that remained of its former glory were the green floodlights at the top, still illuminating a small cylindrical observation spire at its peak—the 101st floor.

That spire, a bare speck from where the two citizens sat, was the last hope of salvation for the City, if only they could reach it.

Squinting through the rain cascading down the windshield, Cross stared up at the tower. He pointed a finger at the green glow at the top, which shone bright enough to cut through the relentless rain.

"I think that's our destination," Cross said.

The albino looked up herself. "That seems likely. I recall seeing a spire of some sort at the top, from a distance of course. I've never been here before."

"Neither have I," Cross said. "I guess this is good, in a way. We both finally get our chance to visit Penance Tower."

The albino sighed. "It seems likely that we might be the last to do so."

Cross ignored that depressing thought as he opened the driver side door. He stepped out into the road, taking his rifle with him. He was instantly soaked by the downpour. The albino exited onto the sidewalk. Together they ran for the front entrance while the rain pattered all around them. The doors were wrought of stainless steel and glass, and as they stepped through them Cross noticed that the glass was all broken.

Cross recalled hearing awhile ago that the tower had been attacked by a group of Truants in order to broadcast their message throughout the City. He guessed now that the Educators had never had a chance to replace the doors after the attack.

Cross followed the albino through the dark lobby. As Iris had said, it seemed the building was running only on emergency power—the only lights were from the exit signs. Then Cross spotted something reflecting one of those lights on the floor, and he walked over to investigate. He bent down and touched the spot with his hand.

It was water.

"Teacher," Cross said, standing up. "Come look at this."

The albino stood beside him and glanced down at the small puddle.

"You think that someone got here before us?" she asked.

Cross frowned. "I don't know. It could be a water leak or something, or maybe some rain that got blown in. There seems to be more of it . . ."

Cross bent down again and traced the direction of the drips with his hand for a few steps. Then he stood up and pointed.

"If it *was* a person who got here recently, I think they were heading for that elevator over there."

The elevator Cross was pointing at clearly stood apart from the rest, and seemed to be meant for maintenance. Most of the public elevators were farther inside the lobby, near the building's core.

The albino shrugged, and then walked over to the elevator in question. Neither the button lights nor the floor indicator seemed to be working. The albino tried pressing the buttons. For several minutes she and Cross waited in silence. Nothing happened.

"Maybe I was wrong," Cross admitted.

"Perhaps," the albino said. "Either way, there's nothing we can do about it. It seems that the elevators are not an option."

"So what are we going to do?"

In response, the albino walked over to a nearby door and pushed it open. Cross followed her inside. He found himself inside a stairwell lit by tiny lights on the walls. Against his better judgment, Cross looked upwards. The stairwell went so high that he couldn't even see where it ended.

"It seems that we are just going to have to walk up," the albino said.

"Um, how many steps does Penance Tower have again?"

The albino brought her hand under her chin as she considered that.

"I think I recall reading that it's something close to two thousand," she said.

Cross sighed. "I guess we'd better get started, then."

The albino took the first step, and together they began their long climb to the top.

As rain poured down the granite steps of City Hall, a soaked Takan looked up at the building. It had never been a match for Penance Tower in terms of scale—it was wider than it was tall, and only thirty stories at its highest point. However, it did seem intimidating enough with the charred hole blown in its side, an angry wound dripping with caution tape.

"Are you coming or not?" Noni asked, glancing back at him.

Takan snapped out of his reverie and hastened up the rest of the stairs. He followed Noni through the glass front doors. City Hall was within walking distance of the Mayoral Mansion, and they hadn't had much trouble getting there on foot.

As he entered the lobby for the first time in his life, Takan noticed that it looked quite lavish—there were leather couches and chairs scattered all over the floor of green marble. A large white fountain stood in the middle, though it was dry now. There was military equipment lying here and there. Clearly the building had been taken over by the Government before the withdrawal.

Their wet footsteps echoed throughout the abandoned space. Takan tucked Iris' folder under his arm. He had been keeping it in a plastic bag, safely shielded from the rain.

"So, what do you think?" Noni said suddenly.

Takan blinked. "Huh?"

"About Iris," Noni said. "You know, when I looked at her, I felt like I was watching the bravest person I've ever met die."

"Yeah, it's a shame. The whole thing is."

"How could we have misjudged her so badly?" Noni wondered. "I don't understand it. I'd never met her before, and I was still ready to kill her—I *did* kill her, with this knife."

Noni drew the weapon and looked down at it.

"You can't blame yourself, after what the Government did to you," Takan reasoned. "We all felt the same way."

"She reminded me of Zyid, Takan," Noni said quietly. "She was really trying to help, and we killed her, doomed the City. I feel . . . guilty."

"I do too."

Noni made a noise of disbelief as she headed for the stairwell. Takan followed, as she looked like she knew where she was going and he surely didn't.

"I doubt that," she huffed. "Did you feel guilty when you killed Zyid?"

Takan shut his eyes. "Noni, I—"

"It was he who brought me to City Hall before, you know," Noni interrupted. "We went over the blueprints together. The controls are probably in the main office, fifth floor."

Takan sighed as he followed Noni up the stairs. He didn't want to be having this conversation now, but it seemed that soon they might not have another chance for any conversation, ever.

"No, I didn't feel guilty. Not at first anyway," Takan said. "That was different, though. Zyid knew about my grudge and he'd agreed to settle it in a fair fight."

Noni snorted. "It sounds like he was a bigger man than you."

"Noni, Zyid didn't want to be leader anymore," Takan said. "He couldn't live with the guilt and the burden."

"I don't believe that," Noni replied. "And even if it were true, Zyid was a better leader than you. He wouldn't have killed Iris. I'm sure of it."

Takan shook his head, realizing now that Noni admired Zyid too much to see the boy's flaws. She had been close to him, but she had never truly understood him. Perhaps that was why Zyid had chosen Takan to succeed him in the end.

"I guess we'll never know," Takan said. "You know, he was worried about you, that night when he knew he was going to die."

They reached the fifth floor. Noni paused, turning to look at him.

"What I told you awhile back was true," Takan continued. "Zyid said you would become unpredictable without him. I think he was worried that you might go off and—"

"Do what I did?"

"Well, yeah."

Noni grunted, pushing the stairwell door open.

"That just goes to show that Zyid knew me better than you did, Takan," she said. "I guess you never really understood me at all."

Takan swallowed as he realized that those were more or less the same thoughts he'd had about Noni and Zyid. It hadn't occurred to him that it might be true the other way as well.

"You're right, Noni. I'm sorry," Takan said. Noni looked at him in surprise, and he continued. "I didn't understand you, but . . . I'm willing to learn. If you'll give me that chance."

In the dim lighting of the corridor, Takan saw Noni turn away. The rest of their walk passed in silence. Soon they reached the main office, and entered inside. Noni fiddled around at each of the terminals as Takan stood watch in the doorway. Then Noni made a small sound of triumph, and Takan heard a switch click behind him.

"It's all done, then?" Takan asked, relieved.

Noni straightened up. "Yes."

"Great," Takan said. "Now let's start broadcasting. Iris can only buy us so much time."

There was silence. It stretched on until Takan finally turned around, and saw Noni looking pale and flustered.

"What's wrong?" Takan asked.

"I don't think there's a way to broadcast from here," Noni said quietly. "There are no microphones. I only turned on the intercom system; we can't use it from here."

Takan felt his heart sink. He'd thought that this whole thing had been too easy. What would happen now? It was hopeless—with no way to get the message out, the people of the City would never know what hit them.

Then there came a scratching sound over the building speakers. Takan and Noni looked around as if by doing so they might see the source. A voice came over the intercom.

"People of the City, this is your Mayor speaking."

Takan and Noni stared at each other, both of them torn by a flurry of different emotions.

"Umasi!" Takan pumped his fist in the air.

"Even now, all of your lives are in great danger—"

"It figures that guy survived." Noni frowned. "I never did get my chance to confront him."

"—evacuate immediately through whatever means—"

"Who cares?" Takan said. "Our part is over now, Noni. The word is out, and the race to escape is on. Let's get going."

"—those who are important to you, and stick together—"

Noni nodded, and headed for the door. Tuning out the Mayor's words, Takan followed behind her. With Iris' directions still fresh in their minds, the two former Truants both shifted their attention to escaping the City. The rest of their issues, they decided, could wait for another time.

When my brother Zyid, leader of the Truancy, spoke to you as I do now, he begged for peace. He warned us that our cycle of escalating violence could only bring us to mutual ruin. We did not heed his words. We did not learn that most important lesson, as he had hoped we would. That cycle has spun out of our control, and now we bear witness to its conclusion.

"I do not believe that this end was inevitable. Had we all been a little wiser and a little less proud, we might have had peace. Mankind at its best, after all, is capable of overcoming great differences. No, I do not believe that this end was inevitable—yet it is the one that we have chosen for ourselves. May future generations learn from our folly.

"I know that I myself am not blameless in this matter. Against my better judgment I allowed myself to perpetuate the conflict. When I should have helped to calm passions, I helped enflame them. Where I should have compromised, I was stubborn. And when I should have made a stand against what I knew to be wrong, I was weak, and I failed.

"Now that failure has been unfairly passed on to this City. Citizens, this is truly your last stand—not against an enemy, or for a particular cause, but for your very lives. You put down your differences in the face of what you perceived to be a common enemy. I ask you now to cooperate with that enemy in the face of total annihilation."

Deep beneath the Mayoral Mansion, in the secret shuttle terminal meant only for the sitting Mayor, Umasi let out a sigh that echoed throughout the City. He leaned forward in his chair, microphone still raised to his lips.

"Soldiers throughout the City, in defiance of their highest superiors, are now waiting to assist your evacuation. Having lost everything, we are left only with our common humanity. We can choose to embrace that bond—or when the dust settles, we can lose even that.

"The choice now is yours alone. From this moment onwards I step down as your Mayor. I was never fit to hold that office."

Now Umasi hesitated. He looked to his left, where Zen stood waiting patiently on the platform. The child waved at him.

"And to milady, if you are listening to this." Umasi swallowed. "We are safe, and we love you."

With that Umasi put the microphone down and reached forward to switch off the broadcast. The system had been installed generations ago in case the Mayor ever had to make an emergency broadcast before fleeing. This was the first time that it had been used.

Umasi was glad now that he had ignored the warning from Colonel Hines and chosen to linger in the safety of the terminal. Iris had sent him a text message updating him on the dire situation. He had then taken it upon himself to issue the final warning to the people of the City.

As Umasi stood up, he briefly wondered why Iris hadn't spoken to him with her voice. Then he shrugged and decided to ask her whenever he saw her again.

"Are we leaving now, dad?" Zen asked.

Umasi nodded. "Yes, if you want to."

"I want to," Zen said quickly.

Umasi smiled and took Zen's hand, leading him over to the shuttle that was waiting on the tracks. He had been learning lately how to ask Zen for his opinion before making decisions that involved him—it was a habit of his mother, or so Zen had explained.

The shuttle resembled a sleek train car, except there was only one car with seats for six people. There wasn't much of a cockpit, just a single lever and a red button that Umasi assumed was the emergency brake. Umasi quickly entered the shuttle behind Zen, his mind focused solely on getting his son to safety.

Then Umasi pulled the lever, and the doors slid shut behind them. As the shuttle began to move into a dark tunnel, Umasi sat back in a seat, watching Zen curl up next to him. Only then did he allow himself to worry about the evacuation, and the hundreds of thousands of people still trapped in the City.

Umasi sighed. He hoped that somehow the bridges and tunnels could be opened before it was too late.

His feet numb from climbing, Cross glanced at the nearest speaker as they passed it by. The Mayor's voice echoed throughout the stairwell. As a Government building, Penance Tower was fully connected to the City intercom system.

The Mayor's speech had begun somewhere around the seventy-eighth floor. Now Cross and his companion were on the ninety-fifth, and it was drawing to a close.

"And to milady, if you are listening to this . . . we are safe, and we love you."

Cross blinked at that, and then turned to the albino, who somehow managed to look graceful even as she was climbing the stairs.

"Does that mean anything to you, teacher?" he asked.

The albino smiled, a momentary look of happiness crossing her face.

"It means that I can breathe a little easier," she replied. Then she shook her head. "But it also means that we have to hurry. The evacuation is already starting."

Before Cross could press her again about the Mayor and his speech, the stairs abruptly flattened out for a final time. Cross turned to see the number 100 painted on the wall. The stairs didn't seem to go any farther. He halted, leaning against the handrail, panting slightly. After the countless steps he had climbed, Cross' legs felt like they might fall off at any moment.

"This is only the hundredth floor," the albino observed, pausing beside him. "I guess this stairway won't take us to the observation spire."

Cross nodded. "I'd heard that the spire wasn't open to the public. It makes sense, if all the important controls are there."

"Still, there must be a way up," the albino said. "Come, let's check the floor we're on."

She opened the door, and Cross followed her inside. They found themselves in a large square-shaped room with glass windows all around. None of the lights seemed to be functioning, though they weren't needed—a bright green glow filtered eerily through the windows on all sides. The floodlights, Cross realized, must have already been left behind on a lower floor.

"Beautiful," the albino whispered.

Cross glanced at her. She was staring out of one of the windows, silhouetted against the green light, her palm against the glass. Cross walked over to her side. Then he looked out of the window and gasped.

Through the streaks of water running down the glass, through the haze of rain outside, the rest of the City could still be seen from up here. The view was unlike anything Cross had ever imagined. Rooftops from a thousand unique buildings formed patterns that seemed both artistic and organic. The faint lines of roads streaked through the city, cutting it up into geometric shapes. Entire blocks were reduced to intricate squares. Dark skyscrapers pointed proudly upwards, contributing to the sprawling vista, all contained by the vast rivers around the City.

It was a breathtaking sight, dark, yet tinted green by the floodlights as Cross and the albino stared downwards. The rain seemed to be falling in sheets now, catching the light, like an emerald curtain fluttering in the winds.

"I never knew," Cross said. "I mean, I'd never thought about how big the whole City was, how it would look from up here. Amazing."

The albino nodded. "It's such a shame."

Cross knew what she meant. He too felt a great sadness in his heart as he remembered that everything they were looking at, everything they had known in their lives, would soon vanish forever. How majestic, how grand was the City from here—and yet as fleeting and temporary as all mortal designs in the end.

The albino sighed, then pulled away and pointed at the river, where the dark shapes of the bridges were still visibly raised.

"I'm glad that we could see this, just once before it's too late," she said. "But those bridges are what we came for. We can't lose focus now."

Cross nodded. "You're right. Let's look for a way up."

Quickly they searched the floor. An elevator in the center seemed to provide access to the spire, but they couldn't get it to work. Then they found what they were looking for; a door to another stairway labeled "Restricted Access."

The albino tried the knob and found it locked. Cross tried kicking the door down, but only succeeded in hurting his foot. They both pushed and pulled to no avail. Finally, frustrated, Cross raised his rifle and tried shooting the door. Dents appeared in the metal surface and the handle bent out of shape, yet the door remained firm.

"It's no good." Cross panted. "It won't open."

The albino sighed. "I guess we only have one option left, then."

"What's that?"

The albino walked over to Cross and gestured for him to give her the rifle. Confused, Cross complied. Then the albino turned towards one of the windows and fired.

Before Cross could yell his protest, the glass shattered and the storm outside burst into the room with a terrific roar. Cross raised his arms to shield his face as the sudden wind and rain battered his body.

"Are you crazy?" Cross shouted over the howling gale.

The albino tossed the rifle aside and began walking towards the newly created opening. Her face was determined as she pushed forward against the wind.

"It's the only hope we have of getting up there!" she shouted back. "There's no other choice!"

"You *are* crazy!"

The albino ignored him, stepping onto a small ledge and into the fury of the storm. The rain drenched her even as the powerful winds threatened to blow her off her tenuous perch. Her Student Militia jacket fluttered violently, and the albino reached up to unbutton it, letting it fly away.

Cross stared at her in shock. Then he snapped out of it and followed. As he stepped through the broken window the wind seemed to double in intensity, the sheer force of it striking him like a hammer. The rain stung his face like little needles, and he was quickly soaked from head to toe. Cross had never felt so cold in his life. He looked down, and then away, dizzied by the height. If they slipped, they would be falling for a long, long time.

The albino was now standing farther down the ledge, looking upwards at the roof, illuminated by the green floodlights. They could see the cylindrical observation spire from here, but there was no obvious way to climb up to get to it.

"Teacher, it's not possible!" Cross called. "We can't do it this way, especially not in this storm!"

The albino shook her head. "We can't give up!"

"We can find another way!" Cross shouted. "Teacher, please!"

The albino ignored him, unwinding her chain. She began twirling it, and then hurled it upwards. Cross' breath caught in his throat as he realized what she was aiming at; a decorative spike protruding from the roof.

A powerful gust blew the chain off course, screeching in their ears, and Cross reached out to grab the albino to prevent her from losing her balance.

"It's too dangerous!" Cross yelled. "We're both going to fall if we keep this up!"

The albino still ignored him, retrieving her chain and throwing it again. It was another miss, and Cross was about to pull her forcefully back inside when she threw the chain once more.

Cross watched in disbelief as this time the ring at the end of the chain caught perfectly onto the protruding spike.

There was a clap of thunder, and the albino turned to look at Cross triumphantly. Before he could even say a word, the albino wrapped her hands tightly around the chain, and then allowed herself to slip from the ledge.

Cross held his breath as the nameless girl began to rappel up the side of the building. She swayed dangerously in the air, at the complete mercy of the winds. Several times she was buffeted by gusts so strong that she was almost horizontal in the air. Yet the albino simply shut her eyes tight against the stinging rain and kept going, pulling herself up the slippery wet chain link by link.

A streak of lightning lit the skies, and Cross began to worry that a bolt might hit the albino as she climbed. Then, with a final tremendous effort, she managed to reach the top, and with the help of the wind she swung herself onto the roof. There she lay exhausted and soggy, the rain continuing to pour down onto her.

"Teacher! Are you all right?"

The albino opened her eyes and crawled to the edge of the roof. She peered over the edge as water trickled from her white mane.

"I'm fine!" she called.

Cross slumped in relief, and a strong gust nearly knocked him off his feet. He steadied himself against an unbroken window, looking up at his teacher.

"Okay, drop the chain down for me now!" he called.

The albino hesitated. She glanced at the spike, upon which the ring was still hooked. Then she looked at her hands, raw and blistered from her painful climb. The wind howled in her ears.

"Come on!" Cross shouted.

The albino shook her head sadly. There was another flash of lightning.

"I can handle it myself now!" she called. "Get out of the City, Cross! I want you to survive!"

Cross stared up at her. "Teacher, wait!"

But she had already unhooked the ring from the spike. With one last glance down at her student, the albino turned and vanished from sight as Cross' desperate shouts were drowned out by the storm.

36

The albino stood alone at the base of the spire, feeling very small amidst the fury of the elements. In spite of herself she shivered—the cold up here was worse than deep winter, the wetness seeming to soak her very bones. The rooftop of Penance Tower was flat and square, the observation spire a cylindrical structure placed in its very center. The spire climbed an additional fifty feet above the rest of the building, scraping the heavens. The albino could see a set of dark windows on each side of the spire.

The floodlights below lit the atmosphere with their green glow. The girl shivered again as a fierce gust of wind battered her body.

Knowing what she had to do, knowing that the fate of the whole City rested in her hands, the albino pushed against the wind and stinging rain. Step by step she brought herself closer to the spire. A metal ladder ran up the side of the structure, leading to a door to the control room, and beyond that, to the roof of the spire.

Tentatively the albino gripped the ladder, and winced as her worn hands touched the rungs. Ignoring the pain, she kept climbing until she reached the door. Gasping for breath now, she grabbed the handle and turned. It was unlocked.

The albino breathed a sigh of relief, then pulled the door open and stepped inside. She closed the door behind her, shutting out the noise of the storm. It was warmer inside, but dark. The girl patted the wall with her hand until she found a switch. She flicked it, and the lights came on.

The control room was circular, and dark. It wasn't cramped, but it wasn't very big either. There was a large locker leaning against the wall, with the elevator in the center. There were a number of dashboards all around the room. The windows offered an even greater view of the City, but there was no time to enjoy it.

The albino walked around the room in a circle, her clothes dripping rainwater onto the floor. She spotted controls to the water mains, electrical utilities, traffic lights, and other things she didn't understand. Finally, she found the dashboard for the bridges and tunnels. There was a switch labeled "Open All Access."

The albino nearly slumped in relief. She took a step towards the dashboard. Then she heard a noise behind her, and turned to investigate—

A gunshot went off.

Pain blossomed in the girl's abdomen as a sudden force knocked her off her feet. Her back slammed against the dashboard. For a moment the albino didn't understand what had happened. It felt like something had ripped her insides out. She looked down and saw crimson stains spreading on her wet clothes.

Then she looked up, and she understood.

Rothenberg grinned. "I finally got you, you little monster."

The large man loomed over her, the large locker open behind him. There was a look of twisted delight on his face. The albino groaned as she slid down onto the floor. Rothenberg had intentionally avoided killing her immediately. Clearly he wanted to savor this moment.

"I bet you regret trying to trick me now!" Rothenberg gloated. "You should've known that someday it'd come back to haunt you."

The albino wasn't listening. Panic and sadness settled in as she thought about the civilians in the streets below. She hadn't flipped the switch. The people of the City were still trapped. The bridges—she had to lower the bridges.

Rothenberg's grin turned into a frown as the albino struggled to rise. With tremendous effort she managed to turn herself around. Her arm scrabbled at the controls—

Rothenberg fired again.

The albino let out a cry as she slid down the dashboard, leaving a red streak on its surface. Her head turned weakly to look at Rothenberg.

Rothenberg smiled at the girl he had once believed to be a phantom. She looked so pathetic lying there; soggy, miserable, defeated. Rothenberg wondered how he had ever let her frighten him before.

Then to his surprise, the albino stirred again. She was still trying to move, in spite of the pain, in spite of her wounds. Her arm twitched feebly upwards, reaching for one of the controls—what was so important about those damn controls?

Frustrated, Rothenberg shot her again. The arm dropped, and the albino only had the strength left to whimper. Rothenberg laughed in triumph, and tried to fire once more. This time nothing happened. He pulled the trigger again, to no avail. The gun was out of bullets.

Rothenberg scowled and threw the gun aside. He didn't need it anymore. Three shots had been enough. The girl now lay in a puddle of rainwater and blood. Her eyes seemed to stare up at him sadly. Rothenberg didn't like that look; it was too much like pity. He wondered if the girl was even still alive. If she was, she didn't have long.

"I knew you could be killed after all." Rothenberg smiled. "This marks the beginning of my reign, girl. I heard the broadcast—it seems I will be the last Mayor of this City. Be honored that you are my first execution."

He chuckled. Then there was a strange noise, from somewhere else in the room. Rothenberg turned to see that the elevator doors had been forced open, revealing the empty shaft.

Cross stood before them, an expression of total shock on his face.

Iris lay on the floor of her study, staring up at the ceiling. She had no strength to return to her chair, and she knew it would be wasteful to try. She glanced at the door once more to inspect her handiwork. She had rigged it up to some grenades—when it next opened, Iris hoped the explosion would be enough to hide her body for a few extra minutes.

Iris turned her head to look at the monitors. The evacuation was proceeding as orderly as she had hoped, the displays showing many different views of the City. In every street it seemed there was a steady stream of civilians being escorted to the nearest bridge or tunnel by the soldiers who had followed her orders. Iris was rather proud of the efficiency with which it was being done.

The only problem was that the bridges and tunnels were still sealed off.

Iris sighed and looked back up at the ceiling. Maybe it had been a bad idea to entrust the Penance Tower operation to a pair of kids. She wondered if the boy and girl had run into some sort of trouble. If they failed, then Iris' whole carefully coordinated evacuation would be for nothing.

Iris glanced at the monitors again. Thousands of people were waiting at the exits now, waiting for an escape that might never come. There was nothing she could do about it but hope.

Iris let her head drop to the floor. She felt strangely cold—the blood loss, she told herself. For that same reason it was getting hard to think. Iris creased her brow in frustration. She already felt faint, and the pain was somehow numb, distant. She didn't have long left.

Oh well, nothing to do now but wait. As the seconds passed, Iris amused herself with recollections from her childhood. She had always dreamed of being a great leader someday, like her father. Iris chuckled. Bleeding out on the floor in a place like this had never been part of those fantasies. She hoped such embarrassing details would be omitted from her eulogy.

It was only getting harder to focus. Iris began to feel that a nap would be very nice. She fought that urge; she wanted to be conscious until the end.

Dimly she became aware of approaching footsteps, outside in the hallway. Iris smirked. It had taken them longer than she had expected, but the Government had finally traced her and sent a squad to retrieve her. She felt bad that they were going to be blown up, but it would help buy the people of the City just a little more time.

Iris shut her eyes, relaxing. No matter how the evacuation proceeded from here, the clock was already ticking. The Government would realize what had happened, and then utter destruction would be on its way. There was nothing more that she could do about it. Her time was up.

With some difficulty, Iris raised her knuckles and brushed them against her forehead for a final time.

Then the door opened, and her life ended.

Cross did not believe what he was seeing. His mind refused to process what his eyes were telling him.

Rothenberg scowled, and then the man turned and vanished from sight. A door creaked open, and for a moment Cross could hear the storm outside. Then the door slammed shut, and all was silent again.

The nameless girl remained motionless on the floor, slumped against the monitor. Her white clothes were stained red. Blood dribbled from her lips, but her gaze still seemed to follow Cross. There was the faintest of smiles on her face. Numbly, Cross realized that she was still alive.

He dropped to his knees before her, tears streaming unbidden from his eyes. The albino looked at Cross. Her voice was so faint that it broke his heart.

"Live," she said.

With that one word she shut her eyes, and Cross knew she was dead.

As the seconds passed Cross became aware that he was screaming. He began to thrash about, and this time there was no one to support him. He was alone. The last of his friends had died. The pain of that loss, the totality of it, was too much to bear.

Then Cross remembered Rothenberg, and a burning hatred welled up in him. He welcomed that feeling, focusing on it—anything to take his mind off the pain. There were no words to describe what his father had stolen from Cross over long years of torment. But this theft Cross could not accept.

Cross rose to his feet. He wanted so badly to just rush out the door and confront his father at last, something he had been unable to do for his whole life. But looking at the albino again reminded him that he still had a duty to fulfill. Their mission was yet unfinished.

Cross walked over to the dashboard, and with a shaking hand flicked the switch. Breathing heavily, he looked out the nearest window. In the distance he could see the dark outlines of the bridges moving.

The mission was over. The people of the City would survive. They had succeeded, and yet Cross could not bring himself to feel happy.

Instead, as he continued to stare outside, Cross thought about the thousands of people who were now escaping. How many of them, he wondered, were even half as decent as the albino girl had been?

Cross glanced again at her body, then swallowed and looked away. There was nothing he could do for her up here, no hope of a burial. He slammed his fist against a wall. The pain felt good, and so Cross did it again, and again. The tears streamed down his face so hot that they were nearly burning.

Then Cross slumped against the wall that he had dented. For several long moments he remained like that, finding it hard to think, finding it blissful not to. Then his mind seemed to clear, and he found that cold hatred remained.

Cross straightened up. The people of the City could now decide their own destiny, but his was yet unfulfilled. There remained one final challenge for him to overcome. He would have to face the demon of his childhood.

Cross walked over to the door, opened it, and then stepped into the raging storm.

Rothenberg stood on the circular roof of the spire, arms raised, staring up at the angry clouds as the winds howled around him. He felt like he was on top of the world, and in a way he was. This peak was surely the highest anyone had ever stood over the City.

There was a clap of thunder, and Rothenberg laughed with triumph. He had destroyed the ghost that had haunted his past—this proved that he was unstoppable, that fate was on his side. Through sheer tenacity, Rothenberg had outlasted all his enemies. No one had ever expected him to amount to much, and yet here he stood, while so many others had already fallen.

The green glow from the floodlights cast Rothenberg's face into relief. He had heard the new Mayor's warning, and he knew that the City would soon be destroyed. He had come to terms with that. From here, he would be able to witness the final moments of what he had come to think of as one big Truancy City. It would all go up in flames with him on top, to watch over it all. A fitting end.

Rothenberg lowered his arms. All that remained now was Cross. Fate had arranged everything so neatly for him, to have the boy show up here now. Rothenberg knew that he would come, if he was worthy.

Minutes passed, and Rothenberg began to wonder if the boy had the nerve. Then a hand reached up over the edge of the roof, and Rothenberg smiled. The rest of Cross quickly came into view as the boy scrambled onto the roof, his red hair fluttering in the wind. Lightning streaked across the skies, and the two faced each other. The rain fell in sheets between them.

Boy and man. Father and son. Student and Enforcer.

For a moment they looked at each other through the storm.

"That's a good look you have on your face, Cross!" Rothenberg said. "I've been waiting my whole life to see that face—I thought it would never come!"

Sure enough, Cross' expression was pure hatred and determination. Not a trace of the fear that had always been there before.

Cross shouted over the storm. "Shut up, you animal!"

Rothenberg laughed.

"Yes, I hated my father too!" he replied. "I finally see myself in you now, Cross! You're just like me!"

"I'm nothing like you, you—"

"Yes, you are, Cross!" Rothenberg insisted. "I've made you like me! I've taken everything from you! Made you strong! Now, you've had my childhood!"

There was another flash of lightning, followed by rolling thunder. Cross remained motionless as he stood there under the freezing rain.

"I wondered if the day would come when you could stand up to me!" Rothenberg continued. "I waited forever for you to face me as a man! Now, you have the nerve! Now, you truly are my son!"

Cross seemed to waver, and Rothenberg grinned widely.

"Take a good look at me, boy! I am your future!"

The wind blew hard at his back, yet Cross did not move from his spot.

"I'm proud of you, Cross!" Rothenberg spread his arms. "Let us stand on top of this City together!"

Rothenberg approached Cross. The boy's head remained bent, his face cast into shadow by the green ambience around them. The winds seemed to screech louder than ever as Rothenberg came to a halt. The man bent down and tried to pull Cross into what would be their first hug.

Cross took a step back.

"You are no father of mine."

Startled, Rothenberg looked again at Cross. No longer did he see himself reflected there. There was only pity and sadness in that gaze. Weak emotions. Things he had fought his whole life not to feel.

Without another word Cross turned around. Turned his back on his father. Rothenberg stood for few moments in shock. His mouth opened and closed like a fish gasping for air. No words came, and so he just stared in silent disbelief as Cross walked back towards the ladder.

Then the surprise wore off and the rage came. A roar ripped itself from

Rothenberg's throat. He charged, thinking only to plunge with his son all the way to the bottom of the City. Cross heard him coming. At the last second the boy stepped aside. He overshot his target.

Lightning flashed. Rothenberg teetered on the edge of the spire. A powerful gust of wind swept over him. He fell.

Cross watched impassively as Rothenberg was swept away into the storm, vanishing as a tiny speck against the dark streets below.

Just like that, the man responsible for untold pain and misery in the City was gone. Cross' encounter with Iris had made him question the notions of absolute right and wrong. However, he was now sure of one thing—if true evil existed in the City, then it had just fallen from the top of Penance Tower.

Cross drew his knife and tossed it to the winds. It sailed away as the storm continued to rage around him. Cross considered what to do next. He searched his heart for purpose, and found it empty once again. In one fleeting moment, Cross considered jumping off the edge as well.

Then he remembered the albino's last word.

Live.

Cross backed away from the edge, realizing that his duty was not yet finished. He still had his teacher's dying wish to cling to, and whether it meant a few hours or many years, he would do his best to uphold it for as long as he could.

As Cross began to climb back down the ladder, he tried to remember what it meant to live. Fresh tears ran down his face, mingling with the rain as he remembered that things hadn't always been as they were now.

There were good memories in his past.

There had been times when he was happy.

When the City was still alive.

ross kicked off the ground and watched the world whoosh by. His stomach fluttered—a tickling sensation. With a creak the swing swung forward, and Cross shut his eyes against the wind.

Cross was on a playground in the Grand Park of District 20, alone on the swings. All around him, other children were going down the slides or jumping on the shaky bridge. All of it was being supervised by a low ranking Educator hired for just that purpose.

Cross did not join in with the other kids—he never did. At age ten, he was the only child there without a parent. Perhaps more important, he was the only child there to avoid a parent. Cross had long since learned to take the subways by himself, and so he had fled here in the hopes that playing would make him feel better.

The swing came to a rest. Cross sat alone, clutching the chains on either side. So far playing hadn't made him feel better at all. He watched the other children spin happily on the carousel, some of them playing with their parents. It only made him feel more isolated. Lonely. Rejected.

Cross couldn't help it. He burst into tears. As he cried, Cross tried to be as quiet as possible. He knew adults didn't like it when he cried loud.

"What's wrong with you?"

Cross looked up, shocked at being addressed. Through his tears he saw a girl his age standing in front of him, uncomfortably close. She was staring at him with her head cocked, as though she were inspecting an alien.

Cross blinked. "It's n-n-nothing."

"Liar," the girl said matter-of-factly. "My name is Floe, by the way. What's yours?"

"C-Cross."

"Nice to meet you, Cross," Floe said. "Why were you lying?"

Cross gulped. "I can't talk about it, it's . . . it's about my d-dad."

"Oh, it's all right to talk about parents," Floe insisted. She pointed over to one of the benches where a brown-haired woman was watching with a frown. "See, *that's* my mother."

Cross buried his face in his hands as he began crying again.

"My f-father hit me," he confessed. "I c-came here to g-get away."

Floe went quiet at that, and for a moment Cross was sure that she would leave now. Then she put her hands on her hips and frowned.

"That's not very nice of your dad," she said. "Parents can be mean sometimes—I don't like mine very much. That's how parents are."

Cross just cried harder at that. Floe looked puzzled for a moment as she studied him. Then she seemed to light up.

"You know what, when I feel sad a hug always cheers me up!"

Floe took a step forward. Before Cross could realize what was happening, let alone mount an effective protest, the girl had pulled him into a hug.

Cross' first thought was to feel intensely embarrassed—no stranger had ever done this to him and Floe was a *girl* and weren't boys and girls supposed to hate each other? Then, strangely, he began to feel warm and fuzzy. His tears dried up immediately. He stopped thinking altogether.

Cross relaxed into the hug, his mind in a haze. Then it was over, and Floe withdrew. She looked at him.

"See, it worked!" Floe said happily. "Are you from around here, Cross?"

Trying to clear his head, Cross shook it.

"No," he mumbled. "I'm from District 18."

Floe clapped her hands together. "Hey, I am too! Maybe we can meet each other around there sometime."

Cross smiled tentatively. "That would be . . . nice."

The first-floor corridors of the District 18 School bustled with quiet activity as students shuffled on to their next classes. These were elementary school kids, confined to the lower floors reserved for them. As the students walked to and fro, one of them paused right next to the door to the art room.

Hung up on the wall were several pictures that the teacher had selected to represent the fourth-grade class. Cross looked up at one of the paintings—a rolling landscape of slides and carousels, surrounding a girl with brown hair. It was his work, painstakingly crafted after many periods of labor in the art room. Cross smiled. He was proud of it.

Suddenly a voice spoke from behind.

"Hey, that your painting, kid?"

Cross looked up to see an older boy standing over him. His hair was wild and brown, his eyes matching it perfectly. The boy grinned roguishly, and his face seemed to sparkle with life.

Cross gulped. He didn't know this boy personally, though he had sometimes seen him among the high school crowd leaving the building.

"Yes," Cross said timidly. "But, uh, aren't we . . . you know . . ."

The older boy bonked himself on the head with his fist.

"That's right, I forgot—no talking in the corridors." He rolled his eyes.

"Well it wouldn't be the first time they caught me at it, so it's no big deal. How about you just keep quiet while I talk?"

Cross nodded, his lips sealed.

"Cool. Anyway, I'm Red, from the eighth grade." Red glanced at the painting. "That's some awesome work right there. What's your name, kid?"

Cross pointed at his mouth and shrugged helplessly.

"Right, I forgot again." Red sighed. "That rule is ridiculous. All right, let's see here . . ."

Red leaned in close so that he could see the name inscribed on the cardboard plaque beneath the painting.

"Cross?" he read.

Cross nodded.

"Well, Cross, good job." Red straightened up again. "You're probably wondering why I'm down here. I'm on my way to see a Disciplinary Officer now. I think they might actually be expelling me this time."

Cross gasped.

"Yeah, guess it'll be a life on the streets for me!" Red laughed. "Well, at least it'll be less dull than life in here."

Cross privately disagreed. Red must've seen the look on his face, for he laughed. Then he reached out to pat Cross on the head.

"Don't worry, Cross. Go on and become someone," Red said. "People like you have potential. Deadbeats like me aren't meant to last, not in this City."

With another confident grin, Red waved good-bye and turned to walk away. The older boy vanished among the other students.

Cross never saw him again.

In an empty lot of District 18, a girl tossed a ball to a boy. They were eleven years old. A few months ago the two children had found each other by chance on the streets, and they had been sneaking out of their houses to play ever since.

As Cross received the ball, he felt that he must be the happiest boy in the whole City. He had never had a friend before, never had anyone to play with. It was difficult to describe his joy at finally knowing what he had been missing.

Floe, for her part, seemed delighted to have a playmate in the neighborhood. Cross threw the ball hard, and Floe laughed as she ran to catch it.

"That was a good one!" she said.

Cross smiled. For some reason he always felt delighted whenever he impressed her. Just then Floe hurled the ball, and it struck Cross right on the face. Cross felt his cheeks heat with embarrassment as the ball rolled out into the street.

"Sorry!" Floe clapped a hand to her mouth. "Are you all right, Cross?"

Cross nodded. The ball was inflatable. The only thing injured was his pride.

"Wait right there," Floe said. "I'll go get the ball."

Not knowing any better, Cross stood where he was and watched her go. Floe ran out into the street, chasing the ball as it rolled along. Then Cross saw it—a red car coming fast down the street. Floe hadn't noticed it yet, her attention still on the ball.

Without thinking, Cross broke into a run. He reached Floe just before the car did, shoving her safely out of the way.

There was a screech of tires, followed by a sudden impact. Cross felt himself get flung aside onto the pavement. For a moment he was dazed and confused. Then he felt a dull pain in his shoulder.

The car had stopped, but only briefly. Seeing Cross lying on the ground, the driver hit the gas pedal. The car accelerated fast down the street.

"You jerk!" Floe shouted at the retreating vehicle.

There was no response. A moment later, the car turned a corner and was out of sight. Floe stood there with balled fists, fuming. Then she looked down at Cross, and her expression turned to panic.

Cross quickly set her mind at ease.

"I'm all right," he said, sitting up and smiling. "I think I just got bruised. My father hits harder than that."

Floe brought a hand to her chest and let out a deep sigh of relief.

"You saved my life," she said, breathless. "Why did you do that?"

Cross concealed the feeling of pride in his chest.

"It was nothing," he mumbled.

Floe placed her hands on her hips.

"It's *not* nothing, Cross," she insisted. "I will pay you back, someday."

Cross was in fifth grade. The whole school had been assembled in the auditorium for a special occasion. Cross had a seat near the door, and as the minutes dragged on he kept shifting his eyes to glance at it. The Mayor himself would be visiting their school, supposedly to administer some kind of award to the faculty.

Cross had never seen the Mayor in person before, though every citizen knew his face from television. Like the rest of the school Cross was nervous, but he was also curious. Teachers and Educators were authoritative enough—what would the Mayor himself be like?

As they continued to wait, the entire auditorium seemed to be on its toes. There was utter silence. Even the faculty seemed unusually subdued. Every preparation had been made to impress. The children were all in their best school uniforms, the teachers were wearing uncomfortable suits. Along the wall near the entrance, samples of the students' artwork decorated the walls.

One of Cross' drawings had been selected for that honor. The sketch hung nearby on the wall, a portrait of the Mayor himself standing larger than life over the City. Cross could see it out of the corner of his eye.

There was a hiss of static over the intercom, and the entire school sat a little straighter.

"Attention. Everyone please rise for his honor, the Mayor."

As one, the entire auditorium got to its feet. A collective breath was held. Cross strained to watch the doors out of the corner of his eyes. They swung open, and the Mayor entered. He was a portly, aging man with a bowler hat. He seemed to be conversing with an aide—a man with brown hair and a mustache, holding a clipboard.

"No, cancel the meeting too," the Mayor was whispering irritably. "Jack, I thought I told you I needed my schedule clear for the evening."

The man named Jack scribbled furiously on the clipboard.

"Yes, sir, it was just a slight mix-up, easily fixed."

"Good," the Mayor huffed. "I'm not going to miss my sons' birthday celebration for another accursed budget meeting."

"Of course, Mr. Mayor."

"All right then." The Mayor sighed, stepping forward into the auditorium. "Now let's get this little ceremony over wi—"

The Mayor paused, staring at the wall. With a pounding heart Cross realized that his picture caught the Mayor's eye. The Mayor blinked at the portrait, and then he laughed and turned to Jack.

"This one is pretty good," the Mayor said. "It suits me, I think. Make sure the kid who drew it gets a commendation."

Jack nodded and jotted something quickly onto his clipboard. The two men then continued down the aisle towards the stage. Meanwhile Cross felt that he might burst with pride.

He never did receive a commendation, but that fleeting moment of recognition had been enough to convince Cross that the Mayor was a good guy after all.

Midsummer. They were twelve years old. The sun beat down hard from overhead. Cross and Floe were sitting together on the sidewalk, their clothes soaked. A broken fire hydrant shot jets of water into the air, the spray creating a rainbow effect. It seemed that half the kids in District 18 were in the street now, playing in the water.

It was a practice discouraged, though not expressly forbidden by the

Educators. Cross and Floe had already had their fun, and now they were winding down in the shade as other kids took their turns.

Cross sighed. "I have to go home soon. My father is coming home this evening and he's going to want dinner on the table."

"He even makes you cook?" Floe asked, surprised.

Cross nodded. "I do all of the household chores."

"That's not fair." Floe pouted. "It's not right what that man is doing—maybe we should report him."

Cross shook his head vigorously at that, splattering water everywhere like a dog.

"He's an Enforcer, Floe," he said. "It wouldn't do any good, trust me."

"If you say so, I guess," Floe said reluctantly. Then she looked at him, still dripping wet. She plucked at his soaked shirt. "Are you going to be all right going home like this?"

"It's fine," Cross said, touched by her concern. "I'll change and do the laundry when I get back."

Floe nodded at that, then turned her head back towards the rainbow spray. As she did, it seemed to Cross that her attention was elsewhere, her eyes unfocused. He decided not to say anything. For several more minutes they remained like that, unspeaking.

Finally, Floe squared her shoulders and looked at him.

"Cross, we're not going to be able to play anymore, soon," she said. "My family is moving away, to District 2."

With those words Cross felt a pain blossom in his chest—an unfamiliar sensation, and unpleasant. It was the first time he had ever experienced the pain of parting with a loved one.

"Are we ever going to see each other?" Cross asked.

Floe grinned at that. She patted him on the head with her open palm.

"Of course we will," she said. "I still have a debt to repay, remember?"

Cross blinked. "Y-Yeah."

"When we're just a little older," Floe said, "we'll meet again, and we'll still be friends forever."

Cross smiled. Then he nodded.

"It's a promise," he said. "Just a little older."

Three years passed. Open warfare broke out in the City. Cross was fifteen and in the Student Militia. He walked down a lonely street at night, his rifle at his side. The Truancy had just been pushed out of his area, and he had been assigned to patrol the streets.

The Educators had declared martial law here. No civilians, not even adults, were allowed out of their homes past curfew. Enforcers were sweeping each block, looking for any Truant insurgents that might have been left behind. Meanwhile Cross and the rest of the Student Militia made sure the streets were clear.

Cross paused for a moment as he heard the sounds of a scuffle. There was a commotion in a nearby alley. He sighed, and decided to go check it out.

Inside the alley Cross saw a pair of Enforcers beating a girl with nightsticks. The girl was an obvious Truant—she was wearing street clothes and was out past curfew. As far as Cross could see she was unarmed, and was hardly a match for the men. She had curled up on the ground, shielding her head from the worst of the blows.

Cross' first instinct was to just walk away. It was none of his business. Dealing with the Truants was the Enforcers' job, and Edward didn't like it when Cross thought for himself. And yet something kept Cross from leaving that alley.

Instead, Cross took a step forward and tried to get a better look at the girl on the ground. There was something familiar about her hair, her hands. Then she looked up at him, and Cross stopped in his tracks.

It was Floe. There was no mistaking that face.

"Hey, you!" Cross called out. "What are you three doing?"

The Enforcers paused, turning to look at Cross. There was a clear look of distaste on their faces. They hadn't yet come to fully accept the Student Militia.

"What does it look like we're doing, kid?" the first Enforcer said. "We're apprehending a Truant."

Cross looked at Floe. Their eyes met, and he could see a flicker of recognition on her face. Her expression was not pleading, but curious, wondering what he would do. Cross swallowed and turned to face the Enforcers.

"There must be a mistake," he said. "I know this girl. What's your proof that she's a Truant? Was she carrying a weapon?"

The second Enforcer snorted.

"Of course she wasn't," he said. "She probably ditched it after the battle. But she was still carrying *that*."

The Enforcer pointed at a red spray can on the ground. Then he gestured up at the alley wall. Cross looked up and saw an unfinished Truancy symbol painted up there—a T tilted clockwise, within a circle with the bottom right quarter missing. Cross frowned at the graffiti, thinking quickly.

"All right," he told the Enforcers. "I'll handle this from here."

Both of the men stared.

"Listen, kid," the first Enforcer said. "Rounding up the Truants is *our* duty. Who do you think you are, anyway?"

Cross stood his ground.

"I'm Cross, second in command of the Student Militia," he said. "If you have any objections, I can bring the matter to Edward. He can settle this."

It was a gamble. If word of this ever did reach Edward, Cross would be in for a world of hurt. The Enforcers, however, couldn't possibly know that. Sure enough, the men looked at each other nervously.

"Ah it's a waste of time anyway," the second Enforcer spat. "Let the damn kid do the dirty work for us."

The first murmured his agreement, and the two men turned to leave. When they were gone, Cross ran over to Floe and helped her to her feet. Floe's clothing was dirty, her lip was bruised, but otherwise she seemed all right.

For the first time in years the two of them looked at each other up close. Both of their gazes were still wary. They each knew who the other was, and yet they didn't know. So much had changed. It was Cross who spoke first.

"Floe," he said. "Are you—are you really a member of the Truancy?"

Floe nodded, looking him up and down.

"And you," she said. "Are you really second behind Edward?"

Cross nodded. Floe laughed bitterly.

"What a miserable irony this is," she said. "The first time we've seen each other in three years, and it had to be like this."

There was a heavy sadness in her voice. It tore Cross up on the inside just hearing it. He bowed his head. There was no way he could bring himself to betray her, even after all their time apart.

"You should get out of here quickly," Cross said quietly. "You should be able to avoid the Enforcers if you stick to—"

"No."

Cross looked up. Floe was looking at him with her hands on her hips.

"What?" Cross asked, confused.

"I'm not leaving, Cross." Floe smiled faintly. "I still have a debt to settle, don't I? Remember the promise we made?"

Cross was speechless. He felt a lump form in his throat.

Floe pressed. "Forever, remember?"

Slowly, Cross nodded. His voice was hoarse.

"Yeah," he said. "Forever."

38

THE END

T he rain had stopped. The summer night was waning. Hours had passed since the bridges and tunnels of the City had opened for the first time in decades. The clouds overhead had begun to thin, though a faint dampness still clung to the air.

Across an old rail bridge, two figures ran as fast as their legs could carry them, the only ones who knew about this forgotten exit from the City. The rails were rusted and overgrown with weeds, and parts of the bridge were so rickety that a vehicle would probably never have made it across.

Thus the teenagers crossed on foot, glancing back once in a while at the City they were rapidly leaving behind.

"I wonder if Cross and that other girl got out all right," Noni said.

Takan frowned. Iris' folder was still tucked under his arm. The maps inside it had led them this far, and had also offered a glimpse of a world beyond the City so large that it had boggled their minds.

"I hope they did," he said. "They're real heroes for getting the bridges and tunnels open—more than we are, anyway."

Noni nodded as she glanced at one of the main bridges in the distance. Tiny dark shapes were still moving over its surface.

"The evacuation seems to be going well," she observed. "I think the crowds are beginning to thin out."

"Most of the citizens must be out of the City already," Takan agreed. "Iris bought us a lot of time. I wonder when the Government is going to catch on."

They had no way to answer that, and so they kept running in silence. Then, just as they crossed the halfway point of the bridge, there was a familiar screech overhead. Takan looked up to see the black shapes of military planes streaking through the sky. The two jets seemed to be heading towards the nearest bridge.

Takan followed them with his eyes. "I wonder if those are on our—"

There was a flash in the distance accompanied by a booming sound. Takan heard Noni gasp as the bridge support blew up. The middle of the structure collapsed, quickly sinking into the river. Takan felt his heart sink with it.

"Not on our side after all," he said. "The Government knows. They're trying to seal off the City before the missile gets here."

"What about the people still left in the City?" Noni said, horrified. "They'll be defenseless! How can we—"

"Wait, look!"

Takan and Noni watched in awe as military antiaircraft guns fired up from the ground on both sides of the river. The planes broke off abruptly, evidently surprised that their own forces were shooting at them. Takan cheered as the fire crisscrossed the night sky, driving the jets away from the bridges.

Noni turned to look at Takan with wet eyes.

"Iris must have ordered her soldiers to protect the civilians," she said.

"Yeah," Takan said, feeling emotional himself. "Or maybe they're just doing it because they know it's right."

The planes looped back the way they came, away from the guns on the ground, which seemed content to see them go. Takan and Noni stood where they were for a few more moments, watching. Then they noticed that the jets were now heading straight for them.

"I think we've been spotted," Takan said. "Run."

The two former Truants broke into a sprint, the rusted rails flying beneath their feet. They could hear the screech of the aircraft drawing closer. The other side of the river was close now, but still too far away. Takan knew there was no way they were going to make it.

Then there was a flare of heat and pressure from behind. For a few moments Takan's world was a confused mess of twisted metal and wooden splinters. He was hurled forward through the air, a roaring in his ears. Then he felt the ground crumbling beneath him, and for a brief terrible second he was falling.

Something stopped him. A hand, tightly gripping his own. Takan glanced down, and beneath him he saw chunks of the old rail bridge vanishing into a frothing river. Then he looked up, and saw Noni holding onto him with all her might. The look in her eyes was fierce and determined—the same look he had always loved.

For a few moments they stayed like that, staring at each other. Takan felt himself sway in the air. His grip began to slip.

"You can let go, Noni," Takan whispered. "Let me fall. Take your revenge, like I did."

The look in Noni's icy eyes intensified. Rather that letting him go, she reached down with her free hand as far as she could. Stunned, Takan grabbed it. Noni braced her feet against the planks of the tracks, and grunted as she hauled him up.

Takan was pulled back onto what was left of the bridge, and then they both collapsed, breathing heavily.

"No," Noni murmured at last. "I forgive you."

Without thinking, the two of them embraced. Takan spared a glance up at the sky, where the planes were in full retreat, abandoning their mission. Idly he wondered how much of this Zyid had foreseen before his death.

For many minutes they remained in each other's arms, unspeaking. Iris' folder, miraculously untouched, lay a few feet away. The two teenagers knew that they had still time to spare before the missile struck, and they were sure that a brighter future awaited them outside the City.

So for now, after all they had suffered individually and together, they were content to be each other's light in the darkness.

The City was deserted. From one corner of the island to the other, a gentle breeze blew through empty streets. Shepherded by the soldiers who, like Iris, had stayed behind, almost every inhabitant of the City had evacuated. Those few that remained, unwilling or unable to leave, made peace in their own ways. It was the calm before the storm.

The wind blew in front of the Mayoral Mansion, stirring the dust that had fallen the day before. Not a single person remained in all of District 1. The twisted streets and occasional corpse were the only evidence of the battle that had transpired. The body of General Iris had finally been recovered by Government soldiers. It had been airlifted out an hour earlier, in highest honor.

In District 57, the wind blew over the last of the deep City refugees, crossing a bridge quickly at the urging of the soldiers. They knew that doom was nearly upon them, that they would be the last ones out of the City. The soldiers waited patiently until the last of the civilians were across. Then they too followed in their vehicles, leaving the danger zone behind.

In District 19 the remnants of a dismantled lemonade stand lay discarded near an old construction site. The wind blew over a lonely grave there, unmarked and unknown except to a boy who had become Mayor of the City. The district had been abandoned for many years before that boy had lived there. Now it was abandoned once again.

At the very base of Penance Tower, the broken corpse of a wicked man lay in the middle of the street. The wind blew a tattered Student Militia jacket through the air, fluttering gently above the empty streets. Finally, the wind subsided like a sigh, and the jacket came to rest on top of the corpse as though covering something indecent.

If a person standing upon that spot had looked straight up at the sky and waited, they could have watched the end of the City arrive. That end had not yet arrived, as it was still soaring beyond the atmosphere.

Yet the end would come.

Like a falling star, it would drop from the heavens, travelling at 150 miles per minute as it returned to earth. It would touch down first at Penance Tower, the very center of the City.

When it hit, the destruction would begin with a flash, blinding any witness with bare eyes. A double pulse of light would rapidly expand from the impact, a fiery shock wave that would consume the City. In its wake would follow blast winds moving at nearly a thousand miles per hour.

Any stragglers left in the City who were not incinerated would be crushed from the inside from the sudden pressure in their lungs. Any who lingered too long or too close afterwards would succumb to the radiation that would poison the land.

This was the Government's most terrible weapon, a nightmarish creation that had no place in reality—yet it was the end that the City now faced.

Eventually the skies opened up, and the end did come. There came a flash.

On the 101st floor of Penance Tower, the body of a brave girl was cremated instantly as an entirely different wind began to blow.

Cross could see the first streaks of dawn on the horizon as he propelled himself forward through the water. The waves were gentle now that the storm had ceased. Cross had never been a great swimmer, yet now he found himself trying to do the front crawl all the way across the wide river that separated the City from the rest of the world.

After descending from Penance Tower, Cross hadn't had any time to reach a bridge or tunnel on foot. Instead, he had headed straight for the waterfront, and then dived in. The river was vast and, he had heard, polluted. It left a funny taste in his mouth, and so he kept his eyes and mouth firmly shut as he swam.

Every now and then Cross would lift his head, and as he gasped for air he would look at the light on the horizon. In spite of all that had happened, in spite of where he was, Cross now felt a strange hope for the future. The darkness was at his back, and he was not sad to know that he was leaving the City behind him forever.

Cross had never loved the City. It was a miserable place where he and all other children had been forced to endure trials they never should have. As the Education City it had been a nightmare. As the Truancy City it had been no better.

Now, as he swam, Cross felt like he was awakening from that nightmare. His childhood demons could not follow him across these waters. He did not know what awaited him on the far shore—be it years of happiness, or swift oblivion. But Cross knew that whatever it was would be better than what he was escaping.

And so he pressed on, no matter how much his muscles protested or lungs burned. He struggled to live on, as he had promised to do. With each stroke Cross took, the dawn light grew a little bit brighter. Finally, he reached the shore on the far side of the river and dug his fingers into the rough sand.

In that moment Cross looked down at his reflection in the placid water and was relieved to see that it was himself, only himself who looked back.

Then there was a flash from behind him, and his whole world turned to light.

The shuttle rumbled onwards.

From the safety of his seat, Umasi gazed out the window at the City in the distance. His sunglasses shielded his eyes as the flash blotted the horizon, and he felt his heart tighten as it did.

The former Mayor watched as his City was consumed by fire. Umasi had seen the bridges lowered and knew now that the people, by and large, had survived. Even so, he could not help but feel a sense of sadness, of loss. The City had been a miserable place, a dark place. It had brought out the worst in most of its inhabitants—as it had been designed to do.

Yet it had been his home. As Umasi saw the mushroom cloud rise into the atmosphere, he shed a tear.

The shuttle rumbled onwards. Zen stirred and mumbled something in his sleep. Umasi looked down and smiled at the slumbering child, glad at least that his son would have a chance at a childhood different from the one the City would have offered him. Umasi could not yet predict what choices Zen might make in his own life, but he would do his best to see the boy grow up to be wiser than his father.

The shuttle rumbled onwards, and Umasi thought about all of those who had died, or whose fates were unknown to him. He remembered the albino, somehow feeling sure that he would never see her again. He thought about the previous Mayor, now gone forever. He wondered now if Iris herself had stayed behind—it seemed like something his selfless sister would have done. He even recalled a boy named Red whom he had known long ago, the first friend he had ever lost.

Umasi then thought about the Government and its misguided leaders; men who had never seen the City with their own eyes, men who knew nothing about the people whose deaths they had ordered from afar. Umasi did not know when or if his path would ever cross with theirs, but if that day ever came he knew there would be a reckoning. The City was not wholly destroyed so long as he lived.

The shuttle rumbled onwards. Dawn light spilled through the windows. Umasi sighed, wondering if any good had come out of the saga that he and his brother had begun four years earlier. Then he remembered the countless citizens who had been saved by the combined sacrifices of so many.

Those survivors would now be united in that shared sacrifice, and in the end they might be wiser for it all. Umasi smiled faintly. He believed they would be. Humanity did have, after all, a great propensity for meaningful education—perhaps outside of the City it would be allowed to flourish.

And when someday the history of the Truancy City was written, perhaps the best that could be said of it was that in their darkest hour, its people finally came together to learn their most important lesson.

Umasi sat in silence as the shuttle rumbled onwards. Then he turned away and looked towards the dawn, with Zen fast asleep in his lap.

Students don't need our education,
it is our education that needs students.

—THE MAYOR